Beads of sweat gathered on her forehead. Her body responded to Jarrid's advances, and she felt his desire. He moved to envelop her, pushed her against the sink to anchor his aggression, the only obstacle to his lust.

Jarrid was magnificent. His body filled the doorway with the yellow and pink mountain flowers framed against his dark-blue peasant shirt.

The dance of dinner was only a ploy to join their two souls, fate dictating destiny, the meal orchestrated, and finished as nervousness filled the room.

"Do we really want to talk about the village tonight? Let's enjoy one another and leave our troubles for another time."

"Okay," Sara answered. Her nerves on edge, she slipped her hands into the warm water. The foam rose above the dishes and lined the sink like pearls, each bubble popping in a chain reaction announcing their watery demise—her senses firing on all cylinders.

Every syllable screamed from deep inside, tearing at Sara's soul. She couldn't stop the words, they rose to the surface, and she willed them into thought, *I want this man!*

Joe Mama In-House Publishing
Ormond Beach, FL 32174
Printed in the United States of America

Contacts:
bloodmoonbook@yahoo.com
www.bloodmoonbook.com
www.facebook.com/Sarah-Kage

BLOOD MOON

SARAH KAGE

Table of Contents

TO CASEY WHO SAID, "GO FOR IT"
BETH MY BETA READER
DEBBIE WHO SAID, "IT NEEDS MORE SEX"
AND MY TEENAGE GRANDSON CHAD, WHO
SAID, "WHATEVER!"

SARAH KAGE

The Dream

The dream was always the same:

Sara struggled to hear the haunted, lyrical melody. Sounds rolled through the fog, like glasses tinkling from a toast. Fear caused her eyes to shut tightly. All the while, she fought to open them desperate to understand.

Mist rose through the air tracing Sara's labored breath. The autumn leaves crunched under the weight of each step. Her heartbeat pounded in her ears, and her legs struggled for balance on the uneven ground.

The air in her lungs escaped with a gasp as icy fingers pulled her through the thick brush; their grip relentless. They forced Sara into the middle of a large clearing, on the side of the mountain.

Her senses acknowledged and categorized each cricket, frog, and night sound; so much so that each one had its unique tune. Sara adjusted her eyes and rubbed them until they stung. She strained for focus to see through the thick fog covering the forest like a blanket.

Sara clawed and scratched at the ground as she moved closer to the vision. Her muscles grew tired, giving a tree root the advantage to bring her face-to-face with the cold, hard ground.

Both feet now anchored, Sara turned toward a quick movement in the nearby trees that demanded her attention. Hues of black and gray formed then disappeared; a shadow slipped under the fog. It was pure-driven-impulse that forced her to follow the unknown into the forest.

Fear drove her to resist the pain, to ignore the red hot ache that throbbed deep in her ankle. Her muscles had their way and formed tight pulls on her stomach, causing the union of dry heaves and tears to flow in constant rhythms. Sara's mind and body faded, struggling against the dream. Electricity shot through her soul and gave her strength to summon her will.

Just as her head rose above the fog, he was there, a presence weighted over her like heavy stones. Before Sara could protest, a large cloaked hand shoved its way in front of her face, beckoning; no doubt as a gesture of help. Sara was in no mood to accept the stranger's chivalry, but the hand shook once again, riddled with frustration and impatience.

Feeling no alternative, Sara reached out to the vision expecting to be pulled out of the fog and onto stable ground, but instead, the sensation of falling took over. Once again, the electricity filled her weary body, and she felt a strange flood of emotions fill her heart.

The stranger's touch filled her with strength and peace. His long brown hair flowed from under the hood of his cloak and fell on his chest in waves. His stature overwhelmed Sara as he pulled her body toward him. She no longer resisted, longing for the safety of his arms, but the moment was gone.

No quicker than it had begun the forest reclaimed its reality, and once again the searing pain demanded Sara's attention. The ache, deep in her ankle, heightened her senses and she realized he was no longer beside her. He had made no sound as he disappeared through the trees.

SARAH KAGE

Ignoring the pain once more, Sara scoured the tree line and searched for a glimpse of the stranger. The fog was thicker and enveloped the trees making it impossible to distinguish between light and dark.

A gust of wind, possibly summoned by Sara's own will, parted the fog just in time to catch a glimpse of his silhouette. Before dusk consumed his shadow, he turned toward her. He didn't speak, but her mind heard his voice, *Sara, look to the wall your face to frame the Righteous One will be the same!* His words bounced off her ears as plainly as if he had spoken them, but their meaning hung in the air, foreign and elusive.

Before Sara could react to this telepathic message, her eyes fell upon the movement of his dark cloak. Like a dance, he slowly reached up and uncovered his head. His shadow seemed to reveal more than mortal attributes and Sara once and forevermore was captivated by the ice-blue eyes staring through the fog of uncertainty and passion.

PART ONE THE VILLAGE

SARAH KAGE
Chapter 1 The Village

Sleep, dreams, and daylight intermingled through Sara's waking thoughts. The muted pink, gray, and black of her sheets blurred the images fading from her mind; curse the morning, the daylight; and especially the alarm clock.

Dreaming took on a new meaning lately. The dreams formed either a fantasy or a nightmare with foreboding and doom. This morning the daybreak interrupted a fantasy and a darn good one too.

Sara threw the sheets back with a loud sigh and forced her feet into her dainty pink feathered slippers. She stomped toward the bathroom with all the grace of a drunken barbarian. Each time a slipper met the floor, another mumble slipped from her mouth. Profanities spewed, her feet entangled, she tripped on the clothes carelessly strewn across the floor.

She fell onto the pink-paisley chair, just outside her bathroom. Fogginess ruled her brain fueled by the vision of the face from the dream. Sara struggled to define the line between dream and reality.

The cotton material cool to her touch, she brushed back the curtain and focused on the morning sun. The drapes reminded her of the day she chose the fabric for her bedroom décor. Her choice dictated pink ruffles with a few polka-dots thrown in for good measure, but her inner Warrior-Princess finally got her way with the creative black border that framed the curtains.

The décor defined Sara's personality, on the one hand, dainty, feminine, and the other cold and calculated. Beautiful, yes! Feminine, yes, but cross her and come to know the soul of a warrior.

BLOOD MOON

It was a dream she knew well. Sara's mumbles filled the bathroom, and she turned to face the mirror. The ringing of the alarm ripped the vision of the man from her dreams. The image was always the same, those striking blue eyes! The details were always a blur, but the eyes burned in Sara's memory. She tried to focus on the vision; *was it a dream or madness?*

It moved in ripples and waves with images unclear and fading. Sara's intense stare distorted the reality of the mirror. *Ringing, what was that constant ringing?*

The room seemed to breathe in and out, and a sudden vacuum pulled her back into her skin. She rushed to pick up the phone, knowing it was probably Alexandra who would no doubt have a few choice words about her ability to disregard responsibilities. She gathered her thoughts and prepared to lie, vigorously.

"Hello," before the 'O' could escape Sara's mouth, the phone started to vibrate in her hand with Alex's familiar and demonstrative voice. "Okay, go ahead, lie! Tell me some tall tale about why you aren't standing here in front of me, at your job, your place of employment?"

Sara waited for the rant to continue, but instead, there was dead silence. She realized Alex was waiting for her to spin a tale of circumstances. Something to melt her anger and calm her tongue, but Sara could not erase the vision of the dream.

Alex's screams echoed from the phone. "Okay Sara, you know I don't even care about your excuse, but I do know Mr. Williams is furious you aren't here. He came to my office looking for you first thing this morning. His face distorted with aggravation, and now you're late. Well, I think you get the picture."

SARAH KAGE

Sara realized that reality was a cold hard sword which must be swallowed frequently and with the vision of the dream fading fast, her words took on a life of their own.

"Okay, Alex calm down. You can be so dramatic. Just get Ted a cup of coffee and tell him I'm on my way. I'm sure the *Daily News* and Ted can survive without me a little while longer."

Sara turned the phone off and laid it on the dresser with the last of Alex's complaints filling the room. The last words she heard, streams of profanity; something about a cup of coffee and she wasn't his secretary. She hurried out the door smiling; the morning games had just begun.

***

Her key, thrust into the ignition and the engine roared to life. Sara hardly noticed the jolt from backing over the curb. Alex's nagging and the thought of Ted's rampage gave Sara's emotions a workout. Thoughts rushed through her mind with every honked horn and hand gesture, from her companion drivers, her senses tingled with aggravation and frustration. Her thoughts twisted and turned under the pressure of her job and the constant searching for that one news story, the one that would put her name on the map.

The traffic snarled and tangled until it came to an abrupt stop. Sara tried to get a handle on the pounding images pulling at her soul. She knew that before she could even get to her office door, the dynamic duo would be demanding multiple explanations for her actions.

The Daily News and Ted colored Sara's professional world for years. Sara and Alex, her number one photographer, worked side by side and complimented one another. It had just worked out that way, straight out of college.

BLOOD MOON

Alex and Sara were a formidable force, although if you asked Alex, she would always put on airs and say she was the more professional one of the two. Arrogant or not, Alex was still the best photographer in the business.

Sara's thoughts scattered like leaves in the wind. A car horn brought her back to the present, and the traffic cleared to reveal a path to the *Daily News* parking lot.

Late, always late! What a way to start the day. Sara's first inclination, reaching her office, was to try and avoid Alex and Ted at all costs, but she knew that would prove impossible. She surveyed her desk, looking for some diversion to her dilemma.

The photos scattered across her desk like autumn leaves; with her next project, waiting for her attention. Sara seriously entertained the idea to leave, to make the next mission her top priority without ever confronting the duo. *Yes, I could slip out the back and avoid the drama altogether.* This thought gained more life with every passing second. Suddenly the office door burst open, and it was clear that the daily spectacle was about to commence.

Alex's persona filled the room like an icy storm. There she stood, arms folded across her chest with a stare that would intimidate most people. Alex immediately realized her glare didn't work, so she tried another tactic, words.

"Sara, what's wrong with you?" The storm moved from the door and circled Sara with great intensity. Before she could answer, another gust blew in her direction. "Don't you care about your job or that your irresponsibility reflects on your co-workers?"

What did I hear? Sara's anger rose in her chest. *Selfish is my crime!* "Okay, that's it I've had quite enough of this!" Sara shivered with anger and poised herself to confront the cold accusation.

SARAH KAGE

The veins in Sara's forehead rose and bulged while she gathered her wit. All of her senses heightened, and her rage formed the words from inside. Her posture took on a new stance, and she confronted Alex. Their faces only inches apart.

"You have no right to insinuate I'm selfish." Sara protested. She searched Alex's face for a sign that her words left their mark, but only a gasp of surprise left Alex's lips.

The room was strangely cold, and the wind stirred through the open window. Stacks of paper on the desk rustled and a photo fell to the floor. It only took seconds for the glossy paper to lodge itself between the desk and the wall. To Sara, it felt like an eternity.

She watched the elusive photo float one way and then the other. Each time it caught the light, the graphic showed itself. Sara commanded all of her strength and dove to retrieve the picture from its resting place. Alex flew past her and landed in a heap against the wall.

Why is Alex always so competitive? Sara knelt to pick up the other papers and came face-to-face with Alex scrambling to get a leg up on the situation.

Short of breath, Alex asked, "Okay, what's all the fuss?" All the while putting on her best, 'I don't care face'.

"It's nothing Alex, just the next assignment." Sara recognized the ploy while acting indifferent and quickly pushed the photo under some papers.

"Don't you give me that nonsense? I know what I saw." Alex slammed her hand on top of the papers. She pinned the documents to the desk and declared, "It was some form of a brick wall. What does it have to do with our next assignment?"

BLOOD MOON

"Alex, why do you always push so hard? Yes, it's our next story, but I don't have the complete details yet, and until I do this is off-limits. Do you understand?" Sara realized she had backed Alex against the wall.

Suddenly a loud booming voice broke the tension, and Ted stormed into the room. "Sara, were you not told that I wanted to see you the moment you arrived?" Ted turned without waiting for a response and stormed toward his office.

Sneering, Alex added, "Yeah, I told her!"

Sara wanted to remove the grin from Alex's face but decided that taking the photo with her would wipe it off soon enough. She smiled a cute little smile, flashed it in Alex's direction, and grabbed the photo from its hiding place on her way out. Ted continued toward his office, pausing briefly to listen for Sara's footsteps.

Her nerves gathered in her throat following him down the long corridor. Sara could hardly contain herself; the smile plastered across her face was at Alex's expense. She'd won the battle and managed to leave without giving Alex any information. The image which caused the grin was of Alex standing in the doorway, mouth gaped open, salivating about the prospect of the next assignment; the Thornfell Village.

The tourist attraction nestled on the mountainside had a very romantic history. Sara had given Alex glimpses into the small community and its people, the living, breathing contradiction that had become part of her life.

The reputation of a tourist attraction, although not its real purpose; it was home to the villagers who clung to the old way of life. Visitors immersed themselves in the simplicity of everyday existence.

Sara came across the quaint village on one of her hikes. Her natural curiosity drove her to seek friendship with the town's people. She'd earned the trust of a few villagers and was becoming a familiar face on weekends.

Some of the elders had confided in her. There was something strange, something evil taking a grip on the tiny village. Sara begged Ted to let her next assignment be on the tourist attraction. He had reluctantly agreed.

Sara approached Ted's office, her heartbeat fast and pounding. Her mind was in turmoil, knowing she would have to defend herself against whatever accusations he threw in her direction. She reached for the cold door handle, took a deep breath, and prepared to do battle.

She entered the office and positioned herself on the edge of a chair, closest to the door, in anticipation of a quick escape. Ted stood up abruptly and with great conviction started toward her. His mere tone of voice pushed her back into the chair. "Do you think this is an example of good journalism?"

Sara was still reeling from the initial confrontation, but she regained her composure and confronted him. "Ted, I think the story is fine!" Sara's words stopped him dead in his tracks. She took a few moments to survey his face searching for a clue to her next move. She thought if she could confront him, he would tell her the real reason, he was never pleased with her work.

He looked surprised; Sara had never been so abrupt. "Ted, why can't we agree to disagree? Alright, so you don't like my work. Just tell me what you think is wrong?" Sara's frustrated words poured from her mouth; she took a moment to re-group and gathered her thoughts.

The lines on his face strained, Ted looked puzzled. He walked around his chair and sat down. It felt like an eternity before he continued. "Okay, Sara, I would like to see perfection in your work." He said with a stern tone.

BLOOD MOON

Perfect, he wanted perfection! Her face contorted.

Before she protested, he continued, "Sara look, I only want you to excel in your career. So I push, and you usually come through. I'm sorry if you're upset, I thought you knew I respected your work, I was only trying to present a challenge." He slumped back in his chair and waited for a response.

Sara thought back on their many confrontations about her work and realized he was indeed challenging her. Lost in thought, Sara looked back at Ted; he was talking, but she hadn't heard a word. With little to no effort, she fell back into the conversation without missing a beat.

***

The photo had been ripped from Alex's hand before she could get a good look. *Yes, it was a picture of a wall. It has the aura of an old and historic building surrounded by forest.* Alex's mind was formulating all sorts of possibilities. *What could the next assignment possibly be? Why was Sara so secretive about the whole thing?*

"Oh!" Sara exclaimed rounding the corner on her way to the lounge, her co-worker appearing in her path. Sara's attitude cocked her mood Froggy, with the success of two battles won, and the morning was still young.

"Well, I see you are soothing your wounds with caffeine!" Sara giggled waiting for a response from her friend.

"What's wrong with you, girl?" Alex inquired between sips of coffee.

"I just had a very intense conversation with Ted, and all of the thoughts are still clouding my mind." Sara stared at Alex. "I must look a little dazed."

"Yeah, dazed is a good description. What did Ted divulge? He respected your work and wanted to see you succeed." Alex's mouth tilted a little at the corner showing the pleasure of surprising Sara with her answer.

The frown tightened across Sara's face. She turned her attention to her cup of coffee and pondered her bruised ego; knowing Alex would take advantage of the situation.

The hot brew burned her lips, a distraction of the task at hand, the defusing of Alex's excitement over the photo, but she was already on a roll.

"Okay, enough with the intrigue. You've already confessed that the photo is about our next assignment, so spill the beans." Alex danced around like a two-year-old filled with the anticipation of a good story.

"Alex, could you try and contain yourself for just one second, I mean really, it's just a photo of a wall." Sara lowered her coffee mug and whined.

"Only a wall," Alex stopped in mid prance and fixed her eyes on Sara's face. "We don't do stories on walls unless something is special or newsworthy. So once more, what gives?"

Sara respected the privacy of the people of the village while pursuing her desire to produce excellent and intriguing journalism. She decided to spoon-feed the info about the story based on a need-to-know strategy, and right now, Alex needed to know very little.

"Okay, you know I love to go hiking in the forest." Sara chose her words carefully. "I already told you that I came across the village just outside of town. It's a quaint and simple grouping of homes, shops, and countryside." Sara spun her tale with general information; while her footsteps inched closer to the door.

"Come on. You know these details will not satisfy my curiosity." Alex was having none of this nonsense, and politely blocked the doorway. "We don't do quaint, and we surely never do simple! So what is the story with the wall?"

"Alex, we have worked together for some time now, and I would hope that you've come to trust me. So now I have to ask you to put that trust into practice. Let it go. I promise when I get the details in order, you'll be the first to know." Sara's answer oozed out in a feeble attempt to patronize her co-worker.

Before Alex could respond, the break room phone rang. Sara made a motion to retrieve the handset, but instead of lifting it, she turned her attention back to Alex. "I give you my promise. You'll be a vital part of this assignment. Believe me; I couldn't even think of doing it without you!"

"This is the Daily News, Sara speaking." The phone call broke the bad juju in the room, and Alex left believing that the biggest story of her career was just on the horizon. She did trust Sara and knew this assignment had all the makings of a great adventure.

Chapter 2 Desires of the Heart

The traffic light turned green, but Sara was reliving the day's victories. The horn from behind aggravated her, prompting the slow, deliberate drive through the intersection. The smirk growing across her face was at Alex's expense. Getting her friend's goat kept that small turned-up-smile beaming on her face the entire afternoon. Sara managed to keep Alex in the dark about the upcoming assignment, but this lull wouldn't last long.

Sara's thoughts relived the meeting in Ted's office. The memory of his words bounced off her ego and stung her soul. Her pain softened just a bit, and she wondered if Ted was romantically involved with anyone.

His wife died a few years back, and she heard there was no one special in his life. She could see he was lonely. He wore it like an old shirt, a feeling she knew well.

The art of flirting and romance took a back seat to the demands of her academic endeavors. Her college days were lonesome. The dating scene never jelled for Sara. She hated games, and the immature schoolboys only proved her point.

Just before graduation, Sara realized she'd missed out on some valuable life experiences. As her friends married and planned their futures, all of Sara's focus was on her career.

The car's headlight beams circled the driveway and pointed toward the garage. Each one shone brighter, its circle of light growing smaller against the door. She stared, mesmerized by the beams of light dancing on the metal door; her foot still on the brake and the car running.

BLOOD MOON

Her mind slipped into thought, and she imagined the tall shadow of her husband, standing on the stoop. She watched with intensity, her eyes focused on his shadow, his hand outstretched to open the car door.

"Why are you sitting here in the dark? I've dinner waiting for us. Come on." The imagined figure stood inside the car door with outstretched arms and motioned for her to join him.

A loud "meow" broke her trance. Sara realized she was sitting in her driveway with the door open, and the car still in drive. Zeus, her black cat, was the only one waiting for her, and dinner was the only thing on his mind.

She quickly shoved the car into park, turned off the ignition, and greeted Zeus with open arms. "That's my good kitty. You love me, don't you, Zeus?"

The black cat purred, cuddled all the way to the front stoop, and only struggled free when the front door opened. He knew dinner was only a few meows away.

Zeus lay in front of the sink, licking his paw and carefully cleaning the fresh tuna from his whiskers. Sara stepped lovingly around the contented kitty, trying to make short work of her dinner. She placed the small steak on the plate next to the string beans with a small scoop of rice. Even the dinner looked lonely.

A whish from behind and Zeus was on the counter, protesting loudly. He nearly shoved her plate to the floor.

"Zeus, no! What's wrong with you?" Sara shooed the pesky kitty to the floor. She'd tried hard to train him against the ways of 'the-bad-kitty,' but he was stubborn and willful, exactly like the men in her life.

Male relationships were Sara's nemesis, her dream of the ideal man, an oxymoron. She needed someone her age; mature, and worldly. This characteristic deemed harder to find than white hairs in Zeus's black coat; why even older men could be shallow and dull. Sara dreamed of a strong dominant personality, but she didn't want to be under his thumb. No, still under his arm would be a comfort.

The men of the village fit this bill with their old-world charm, and charisma. Their customs reminded her of days long past. She felt at home among the tiny houses and small shops. The simplicity of daily life lured her back again and again.

Zeus' loud purring cleared her mind. "Come on, Zeus, it's time for bed. I have to get up early and drive to the village." The black kitty meowed his approval and chased the tie of her housecoat through the room. He jumped onto the bed, curled up next to Sara, and they both drifted off to sleep.

***

Stones and twigs crunched, announcing Sara's car tires gripping the cobblestone roadway. Fallen leaves of red and orange paved the way like a ragged blanket, offered up because the summer wind had lost its warmth.

One of the village's attributes was its obscurity. So was the story of the cobblestone road ending just in a grove of Elms? Only a small dirt road offered itself to visitors, and showed the way to the past.

The climb by foot was steep and colorful. The path was narrow and blanketed by tall trees on each side. The wind brushed against Sara's cheek, caressing her skin with each step up the winding lane.

Sounds of laughter and merriment traveled through the boughs of the trees and rung with clarity and joy, but no one was around. It was the wind whispering the memories of the past, playing the leaves like tiny strings on an invisible violin.

BLOOD MOON

Sara stopped to catch her breath and raised her eyes to the tops of the tall trees. The hair on her arms raised, the wind rushed around her to reveal the foreboding wall and its tall turrets, disappearing into the mountainside; it was the Fortress.

Folklore painted each brick and stood as a reminder that magic and danger could be just around the corner. Sara had listened to the villagers spin the tales about the secret passageways, the many rooms scattered throughout the ancient site, and had considered it intriguing.

However, the villagers were anything but intrigued. Only the stories passed through generations kept the old magic alive. The walls were nothing more than an old landmark that gave the village its spooky reputation. Some of the best storytellers lived in the community, and the Fortress always prompted the tales to flow.

Around the corner, the village appeared, like a veil in-between time. The storefront of the old five & dime that included the local grindery, with its peddler Mr. Choate, was the center of the hustle and bustle. Dr. Willows was always available whether in his office or on house calls. Each citizen was an essential cog to the community's health and well being.

The women busied themselves with the chores of the day while the men worked in the fields. The village had no supermarket, gas station, or any modern conveniences. The daily bread baked in wood-burning stoves. The cattle were fed and butchered; the fields yielded the bounty on which the villagers feasted year-round.

Even the children knew little of idle time, for they too were an important part of everyday living. The people were early to rise and early to bed. No electricity or central heat comforted the simple houses. Only candlelight and firelight graced the presence of the quaint rooms.

"Sara, Sara," the words rose and fell on the brisk wind and circled the fountain in the middle of the village square. Mr. Choate waved his towel in the air and motioned for her to come closer. He reached out his hand and pulled her through the crowd. "And what brings you here, my dainty lass?"

"To see the wildflowers, smell the wood burning in the fireplaces and the scent of fresh-baked bread. I'm hoping to wash away the frustrations of the week with some lively company." Sara replied girlishly.

Mr. Choate let out a belly laugh, his eyes flashing. He guided Sara to the front of his shop. His chuckle seemed to vibrate the door, his energy surrounded her, and they walked across the room to the counter.

It only took a few seconds for the wide grin to leave the old man's face. Wrinkles formed and intertwined with the corners of his mouth to droop, forming a weathered frown.

"Laughter suits you much better, old man. What's upsetting you so?" Sara settled in the chair, waiting for the old store owner to unburden his soul.

The old peddler was reluctant to confide in an outsider, but brushed aside his distrust and decided to let her in on his secret. "The council has asked all of the elders to investigate the mutilation of the town's cattle."

He waited for Sara's reaction, but she was a trained journalist and gave great poker face. "Cattle mutilation?" she queried. "Can you describe mutilation?" The inquiry was just a ploy for Sara to gather her wits. The questions lined up and fought for position in her mind.

BLOOD MOON

"Do I have to spell it out for you? Butchered, castrated, and mutilated. How else can one say it?" Mr. Choate asked his frustration obvious.

"Who do they think is doing the mutilating, and for what purpose?" Sara ignored the sarcasm and asked the most obvious question.

"Oh, we think the purpose is pure evil. The villagers think that the culprit is a banshee." Mr. Choate shot back.

Finally, the unthinkable happened. Sara's poker face morphed into pure disbelief, *a banshee? I know the villagers are superstitious, but really. There must be a better solution. Usually, the simplest answer is the best one. The supernatural is not a simple answer.*

The door to the shop vibrated to life. A customer passed through and broke the tension in the room. Mr. Choate shot Sara a harsh glare and moved to accommodate the wishes of his patron.

"Well then, Mr. Choate," Sara looked down at the floor to avoid his stare. "Thank you for your rousing conversation. I'll talk to you again soon."

Outsiders were rarely invited into the village because the people didn't trust their motives. Mr. Choate's suspicion raced across his face, his frustration building. Sara saw this in his eyes and left him to his wares.

She rushed out of the store, wanting to put distance between Mr. Choate's conversation and her disbelieving reaction, *but really, a banshee?*

The warm sun and friendly faces softened Sara's mood. She headed toward the home of Mary, the older woman she had met on her last visit.

She had given Sara a friendly smile and then talked to her like they were old friends. Their conversation had been lengthy, stories of the many customs sprinkled throughout the lives of the villagers.

Mary was a widower. She had two sons; one was twenty-five, and the other twenty-one. On the day they met, Mary's family hadn't been home, so today, in walking past her house, she felt like saying hello.

Sara knocked on the door. To her surprise, it burst open, putting her on the ground in the most un-ladylike position. She scrambled to regain her composure when Mary rushed out and almost knocked her to the ground again.

"Jarrid, stop, come back!" Mary screamed at the top of her lungs. "Joshua, please," she cried.

The two brothers were on the ground wrestling, squirming and wiggling. From where Sara stood, they looked like one form.

"You will stop this very instant!" Mary rushed over, towered over the top of the two culprits, and with a stern voice commanded, "Stand up and act like men." To Sara's surprise, they jumped to their feet. It was the first time she had seen Mary's sons. She determined Jarrid was the oldest. He had a dark complexion and a sturdy build. It was apparent he respected his mother, *the desired quality for a man.*

The youngest, Joshua, wiggled and answered, "Mom, Jarrid started it. I was defending myself."

"Please dust off," Mary said, out of breath. "And acknowledge this proper lady."

The fire burned hot in Sara's cheeks. She stared at the ground waiting for them to approach. Her eyes raised to meet Jarrid's stare. He moved to take her hand, but she pulled back a knee-jerk reaction.

Mary recognized the tension and said, "Why don't we all go inside and have a nice cup of tea?"

BLOOD MOON

"Yes, thank you," Sara replied, avoiding Jarrid's stare.

The romantic setting of the roaring fire and the sweet smell of wildflowers made Sara uncomfortable. Mary rushed to ready the small table. Jarrid raised his hand and motioned for Sara to take a seat. His stare burned her gaze. The chair pulled out, his act of chivalry.

"Jarrid, Sara is a journalist for '*The Daily News*.'" His mother tried to soothe the heaviness in the room. "We met when she was visiting Mr. Choate."

"Yes," Sara swiftly interrupted Mary's introduction. "He and I have been working on an article."

"What sort of article? Mr. Choate is not a man of idle words or frivolous notions." Jarrid's stare intensified, filling in his facial features while he repositioned himself in his chair. "What could he possibly want to tell *The Daily News*?"

"You know how his shop is the center of the tourist trade and the quaintness of the village." Sara found herself in an awkward position and tried to make light of her explanation. She raised her eyes to scour Jarrid's tightened face for any sign he was satisfied with her answer. It was clear; he was not!

"Jarrid is head councilman." Mary broke the tension and proclaimed. "I am very proud of him." He shot a warm and loving smile in his mother's direction.

This small gesture calmed Sara's nerves, and she confronted the oldest son. "Aren't you too young to be head of the council?"

"Hmm, aren't you too young to be a journalist?" Jarrid barked, his smile turning into a manly frown.

His fiery words rose up in Sara's heart, and the Warrior Princess started to emerge, but she gained control and answered, "Not at all."

Jarrid locked his blue eyes across the table, waiting for Sara to back down, but this was not in her DNA.

She cocked her head, bit her bottom lip gently, and proclaimed, "I'm as good a journalist as any senior partner at my newspaper. Besides, I bring a younger point of view to our readers. It's what sells papers."

"My point exactly," Jarrid smirked. The two held their ground for a moment more, to settle this dispute of maturity.

"Now then," Mary added and made a move to pour more tea. "Let's have another cup and get to know one another a little better."

"Thank you, but I must go now." Sara quickly positioned her hand over her cup to discourage Mary. "It's a long walk back to my car." She pushed her chair from the table and moved to say goodbye.

"It was a pleasure to meet you, my Lady." Joshua spun around the table to meet Sara before she could reach the door. He took her hand and kissed it softly while he stared at Jarrid. "I must apologize for my brother's actions. You see, he doesn't entertain the company of beautiful women, and has no idea how to treat one so intriguing."

"Thank you, Joshua." Sara took this gesture like that of a young boy trying to one-up his older brother. "It has been very nice meeting you."

Sara retrieved her hand and said goodbye to Mary. She turned and watched Jarrid walk toward the door. It squeaked, he propped it open with one hand and motioned for her to exit with the other.

She pushed past his massive body leaving only the sound of "Goodbye to you, sir," ringing in his ears.

Her stride brisk, she hurried down the streets of the village and turned on the familiar dirt road. From a

23

BLOOD MOON

distance, she heard, "Sara! Sara! Wait up." She turned to see Jarrid running down the dusty road after her. She turned toward him and took a position of defiance.

"Wait, please." Jarrid called out with labored breaths, "Look, I apologize for my rudeness. It is just that my brother brings out the worst in me."

Her frustration took the form of folded arms together with the nervous tapping of her foot. She wanted to lash out and tell him what she thought of his behavior.

He slowly stopped just short of her icy stare, pushed the dirt around with his foot, and brought his eyes up into her cold gaze, saying, "Sara, I truly apologize. Can we please try and start over?" He knew enough about women to keep his mouth shut from this point, and waited for her to show him his next move.

Sara called on her inner strength and struggled to stand her ground. She was angry with this beautiful, stunning, masculine male specimen who had chased her down the mountain, trying to apologize. Her anger and rage slowly replaced with curiosity.

Are these words truly coming out of my mouth? "Yes, Jarrid, I accept your apology. I want to get to know you better, so let's start over." Sara made the first move to start down the mountain with Jarrid following close behind. She was the first to speak, "So, it must be invigorating being a part of the council. You surely have your finger on the heartbeat of the village." Sara didn't wait for the answer but continued, "Maybe you could tell me some of the stories about the wall sometime. I'm not a tourist, but still, I would like to know the history."

He put his hand on the small of Sara's back to steady her down the steep road. Jarrid reached deep into his being and tried to show his best side. "I would be honored to tell you about our history, but I do not want

24

what I tell you, scattered on the front page of your newspaper."

"I'd never print anything you tell me in confidence; my reputation is the core of my being." She pulled away from his touch and spoke with authority. "My job relies on the fact that I can keep my personal and professional life separate."

He'd done it again, miffed her with the least bit of effort, brought her fire to the surface which emphasized her beauty, and stirred his emotions so easily.

Sara gained her composure and started back down the road. The walk was brisk, and her emotions bounced from anger to excitement. Jarrid's attitude truly aggravated Sara, but his mere existence was titillating.

She reached the car first, eager to say goodbye once more. She needed to corral her emotions and get a handle on how she felt about this walking contradiction that had her senses firing on all cylinders.

Jarrid rushed past Sara to reach the car door first, opened it, bowed, and said, "Well, my Lady, here is your chariot, allow me."

Sara also reached for the handle at the same time but pulled back to let him achieve his mission. As he reached for the door, their faces connected, and a bolt of electricity shot through Sara's heart. A small gasp left her mouth, and she noticed a look of shyness flood across Jarrid's face. Sara smiled and beamed from ear-to-ear. *He is shy, something unexpected in one so bold.*

"Please, Sara," Jarrid's strong hands closed the door; he bent down to say goodbye. "Don't let my arrogance of the day keep you from revisiting my family. I shall be happy to speak with you the next time you visit."

He made a slight move toward her, a small gesture of apology or insurance that she would indeed return. She could imagine his warm touch, could see he was contemplating the movement, but alas he stood up, put his hand in the air to wave her on, and turned back up the mountain. Sara started the car and slowly watched him disappear into the magic of the village.

The day was almost gone, and the sun was sinking behind the mountains. Sara drove down the pass, she thought over the day and the memories she'd made. *Would Jarrid become part of my future? Was the dread growing in my heart connected with Jarrid and the village?* These thoughts constantly haunted her. She brushed aside these questions and turned the radio to her favorite station. Maybe she could drown her haunts with music.

SARAH KAGE
Chapter 3 Spirits Awakened

The sun's setting announced itself with soft pinks and greens laid on the horizon like satin ribbons. Sara sat cross-legged in her favorite chair, sipping on a warm cup of coffee to ease her chill. Zeus curled himself around the papers and books strewn across the coffee table, each heavy purr coaxing Sara to drift into a dream state.

Sara's breath matched each of Zeus's purrs, and the warm coffee gave way to sleep. Mr. Choate's words came to life, playing like a movie in her mind. Even dreaming, her unconscious was trying to understand the revelation of the banshee.

Sleep directed her thoughts. *There on the bottom shelf of the bookcase, yes, the old English dictionary given to me by my Scottish grandfather. The leather-bound cover, torn and tattered, opened to reveal the meaning, [Ban-shee n. In Ireland and W. Highlands of Scotland, a fairy-elf who, by shrieking and wailing, foretells the approaching death of a member of a family.]*

The vision of Jarrid's face overshadowed the tattered dictionary; Sara watched his words floating in the air. *Old wives' tale, the logical explanation for the mutilations and disappearances is the best answer.*

Mr. Choate's likeness came from behind to fill her mind and argue his point. *Jarrid, you have been raised on these stories and myths. Your ancestors demand that you believe.*

Zeus, looking slightly annoyed, jumped into Sara's lap, causing her to drop her cup. "No, Kitty! Oh, Zeus, you're lucky the cup was empty."

The clink of the porcelain on the table startled Zeus and caused him to leap from Sara's lap. She bent down, scooped the frightened feline into her arms, and

BLOOD MOON

enlightened him. "We know there are no such things as banshees." She didn't wait for Zeus's response but agreed with herself that indeed it was an old wives' tale. However, the journalist in her knew anything was possible.

Sunset was replaced by darkness, which spilled into every void of the room. Sara tugged on the chain of her favorite lamp, waiting for the beam of radiance to show itself. Dust particles drifted in and out across the cylinder of light and colored Sara's view, a distraction to her debate of the possibilities of the day.

It started slowly and then became relentless. The ringing of the phone jarred Sara's thoughts, and she lunged to stop the shrill attack on her ears.

"Okay, so tell me," Alex's voice spilled from the handset, "are we going to the council meeting or not?"

"Yes," Sara sighed and answered before Alex had a chance to continue with her questions. "We've been invited to the council meeting on Friday night."

The line went silent except for a distinct sound of air rushing in or out. Sara wasn't sure. The wind gathered in a gust, the fuel for Alex to spill her excitement into the earpiece. Each question dropped before the thrill pushed her to ask the next. "Do you think we'll...I mean, are we going to get the... Oh, am I going to get photos of the village, finally?"

"You have to promise me you'll take my lead and not dominate the meeting, Alex." Sara dropped her words like an anchor set in a thunderous ocean, "We have to move slowly with this."

The anchor slowed Alex just briefly, before she answered, "Okay, but what a great story. I can feel it in my bones."

SARAH KAGE

***

The elevator creaked, moaned, and stopped just across from Sara's office. Co-workers mingled and scattered in front of the open doors, immersed in the daily grind. A sea of suits and high heels gave way to a foreboding form standing just inside the parting doors. Sara barely had time to lift her eyes to see the approaching storm.

"Banshee," Alex almost tripped in her excitement to say, "Are you serious?"

"Damn!" The exclamation rolled off of Sara's tongue. She guessed telling Ted earlier not to mention Mr. Choate's conclusion was a moot point.

"Oh boy, what a story!" Alex's eyes bulged in their sockets only eased by breath escaping with each exclamation, "What a jolly good investigation this will be."

It started from deep in Sara's soul, her declaration. She had offered herself as the village's protector and protect she would.

Her words spoken with a low moan gathered momentum and filled the room like a thunderbolt. "NO WAY!" Sara's words weren't meant as an argument or even a disagreement.

The sound of babies' giggles, her daughter's familiar ringtone, filled the room. Alex moved to answer her cell phone. "What is it, Lizzy?" The movement of Sara's hand, a gesture to shoo her out, was ignored. Alex stomped her foot and commanded, "Lizzy, put your grandmother on the phone this instant." She muffled the phone and blurted her demand. "Don't think this is over Sara. I will have my way. We will cover this story."

"And you shall have your way," Sara muffled her words and proclaimed, "But only on my terms."

BLOOD MOON

The room buzzed with Alex's conversation, her frustration palpable, she turned toward the hall and trudged out the door, her words animated. "Mom, please, I'm working…"

***

Avoidance was the name of Sara's game, played well, slinking from the copy room to her office. She expected Alex's face to show any minute. Her eyes stared straight ahead, full of un-controllable anticipation, but all remained quiet. Of course, it was only the calm before the storm, and the morning had only just begun.

The slamming of the door was the first indication Alex had entered the room. She stood poised in front of Sara's desk and waited for an acknowledgment. It didn't happen.

"Good Morning," Alex greeted.

"Are you okay, girl?" Sara responded, "You look like you swallowed a firecracker." Sara's words ignited the fuse, and all restraint was lost.

"How can you be so calm about all of this, Sara?" Alex couldn't contain her spirit any longer. "You act as if we're going to do a story on the Girl Scouts." Alex continued, "Look, I have it all planned. This weekend we can get to the bottom of the mystery. We'll interview Mr. Choate, and maybe he'll shed some light on the mutilations."

How am I going to do it? Keep Alex in check and respect the fine line between professionalism and the feverish desire to write the story.

Alex was not the only one with enthusiasm. Sara knew much more was at stake. Her soul reminded her daily.

A loud bang shook the room. A book slid off Sara's desk and landed in front of Alex. They both stopped for a moment, mesmerized by the loud noise.

SARAH KAGE

"What the heck?" Alex spoke first, "How'd that happen?"

"I did it," Sara confessed, "moved it with my mind, willed it to slam in front of you, anything to shut you up!"

Alex searched Sara's face for a giggle or some resemblance of a smirk. There was nothing but a confident smile.

"Oh, so now you have superpowers?" Alex spoke, breaking her silence, "Guess that ability will come in handy when we attack the wall."

"Attack?" Sara replied, "Seems like an aggressive word for our investigation."

"You know what I mean," Alex giggled, "yes, our investigation. Hey, I have an idea. I think the kids would get a kick out of the village. Let's take them with us."

Yes, Sara embraced the idea; *maybe Alex's kids would keep a wrap on her tongue.* "Alex, you have to promise me you'll keep everything low-key. Maybe the children can help us to fit in with the village families."

Ah, finally something they could agree on. Lizbeth, eight, and Chad six were Alex's children from a previous marriage. They were full of enthusiasm and loved life, just like their mother.

"Do you think Mary will mind if we bring the children?" Alex fidgeted with the paperclips on the desk.

"No," Sara reached across the desk and swiped the container from Alex's hand. "She is very hospitable, and I've heard her say that children make for a joyful household."

"Okay, it's set. I'll tell the kids tonight." Alex turned on her heels to leave and stopped dead in her tracks, "Oh no, Sara. Do you think it's safe to bring the kids? I mean, shouldn't we think about this?"

BLOOD MOON

"I feel very safe inside the village." Sara quickly answered, "All of the trouble is at the Fortress. They'll be fine."

Alex paused. Soon the enthusiastic smile returned to her face, "You're right. Everything will be okay."

The slamming of the office door mimicked the distant thunder. A bolt of lightning lit the room. *How beautiful the clouds appear as they roll across the landscape, the lightning enhancing the edges of the storm. How could something so beautiful hold a dark and dangerous threat? Good and Evil, Yin and Yang, the ancient struggle.*

The rain, soft at first, lulled Sara as Nana's words echoed from long ago. *Child, you must mark my words. You are unique; the gifts you possess will always show you the way to the light*. The vision faint and lofty, curls of white hair falling across Nana's forehead. *Evil is part of your destiny, but you possess The Spirited Sword of Purity*. These words always rang in Sara's ears anytime she was tempted by her inner desires. The same words kept her pure even into adulthood.

The memory of sitting cross-legged in front of her grandmother, fidgeting, and straining to understand the words revealed in the glow of love, floated across her mind; the conversation remembered word for word. It had little meaning to a child, but as it drifted across her mind, being punctuated by the fierceness of the storm, it rang crystal clear. She must remain pure!

Nana preached relentlessly. Sara knew her grandmother was serious when she stressed the importance of her virginity, but not until this moment, this very snapshot of time did she truly understand the meaning.

Evil poured from the fortress wall like a river of doom. The prophecy tied to Sara, threatened her very soul. In her mind, the words formed. She spoke out loud, "Yes, I will accept *The Spirited Sword of Purity*."

Rain drizzled outside the office window as the storm rolled away, losing its power and rage. Sara's thoughts cleared, and she heard herself speak the vow brought on by the memory of her grandmother.

Her breath slowed, the memories faded, and her thoughts snapped back to the present. She watched the rays of sunshine burst through the window to kiss the top of her desk. Surely as the rays of light warmed the wood, Sara knew destiny would dictate her life from this moment forward.

"Wow that was some storm!" Ted exclaimed as he fell into the chair in front of her desk.

Sara was oblivious to his entrance. He perched himself on the edge of the seat, his arm stretched across her desk, snapping his fingers in her face.

"Hey, get a grip I have a significant assignment for you girls." Ted slumped back into the chair and repositioned his tie while he waited for a response.

"Sorry, Ted," Sara cleared her throat, "guess I was mesmerized by the storm. What assignment have you cooked up now?"

Ted jumped from the chair, paced in front of the window, and spoke, "Mr. Jones, a friend of mine, hired a local builder to renovate a downtown warehouse that he's turning into condos. Mr. Jones' condo is the first unit renovated, and I want to feature it in tomorrow morning's edition of *House Beautiful.*"

Sara was use to Ted's manipulations. He often gave his friends write-ups in the paper. She saw it as a way for him to get his foot in the door with the local hierarchy.

BLOOD MOON

Ted was standing over Sara's desk with a grin plastered across his face. The standard procedure for when he wanted her to think his idea was good for her.

"This is a prestigious opportunity and will look good on your resume. Besides, I'm doing you a favor by allowing you to do your little story on the village. So you owe me." He tossed the address and the contact information on her desk and left without her approval.

How arrogant. Oh, and don't shut the door or show me any respect at all, just demands and over-bearing leverage. Ted's cocky confidence only fueled Sara's anger, but it gave way to one realization. She would, indeed, comply with his request; after all, she owed him.

Sara was still steaming when Alex popped her head around the door. "I just saw Ted in the hall, and he said we have an assignment. He seemed pretty excited. Is it a good story?"

Sarcasm brimming, Sara replied, "Oh, yeah, it will put us on the map as the best journalistic duo in history. Just gather your stuff and meet me at the car." Sara's tone meant it was time for Alex to be uncharacteristically quiet.

Alex grew to revere and respect the dragon. She helped Sara load the equipment and looked for signs of smoke to let her know Sara was once again in control. Alex held her tongue as long as she could and finally dipped her toe into the proverbial waters to test their acidity. "Where are we going? Ted told me nothing about this assignment."

Silence circled inside the car like waves of fog. Sara took a deep breath and cleared her anger. "We are going to an old warehouse in the middle of downtown. Ted's friend talked him into doing a spread on the renovation of his condo. Heaven only knows what sort of payment Ted will demand for his favor."

There it was sarcasm, the telling sign that always followed Sara's rage. Now Alex knew it was safe to press her friend for more details. "What's so special about this condo? Why couldn't Andy or Bill have done this spread? It seems more under their job description."

"Beneath our capabilities, is that what you're saying, Alex? Well, it seems I owed Ted for allowing us to do the story on the village. Imagine that."

The warehouse loomed over the downtown street and blocked out the sun as Sara turned the car into the underground parking. Ted had instructed Sara that Mr. Jones would not be able to meet her until later, but the door would be unlocked.

Construction of the condos was underway; however, no workers were present, so Sara looked for a dolly to load the camera equipment. "Come on, Alex; let's just get this over with."

The condo was located on the top floor, apparently nothing but the best for Mr. Jones, the front door looming at the end of the long corridor. The two sleuths tugged, pulled, and maneuvered the dolly down the hallway toward the service elevator. Alex's finger stuck to the duct tape covering the penthouse button and sarcastically said, "Hope it's fixed before opening day."

The old doors resisted, creaking and moaning. The pulley system jerked to life, pulling the elevator; slow at first, upward to the twelfth floor. The noise and commotion made conversation impossible, while the two women stared at each other.

Then, in an instant, everything stopped. Alex was in mid-smile, hands positioned above the dolly, her face

BLOOD MOON

riddled with questions. No more noise or movement, the moment frozen in time.

She moved under Alex's upraised, motionless hand and marveled at the site. She moved from side to side, trying to get a different perspective on the predicament. *How was this possible?* Her mind could not grasp the reality painted across this sliver of time.

The hair on Sara's arm raised and stood at attention. From the corner of her eye, it appeared, hazy at first, but soon in full view.

The vision of a woman appeared in the corner of the old elevator, draped head to foot in a cape that obscured her face. Time ticked in Sara's ear, each second was slower than the last.

Sara tried to look back at Alex, but the woman's glare prevented it. Her ghostly arm rose, she pointed her finger at Sara and spoke, "Are you afraid? I do hope so. Just try and contain your fear for now. I am the woman from your dreams." Only Sara's eyes followed the entity. The vision moved closer to trace her face with the outstretched finger.

"Such beauty for one so young, but it will not be enough to fulfill your destiny. Oh, I know you have faith and virginity, but your purity will not stand against my dark magic."

Once again, the woman circled Sara. Then she returned to the corner where she had first appeared. Sara felt the atmosphere change, reality slowly taking over once more.

"Watch out, Sara!" Alex's scream poured slowly from her mouth, "What is that?"

The apparition addressed Alex directly, "You should relish in the moments of your life, Alex," Sara turned once more watching the ghostly entity fading into the light, but her last words, directed at Alex, stung Sara's soul, "for your destiny is written in the stones of the Fortress wall."

Again the elevator moaned, and the ride came to an abrupt stop. The dolly lunged forward and pinned Sara's leg against the rusty metal doors.

"Come on, girl," Alex mustered all of her strength to pull the dolly off Sara. The doors opened, revealing the penthouse, "are you waiting for a personal invitation? Let's get the hell out of here."

Sara's hand touched the condo's front door and turned the handle in what seemed like one motion. Once inside, Alex pushed the dolly against the door, "Quick! Push that chair here."

The two dropped to the floor with their feet plastered against the heap of equipment and furniture. "Nothing's getting through this," Alex grunted. She positioned her feet once more against the makeshift barrier and heaved with all her might.

"You do realize that was a ghost." Sara touched her trembling hand to Alex's arm, "I mean she came right through the wall. I'm not sure this defense is going to work."

Sara was still reeling from the ghostly encounter and the entities words spoken to her friend. She decided not to tell Alex the dark words directed at her by the entity, but they weighed heavily on her conscience.

"A ghost, you say? I didn't see much of anything. One minute you were in front of me and the next the dolly had you pinned."

Good! She hadn't heard the foreboding words spoken to her. Alex didn't see or remember what happened, and Sara planned to keep it that way. But these thoughts could not erase

BLOOD MOON

the fact that the ghostly vision resembled the vision of Sara's dreams.

"Hello," Sara's mental cobwebs gave way to the encroachment of the front door, moving the only thing standing between her and the elevator. "It's Mr. Jones. Sara, is that you? What's in front of my door?"

"Quick, Alex, help me move the equipment. Sorry, Mr. Jones, just a minute while we get our gear from the doorway."

The door burst open, and Mr. Jones fell into the room. The two culprits stood in unison, red-cheeked and breathless. "We were just getting started," Sara smoothed her hair and walked toward the center of the condo.

"I hope you can appreciate the beauty of this space." Mr. Jones pushed past Alex and proclaimed, "My architect is the best in the business, and I spared no expense. Why I spent more money on my bedspread than you probably paid for your car."

Great two arrogant men in one day, Sara flashed Alex the look, *I feel like I just won the lottery.* "Oh, I assure you, Mr. Jones, your condo, will get the recognition it deserves." then mumbling under her breath, "but I wouldn't want to be you when Ted collects your debt."

"Mr. Jones, I think we have all we need." Alex mumbled, browsing through the photographs on the digital camera.

Sara's interview was short and sweet. She nodded at Alex and stated. "I think we're done here."

He shot an arrogant smile in her direction, "I just want to make sure my home reflects a glamorous ambiance."

"Oh, and indeed it will, Mr. Jones. You have my word." Sara's voice cut the air like a knife.

With that, Mr. Jones herded the women to the door, "Okay, ladies, thank you very much. Please be careful when you collect your equipment. Hurry now, off with you."

Sara and Alex maneuvered the dolly out into the hall with the front door to the condo shutting noisily behind them. They both froze, each one staring at the elevator. "What do you say we carry the equipment down the stairs, Alex? We can get in some much-needed steps."

"I'm with you, girl. I've had enough adventure for one day."

There was silence in the car, not due to Sara's anger but more attributed to the strange vision.

"Sara, what really happened in the elevator? Honestly, I didn't see a thing."

"Alex, I don't want to talk about it. Let's focus on getting this riveting story back to Ted before our deadline."

Her friend reluctantly agreed and started jibber-jabbering about the upcoming council meeting. The dreams, the village, and the evil words of the entity swirled around Sara's mind, fitting into a puzzle that had not yet revealed itself.

BLOOD MOON
Chapter 4 The Council

The sun shone through Sara's office window and draped its golden rays of light across her desk. The clock on the wall struck four as a sunbeam kissed the crystal vase on the credenza and lit the room with a rainbow of colors.

Alex entered the office and broke the colorful prism, scattering hues of blues, greens, and yellows in opposing directions.

"So, are you ready for the council meeting tonight?" Alex took a position on the edge of her chair as if she were ready to leave that very moment and queried.

Her excitement evident; Sara could only smile and quip. "Cool your jets, Ms. Detective. Before you get all giddy, we must agree on some important ground rules."

"You know, you can really put a monkey wrench in a girls' fun." Alex slumped back in her chair and snorted, "Okay, give them to me slowly. I don't want to miss even one."

"You're going to have to take this seriously, Alex." Sara's chair bounced off the wall. She rose and took a stance in front of the window. "These people are my friends. Individuals I respect and trust, and in return, they welcome me into their lives. The balance of the tightrope we must walk, between our story and their right to privacy, is the cross I must bear."

"Yes, I'll be professional." Alex moved to stand by her friend. "You can depend on me. I'll put my pride aside and follow your lead." She touched Sara's shoulder to seal the promise.

SARAH KAGE

The prisms of light danced across Sara's back, parading across her skin, she turned and sat down at her desk.

"Look, Alex, think before you speak, that's all I ask. I'll pick you and the kids up around six. Just be ready." Sara squared her shoulders, pushed Alex toward the door, and said, "Go now, I have work to do before we meet Jarrid."

The words came out of Sara's mouth and dribbled across her brain like letters in alphabet soup. *Oh no, I said his name. Why did I let that slip? Maybe the inquisition will pass and not gather strength.*

This thought had not echoed in the chasms of Sara's mind before Alex pounced. "Who in blue blazes is Jarrid? Why did your mouth make that funny little pout at the mention of the name, J A R R I D? I think it's time for you to spill your beans."

Sara wanted to lasso the words before they poured from her mouth, pull them back into the space from which they were born, but it was too late. "It's no big deal, Alex. He's just someone I met in the village."

Electricity seemed to dance all around them to combine with the pale rainbow of colors fading in the dusk. "He's just someone, huh?" Alex quipped. "I guess your face lights up for every stranger you meet? Come on, Sara, give me something here before I bust."

"Oh, we wouldn't want that to happen," Sara obliged. "Look, he is the son of my friend Mary. Now, we must hurry, or we'll not be able to meet Jarrid in the clearing."

"The clearing, at night...?" Alex's demeanor changed like the deflation of a party balloon, "with a banshee on the loose? You're kidding, right?"

The grumble started low in Sara's chest. "Alex, please, give me a break here. Calm down. There's nothing to worry about. Stop letting your imagination run wild. Put that energy into something positive like getting the hell out of my office."

"Gosh, girl..." Alex straightened her jacket and demanded, "Must you be so pushy? All you had to do was ask." With that, Alex scurried off, leaving Sara in a heap of frustration and regret, punctuated by the slamming office door.

***

"Aunt Sara, are we there yet?" Lizzy asked, twirling her hair into spiral ringlets.

"Almost, are you excited?" Sara caught a glimpse of the young girl's eyes shining in the rearview mirror. It was as if she'd swallowed jumping beans for dinner, and they were multiplying with every second, so much like her mother.

"Oh, yes," She responded without a moment's hesitation. "Auntie Sara, very much so," she continued to fuss with her curls, reached over and punched her brother, just because she could, and continued. "But Chad is scared, he told me so."

Chad had been kicking Sara's seat, relentlessly all the way up the pass. He stopped only briefly to protest. "Am not," He returned his sister's blows and picked up the kicks right where he left off.

"Alright, guys," Alex turned just in time to see Lizzy land a right punch square into Chad's shoulder. "That's quite enough, you two must behave, or we'll not go to the village. We can turn this car right around and go home. So what's it going to be?"

"Okay, Mommy, but I still think he is scared." The impish girl pulled her curls and let them snap back toward her head in frustration.

SARAH KAGE

"I am not scared!" Chad exclaimed, pointing his frown in Lizzy's direction.

"We're here." Sara chimed, breaking the tension in the backseat. She slowed the car and turned onto the dirt road leading to the clearing.

Lizzy was the first to unfasten her seat belt, but Chad shot like a bullet to the front of the car. Alex nervously called to her son, "You stay right there where we can see you."

Jarrid's figure rose and fell in the headlight beams. Sara could see him coming down the mountain, his tall silhouette formed from the lantern's light. Alex gathered the children and joined Sara to watch Jarrid's approach.

"Hmm," said Alex, watching Jarrid's physique in the headlights, "Just someone, huh?" Sara brushed Alex off and stepped forward to greet him.

"Hello, everyone, welcome," Jarrid spoke first. His strong words addressed his visitors. "And who do we have here?" Jarrid knelt, so he was eye-to-eye with his small guests.

"My name is Lizzy." She scurried right up and took his hand. "Pleased to meet you, sir," She reached over, snatched her brother's arm and pulled him toward the stranger. "And this is my little brother, Chad."

"Very nice to meet you, Lizzy and Chad, my name is Jarrid." The young boy pulled away from his sister and bobbed his head toward the tall man, still not sure of the situation.

Lizzy wasted no time and chimed in, "Don't mind him. He is scared." Chad didn't even bother to dispute this fact; he ignored his sister and grabbed his mom's hand.

Sara joined the group to hover in the headlights. "Jarrid, this is my co-worker, Alex."

43

BLOOD MOON

"It is so nice to meet you, Alex. Your children are delightful." Jarrid took her hand and gently kissed it.

"You are kind sir, thank you." Alex smiled, surprised by the act of chivalry. "I hope you don't mind, but the children wanted to come, and I didn't have the heart to disappoint them."

"Certainly…" Jarrid was magnanimous; "Mom would love to have them. It has been a while since children's laughter filled the cottage."

"You guys need to wait for us," Jarrid called to the children. "I brought a lantern to light the path. We should all stay close together."

Lizzy pranced in the light, her curls bouncing, her excitement unleashed. She jolted past Jarrid leading the way with Chad coaxing his mom to follow.

The lantern broke the darkness. Sara turned off the car lights and joined the others. "Yes, I'm glad you're here, Jarrid. The walk would've been a little unnerving without you."

"Okay, up this way, not too far." Jarrid pointed the lantern in the direction of the path. "Mary is waiting for us. She can take the kids to our cottage, if that is okay with you, Alex?"

The soft light of the lantern fell on Alex's face, a nod, showing her approval. She followed his shadow down the path. Sara noticed Jarrid had impressed Alex. She walked past her to catch up with the children. Alex pulled on Sara's sleeve and whispered, "Just someone from the village, my ass!"

The soft glow enhanced Sara's smile to beam just a little too broad. "Oh, Alex, technically he is; just someone from the village."

Disapproval sprang from Alex's throat, "Right," She shook her head in the darkness; the light of the lantern missed the scene as its beam followed the children.

"Ladies," Jarrid coaxed. "You are letting us beat you." The lantern's light danced just far enough ahead to reveal the outskirts of the village.

"Come on, Chad. I'm winning." Lizzy's laughs goaded her brother.

"Keep up…" Jarrid kept an ever-present eye on the children prompting the women, "I don't want you two bringing up the rear." He pushed his elbows from against his body, an open invitation. "We are almost there, come and join me."

Sara didn't need a special invitation and accepted his gesture with gratitude. Warmth and strength radiated from his arm to extinguish the night chill.

"Keep up, Alex; it's much brighter in front of the light. You don't want to face the dark, all alone." Alex hastened her steps and accepted Jarrid's other arm while flashing a smirk in Sara's direction.

Lizzy's steps mimicked the light from the sway of the lantern, a few steps forward and then backward. She giggled and teased the light, pretending it was an imaginary friend, being ever careful not to venture outside of its beam. Then she stopped, letting the friendly light go ahead. Jarrid raised the lantern to reveal the edge of the village.

A figure stood just in the light. Mary called out, "Jarrid, is that you?"

"Mom?" the word spilled into the night air but was interrupted.

"Is that your Mama, Jarrid?" Lizzy rushed toward the stranger and engulfed Mary's legs with a bear hug. "Oh, hello, Jarrid's Mama. I am Lizzy." Before Mary could say

45

a word, Lizzy was off to instruct her brother. "Chad, come and meet Jarrid's Mama."

"Hello, Mary." Alex gathered her wee ones close. "I'm Alex, Sara's co-worker."

"It is a pleasure to meet you." Mary reached out and took Alex's hand.

Chad escaped Lizzy's grasp and hid behind Sara while she spoke, "Hello Mary, I guess you see we brought you some wee guests. I hope you don't mind."

"Oh, no…" Mary chuckled, her round belly bouncing with laughter. "It will be a pleasure, and I do not think they will refuse my offering of fresh cookies and milk."

"Oh, thank you." Lizzy once again planted herself around the robust woman's legs, squeezing with all her might. "I do so love cookies and milk. Can Chad have some too?" She only turned loose to wait for Mary's response, her eyes shining bright with childish anticipation.

"Why if you are not just the sweetest little thing, of course Chad may have cookies and milk too."

"Come on, Chad." Lizzy, confident she had procured treats for her brother, took the woman's hand. "We are going with Mary," skipping she chanted, "There will be two cookies for Chad and two for me, right, Mary?"

"This is very true, my dear. Now, take my hand, Chad, and we will see to the treats."

The young boy scurried to Mary's side and only paused a moment to look back at Alex, nodding in his direction. "Well, I think Mary has won them over, bribes always work."

"Yeah…" Jarrid pointed the lantern toward the old church, "Especially when they are in the form of cookies and milk."

SARAH KAGE

The steeple bells rang out, breaking the silence of the night air, each toll underscoring the importance of the council meeting. The children's laughter and innocence gave way to the heaviness that resounded in the dark wood of the church doors, creaking noisily to announce the trio's arrival.

"Please…" Jarrid stopped just short of entering the church, turned and addressed the two women. "I brought you here tonight to listen and learn. You will be given a glimpse into the very private world of our village. I must know that you will respect the elders and me, for I am the Word."

The authority of Jarrid's words was so strong that Sara and Alex could do nothing more than obey, following this man into the unknown, bowing to his wishes and demands, something very alien for both of these strong-minded women.

Jarrid turned and led the way through the sea of men. No village women were allowed at these meetings, so the fact that he led two strange females into the church escaped no eye.

The walk down the long aisle was never-ending. The Village Elders called out, "Jarrid, have you lost your mind? Women do not belong in these proceedings!"

The stares and rude gestures spilled over the pews and landed on Sara's ears like daggers. Alex defiantly moved ahead, not cowering to the poison being belched in their direction.

Sara could only watch Jarrid, the determination in his shoulders; he seemed taller and more foreboding. He reached the end of the aisle and pointed toward the empty pew in the front row. There was no question the seats were meant for the women.

BLOOD MOON

A long table and eight chairs graced the church stage and set the scene for the elders to conduct the meeting. Sara watched Jarrid, her stare fixed; she sat down, feeling the comfort of Alex by her side.

Each man bowed and removed himself from Jarrid's path. He moved through the crowd of men parting the way with his every step. Sara watched with labored breath, the long strides of muscles and sweat commanding respect.

Jarrid took center stage and positioned himself in front of an ornate chair, which had the appearance of a throne. Sara's heart pounded in her ears, the moment anticipated. Jarrid reached for the gavel, beads of sweat glistened, and dropped onto the table. He raised the wooden mallet with a mighty gesture and brought the hard round head down upon the wood surface. Drops of sweat flew into the air, his strong hand once more bringing the tool of authority down to find its mark.

"This meeting is now called to order!" Sara felt the air leave the church with Jarrid's words exploding from his lips.

The elders took their places; the villagers ceased their murmuring and found their seats. The quiet lasted for only a few moments.

One of the elders approached Jarrid and draped a purple cape around his shoulders. The Head Councilman gave the regal material a quick flick and took his place as the head elder; shouts came on strong from the center of the church. "What are these outsiders doing at our meeting? Why did Jarrid bring them?" The angry shouts joined in unison, "Yeah, he needs to answer for his actions."

"I am responsible." Jarrid rose from his perch with such strength the large chair almost toppled over.

A united gasp rose from the men, but he continued, "They are my guests, and protected by me." Jarrid's eyes gazed upon Sara, his nod to let her know they were welcome. The mere tone of his voice told the men there was no reasonable argument to give, and they took their places. Each man indicated his respect for Jarrid, their leader.

"Why would Jarrid be the head elder?" Alex whispered. "Wouldn't the older men hold that title?" Alex put her hand on Sara's arm. "Don't you think that's strange?"

"Yes, it's peculiar." Sara's thoughts scrambled in her head, each one placing itself in the proper index. She remembered Mary's proud words, but the fact he was Head Councilman hadn't registered.

"Everyone, please..." Jarrid spoke, "emotions are running high tonight. There are things you need to hear. They will not be easy for you to accept."

One of the men interrupted, "You know what is killing the cattle and causing the disappearances of the tourist!" The villager was almost screaming, "You know what is going on, but no one is talking about it. Is it because of the strangers who are among us?" He turned in the direction of Sara and Alex staring intently he continued, "We have to talk about it. Our women and children are afraid to venture into the woods."

The angry man turned his gaze toward Jarrid and proclaimed, "It is better to discuss it instead of letting the people bring their fear to the surface with their imaginations."

Jarrid rose, leaned over the large table and with a voice that was deep with emotion, commanded, "Silence, all of you! Be quiet and listen to what I say."

BLOOD MOON

"Yes…" Sara could feel Jarrid's eyes piercing her soul, he continued to speak, "We have strangers among us tonight, but they are here to bring our story to the outside world." He stepped out from in front of his chair and walked behind the elders to continue, "If we keep the evil only unto ourselves, and if it envelopes us, we will become one with the dark side. Then how will the outside world know what awaits them? These women are here to keep reality in our reach." A hush fell through the church, and no one stirred.

Sara pried her eyes off Jarrid for a moment and realized Alex was stone quiet, such an unusual state of affairs for her partner. "What are you thinking?"

"For the first time in my life, I believe the supernatural world exists." Alex turned to Sara with a sober look and continued, "I feel we are very near to it, and it is reaching out to me." Sara noticed the gray, almost ashen reflection in her friend's face. Alex's fear gathered in her eyes.

"We've known the presence of darkness will always be." Jarrid's voice started low at first and then thunderous, bouncing off the ceiling of the old church, it's every syllable washed over Sara. His speech continued, "Whether it is supernatural or magic is no longer a question?

"As children, we are taught, evil will always battle good, and even though the evil can win the battle, good will always prevail. This single belief is our weapon against the vile presence that dwells among us."

Each of his words stronger than the last, Jarrid paced across the stage with the speech pouring from his mouth, his purple cape giving way to his stride. "We have been taught that the spirits of many people inhabited the Fortress before us, and I say to you without hesitation, evil is spilling over the great walls and infecting our village. I believe the mutilations are a warning of much tribulation. And now I say to you, these people you call strangers, are the very ones who will be your deliverance."

The room broke into madness. Fists rose, and angry words spilled into the air. Sara could not stay in her seat; anger pushed her to stand, wishing to be anywhere but in this church. She shoved her way through the sea of men waiting for no one to lead the way.

The angry mob pushed from behind. Alex caught Sara's sleeve and screamed above the crowd, "Sara, did you hear what he said?"

"What, what did you say?" the crowd was deafening. At that same moment, Sara caught Jarrid's gaze as a laser pointed straight into her soul. Her mind played back his ominous words. She fought even harder to reach the wooden doors.

"Come on. Let's go." Sara gathered Alex like a belonging and shoved her through the crowd. The church doors offered no resistance. No lantern lit the path; only darkness greeted them, as they stumbled down the village road toward Mary's cabin.

"Sara, Alex, wait up!" Jarrid yelled, "Please stop. I want to talk to you." Sara didn't pause but guided Alex down the path with Jarrid's words rising above their heads. "Sara, what is wrong?"

This silly question stopped Sara dead in her tracks. She turned to face him, her mouth poised to speak the only answer she could muster. Her stare was deliberate, her voice strong, "Why did you say those things about us? We are only here to write a story. How could we be involved with the evil?"

BLOOD MOON

"Look, Sara," Jarrid answered. "I do not know why, but be sure that you are indeed involved with whatever is going on. I do not know how I know. I just do. Were you not the one telling me about the dreadful feeling you have been experiencing lately? Please, do not be angry with me."

"I'm not angry," Sara said, looking into his eyes. "You're right. I have a feeling of doom, but what could it have to do with your village and the mutilations?"

At this point, Alex interrupted, "Look, guys, I don't know what's going on either, but you can be sure that we'll report one hell of a story."

"NO!" Jarrid yelled, "Not yet. I want you to tell the whole story, from start to finish the way it unfolds. You will not write anything until it is over." The force in his voice was so compelling all Alex could manage was a nod in his direction.

"Okay, Jarrid, cool your jets." Sara broke into the conversation, "I don't know what any of this means. I'm confused and weary of this whole matter."

Alex agreed and walked ahead with Jarrid shining the lantern down the village road. He let a little distance come between them, prompting Alex to walk ahead, chose his words, and whispered to Sara, "Please, you have to believe me. You are in great danger."

"What kind of danger?" Sara turned and asked, watching tiny lines form in the lantern's shadow falling across his face. A shiver ran up and down her spine, for she knew, in her soul, he was right. "Jarrid…" her mouth poised to continue.

He put his finger upon her lips and said, "Sara, when the time is right, you will know your part. That is all I can say."

SARAH KAGE

Even though Sara wanted to push the matter, she found she couldn't. It was his spell, a force that both excited and terrified her. But Sara couldn't resist his request to stop and speak of it no more this night.

***

Candlelight shown through the tiny cabin windows and lay on the porch like soft ribbons. Alex's steps echoed on the wooden stairs, the screen door burst open, and the children's laughter filled the night air.

"Look, Chad, its Mommy." Lizzie's smile beamed even brighter than the candles. She gathered Alex's hand and proclaimed. "Come on, Mommy. You must try Mary's cookies. They are divine."

Jarrid positioned himself behind Sara, so close that not even the night breeze could pass between them. He paused to squeeze her arm and whispered in her ear, "Follow my lead."

A small gasp passed over Sara's lips, and she pressed herself into his chest. A slight quiver arose in Jarrid's voice, "Alex, go on ahead, Sara and I are going to…" his voice cracked, "take a walk." Alex nodded with the two children guiding her toward the kitchen and the waiting treats.

The lantern scraped the ground as Jarrid discarded the light. Its sound dug at Sara's ears, and she snapped back from the hazy realm of Jarrid's chest. Beams of moonlight rose over the fortress wall in the distance and lit the winding path. Their fingers laced together, Jarrid led Sara toward the ancient Fortress. Crickets sang their nightly song with an occasional bullfrog to bring in the bass. Words would've been foreign to Sara at this point.

A hoot broke the night air with an owl landing in the tree above, its wings shining in the moonlight. Jarrid took advantage of Sara's upward gaze and slowly buried his

BLOOD MOON

face in the small of her outstretched neck. Her tiny sigh slid over his ear, encouraging him to continue. A still fell over the forest, their passion stealing the attention of every being in the dark.

Sara's resistance was gone, and she had no free will. She fell into his mold, lying against every muscle and form of his body. Then he spoke low with mammalian tones, his breath light to brush against her skin. "You are my deliverance. The only one I see. You are my destiny."

She gasped, Jarrid's body pressed against hers, the only restriction she felt was the cold, hard, stone wall bringing their bodies closer together. He engulfed her with his arms—all of her.

His head buried deep into her shoulder, breathing short, calm wisps of breath tunneling toward the rise of her breast. His lips leaving small traces of the kisses pressed ever so gently on the length of her neck. It was the moment she knew she could be lost, all of her control gone like hot breaths in the cool night air.

The dance continued. Jarrid slowly searched for the moistness of her lips, pausing only a moment before exploring the depth of her kiss.

Sara waited all her life for this kiss, her body responded. There would be no resistance to it; only the sweet surrender of her beating heart to this one man.

His grip tightened, Jarrid hoisted her upward against his body only to let her slide back down slow and deliberate until once again their lips entangled.

Sara's passion draped across her body like fire on a blazing mountain, licking and flirting with the night, not to be smoldered. Once again, Jarrid's voice echoed in her ear, "There will be no walls between us."

Her brain was calling, screaming to get her attention. *What are you doing? Quick, you must gain control.* This thought interrupted by a low growl coming from deep within Jarrid's soul. His urge of release fell upon him, the evidence on his face, ebbing and flowing like the pull of the ocean tides themselves.

Faintly, a call rose through the forest, "Jarrid, Sara, are you there?" Mary's voice echoed across the pines and disturbed the owl. It flew from its lofty perch; the flapping wings gave rise to the sounds of the night once again.

Jarrid released Sara's trembling body and called to his mother, "Yes, Mom, we are here." Jarrid stared deep into Sara's eyes and continued, "We will be right there."

Every sense was heightened and on fire. Sara stood in the clearing, her body foreign to her. There in the shadow, Jarrid reached for her hand and guided her down the path. No words were necessary; the night had spoken. His touch electric and their relationship changed for all eternity.

BLOOD MOON
Chapter 5 Dreams Unleashed

Jarrid brushed past Alex with two sleeping angels, one in each arm. Mary beamed from ear to ear, exclaiming, "Please be sure and bring the little ones back for another visit. They are such a joy." Sara and Alex hugged the chubby elf-like woman and started after Jarrid.

"Oh, such a strong man, Sara, and such a heart. This one is definitely a keeper." Alex whispered. Sara frowned and tried to show a neutral position toward the mountain of a man with a sleeping child in each arm.

"Hmm," is all she could muster, hurrying to catch up with her knight in shining armor?

Jarrid placed the sleeping angels in the back seat of the car without a single eye opened. Alex was on a sugar-induced high, causing her to gush words of praise, "Jarrid, you're a dream. Thank you so much for your help."

He guided Alex to the front seat and said, "It has been my pleasure," all the while, he stared directly across the car's rooftop and straight into Sara's eyes.

She broke his stare, sliding into the seat, hoping to avoid a lengthy goodbye. The car rolled only a few inches. She felt his strong hand on her shoulder. "Sara, please drive carefully and remember my words. Keep them close to your heart."

The emotion Sara felt was surrender, but her mind hinged on fear and confusion as she spoke, "Yes, Jarrid, I do feel the same." She removed her foot from the brake. The night's connection was over. Jarrid stood in the dark and watched the distance grow with the car lights vanishing into the night.

SARAH KAGE

Lights of the passing cars invaded the darkness and revealed Alex's relentless stare, "Is something wrong, Sara? Are you mad at Jarrid? Why is there so much distance between the two of you?"

Sara shivered at the word distance. *Wasn't that much space between us, nope not at all, if Alex only knew the truth of the night.*

"Aren't you bothered by the council meeting, Alex?" Sara shoved her rampaging emotions aside and put on her journalistic hat. "I mean, it was pretty intense, don't you think? Jarrid has this desire to put us front and center in the terrible evil raining down on the village. I'm so confused about our part in it all."

"Yes," Alex considered her answer and spoke, "but my professional spidey-sense is really tingling. I mean, we are in a perfect position to get a scoop. Aren't you excited?"

"Well," Sara's voice rang with a little sarcasm, "I have some kind of sense tingling, but I'm not sure what it is."

Her comment was Alex's cue, "Oh, and does that tingle have anything to do with Jarrid?" Alex was pleased with her question and continued, "Look, you know I love to tease you, but on a serious note, I think Jarrid is…"

"What?" Sara waited in the dark with the sound of the passing cars ticking away the seconds. She continued, "Jarrid is what?"

"It's true that I'm impressed with Jarrid." Alex took in a deep breath and let her concerns pass through the silence, "But at the same time, I don't know? There's something dark about him. Something deep in his personality that scares me."

"Are we home, Mommy?" Sara pulled into the driveway just as Lizzy started to stir.

BLOOD MOON

"Yes, my precious," Alex answered, collecting the two half-sleeping bundles. Lizzy wiped her sleepy eyes and gathered Chad, guiding him down the sidewalk and toward the door.

Alex stood on the front stoop fumbling with kids and keys; she waved back toward Sara and flashed thumbs up.

Darkness surrounded the door with only the interior hall light to illuminate the entrance. A strange glow seemed to surround Alex's head, radiating out in every direction, capturing Sara's attention. Her thoughts, jumbled and fuzzy, searched for an explanation of the halo-like beam draped around Alex's head. *Am I going crazy? What could this mean? It's so unusual.*

No rational explanation could account for the strange light. Alex turned to slip inside, and the beam disappeared as if snuffed out by some hidden hand to obscure it from human sight. Sara rubbed her eyes and chose denial as the best solution.

The traffic light broke Sara's trance. She slammed on the brakes and realized she had started the car and headed in the direction of home. This day would go down as one of the most unusual in her memory. Sara ached for the comfort of her bed and the possibility of a dreamless night.

***

A meow broke the silence of the room, "Oh, Zeus, are you ready for bed?" The sheets folded around Sara to envelop her with the soft promise of sleep, with the black cat settled down beside her. She drifted off into that space between wake, and dream where the mind is a little fuzzy, floating just beyond reality.

Drip, drip, the small droplets of water fell through the air and landed on the porcelain bowl, the sound relentless, the next drop took its place in the bathroom basin. Thoughts of porcelain, cold and hard flowed through Sara's dream, the feeling rising to find its way to the tops of her shoulders.

Her warm bed was a distant memory with the rocks lashing out against her body from all sides of the dark cave. Only shapes and colors made it through her sense of sight.

The moisture fell from the rock formations with a constant drip. With each drop in unison until it reminded her of a familiar tune rising and falling through her memory.

Beads of sweat trickled down her face; the dream demanded Sara's attention. A light in the cavern directed itself into a beam to show the middle of the large cave. It pulled at her gut and forced her into the direction of the stone altar. A beam of light shining from above lit Jarrid's naked body draped across the altar's cold, bare surface.

"No, no, stop!" The words rose from the depth of Sara's soul and echoed throughout the cavern, bouncing off the wall behind her. She couldn't move, pinned to the stones by some unseen force.

There in the shadow, a woman draped in black stood over Jarrid. Her hands clasped around a long dagger, its steely blade shimmered in the light. Demonic voices oozed through the walls, and the words of ancient incantations circled Sara's thoughts.

"Jarrid…" Sara's breath fueled the scream from deep inside her core, but the glimmer of the blade didn't show her reflection. No acknowledgment of Sara's presence existed. She was a mere shadow, only an observer of this fiendish act.

The woman threw her head up and cried out to the Dark One, "I sacrifice this mortal soul to you, my prince.

BLOOD MOON

Bless our immortal union and grant us the title of your King and Queen of Darkness."

Sara's anger fell upon her like fire. She fought the invisible hands twisted and gnarled around her body. Her head rose, the scream poured from her mouth and echoed from every crevasse of the cave.

Then, as if someone had taken a snapshot, every movement, sound, and echo ceased. Sara's eyes fixed on Jarrid's naked body, while her mind took inventory of each Kodachrome detail.

His eyes opened, their blueness pierced the stillness of the moment, and they stared straight through Sara. The room spun, images twisted, and smeared across her mind.

Sara strained to hear the shrill scream coming from a distance. Her arms and legs twisted and held captive by the bed sheets. She struggled and gave one last attempt to free herself from the night's terror—every fiber of her being enveloped the image still burning in her mind.

Sara raised herself in the bed; the room still spinning; she struggled to capture the last moments of the nightmare. Zeus jumped off the bed and screeched, heading for the closet.

Sweat poured from every pore, her long red hair swept from her wet face. She tore at the sheets ripping and pulling their last restraints from her body.

She sat, her knees pulled close to her torso. Sara rocked and waited for her heartbeat to slow. The taste of metal wrapped around her tongue, her breathing slowed, and her mind calmed. Sleep would not come this night only the weary tossing and turning of the reality of the nightmare, or was it an omen?

SARAH KAGE

***

"Are you there, Sara?" Alex answered the phone with her usual sarcastic charm, "Hello. I know it's you I recognize the number. Are you alright?" Sara had dialed Alex's number, while she drove, still in a trance, reeling from the restless onslaught of terror otherwise known as sleeplessness.

Brake lights loomed, their redness assaulted Sara's eyes. She almost dropped the phone into her lap, while answering Alex. "Yes, I'm here. I called you, didn't I?"

"Okay, it's your nickel." Alex snorted and teased. "What's up?"

Sara rolled her eyes, growing impatient with the traffic and Alex's teasing.

"Look, I'm coming to pick you and the kids up. We're going to the park. I need to talk to you." Sara didn't wait for an argument, but continued, "You can't say no, I need to vent."

"Oh, well, in that case, okay. The kids would love a morning at the park. Alex conceded. Hey, this couldn't have anything to do with the way you left Jarrid last night?" Sara could hear the small undertone of Alex's whisper, "I hope, I hope."

"Really, Alex, men," Sara's wits were frayed and on edge, evident by her tone, "Is that all you ever have on your mind?"

"Okay, cool your jets, Miss Primadonna." Alex heard the desperation in Sara's voice and changed her tune. "Is it about the village?"

Sara squeezed the phone so hard that her hand started to ache. She composed herself and answered, "Yes, no, I don't know? Just put your efforts into being ready. I'm only a few blocks away."

BLOOD MOON

She waited for Alex's goodbye or at least a sarcastic comeback, but only the tone of an ended call buzzed from the phone.

***

Fall was in full bloom. Sara walked through the grass with the fallen leaves pricking and digging at her ankles, driven by the cold wind of autumn. The breeze caught her hair and flung it hard against her face, swirling to lift it above her head like a red kite bursting to free itself. The atmosphere dulled her sense that summer had given way to fall.

Leaves fell from a nearby tree, like jewels from a king's crown. The red and gold of the foliage, like Christmas wrapping, crumpled and tossed aside by a child in his haste to reveal the present carefully wrapped inside.

The front door opened, and Lizzie spilled out in all of her splendor, "Auntie Sara, you're here."

"Don't go in the street, Lizzy!" Alex's concern melted away as Lizzy wrapped herself safely in Sara's arms.

A fierce wind blew from behind and tousled Alex's unruly hair. She brushed it from her face and tugged at the last holdouts, plastered across her lips, to release them from their entrapment.

Alex flung out her keys to lock the front door, looked back over her shoulder, and noted Sara's peculiar expression.

"Well, girl, you look worse for the wear. I guess our visit to the village took more out of you than I thought," Alex proclaimed, gathering her hair into a ponytail.

"No," Sara exclaimed, "it wasn't the meeting." She stopped for a moment wrestling with the decision to tell Alex about the nightmare.

SARAH KAGE

"Hurry up, Chad," Alex took Lizzy's hand as the young girl skipped and taunted her brother. "Aren't you coming with us?"

"Guys, you're pulling my arms out of their sockets." Lizzy on Alex's right and Chad on her left, the two kids swung and jumped, each one trying to outdo the other. Alex bent down, bringing them together and then rose up, her eyes opened wide with enthusiasm. "Oh, yeah, you wanted to talk about last night, right."

Sara froze, the words cascading through her mind, *the halo of light, the passionate kisses, and the premonition. But which one do I really want to reveal?*

"Hey, guys. Who wants to go to the park?" The children scampered to the car with screams of joy spilling into the air.

"Okay, I guess the talk can wait until the children are safe on the jungle gym, an oxymoron, you understand." Alex threw her hands in the air and motioned onward.

"You must walk the plank, Captain Ron." Lizzy took the role of Blackbeard and taunted Chad. She pointed to the edge of the slide and prompted him to take the watery exit.

The warm wooden bench gave solace from the cold, windy breeze. Alex waited for Sara to speak. She couldn't contain herself any longer. "Listen, we only have a finite number of hours here, so could you please just spill your beans."

Calm stirred through the breeze, or maybe it was the laughter floating on the wind, whichever, the atmosphere engulfed Sara's troubled soul, and she spoke, "Alex, I know that the fingers of evil surrounding the village envelopes us and threatens our lives. I think the future revealed itself to me last night in a dream."

BLOOD MOON

"What, a stone altar," Alex's expression widened with every detail, "with Jarrid naked and a woman sacrificing him to the Devil…" Alex's mouth fell open.

"Yes," Sara placed her hand on her friend's arm. "Something about them being the King and Queen of the Underworld."

"Hold that thought." Alex rose from the bench with such intensity that it reacted like a teeter-totter. She rushed the playground and scolded Lizzy. "Let Chad be the pirate. It's his turn to take charge." Alex walked back to the bench, slumped down and braced herself.

"But, that's not all." Sara waited for her friend to process the horrible accounts and then continued. "Last night when I dropped you and the kids off, I had a vision"

"Don't sugarcoat it. Are we going to die?" Alex exclaimed, with fear in her eyes.

"Oh, my Drama Queen," She wrapped her arms around Alex's sunken shoulders to reassure her friend. "I certainly hope not."

"Wait…" Alex burst into a verbal explosion, "we're talking about demons, the Devil, and ancient incantations. Do you hear yourself?"

The wind slapped Sara directly in the face causing her to rise from the bench. "Look, all I know is that there are things I can't explain. This nightmare was not a dream but a warning."

"Come on, guys." Alex yelled, "We're leaving." Sara stopped short and searched for just the right arrangement of words to tell Alex about the vision of the halo.

Before the kids crossed the playground to complain, Sara confronted Alex. "You're going to stand still and listen. You might not want to hear these things, but I'm compelled to tell you anyway. Last night when you were on the steps, fumbling for your keys, I saw a halo of light, around your head; shinning so bright I had to look away. Now, I have no explanation for this other than a vision. If you have any other ideas, please feel free to enlighten me."

The kids chose to ignore the request to leave and continued playing. Alex confronted her co-worker, the fear rising in her throat. "Damn it, Sara, I do believe what you're telling me, and I'm afraid, and that pisses me off. My career should always be front and center; instead of fear, I should be rushing to the office to gather my equipment. Instead, my nerves are shot, and my courage is gone. That's just how much I do believe you."

Have I gone too far..., Sara stretched out her arms and hugged Alex, *given up too much information?* "Okay, maybe my imagination has run away with me; probably too much late-night TV?"

"Yeah," Alex let a nervous laugh slip past her lips. "But, it's probably me, the ultra Drama Queen." She wiped her eyes and moved to lighten the moment.

"Come on, you two," Alex yelled for the kids, "it's time to go."

The typical moans and groans of the rambunctious kids helped Alex calm her fears and gave her the strength to face each one head-on. "Look, we'll approach the story like we always do, just the facts' ma'am." She deposited the two wiggling bundles, also known as Lizzy and Chad, in the back seat and gave Sara a quick wink.

The cold air and jungle gym took its toll on the two cherubs, and they slumbered, piled one on the other in the back seat. The lyrics to *Witchy Woman* spilled from the radio as Sara thought, *how ironic?* Her mind toyed with the thought of revealing her plans to investigate the

BLOOD MOON

Fortress that very night. Should she ask Alex to join her, knowing the fear her friend now held in her heart?

The lyrics of the song motivated Sara to raise the subject; she reached for the radio knob with the lyrics trailing off. "Okay, I'm going to ask you something…"

"Huh," Alex stirred, wiping the car induced nap from her eyes. "What is it now?"

"We have a job to do," Sara proclaimed, "which is the nature of the beast. No personal feeling, fears, or judgments' can cloud our ability to do our job. Would you agree?"

"Yes, I agree, don't mind me." Alex sat up and uncrossed her legs, "It's just that was a lot to take in. You've had a few days to process all of this. I've had my head in the sand, but rest assured, I'm back on my game."

Courage flooded back into her friend's eyes, a cue for Sara to continue. She put both hands tightly on the wheel and spilled her beans. "I want to go to the Fortress tonight to investigate it for myself, without Jarrid or anyone from the village. Are you with me?"

The silence in the car was palpable. It seemed like an eternity until Alex spoke, "So I guess your thoughts are that you and I will sneak into the Fortress, where all the evil has taken place, without Jarrid, the Village Warrior, and oh, I don't know; do some investigating? Does that seem about right?"

Alex's sarcastic response took on a life of its own, so Sara asked the most crucial question of the day. "Are you in?"

Her answer bounced off the windshield, "When have you ever known me to back down from a challenge, evil spirit or not. Hell yes, I'm in! The kids can stay at Moms tonight; we'll pick them up in the morning. Let's go be journalists."

It was a calculated decision not to invite Jarrid to join the night's adventure. Sara's black and white analytic mind reasoned if he didn't enter the Fortress, he could never become a sacrifice. It was the only way she knew to keep him safe.

Even though Alex had agreed to Sara's hair brain scheme, her exact words, she was still a little hesitant. "Hope we're doing the right thing going alone?"

"It's the only way, Alex." The oncoming cars shed their light into the car, falling upon Sara's worried face. "We'll be fine, trust me."

***

It was colder than usual. Old Man Winter had overpowered autumn, blowing across the mountain, sending a frosty chill over the village. The car ride was silent without the taunts and giggles of the kids. "Did Lizzy complain about being left behind?" Sara inquired, looking over her shoulder to change lanes just before she turned onto the village road.

"You know my daughter." Alex quipped. "Of course she did." The car lights spread out into the tree line, casting eerie shadows across the field. "Mom bribed her with cookies, works every time." She sat back in her seat and continued, "Besides, Mom agreed my work is important. She was glad to help."

Sara pulled the key from the ignition, leaving the car in silence. Sara and Alex sat quietly with the dashboard lights slowly fading, as the car headlights vanished, leaving only the darkness.

The extra layers of clothes lay on Sara's shoulders like boulders meant to drive off the cold autumn night. They didn't help the shivers that raced up and down her spine.

BLOOD MOON

"Okay, this is it." Alex reached across the console and grabbed Sara's hand. "Either we are brave, or we're not. I vote for brave."

Before Sara could respond, Alex opened the door to face their cold reality. "Um, I'm standing in the dark, alone. Would you care to join me?"

Sara felt for the side of the car, circling to stand next to her partner in crime. There could be no lights guiding them to raise suspicions among the villagers. The reporter and the photographer were in stealth mode.

"This was well-thought-out." Alex started to walk, feeling the ground with her foot. "How are we supposed to see?"

"Let your eyes get used to the dark and then look straight ahead." Sara took Alex's arm. "Can't you make out the trail between the trees?"

The two women walked in unison with each other. Sara pushed forward as though she had a sense of direction.

Frustration rose in Alex's voice, "Where're we going? I still can't see a thing."

"We need to head in that direction." Sara stopped and pointed to a bright star in the sky. "It'll lead us directly to the fortress wall."

Sarcasm, Alex's one tool of courage poured over her lips, "Oh, so we're astronomers now, are we?"

Sara drove her finger into Alex's side to raise a giggle, but the layers of clothing adorning her torso foiled the attempt.

They headed up the dark path and around the corner from where the fortress wall loomed up straight and dark. Alex pulled back on Sara's arm, seconds passed before she spoke, "We are justifiably nuts. You do know this right. I mean all this time we've been worried about the supernatural not even entertaining the idea that the killer could be human; with a gun."

"This is just an adventure, Alex." Sara's fears welled up inside, trying to steal her courage. "You know, like when we were kids. We're just investigating this old relic, at night, in the pitch dark. Okay, I see your point." Sara reluctantly concurred.

Her fears formed words running across her mind, *not so much a person with a gun, but the possibility that Jarrid could meet his death in the walls of the Fortress. I have to know more, who was the woman in my dreams? Does Jarrid know her? When will her identity be revealed?*

All at once, Sara's thoughts fell into the abyss of her mind. Alex was pulling on her arm. "Look, up there on top of the wall. It's a light. Do you see it? I've never noticed it there before. Do you think someone's in the Fortress?"

"Looks like a candle or lantern." Sara walked the length of the wall feeling with her hands for the gate that would lead to the inner corridor of the Fortress. "There's no electricity for lights." Just at that moment, her hand felt the old metal latch, and the gate swung open.

The creak echoed through the dark and bounced off the inner walls. The two women stood, just in the doorway, waiting for some ancient entity to appear before them in the darkness.

And there it was the familiar sarcasm spilling from the one person Sara was glad she brought along. "Well, Missy, put on your big girl pants, and let's go save the world."

BLOOD MOON
Chapter 6 Whispers on the Wind

Silence gave way to the crickets and night serenades. Darkness fell across the hall as it wiped away any clue that led into the inner chambers of the Fortress.

Alex crept up from behind to get a closer look as Sara stepped back, unsure of her next move.

"Watch out," gasped Sara feeling a hardness bury into her back. "Alex, what the hell is that?"

"Look," Alex slowly moved the layers of clothing aside as the moonlight bounced off the hard steel barrel of the gun resting in her waistband, "we could be confronting a crazy person, hell-bent on putting another notch on his belt. I came prepared."

"Oh, my God! Do you know how to use that?" Sara touched the steel barrel and realized Alex was right. She'd been so busy contemplating the supernatural that just an everyday crazy person, with a gun, seemed too typical.

"Hell, yes. Of course I do." Sara's focus was interrupted as Alex's answer rang through the night. "You don't think I would've brought it otherwise."

"Yeah, okay," Sara retorted. "I guess you'll have to fill me in on your Annie Oakley tendencies later, but for now, just keep that thing close."

Quiet lingered, a stillness that lent itself to the task at hand. Sara took Alex's hand as she felt the wall for the direction of the inner chambers. Their footsteps echoed as each shoe raised and dropped on the pebbles strewn across the path. Each forward motion was in anticipation that the mere sound would set in motion some dreaded evil encounter.

SARAH KAGE

"Stop, listen." Alex squeezed Sara's hand and whispered, "I think someone or something is behind us, but I'm too afraid to look."

Sara reached under her coat and took out the tiny flashlight, her contribution to the weapon arsenal, which seemed pretty silly next to Alex's glinting, deadly weapon. Its use deemed necessary by a dire emergency, and this situation qualified.

"Look, we will both turn around at the same time." Sara turned and pointed the tiny beam down the hall. The tube of light raced down the sides of the corridor for what seemed an eternity. Then something broke the beam, diffused its light snuffing out the only ray of truth in the darkness.

"Did you see that, Alex?" Sara heard Alex's chest rise and fall as shallow, fearful breaths shortened her answer.

"Yes, yes, I did. What was it?"

"We're going to find out where this leads." Sara once again pushed Alex forward toward the answers waiting in the darkness. "I'll not leave without knowing." Sara's mind filled with possibilities. *It was probably just the old wooden gate swinging closed, nothing to worry about.*

Even when Sara pulled at Alex's sleeve, she knew the words were only thoughts offered up to the night, something to fuel her bravery. They hastened their steps as the uncontrollable impulse to move deeper into the Fortress enveloped their every sense.

Each step echoed in Sara's mind reminding her of the altar with its deadly consequences. Her primal drive for self-preservation married with her need to get to the truth.

Sara dug in her heels, stopping her forward motion, and tousled Alex to the ground with a thud. "Hey, what's wrong with you?" Alex shouted, "Okay, now you're scaring me." Alex jumped to her feet to confront Sara but found her friend standing like a stone statue. She grabbed the tiny flashlight from Sara's grip and pointed it directly into her eyes.

The light danced across Sara's face and showed no life. Alex ignored the condition and spoke, "Sara, we need to get out, to abort this crazy, suicidal…" Only the sounds twirling around her tongue and passing through her lips danced across her eardrums.

Sara's inner voice screamed with urgency. *It's the demon woman, the one from my dreams, her voice low and evil spewing the night's secrets.*

The wind pushed down the mountainside and over the Great Wall to rush in front of Sara's frozen face. Her eyes fixed without life, no movement, just the demon's voice that rose from deep in her throat. "We are headed to the altar for *The Feast of Souls*. We must have this one if we are to accomplish our mission."

"What are you talking about?" Alex screamed.

The violent shaking erased the sounds while Sara's head snapped forward and then back, her eyes coming into focus just in time to see something tackle Alex from behind and wrestle her to the ground.

Still shaken from the trance, Sara screamed, "No, no, leave her alone." She struggled with the cloaked entity pulling it away, the flashlight falling and spinning on the ground, each revolution of light fell on the face of the attacker and revealed his identity.

"Jarrid, what are you doing here? Stop! You're hurting Alex."

The pummeling of Sara's fist against Jarrid's back caused him to spin in her direction. He offered a hand to Alex and answered Sara, "I was in the woods and saw someone enter the Fortress. I came to investigate, and pray tell what the hell are you two doing?"

"We're doing our job if you don't mind." Alex pulled and tugged at her coat, covering the barrel of the gun.

"You can't be here," Sara jerked his hand and commanded, "behind the walls. You must never be behind the walls."

Alex brushed off the fear and turned her attention to the standoff that was in full swing playing out in the cold night air. "Jarrid, did you hear her? What Sara was saying, and the voice it was something evil."

Jarrid tried to pull Sara close, but her growl, a low guttural warning, oozed from her throat, a leftover emotion coursing through her veins.

"No, Alex. I was too busy trying to protect myself." Anger tinted his words, "Sara, do you remember what you said?"

Sara stood for a moment, trying to remember what she heard. "It was the voice of the woman from my dreams."

"Yes," Alex agreed, "she was talking about sacrifices and altars, but in a strange voice, no voice I ever want to hear again; something about *The Feast of Souls*. Honestly, it just seemed like gibberish to me. It wasn't so much what she said, but that unholy voice."

The remaining effects of Sara's trance faded like a movie restarted in slow motion. Her thoughts replayed the nightmare and the fact that Jarrid was standing in front of her in the Fortress.

"Jarrid, we have to leave now. Your life is in danger."

Sara pulled on Jarrid's sleeve frantically trying to get him outside of the Fortress. He realized the fear was real and coaxed the two women to hurry, bringing up the rear for protection.

BLOOD MOON

Urgency spurred Sara on, and she led the way to the old wooden gate, looking back to make sure Jarrid had heeded her warning and was leaving the Fortress.

Jarrid slowed to secure the latch before heading down the path calling to Sara, "Wait up. You have to tell me why you were here. You cannot do this on your own. It is too dangerous."

His words fell on deaf ears, his command ignored. Sara trudged down the mountainside with Alex close behind.

Sara's mission was to get Jarrid as far from the Fortress as possible. She stopped briefly to make sure he was following them to the car.

Jarrid finally caught up to Sara before she reached the car door. He lunged and grabbed her arm, pulling her away from the handle. "Jarrid, you're hurting me."

The words caused Jarrid to loosen his grip and pull her up into his arms. His words fell softly on her neck, "You must promise me that you will never go into the Fortress again without me."

Sara wiggled out from under his arms to confront him directly. She knew he must understand how much danger surrounded his very existence.

"You were right, Alex and I are very much a part of the evil here, but you must understand that you are also involved. You must heed my words, Jarrid; I'll never go inside the Fortress walls with you. Your life depends on it. My dreams have shown me the future." Jarrid stepped forward. Sara placed her hand on his chest and made her point. "I have seen your death. You must never go inside the walls. Do you understand me?"

Sara broke down. Jarrid gathered her into his arms and proclaimed, "Okay, Sara, I promise."

SARAH KAGE

Even as the words poured from his mouth, a sharp pain rose in his heart, for he knew it was a promise he couldn't keep.

Jarrid's goodbye lingered in Sara's mind. Her heartbeat mimicked the cadence of the white lines, reflecting in the car headlights. The heaviness of the night echoed through the car, no explanations or theories painted the darkness; only dead silence. There were no words; souls intertwined with the evil and circumstances that surrounded the very existence of the village.

The brakes squealed, and the car slowly kissed the curb outside of Alex's apartment. She reached for her friend's hand. "Okay, I get that you don't want to talk about tonight, but we'll have to discuss it soon. I'm committed to getting to the bottom of this story." She gave Sara's hand a little squeeze and left the darkness of the car.

Sara watched the hall light engulf her friend and expected the halo to surround her with its loving glow, but no such comfort offered its self this night.

***

The click of Sara's heels on the hard floor brought her closer to the start of her day. Her office door offered no resistance as she brushed through the doorway and headed toward her desk, just like she'd done many times before. Today it all seemed black and white, with no colors or brightness, only the constant haze and dullness that had invaded her once peaceful existence with the fear of the future.

She rounded the corner of her desk and slumped into the chair, staring out the window, searching for some sign of beauty. Her eyes reluctantly gazed across the papers on her desk, each one a hue of gray in varying tints and patterns. But there, anchored on top of the colorless stack, a vibrant square of yellow notepaper beckoned for her attention. It demanded respect like a sunflower waving in the breeze as it followed the sun across the morning sky.

Sara couldn't muster passion or inspiration as her fingers pushed the corners of the yellow note down against the desk, only to have it curl back up against her will. Frustration tinted her view with the letters falling across her mind; *Love, Jarrid.*

The pull to examine the clue, started deep in her stomach, color once again filled the room. She grabbed the note to acknowledge its author, while she waited for the waves of light to focus on the words so neatly printed on the yellow square.

Sara, please meet me at the Mountain Pass Restaurant today at 5:00 p.m. Love, Jarrid.

His name ran through her mind. The room filled with vibrant and dominant emotion, his spell cast with potent results. *How did he get into my office to leave the note? The building is locked.*

Ted burst into the office, tie flying and hands thrown through the air proclaiming his arrival. He slipped into the chair and waited for her acknowledgment, but she only stared at the yellow square.

"One would think an employee would be eager to know why her boss has just invaded her office."

"Okay, I'll bite." Sara raised her eyes enough to see the smirk rise and fall on Ted's face. She carefully folded the note and slipped it in her pocket. "What brings you here? A favor, I suppose?" She snapped sarcastically.

"You guessed it, a favor indeed." Ted jumped from the chair, sauntered over to the window, and ran his fingers through his hair. He turned to survey her reaction, not really waiting for an answer. "This is strictly professional, you understand?"

"Ted, please just spit it out." Sara wanted to re-read the note, to try and understand how Jarrid had managed to pull it off. It wasn't like him to leave the village. "What is professional, Ted? What do you need?"

"Well, you see, it seems that prominent people in the community have recognized my talent and have seen fit to nominate me for Newsman of the Year." Ted pulled his sleeves down to show off the diamond cuff links adorning his designer shirt. "There is a banquet tonight for all the nominees; the winner's announcement following the dinner."

Acid rose in Sara's throat, burning her vocal cords, causing gruffness as she spoke, "What does this have to do with me?" She choked on the words, for she knew he was asking her to accompany him.

Smugness smeared over his face like petroleum jelly distorting his arrogance as if to hide his motive. "I think we'll make quite the statement, a highly recognized News Anchor and his lovely assistant."

The word assistant swirled around and fought for Sara's attention, while the lines of Jarrid's note mingled with her frustration. "Now listen, Ted, I wouldn't mind attending this gala occasion. The most talented people in the news world will be attending. It could be good for my journalistic career. My name frequents the stories that you so eloquently bring to the public. My reputation precedes me. Yes, I would be glad to accompany you as the lead journalist for *The Daily News*."

Ted's face grimaced as Sara's words made their mark. A long sigh expelled across his lips as if she had punched him in the stomach. Not quite the admiration he had hoped for, this revelation fell upon his face like a mask.

BLOOD MOON

"Besides…" Sara took her cue and continued, "I have this long formal that I've been dying to wear, and this event is the perfect opportunity to do so."

Ted headed for the door with his shoulders slumped, the air being sufficiently let out of his arrogant persona. "I'll pick you up at 6:30 p.m." More a statement than useful information, but Sara didn't mind, she was doing this for her career and a chance to wear her red satin gown.

It took seconds for the vision of the note to float to the top of Sara's mind. *He will be waiting for me tonight at 5:00 p.m. How can I be in two places at once? I'll have to dress before meeting him at the truck stop; in my red satin gown.*

The thought of walking into the truck stop in a revealing formal dress suddenly caused her fear to run rampant. She could imagine the eyes staring, words whispered, and her heart beating as her eyes met Jarrid's stare. She shook off the thought, gathered her things and headed for home.

Steam hung on the bedroom ceiling like clouds gathering with an ominous light. Sara swung the closet door wide as the billows of heavy moisture rose and fell against her damp skin.

She pushed aside her work clothes, jeans, and hoodies to reveal the vibrant red formal. Standing in nothing but a black lace thong and a push-up bra, she brought the shiny satin up to her waist and twirled magically about the room.

Her foot caught the edge of the rug. She stopped mid-twirl, her mind playing out the truck stop scene. The emotions rose fast and hard, as she imagined whispers carried on the scent of hamburgers, French fries, and burnt popcorn. She visualized, taking the hem of the satin dress in her hands, trying desperately to keep it from dragging on the greasy floor.

The closet door slammed shut with a thud; the vision faded with the leftover steam in the room. Sara cleared her throat and tousled the fabric over her head, feeling each seam of the dress find its resting place against her curves. One glance in the mirror, and she was off.

***

The sound of semi horns and loud masculine voices attacked Sara's ears before she could get out of her car. Parking spaces were at a premium, her payment being made by the long walk through the rows of big rigs. Catcalls and loud whistles broke the crisp night air as she made her way to the front door. It had begun.

Sara couldn't suppress the awkward feeling as she approached the entrance, and parted the sea of beards, whiskey, and large round bellies. Two of the men were engaged in a heated argument and blocked the door. One of the heavy bearded men stepped forward. "Gentleman, can't you see this beautiful lady needs to pass."

Frustration passed through the men in huffs and grunts as they reluctantly moved aside and opened the door.

The noise of the restaurant pushed past Sara as the door's breeze circled the red satin trailing behind her like a banner. Every eye fastened its gaze on her dramatic entrance. A hush fell over the room, not exactly how she'd planned to start the night.

The conversations were slow to resume as Sara searched the room for Jarrid's face. She pushed her shoulders back, raised her head, and started toward the back of the restaurant wanting to put distance between her and the stares of the patrons.

BLOOD MOON

She was methodically putting one foot in front of the other, concentrating on her mission to reach the back of the room, when a large trucker pushed a chair in her path. He jumped up and towered over her small frame. "Well, well, what have we here?"

He pushed closer to Sara's face, his massive chest puffed out with a seductive grumble directed toward her body. The words gathered in her throat, she opened her mouth, scolding the unruly barbarian, but his loud thunderous voice echoed in her ears and thwarted her words.

A large hand landed on the ogres' shoulder. "You best step aside, man, and let the lady pass." Jarrid proclaimed with authority.

The trucker turned with his fist in the air, but as soon as he saw Jarrid's face, his arm went limp, "Um, sure thing. I didn't mean no harm. My apologies, Miss."

Jarrid placed one hand on his shoulder, anchoring him to his chair, while he outstretched the other to Sara. "Man, this is a lady. You would not treat your mother that way, would you?"

Sara brushed past the smelly heap of hair and sweat, the ruffian's head hung in shame. She was a little put out as her rousing speech still lay on the tip of her tongue, "You know Jarrid, I had that situation completely under control. I could've handled that brute quite easily. I have a silver tongue for just that sort of thing."

"A silver tongue indeed," Jarrid turned to face her with his words rolling over his lips, "but all that man could see were your breasts bulging out from the restraint of your bra and the curves of your hips swaying from side to side, an open invitation for someone of his character." He didn't wait for a response, taking her hand and guiding her to the back of the room.

SARAH KAGE

Jarrid had picked a table away from the kitchen with a little privacy. Sara pushed and tugged at her dress, trying to push its fullness under the tiny table.

She was preoccupied with this ritual until she noticed the stare that billowed across the table. Jarrid's ice-blue eyes burned into her soul. "Yes, may I help you?" She smirked.

"Are you not a little overdressed for a truck stop?" Jarrid cleared his throat. "I have guessed that you must have another engagement. Would it be too presumptuous to ask with whom?"

The words took Sara by surprise; *did I hear jealousy in his question?* "Why no, I don't feel it's too forward at all. I'm attending a banquet for work with Mr. Williams, my boss."

Sara watched as the frown lines left Jarrid's brow. "Well, Mr. Williams is a lucky man this evening."

"I'm doing this for my career." Sara chimed; "It's an excellent opportunity to mingle with my peers."

The hour passed as the orders from the kitchen floated across the room. Jarrid ceased the lull in the conversation to ask, "So, I got your note. I was a little surprised that you wanted to meet at the truck stop."

"My note," Sara almost choked as the soda spewed from her mouth, "don't you mean your note asking me to meet you here at 5:00 p.m."

Jarrid's face contorted into waves of disbelief. "Sara, I sent you no note. What is happening here? Are you seriously telling me that you did not send me a note?" All Sara could muster was a profound nod of the head.

"Okay," Jarrid spoke first. "I guess we will chalk this up to another weird and wacky thing that seems to happen between us. It is like someone else is in control of our destiny."

BLOOD MOON

"I'm sorry, Jarrid," Sara interrupted his thought, "I have to leave if I'm going to arrive on time for the banquet. Please forgive me."

She pushed the chair away from the table, letting the fabric fall and flow until it took its place arranged around her curves, gave it one final tug and said, "Look, I don't think we're finished here."

She took the pen from the table and wrote her address on the back of the bill and reluctantly handed it to Jarrid. "Would you be willing to come to my house tomorrow night for dinner?"

"Oh, madam, you and I alone at your house; do we dare tempt fate?" Jarrid chuckled as he walked her to the car, past the uncharacteristically quiet truckers. The night air swirled as Jarrid reached for Sara and closed the distance between them. The heat from his hand lingered on her chin as he pulled her lips into the shallows of his waiting kiss. Slow and gentle, touching but not, only to climax into a sweet surrender in the nape of her neck as he whispered, "Until tomorrow, my Lady."

Sara reluctantly loosened her grip on the lapels of his shirt and watched him fade into the distance; *tomorrow night indeed!*

SARAH KAGE
Chapter 7 Terror Reigns

His red sports car sat at the curb, engine idling, his impatient glare aimed at the parking attendant. Sara brushed her hair from her face and turned just in time to see the keys being handed off to her male companion. A chill swept her arm. She'd waited there in the cold, expecting Ted to open her door graciously. The award winners and losers filed past with trophies and regrets lingering on the night wind.

"Hey, are you going to stand there all night gawking, or are you going to get in?" Ted asked. He leaned up against the driver's side of the car, arms crossed with his fingers drumming the roof.

Small waves of anger crossed Sara's face. She reached for the door handle and mumbled, "Some gentleman, too much to expect, I suppose." Sara gathered her skirt, coaxed its fullness, pushed it inside the door, and slipped into the car.

She'd barely closed her door before Ted spun off in a cloud of dust. "What do those people know? They wouldn't know talent if it..." Her face distorted, no compassion, a sign that she didn't think he'd been robbed. Her disagreement formed a cold, hard wall of silence, the only thing she could offer.

It was a short ride. Sara was truly thankful when the car came to an abrupt stop in front of her house. "Goodnight, Ted. I hope you'll take some positive direction from your loss and use it as a learning experience."

"Okay, enough of your Polly-Anna attitude. Off with you. Be in the office bright and early tomorrow." His stare cold, he waited for her to exit the car. She gathered

BLOOD MOON

her dress and her dignity and left him with his arrogant persona.

Sara draped the red satin formal across the bedroom chair. She made her way to scoop up Zeus; his squirming prompted her to lay him on the bed. The blankets piled in mounds, beckoned for her to embrace the night. Zeus complained when she tousled the bed coverings. Finally, he made two spins and plopped down by her side. The nightly ritual had begun. Each stroke of Zeus' silky, black coat brought Sara closer to sleep.

Deliberate slow breaths erased the memories of the night with a faint glow of warmth centered on the thought of tomorrow's dinner. Zeus gave one final meow, and the two dream partners drifted off to sleep.

It started low at first. Notes floated across the air; harpsichord strings were being plucked to reveal the wedding march echoing throughout the large church. The white dress rustled with every step toward the altar, Sara's eyes focused on the lace of her sleeve mingling with the pin-striped suit of the man who escorted her down the aisle.

She wanted to push the veil aside to see the face of her guide, but her bouquet of white and pink roses draped her hand. Trails of green ivy pressed against the fullness of her lacy skirt.

White doves flew across the expanse of the old church and landed on the altar, their flight a part of the wedding party, cooing one to the other in soft tones of welcoming enchantment.

The notes of the harpsichord grew louder, the groom nervously waiting for his bride. He stood like a giant, grounded at the altar by the sheer beauty of the vision. She was only steps away—the union their destiny.

SARAH KAGE

Sara's eyes couldn't focus on her groom. Desperation clouded the sacred moment. But she wanted to see him. Her last step revealed the illusion as the scarred and grotesque face turned to receive his bride.

Terror gripped at Sara's heart. She threw the bouquet across the pews and ran down the long aisle. Every step was a forced attempt to put distance between her and this dreadful vision.

She grabbed at the fullness of the dress, trying to coax it to yield to her desire to run. The more she grabbed, the fuller the dress became until it engulfed her. All she heard were her screams echoing through the night.

Zeus arched his back and hissed, his tail fluffed out to show his surprise. Sara sat straight up in bed with the last syllables of her scream bouncing off the bedroom walls. What started as a beautiful dream had quickly morphed into a nightmare.

Sara took Zeus into her arms to calm the frightened feline. "There, there kitty, it will be alright." She stroked and rocked the black cat until purrs echoed into the dark, "Oh, Zeus, who will comfort and protect me?" She whispered.

The black cat tucked himself under Sara's arm, his version of applying for the position, offering his support. She could feel the rattle of his purrs across her chest, coaxing her to give into sleep once more.

***

The aroma of coffee wafted down the halls of *The Daily News* and brought a steady stream of suits and heels to indulge in the office ritual. Sara placed both hands around her cup, feeling its warmth. She closed her eyes and took a slow sip.

BLOOD MOON

No announcement, warning, or word to let her know that Alex was standing behind her. "Well, I see you survived the juggling act last night."

"Really, Alex," Sara jumped and almost sent the coffee into the next room. "I think we need to hang a bell around your neck. You know, like they do with cats."

"Oh yeah, and what fun would that be?" Alex pranced to the coffee machine and poured a cup. "So, come on. How'd you manage two men at once, hmm, your Padawan is dying to learn your secrets?" Alex stood cross-legged, acting like a child waiting for instructions.

"I'm glad you think so highly of my abilities, but I told you Jarrid's meeting was at five, plenty of time for both events." Alex started to speak, but the sound of the water splashing over Sara's cup muffled her inquisition.

"So," Alex shivered like a bird ruffling its feathers in frustration, "did Ted win? Please tell me he didn't. It would make him more arrogant, and that's not acceptable."

Sara smirked, remembering the look on Ted's face when the announcement of the winner filled the room. He was already half-way up from his chair when the words poured over the speaker. Bruce Torrence had won the prestigious award. It was a memory she would hold sacred.

The smirk stopped Alex dead in her tracks. "So, he didn't win? Oh my, he will be a real pill for the rest of the year. Maybe his ego will be a little deflated, that would be quite the novelty."

"Okay," Sara patted Alex on the back and headed for the door. "I've lots of work to finish. See you later." Her attempt to leave the room without the rest of her story was an epic fail.

SARAH KAGE

"You've left out the good part." Alex filled the doorway and blocked Sara's exit. "Why did Jarrid want to meet you?"

"Look, Alex, not now." Sara deflected her curiosity. "I've too much work to do. I'll call you tonight after Jarrid leaves for the village."

The two women pushed through the doorway at the same time. Alex emerged first and straightened her jacket. "What do you mean? Is he coming to your house?"

"Yep, and you aren't going to get the details until later tonight." Sara turned and walked backward toward her office and said, "What do you think about that?"

Sara left Alex standing in the hall with her feathers ruffled once more. "Are you going to call me later?"

The victor raised her arm and swished her wrist with a 'yes' motion. She sauntered to her office with a smile that beamed from ear-to-ear. It had ended up being a great day.

***

Zeus meowed and purred, darting in and out of Sara's legs, his demand for dinner. "Okay, Zeus, give it a rest, I know." It was a ritual, Zeus' can of tuna. The only way Sara could have any peace before she threw off the shackles of the day.

The smell of pot roast from the crock-pot was delectable; it was her crowning glory in the kitchen. She hurried to plate the steaming meat being careful to ladle the small potatoes around the succulent beef. Next, she gathered the asparagus and placed them around the sides of the plate. She brought out her grandmother's gravy boat and filled it with the liquid gold. It was perfect.

Sara hurried through the house lighting candles, heading toward the bedroom. She chose a mini-dress that complimented her sleek legs, gave her hair a toss, then

BLOOD MOON

one quick look in the mirror and re-applied her lipstick. She slowed her breaths to calm her ragged nerves.

Zeus lay in his bed content for the night. "Alright, kitty, you be good. I'll see you later." She closed the bedroom door to sequester him to his slumber.

"Eight, nine, and..." Before she reached ten, the doorbell rang, and calm vanished from her body. She hurried to the door stopping for a moment to adjust the lighting in the room. *Oh, I hope this isn't too suggestive.* Sara stood at the door, ran her fingers through her hair, and turned the doorknob.

His body filled the entire doorway width and height. Sara noticed his dark blue shirt tucked into the most attractive jeans she'd ever seen. Blue, green, and yellow poured from his outstretched hand. Wildflowers picked from the mountainside with sprays of baby's breath to soften the stems. "I know you love mountain flowers."

"Thank you so much, Jarrid." Sara took the bundle of scent and pushed the door further open to invite him in. "These are my favorite." She brought the flowers to her nose and inhaled the fragrance of each petal.

Sara peeked over the bunched flowers leaving Jarrid to shut the door. His muscles rippled, leaving patterns that ebbed and flowed across his back. Her eyes fell upon the stark contrast of his belt just above the tight blue denim that clung to each rounded muscle.

A gasp left her throat and escaped through her tight lips. "Oh, yes. Dinner is ready, are you hungry?" She quickly cleared her thoughts and headed in the direction of the aroma oozing from the kitchen.

"How could I not be?" Jarrid covered his smirk with his hand, "What are you cooking? It smells insane."

Sara putzed with the flowers and watched Jarrid stroll into the kitchen. He raised his head to sniff the air like an ancient wolf following the hunt. She realized that she'd left his question dangling between them, "Oh, just a southern pot roast, my grandmother's recipe."

She moved toward the dining room, knowing he would follow close behind. Silence hovered in the room, with an air of tension circling the dining room table. The places set, a romantic dinner for two.

Jarrid moved to break the silence. "Here, allow me." The chair made a scraping sound, its complaint to being pulled away from the table.

The candles had been cropped low, so the couple's conversation wouldn't be hindered, or perhaps it was a ploy for her to look into those blue eyes? Sara settled in and watched Jarrid take his place.

He tugged at his napkin and placed it across his lap, returning Sara's stare. The candlelight flickered and left shadows that danced across his chiseled face. There was magic in the air. Sara couldn't deny the animal magnetism that flowed across the table.

Jarrid filled his plate with all the grace of a Viking returned from the battle to enjoy the offerings of his wench. He loaded his fork and pronounced, "I have never tasted asparagus prepared this way. They are robust."

"I'll take that as a compliment, my lord." She smiled nervously. Then it happened, a change in the atmosphere, like someone flipped a switch. Objects in the room seemed to suspend in time and space.

Her heart raced, and all she could do was watch Jarrid place the meat slowly into his mouth. His blue eyes burned bright, the candlelight bounced off his face and danced across his brow. Every sense screamed from deep inside, tearing at Sara's soul. She couldn't stop the words, they rose to the surface, and she willed them into thought, *I want this man!*

Slowly, Jarrid raised his glass. "A toast to you and this meal fit for a king." Sara raised her glass to meet his gesture. It seemed like minutes before the two glasses came together in a loud, crisp ring, magic filled the air, and then the spell was broken.

Jarrid tipped his glass to his lips, stared at Sara, and sipped the sweet nectar. His eyes penetrated her soul; his stare prompted her to clear the table. "So Jarrid, what's the news from the village?" She hoped the small talk would lighten the feverish mood.

The sound of dishes being stacked one upon the other clattered from the dining room. Jarrid gathered the remaining plates; his voice announced his entrance into the kitchen. "Do we really want to talk about the village tonight? Let's enjoy one another and leave our troubles for another time."

"Okay," she answered. Her nerves on edge, she slipped her hands into the warm water. The foam rose above the dishes and lined the sink like pearls, each bubble popping in a chain reaction announcing their watery demise—her senses firing on all cylinders still engaged from the toast. Jarrid reached around her to set the stacked dishes on the sink intruding on her very existence.

She turned to face him. He cupped her elbows in his hands and pulled her closer, eliminating any space between them. His stance broadened, and he moved to steady himself against her trembling body; he held her fast. His control was undeniable. She did not resist.

He strummed each arm with the backs of his fingers touching ever so softly, each hand in unison, like playing an ancient instrument. Sara felt his breath, hot against her ear.

His hands cupped her elbows once more. He pulled her up on her tip-toes and buried his face into the small of her neck. He loosened his grip to let her slide down the length of his body to rest against his chest.

Jarrid wrapped his arms around her waist to steady the union. His lips lightly caressed the whiteness of her shoulder; his kiss flickered on her skin like hot embers.

Beads of sweat gathered on her forehead. Her body responded to Jarrid's advances, and she felt his desire. He moved to envelop her, pushed her against the sink to anchor his aggression, the only obstacle to his lust.

A gasp was her feverish response to his hand running down the length of her leg, slowly pulling the material up and exposing her moistened thigh. She was powerless to his touch.

Lost in the moment, Sara reached up and pulled his head into her shoulder. "Jarrid, please..."

Lust, a mammalian affliction, fueled their human condition and intensified the moment. Each caress burned like an uncontrollable fire, to consume and unite their passion. She threw her head back, trying to recover from the overwhelming demands of her arousal, her head flew forward to see the embers smoldering across his face. "Sara, you have the passion of the ancients. Your lust fuels my soul," he whispered as he searched for the warm, tender taste of her kiss.

Her fight to resist was overwhelming. She knew what was at stake. *How can I give into my lust?* Sensual rhythms pulsed through her veins. The dance continued; each movement drew her closer to no return. Her desire for release was evident; her yearning demanded it to be so.

BLOOD MOON

Her reaction to his lust, giving in to her desire, she fell hard against his need.

The sound was sharp and echoed through the room. Sara slumped into Jarrid's arms limp and spent. He gathered her up like a rag doll, with his passion flowing down to his feet. "It is the doorbell." He proclaimed.

Sara laid her head on his shoulder, waiting for the air to come back into the room. Jarrid moved to steady himself against the sink. She composed her thoughts, straightened her dress, and answered the door.

Just moments before, Sara's emotions had pooled in her eyes like rivers of fire and ice. But now, peeking through the peephole, with the site of Ted standing on her doorstep, her passion waned. Ted's finger pressed relentlessly on the door buzzer. Sara's shoulders drooped, with the weight of reality, cascading down around her.

"Ted, for God's sake," Sara couldn't open the door fast enough. "Why are you camped out on the buzzer?" Jarrid came from behind just in time to keep the door from slamming through the wall catching it in his grip. He stood behind Sara, glaring at the man, the intruder.

"Hello, my good fellow." Ted, oblivious to his lack of courtesy, pushed past Sara to grab Jarrid's hand. "Hope I'm not interrupting anything." He shot a wink in Jarrid's direction, sauntered into the dining room, turning to face their impatient stares.

"I was just in the neighborhood and thought I'd pay a little visit to my favorite journalist." Ted took a glass off the table and poured the red remnants of the night's festivities, shaking the bottle to release the very last drop. He slowly took a sip of his spoil while he sized up the tall stranger, now staring him down with great intensity.

"We haven't been introduced." Ted took a long stride toward Jarrid and outstretched his hand once more. "My name is Ted Williams. I'm Sara's boss." Jarrid stepped forward into Ted's grip. The motion unhinged Sara, and a dizzy feeling enveloped her mind. The sound of the two men's hands connected with a snap, the gesture sickened her, and she fought back the impulse to shove Ted out the door.

"Ted, this is my friend Jarrid." Sara willed her words, "He's from the village."

"Very nice to meet you, Ted," Jarrid finished the handshake and acknowledged the rude man, "Sara has mentioned you often."

"I'm sure it was all good," Ted smirked and placed his empty glass back on the table. "Sara is a little enamored with my style and accomplishments, but then I do consider myself her mentor."

Sara felt the tide of nausea rise in her stomach with each egotistical word that flowed from Ted's mouth. The fire and ice were once more pooling in her eyes, but this time anger and disgust swirled in her veins, *my mentor, indeed.*

The silence in the room was obvious. Both men stood their ground, sizing up the competition. Sara swallowed hard and motioned for Ted to take a seat. "Is there something I can do for you, Ted?"

"Oh, I just thought you might be lonely and decided I'd stop in and keep you company." Ted sat in the middle of the couch, occupying most of the available space, flipped his hand in the air, and spewed his arrogance into the room.

Jarrid sat next to Ted, using his massive body to encourage the arrogant man to rethink his position. Instead, Ted jumped to his feet and honed in on Sara.

She positioned herself next to Jarrid on the couch, trying to diffuse this male exhibit of testosterone. Jarrid's

BLOOD MOON

hand softly brushed her arm, and the feeling of electricity shot through her being, sensual emotions filled the room.

Ted shifted from one foot to the other. His body language was a clue that he might be feeling a little out of place. The thought that he had indeed interrupted something took root and prompted him toward the door.

"Well, I think I'll be on my way. I have another engagement to attend." Ted rushed to the door with urgency, the rise and fall of defeat in his steps, like the younger sibling who realized he was no longer the family favorite.

"It was nice to meet you." He stopped at the door and motioned to Jarrid. "I hope we meet again."

"Okay, Ted," Sara circled the obnoxious visitor and corralled him onto the stoop, "you don't want to miss your engagement." Ted was still mumbling when Sara slammed the door, turned and pressed her back against the solid wood between her and the most arrogant man she knew.

"Wow," Jarrid couldn't help but laugh with his words spilling beyond his grin, "you could not get rid of him fast enough. I think he may still be saying goodbye. Is that because you want to take up where we left off?"

"Oh, that man makes me so furious." Sara pushed past Jarrid ignoring the last melodic laugh that spilled from his Cheshire grin. "He's so arrogant and delusional, my mentor? I've saved his professional butt so many times. Why the audacity! Not to mention, he has an ego the size of an elephant."

"Now, just let those thoughts wash over you and answer my question." Jarrid rushed to stop her forward motion, took her arm, and pulled her close.

"What do you mean? Where we left off doing dishes?" Sara's laughter filled the room. Jarrid moved to envelop her, to keep her safe from all harm. She could feel the difference in his touch. Lust was replaced with a calm, caring, and protective stance.

He took her hand and led her to the couch. "I need your attention for just a moment. I wanted to see you tonight, to spend time just the two of us, but I also have something of great importance to tell you."

"Please don't get upset." Jarrid pulled her arm to coax her onto the couch, "What I have to tell you will be hard for you to believe."

"I've told you some fabulous tales, and not once have I ever felt that you didn't respect and believe me, Jarrid," She watched and waited while his quiet expressions lingered on his face, "so you have my attention. What is it?"

"I am having dreams of a woman who walks in death." He cupped her hands into his and laid their entangled fingers in her lap. "She tortures me in an unfamiliar place, but that's not the worst part. You're there, and I can't protect you. I keep calling the devil woman's name, but I do not know her. Do you hear me?" He gazed into her ashen face.

"Yes!" Sara nodded her head, opened her mouth, and revealed her secret. "Her name is Luna."

The air forced itself out of Jarrid's lungs with a loud moan. "Sara, no! How could you possibly know her name? I have told no one of my dreams."

"I know her because she is the same woman in my nightmares." Sara bolted from the couch to the center of the room. "I've watched her torture you inside the walls of the Fortress. That's why I told you not to go inside the walls. I am afraid for you."

"Do not concern yourself." Jarrid moved to comfort her the only way he knew how. His arms circled her body, trying to protect her from all assaults, both real and evil. "I am strong enough to protect us both, from whatever evil crosses our path."

Sara buried her head into his muscular chest and decided to let him believe this declaration, but she knew they possessed only two of the three tools to defeat the evil behind the fortress wall; their love for one another was the first tool in their arsenal. This love couldn't be consummated in an unholy union, the condition of *The Spirited Sword of Purity*. She knew the second tool; their holy union was in jeopardy each time they came together. The third tool was their faith in God's love; with Him, all things are possible.

The grandfather clock in the corner struck the hour. Jarrid raised her head and gently kissed her tear-stained lips. The words spoken to accompany the kiss gathered in his heart. He quietly whispered, "We will be victorious."

Sara rested her cheek against his chest and heard his heartbeat soften. They had shared a night of emotional intimacy, something she would cherish forever.

She wished he would stay if only to ward off the screams of a nightmare, but alas, he was of the village, and he wore the old ways like a weathered shirt.

"Thank you for a wonderful dinner." Jarrid pulled away and moved toward the door. "I will see you soon." He laid his hand on his heart, bowed and with a flash, was gone.

Zeus' loud meows echoed through the hall. "Yes, kitty, I'm coming." Sara wiped the emotional fog from her mind and turned to rescue the other man in her life.

The purring resounded through the bedroom door. "Alright, come on then." She scooped him up and declared, "I know you love me too." Her eyes fixed on the front door, remembering the vision, his jeans, and those blue eyes. It was surely a night of passion, the likes of which she would never forget.

BLOOD MOON
Chapter 8 Evil Becomes Her

The coffee pot clanked loudly, its complaint of being lifted from the hot, round surface that pumped its aromatic steam into the office break room. Sara leaned against the countertop, a barrier that formed the wall between reality and vision.

She planted her hands on the counter's smooth surface and braced herself against the voices in her head, which demanded her attention. The cup of coffee swirled into a vortex of black liquid, which filled her senses with darkness and despair.

Its demonic face rose from the bottom of the dark swirl, spewing words as it chanted, "You will fear me! Your sacrifice will consummate *The Feast of Souls*."

The room filled with stench as the entity rose to tower over Sara. Its existence forced her head up toward the ceiling; the black liquid mass poured into Sara's mouth, filling her with the vision. Sara's mind wrapped around the evil words spoken, *The Righteous One has been foretold, but evil will possess their soul.*

The sound of boiling liquid percolated through Sara's ears until silence snapped her back into reality. Her eyes fixed on the spoon in her cup that swirled around in the black liquid as if some unseen hand had brought its content to a fevered spin.

"Whoa. Are you okay?" Alex appeared just as Sara slumped to the floor. She guided her to a chair and knelt beside her friend. "What's wrong, Sara? Look at me. Here, focus."

Sara only stared past Alex, void of any emotion. Then, it started from the bottom of her lungs as each facial expression grew with intensity, and the scream rang out across the room, forcing her to rise from the chair.

She grabbed Sara and held on tightly to stop the uncontrollable shaking. Tears fell down Alex's face as the emotions poured from her friend.

"There, there. It's okay." Alex spoke softly. With each word spoken, she hugged Sara harder and continued, "Whatever it was is gone now. You're safe." Alex gently sat Sara back into her chair and offered a tissue for her tears.

"Can't you tell me what happened?" Alex reached across Sara's lap and took her trembling hand. Their eyes met, and all Sara could do was shake her head. "You'll feel better if you talk about it." Alex's words were met with short sniffles as Sara regained control.

The forced smirk and laughter echoed in the room as Sara threw her hands in the air. "Well, I guess its official. I've gone and slipped off my rocker. It's bad enough that the dreams invade my sleep, but now I'm hallucinating at work." Sara paused a moment as she wiped the moisture from her cheeks.

"Hallucinating," Alex chose her words carefully and pushed on, "girl, what are you talking about?"

"Fear her, indeed." The anger rose from deep inside, coaxing Sara from her chair to pace across the floor "I am fearless! The words flowed wildly from her lips. I'll not give in to it, never."

Alex's face screwed into a question. "Fear who?"

Sara slid into the chair and planted herself firmly into the mold of the seat. "The woman from my dreams, Luna, and this *Feast of Souls* she keeps taunting me about."

"Okay, slow down. Who is Luna?"

BLOOD MOON

Sara's mouth formed the sound of her next word, but Alex wasn't listening. The commotion directed her attention to Ted's office. She rushed to the door to get a better view. The entire staff was huddled around as someone turned up the TV.

It was an anchorwoman from their rival station. Alex only paused to glance at Sara. "Hold that thought. Are you coming? Something is going down outside of town."

"Give me a second to compose myself. You go. I'll be right behind you." Sara threw a half-hearted hand gesture in the air to wave her on. Alex almost sucked the door facing off as she flew through the opening, never looking back.

The atmosphere was solemn as Sara pushed her way through the crowd and joined Ted and Alex at his desk. "Hey, what gives? Are we watching our rival station now?"

Ted glared in her direction and motioned for her to shut up. "Would you please be quiet? Something is going on outside the village." He pointed his finger sternly in her direction and then turned his attention back to the broadcast.

The hairs on Sara's arms rose with the syllables of the word *village* pouring across her mind. Alex grabbed her arm and pulled her to the side. "They found a boy right outside the Fortress near the highway." Her eyes widened with horror as she continued, "Sara, he was mutilated!"

A gasp escaped Sara's lips as Ted bellowed, "Please! Would the two of you shut your traps and listen. This breaking news could be the story of the year."

Urgency bubbled up in the voice of the broadcaster, and all ears tuned in to her report. "Yes, Bill. We have been on the scene now for about twenty minutes. When we first arrived, there were reports of murder; someone ripped apart."

Their exuberance flowed, and a low mumble rolled through the room. The journalists and photographers were excited; it was like being in a candy store.

"The atmosphere was low key at first," The broadcaster continued, "but then someone reported that something was lurking inside the drain. Now law enforcement has surrounded the location."

It was strangely quiet in the room; no sound punctuated the importance of the story that was unfolding before their eyes. They say a dog whistle is just beyond the frequency of the human ear. The tone that pierced through the TV was barely below that sound. The shrillness of the scream caused everyone in the room to cover their ears for protection.

The broadcaster covered her ear with one hand as she tried to continue, "It sounds like some kind of injured animal. Folks, I'm not sure what's causing this horrific sound. I'm going to give this broadcast back to the anchor room. Stay tuned. We will keep you updated on the outcome of this story."

Ted turned the TV off and shouted, "Why are the two of you standing in my office, watching our competition deliver the news story of the year? Aren't you already gone?"

Alex grabbed Sara's arm and coaxed her co-worker toward the door. "You heard the man. Aren't we there yet?"

She hardly noticed her speedometer registering ninety miles per hour, or the fact that Alex bounced around in her seat like a two-year-old child. Sara's thoughts were cascading over each other. *Where was Jarrid? Was he aware of the drama unfolding just outside his home?*

BLOOD MOON

"Are you listening to me? Really, are you oblivious to how important this story is, Sara only ninety miles per hour? Can't you get us there any faster?"

"Not if you want to arrive in one piece. Look, we're almost there." Sara fought the wheel as she turned it sharp, and the car arrived in a cloud of dust.

The commotion was not hard to spot. Sara drove past the officials and headed toward the scene. The area was taped off, but one of the officers approached the car. "Ladies, I'm going to have to ask you to leave this area." His flashlight lit Sara's face as she flashed her badge. The light bounced off the plastic. "The reporters are gathered about sixty yards back. I suggest you do the same."

Sara could feel Alex rising from the passenger seat. She put her hand on her arm and squeezed. The charm oozed from her lips, she smiled and addressed the officer, "Thank you, we will join our peers and leave you to your work."

The whine of the reverse gear only agitated Alex, and she protested, "No, No, Sara. Go back. We need to get closer to the duct and get a video of whatever is making that horrible noise."

"Just cool your jets." Sara retorted, "Have you ever known me to back down from a story?" The screaming still cracked the night air. Sara steered the car in the direction of the attack on their ears. She knew the area pretty well and was able to maneuver the vehicle behind the drain. She turned the headlights and the engine off as the car, camouflaged by the tree-line, coasted and stopped just in front of the officials.

Chirps of crickets drifted through the darkness that enveloped the front seat of the car. The screams no longer pierced the night air. Sara rubbed her eyes to focus on the huddle of officers gathered just in front of the drain and the source of the chaos. The night sounds lulled Sara, her heartbeat slowed, and a gentle rocking soothed her mind, but the peace was short-lived.

The car rocked from side to side; it shook Sara into the moment. "Alex, what are you doing?"

Muffled syllables flowed from the back seat with Alex struggling to retrieve her camera equipment. Most of her body, draped across the seat, derriere planted toward the moon. "Just trying to … want to get my equipment …"

Sara grabbed a leg and gently tugged her back into the seat. Alex slid down and clutched the equipment to her chest as she mumbled, "Just wanted to …"

Sara's gaze shot through the windshield as she reached for Alex's chin to point her face toward the ten or fifteen police officers, gathered in front of the drain with guns drawn. "Okay, you have my attention." Alex made one more move to embrace her cameras. "Are those guns pointed at us?"

The officers had positioned themselves in front of the culvert. Every man held a pistol or rifle pointed toward its opening and in the direction of the car. Alex whispered, "I should be filming this, huh?"

"Alex, we have to get out of the car and find a better vantage point. Do you think you can manage to do that without being the center of attention?"

Sara was sure that a rolled-eye-glare had been pointed in her direction in the darkness of the car. "Come on. Follow me, and please be stealthy."

The quietness of the moment only amplified Sara's attempt to open her door. "Alex, follow me to the back of the car. We need to decide on a plan."

The photographer in Alex wanted to bring all of her equipment, but she quickly decided on her smallest video camera. She slithered out the door and joined Sara

BLOOD MOON

behind the car. The moonlight bounced off the paint of the trunk and illuminated the area. Sara touched Alex's arm and pointed toward a grove of trees to the left of the car.

This vantage point provided more cover while still allowing the officer's conversations to drift on the gentle breeze and ride the direction of the wind.

The crunch of a dry pinecone broke through the air. "Alex, be quiet. I'm trying to hear what they're saying."

"Did you get a good look at that thing, Roy?" Two officers asked at the same time, "What is it?"

His gun still pointed toward the culvert, Roy asked, "What kind of animal was that?" He never took his eyes off the drain's opening as he spoke.

One of the men jumped up and yelled, "That's no animal. Can't you see? Don't you have eyes?"

Roy lowered his weapon to address the other officer. "Okay, it's not an animal. What the hell do you think it is?"

The officer closest to the drain, crouched down with his rifle pointed directly into the mouth of the culvert. The creature had been in his site since he arrived on the scene. Never taking his eyes off his target, he answered Roy's question, "It's straight out of Hell."

The same pinecone rustled and cracked under Alex's foot, announcing her standing to position her camera. Sara pulled her back down by her side. "What are you doing? Were you planning on, oh, I don't know, strolling up to the scene like you were taking Sunday pictures?"

Alex yanked her arm away from Sara, she stood and leaned against the tree to adjust her stance for the best position to start filming, but instead, she raised her knee against Sara's arm and motioned toward the woods.

SARAH KAGE

The dense growth of trees swallowed the sleuths as the forest gave refuge. "Can you believe it? Did you get a look at that thing?" Alex whispered at the top of her lungs.

"Not really," Sara climbed the hill and collapsed on the ground. "But did you hear the comments? They don't think it's an animal." Sara shivered at the thought, or maybe it was the cold night air.

Alex kneeled and let her camera rest on her knee. "Well, it certainly wasn't human, kind of running out of species. Wait, 'from Hell,' you mean like a demon." Her syllables circled like a vortex, her words sliding off her tongue.

Sara jumped to her feet and searched her mind for another topic. She stood in the middle of the black forest surrounded by its creepy night sounds and exclaimed, "Hey, did you notice how close we are to Mary's house? I wonder what Jarrid thinks about the huge drama that's playing out right in his backyard?"

***

Helicopters rarely flew over the village, but this night the vibration of the propellers rocked the vase of flowers on Mary's table. Jarrid opened the front door to hear the distant voices of police officers, with their car's blue and red lights dancing across the front porch.

Jarrid made a sudden move to retrieve his jacket from its hook. Mary confronted him with tears in her eyes. "Jarrid, no, let the officials handle it."

He took her by the arm and hugged her. "Mom, it's okay. Just lock the door and wait. I will be back soon." Mary could only watch Jarrid run into the night and disappear into the shadow of darkness.

The front door groaned, she coaxed it closed and followed her sons' instructions. The hard metal bolt

105

BLOOD MOON

scraped and fell into position, placing the barrier of a thick wooden door between her and whatever awaited her oldest son.

The candles flickered and painted shadows across the walls. Mary's tears fell from her weathered face and pooled under her eyes as she brought the hem of her apron to her face and remembered. *The drawer, just there by the door, the artifact holds a place of honor, the family medallion.*

Mary made her way to the medallion's resting place. Each step brought back a memory of the day Jarrid's father had entrusted her with the legacy of the family crest. *It is our heritage, but much more than that—it is our protector. Each generation has respected it, given their lives for its existence. Some day Jarrid will be responsible for its preservation.*

The drawer resisted Mary's attempt to cling to the protection of the circle of metal that was foretold to conquer evil. Her mind opened like the petals of a flower to reveal the memory of the day she gave the medallion to Jarrid. He was so young, just barely a man, given the responsibility of the household as well as the head of the council, to rule in his father's place.

The memory of her husband's words stung as they floated across her mind. *I cannot give you what you want, Mary. The city calls to me, but I cannot ask you to leave your home.* She could still feel the pain clench and pull at her heart even with the passing of time.

She tried to make her oldest sons' life joyous and normal. She succeeded for the most part. Until the day she handed the medallion to Jarrid, with all of its responsibility, and declared him the head of the village council.

The drawer no longer resisted; it opened and cleared the fog from Mary's brain. She blinked her eyes and tried to focus on the vision of the medallion, but it wasn't there.

***

Jarrid had wasted no time. He plucked the circle of metal from its resting place and concealed it under his shirt next to his bare chest. He was never sure if he believed the stories that his mother told him, this tale of good and evil. Was the medallion more than just a cold hard trinket?

Jarrid remembered the words Mary had burdened him with the day she gave him the family relic. They poured through his head as he rushed off the porch. *These revelations are for your ears only. Jarrid, hold the crest dear to your heart. Guard it with not only your life but with your strength and faith or evil will prevail. I have seen this in a vision.*

He knew the clearing well, but the darkness and the voices played tricks on Jarrid's mind, and he struggled to make his way. Again, Mary's words impressed themselves upon his thoughts. *The medallion has many powers used for both good and evil. It depends on the soul that possesses it. She will be successful in her attempt to steal the family treasure. With it, she will be able to fulfill her destiny.*

The words *her destiny* resounded in Jarrid's mind and bounced off the constraints of his thoughts. Mary had spoken her words clear but never gave a hint as to whom she was referring.

Thunder echoed through Jarrid's thoughts as one sentence burned, its flames flickered in his memory. *The medallion's purpose is to form a pure union and bring the world from the depths of Hell.*

The clearing lay large and dark, its shadows combined with the night's breezes to wake Jarrid from his inner mind. He stopped in the middle of the tall grass. His eyes focused on the tree-line ahead.

BLOOD MOON

A woman emerged from the tangle of trees. Her black cape danced and mingled with the grass. Jarrid stood mesmerized by her beauty. Her fingers coaxed the black hood to fall upon her porcelain shoulders; she called his name.

Jarrid recognized his childhood friend. "Anuk, what are you doing? It's not safe. You should go back to the village."

She seemed to float through the grass, her stride long, falling into his chest. "Oh, Jarrid, I'm frightened. Why are the police searching the woods?"

Jarrid pulled her close, only to comfort her. Anuk melted into the very shape of him. Her hands traced the muscles of his back, and she nuzzled her head into his neck. Sweat beads intermingled with the gold chain of the medallion and ran down its length to drop and make its way down his chest.

He responded, even though his brain screamed for him to stop. His desire draped upon him like a ball and chain. Her thoughts pierced his mind, tangled, dark, and evil. "Jarrid, you will be mine."

His fingers clutched her arms and dug deep, pushing her away. The world stopped as their bodies separated, and she fell away in slow motion. Jarrid opened his eyes just in time to see her reach and tear the medallion from his neck.

***

Alex paced back and forth as the tall grass crushed and bunched at her feet. "This isn't getting us anywhere. You know, I'm not sure why Jarrid isn't smack dab in the middle of all of this, but we don't need him."

Sara mumbled, "I don't know, it might be nice to have a little backup."

SARAH KAGE

The darkness morphed Alex's frown. "Okay, where's the Warrior Princess that I know and love?" She grabbed Sara by the arm and coaxed her forward. "What do you say we put on our big girl pants, stroll down this hill and meet this creature?"

"Warrior Princess indeed, I'll show you just how badass I can be," Sara's voice rang out as she shook Alex off like a banana booger. She brushed past her partner with a soldiers' stride. "Hey, you got your pants on yet?" Sara snickered. "Come on, stop bringing up the rear."

The sound of shouting rose up the hill, soft at first, then urgent and chaotic. The opening of the culvert drew Sara's attention. The officers scattered in a large circle and backed away in unison. "Sara, look, it's crouched on the top of the drain. We've got to get down there." It was a command, as in now-or-never. Alex had taken the lead in the charge down the hill, but something stopped her; an obstacle only visible to her eyes, then the creature came into focus.

The armed men shouted, "Get back! Shoot it!" The gray troll confronted the men then suddenly turned, escaping down the length of the culvert and up the hill. Alex found her footing and started to back up. "Look, it's coming up the hill, straight toward us."

"Isn't that what you wanted, a video? Well, start filming." Sara's eyes focused on the creature. "You don't have long. It's really moving."

Then, like someone had dropped a red flag, the armed men took aim and started shooting, but the creature only turned and confronted the assault with its piercing scream. "Hold your fire. It's out of range." One of the men yelled.

"Alex, are you getting this?" The evil scream cut off the last word of Sara's question. "Why aren't you

BLOOD MOON

filming?" Alex released the record button and slowly dropped the camera to her side.

"Are you out of memory? Is there something wrong with the camera?" Sara waited in the darkness for her answers, but instead, she heard a low growl, its tone getting angrier with every passing second. To look was against every fiber in Sara's being, but look she did.

The creature was small in stature. Asymmetrical features were smeared across its face as if painted by a cruel artist. It was close enough to smell, a pungent odor rising from its gray hairless skin. Two pointed ears drooped, one to the front and the other to the back. Alex stepped backward to take Sara's hand, "What does it want? Why is it just standing there?"

Each time it growled, its upper lip trembled, revealing a row of sharp pointed teeth. "Alex, why aren't you filming this?"

"Are you kidding me? I'm too scared to move. I got enough of it rushing toward us." Alex gasped as the creature moved closer.

It crouched down, but instead of sitting, it used the movement to summon another scream from the bottom of its gullet. Grotesque hands pointed to the sky as the shrill wail penetrated the forest. The howl summoned the wind as it roared past Sara, and caused her hair to whip Alex in the face as it shook the atmosphere.

The sounds of the forest became silent. Alex still clenched Sara's hand. "It's just staring at us. Sara, start backing up, slowly."

Alex was right; the creature slumped toward the ground as the last sound of its wrenching scream withered in the darkness. Its gray body fell in a heap; each belly wrinkle folded like an accordion and laid one on top of the other. The arms that reached toward the sky, now lying lifeless, its hands puddled on the hard ground. The blank stare of the red eyes focused straight ahead. It looked almost dead.

"Okay, back up slowly…" Sara whispered.

"Sara, is it dead?" Alex asked, planted like a mighty oak. "It almost looks like it was crying."

"Now is not the time to go sentimental on me. Move it." Sara pulled on Alex's sleeve, but could not ignore her comment. The red-eyed stare was relentless. Sara's actions were not her own as a force dominated her moves and caused her to stare back at the gray entity.

It rose over Sara like a wave, the sad almost human emotion that flooded from deep within the creature's eyes. She was mesmerized by the flood of hurt and almost felt sorry for this grotesque freak of nature.

The shouting from the bottom of the hill broke her trance as the officers' stormed the hill and shouted, "There it is. Shoot it!"

The words *shoot it,* rang through the night air. Alex cried out, "NO, no, don't shoot!"

Sara's eyes focused on the flare from the gunshot that lit the area with a flash of light, just in time to see the creature leap in her direction. Its foot grazed her head as it landed behind her and headed toward the Fortress.

Alex pushed Sara to the ground and screamed, "No, no. Don't shoot! The creature is gone. Hold your fire."

The officers gathered as "Stand down," echoed through their ranks.

"We need help up here. Someone's been shot." The lieutenant called to his dispatcher.

Sara jumped to her feet. "Alex, it's just a flesh wound. I think the creature tagged me when it jumped." She placed her hand to her head and felt the warm blood oozing from the wound.

BLOOD MOON

One of the men offered a handkerchief. "Ah, no ma'am, it looks like a bullet wound, but it only grazed you." He placed the cloth on her head. "Just put some pressure on it. The bleeding will stop."

The remaining officers joined the group as the words flowed through the crowd, "Where is the creature?"

Alex took the handkerchief from Sara and continued to apply pressure. "Look, its over. That thing has vanished over the fortress wall. I think your hunt is over for the night. You've already wounded one of us. I think our objective now is to see that my friend gets medical help."

It started as a low grumble, the commotion rising from the bottom of the hill. The sequestered reporters gathered behind the officers.

Alex slid the small camera into her pocket as she turned Sara toward the village. "Thank you, officer. I think I can handle it from here. We will seek medical help in the village."

Sara wobbled on her feet and protested, "Where are we going?"

Alex grabbed her up like a rag doll as she explained, "We're going to Mary's. We're way too close to the cameras of the other reporters. I'm sure they suspect that I have footage of the creature."

Sara's mind raced back to the images of the demonic entity they encountered in the forest. Her head throbbed as the visions blurred in and out of focus. Under her breath, she mumbled, "Alex, what have we gotten ourselves into?"

Chapter 9 Before The Full Moon

The golden symbol ripped from his chest. Links of chain flew before his eyes. The sound of the metal scraping the medallion rang out, deafening in Jarrid's ears. Anuk ran through the clearing with an evil laugh that rustled the birds from their nightly perches, leaving him alone in the forest with his defeat.

Jarrid fell to his knees and let the dark close in around his lust and shame.

Anuk slipped away like a misty vision in the wind. She had taken parts of his soul, intertwined with the golden emblem, stolen in the night.

His failure to protect the heirloom weighed heavy on his heart, and with a tremendous wrenching scream, he cried out in the night, "Why?"

Nothing else mattered. Jarrid was broken, left to realize that his childhood friend, Anuk possessed the medallion.

The night air blew crisp. Jarrid's head leaned backward, his face pointed toward the night sky, still on his knees, anchored to the cold ground. His eyes opened to focus on the stars scattered through the darkness, forced to watch them fall to their earthly deaths. Silence crept slowly into the clearing, giving the starry night the attention it demanded.

One heavenly light pulsated, in the dance of celestial bodies, and fell to circle the darkness. The other, smaller stars joined in to follow in a tornadic, rhythmic descent to earth.

Jarrid was frozen in time, only to watch their lights drop to their climatic death. Faster and faster, they fell, but he didn't move. He seemed to give in to the

BLOOD MOON

possibility of being wiped from existence by the falling celestial bodies. He would accept his punishment for the lustful thoughts and the inability to protect the medallion. *His mother's warnings were coming to pass.*

The gunshot pierced the clearing with a distinct '*pop*'. Jarrid's strange vision was wiped away by the sound. His ears recognized the noise before he jumped to his feet. He physically shook off the pure, raw emotions that coursed through his veins.

Jarrid ran toward the direction of the sound without hesitation, still affected by the vision born of guilt and despair. He stopped short, straining his ears to hear. *The gunshot came from the direction of the red and blue lights.*

The sound of the bullet still rang in his ears. Alex called from the edge of the trees, "Jarrid, is that you?" She stopped briefly to let Sara catch her breath. "Here, come quick. Sara's hurt."

He sprinted toward the two shadows and stopped short, sending gravel into their path. Sara stood with the handkerchief still pressed to her forehead. "Slow, down." She said. "I'm okay. It's only a scratch."

Jarrid's grip was hard and forceful. He scooped Sara up and headed toward the village. "Wait! Put me down, for the love of goose feathers!" Sara screeched, "What's gotten into you?"

It was the feather that broke the proverbial back, or so to say. Alex couldn't contain the giggle that bubbled up in her throat. Silliness reined, even Jarrid couldn't contain his reaction to the ridiculous phrase. He gasped in between laughs and slowly lowered Sara to her feet.

"Great, that's just great." Sara stood in the clearing and watched her colleague and knight in shining armor give in to the uncontrollable laughter. "I guess a few silly words can wipe away your concern. Well, I'm fine if anyone is still wondering."

"I'm sorry," Jarrid spouted. He pulled her closer. She melted into his chest, feeling the last bouts of laughter leave his stomach. "It's just those words coming from a serious journalist, in a life and death situation…" He took her hand and guided her toward the cabin. "Well, anyway. We better get going before the cops' storm the clearing." Jarrid didn't wait for her approval and hurried her along.

"Right," Sara looked back just in time to see Alex compose herself, "don't want this video to get into the wrong hands."

"What video?" he asked, his eyes intent on Alex's face, his reaction abrupt.

He felt Sara's familiar touch rest on his arm. "Don't you know what's going on?" She gave his hand a slight squeeze, a simple gesture to soften the news. "They found a boy mutilated just outside the Fortress."

The word 'mutilated' forced all laughter from Jarrid's stomach. "Was he from the village?" He asked with concern.

"No," Sara quickly spoke. "I think he was from the city. I overheard the police discussing his clothing."

"Even so," Jarrid paused, "someone died. The threat is affecting the outside world. The council has to do something to stop the threat, and since I'm the head councilman, that responsibility falls solely on my shoulders."

"Wait, that's a lot of police for a murder investigation," Jarrid took a few steps forward to confront Alex. "What else is going on?"

"Funny you should ask." Alex moved closer to Jarrid and continued; "You see it's like this…" She led with the

BLOOD MOON

star of the story, the gray entity. She spun her words peppered with only the highlights.

"You saw a creature?" Jarrid's eyes were flashing with intrigue.

"Ah, yeah, just before the cops starting shooting at it, right in our direction." Alex quipped, "They didn't see us at the edge of the clearing, hidden in the trees."

"Didn't you see the guns pointed in your direction?" Jarrid threw all caution to the wind and confronted Sara. "Did it ever dawn on you that you were in the line of fire? What were you doing there in the first place?" Jarrid heard the words fall from his mouth and turned from her gaze.

Each question insulted Sara's intelligence, and she complained, "Excuse me, but I was just..."

Frustration tightened Alex's throat. She interrupted Sara in mid-sentence, "Oh, I don't know our job!" Alex shouted angrily. "We don't live in your world. We must bring the news to the people, and this is a damn good story."

"Story my ass. It affects my life." Jarrid took Sara by the arm and rushed her toward the village, with his anger seeping through his teeth. Jarrid turned back and confronted Alex. "The deaths of my people are what make your paycheck." His sudden movement caused a torrent of dust and gravel to fly in her face, and then he asked, "Is that what you're saying?"

"This is our job, Jarrid," Sara pushed through the dust to place herself between her friends. "But you know that we, you and I, are affected by these events. Can you deny this?"

"No, I didn't mean to—look, let's just get to the cabin, and then I want to know what you know." Jarrid started up the hill, past Sara leaving her to gather Alex and follow behind.

"Wait up, Jarrid." Sara ran ahead to close the distance between them. He shortened his stride and took her hand. Her words whispered in the night. "This can't be easy. Our destinies are on a collision course, and someone just pushed fast forward."

Jarrid didn't answer. He pulled her arm around his waist to bring her closer. They walked in unison together, one shadow in the night. His heart was pounding beneath his shirt. He responded to her touch, grabbed her other hand and placed it on his chest, the illusion of the hard metal still stung against his skin, only to remind him of the night's failures and his guilt.

***

"I can't believe you let Jarrid go alone." Joshua stood at the window with only the light of the flickering candles to show his silhouette. "Why didn't he wait for me?"

"It's Jarrid's job. He's head of the council." Mary rested her hand on Joshua's shoulder. "He must protect everyone in the village, and that includes you."

He pulled away from her touch and ran to unbolt the door. "Jarrid's coming, and he has the girls with him."

"What happened to Sara?" Joshua tripped down the porch steps and stumbled right into Jarrid's path. "Is she okay?"

"Yes, Joshua, it's nothing, just a little scratch." Sara waved the blood-soaked handkerchief in the direction of his inquiry. "You mustn't fuss, really, I'm fine." Sara grabbed his arm and hurried him along.

"Wait, Joshua," Jarrid tugged on his sleeve. "I have a big favor to ask you, my brother." Sara stared at Jarrid, a puzzled look across her face. "Look, Alex needs to stay at the hotel in the village tonight. She has to do some editing, and she will need privacy. Can you walk with her and make sure she gets safely to her room?"

"What, editing…" Alex caught up with them and complained, "I don't…" Alex caught Sara's wink and understood. "Oh yeah, I've work to do, and I'll need the quiet of my room, with no distractions." Sara's glint spoke volumes, threes a crowd, and one too many. "Okay, let's go, and Sara, by the way, you owe me big time!" Alex turned and headed for the hotel.

"Here, just rely on me." Joshua puffed out his chest and offered his arm to escort Alex. "I'll make sure you get there safe and sound."

"Escort indeed." Alex ignored the chivalry. She brushed past the young knight and scolded him under her breath, "What, you think a demon running around on the loose scares me? I'll make it to the hotel just fine, thanks."

"Wait. Wait for me." The word rolled off Joshua's tongue, "What do you mean 'demon'?"

***

Mary stood in the doorway of the quaint cabin, patiently waiting for Jarrid and Sara. She called to them before they reached the porch. "What's going on? Are you guys okay?" A beam of moonlight crossed Sara's face and erased the shadows of the night.

"Sara, you're hurt." Mary gasped. "Come, Jarrid, bring her to the table. That needs to be taken care of immediately."

The door acted as a magnet to force all of Sara's strength out through the bottom of her feet. She slumped and fell onto the chair. Jarrid crouched down to catch her.

SARAH KAGE

"I'm okay. It feels terrific to sit." The sweat dripped from her forehead and down into the corners of her mouth.

"I must stitch that up, you don't want it to scar," Mary commanded. She placed her supplies on the table and began to tend to the wound. She didn't take her eyes off Jarrid, her stare relentless. She squeezed Sara's shoulder, "So, how did you get this nasty little gash?"

Not now, Mother! Jarrid stood up abruptly to break Mary's stare. It was a look between mother and son—a thought punctuated by his eyes.

"Oh, never mind, dear. I'll fix you up, right and tidy." Mary dropped her stare and continued to clean the wound. "There, there, that's better. Don't think it needs stitches after all. Just need to put some antiseptic on the wound."

Mary spun around to get the tincture from the shelf. She retrieved the blue bottle from its resting place and turned toward Jarrid. His mother stared him down until he met her eyes. Mary placed her hand on her chest, with her eyes pleading the question. *"Do you have the medallion?"*

Jarrid knew immediately what his mother was insinuating. The silence of her words spoke volumes. The shame and disgust rose up in his throat, a reaction to his failure to protect the family heirloom. He waved his hand to dismiss her stare.

"Sara should stay with us tonight." He insisted. "Alex is getting a room at The Thornfell Village Hotel; she needs to coordinate with the newspaper before the story can be written and released." It was a declaration, given by the head councilman. Mary didn't argue.

She took Jarrid's arm and placed her hand on his chest. "I guess we'll know more about the incident tomorrow?" She patted his arm and turned to Sara. "Hope you sleep well, my dear."

"Yes," Sara hugged the robust woman then answered, "I'm sure tomorrow will shed more light on the night's events." Mary straightened the doilies on the back of the sofa and spun on her heels in the direction of her room. She yawned as the words rolled over her tongue, "Night to all."

The flames of the candles flickered in the darkness to shine a light on Jarrid's guilt. Sara's head pounded to mimic each one of Jarrid's steps. She grabbed his hand to stop the forward momentum. "Jarrid, your pacing is giving me a headache. What's wrong?"

His reluctance to answer, and the pain in her head, coaxed her to sit at the table. He stared in the dim light of the candles, right past her, and into the middle of the room. He stepped in front of the window and peered into the night. The fireplace light danced and kissed the hearth to illuminate the emotions that hung heavy in the tiny parlor. The mood flowed over Sara like a wave stirring the dread in her heart.

The closeness of the table restrained her. She slid out from under its control. The squeak of the chair reminded her to breathe. The air in the room seemed to replace itself as though the tiny cabin took a breath.

Sara crossed the room to stand at the window with Jarrid. She nuzzled against his side. His voice low, he whispered, "It's been a hell of a night. Wouldn't you say?" A nod was all Sara could muster, her head buried in his chest, protected by his arms.

***

The elevator doors of the village hotel creaked and moaned to reveal the hallway. The décor draped across the hall in all of its modest styles; the red and gold carpet, tattered and worn. The golden candelabra's, hung on the wall, spaced between each room. It was the one dwelling in the village renovated with electricity and running water for tourists.

The hotel, elegant in its simple beauty, spoke to Alex, and she yearned for the quietness of her room.

"So, creature, huh, and you got it on video?" Joshua asked, clamoring through the elevator doors and out into the corridor, asking questions one after the other. "What did it look like?" He didn't wait for her answer; he was more concerned with being the gentleman and the act of opening her door.

Alex slung the backpack over her shoulder and pushed past Joshua. She ignored his incessant mumbling about how the man should open the door for a lady. Alex grabbed the key from his hand and thrust it into the lock. She turned, hoping to discourage him from wanting to come in, but it didn't work.

"So, can I get a look at the video?" Joshua barged into the room and planted himself in the Victorian styled chair.

She smirked and shot him her best answer, "When pigs fly." She didn't wait for his response and continued, "Okay, well, thank you for escorting me, but I'm fine now." She stood in front of the open door, hoping he'd get the hint.

"You say the creature was small, about the size of a monkey, and gray. In your description, you used the word demon. That paints a pretty good visual." Joshua scratched his head and ignored Alex's invitation to leave. "When I was a child, some of the elders told stories of the gray trolls that lived behind the fortress wall."

Joshua settled onto his chair, ignoring Alex's attempt to direct him through the open door. Defeated, she closed it, flicked her hair, crossed the room, lowered her backpack to the floor, and sat down in the opposite chair. "Stories, like fantasy?" She shoved her glasses up the length of her nose, crossed her legs up under her, and waited for his answer.

"Oh, no, these stories were told to the children to assure the preservation of the ancient knowledge." Her attention captured Alex hung on Joshua's every word, something he'd tried to accomplish on their walk down the hill to the hotel.

"So, what's the story of the trolls?" Alex flopped backward into the massive cushion while Joshua moved to the edge of his.

"That was a long time ago. I was only six or seven. The story goes that the trolls inhabited the Fortress behind the inner walls, and they sometimes ventured into the village." Joshua fidgeted around in his chair, his nervous reaction to Alex's presence.

"Yeah, Sara told me about a banshee. She heard the story from Mr. Choate, but her description doesn't fit what I saw." Alex reached for the backpack, pulled the satchel into her lap, and put her hand on the camera inside.

"I think the description comes from the wailing." Joshua wiggled around in his chair, antsy and awkward he offered his wisdom, "They have an awful scream, similar to the banshee legend, but they're a different creature altogether, and according to the elders, not something to mess with." The cushion of Joshua's seat sprang upward, like a catapult it directed him toward the door.

"You realize the video puts you in real danger." Joshua's hand rested on the doorknob, he paused for a moment, and then turned back toward Alex. "If other members of the press have any inkling the footage exists, you know they won't stop until they possess it."

"You're concerned, how sweet, but I'm a big girl, and no one ever said journalism was a safe job. I live for intrigue." She gave a pouty little smirk and shooed him through the door. "Away with you, and be sure to watch for things that go bump in the night." Alex left Joshua in the hallway to ponder his next question and closed the door to end his act of chivalry.

Scents floated through the air and mingled together, dispersing through the room. *Was that meatloaf, oh, and maybe gravy? Possibly homemade yeast rolls?* Alex leaned against the closed door. The fragrant aromas teased and burst in the air, intensified with each breath.

The rumbling of her stomach echoed across the room. The aroma beckoned her toward the hotel's diner. She grabbed the backpack and headed downstairs.

Syllables of small talk swirled around Alex, with the guest departing from the diner one-by-one to retire to their rooms, leaving an air of emptiness punctuated by the sounds of the kitchen.

The nightly special was the culprit of the aroma that had wafted through her room. It was the advertisement for the plate of meatloaf, mashed potatoes, green beans, and apple pie that sat in front of Alex on the diner's table. Each of her bites accompanied by a glance to assure the backpack was in no danger.

"May I take your plate, Miss?" Alex nodded her head and slipped five dollars into the busboy's hand. "Thank you," he mumbled while brushing the crumbs into the plate. "Please be sure and dine with us again." Dishes rattled around in his tub, the sound waning to announce his exit from the room. The emptiness pulled at Alex and prompted her to head toward the elevator.

BLOOD MOON

The backpack bobbed and shook against her back, marking each step from the elevator to her room. The door stuck and protested. She gave it a push and forced it to burst open with a loud swoosh.

A warm atmosphere bathed her room in tones of gold. The light from the bathroom flooded the floor with soft shadows. Alex flopped in the chair, facing the window with the taste of the warm apple pie still caressing her taste buds. *Okay, I don't want to leave the camera out in the open. What if someone confronts me about having the video? Don't want to make it easy for them.*

She balanced precariously on the edge of the chair and plucked the camera from its case. *Wait, what if I didn't get the creature on film? I know I was recording, but it all happened so fast.* She flipped the viewer out to the side, took a deep breath, and pushed play.

It was only about thirty seconds worth of video. The screaming pierced the room. The sound was so intense it pushed Alex back into her chair. Her hands fumbled until her fingers ended the horrible noise. "Okay," she mumbled, "There's no doubt we have it on video, time to put this away for the evening."

The cell phone rang, causing Alex to nearly jump out of her skin. "Hel…" Her dinner complained in the form of a belch that rose from the bottom of her stomach. "Oh, please excuse me. Ted, is that you?"

His voice cracked, the anger flowed out, and he shouted, "Where the hell are you? I send you guys out to get the story, and you go AWOL for hours."

"Please, Ted, you don't understand. The police shot Sara by mistake." The silence was deafening. "Are you there?" Alex paused, listening for his answer.

"What'd you mean? Is she okay? Did you get the story? I mean, how did she get shot?" Ted stuttered.

SARAH KAGE

"She's fine. We decided to stay the night so she could get medical help."

A few seconds passed before Ted broke the silence to ask the question. It bubbled up deep in his throat, and he could no longer contain it, "Did you get it on camera, the creature?"

Alex froze; she wanted to scream, *No!* The syllables rose to the surface, her mouth formed the word, but instead, the truth rang out. "Yes, Ted, I got the video."

Enthusiasm filled the air and flooded across the phone. "Alex, do you understand that we have the only video of that, that thing? Your story will put us on the map. National exposure, we'll be top dog."

The hairs on Alex's arm rose, and she blurted, "We have? Don't you mean Sara and I have?"

"Well," Ted cleared his throat, "of course that's what I meant. When can you get the video to me?" His exuberance rattled the phone; there was a slight laugh to punctuate his joy while he waited for her response.

"Ted, let's think about this for a moment." Alex had no intention of giving the video to Ted until she could plan her next move. "No one else has proof of this creature, and the story is still unfolding. Wouldn't it behoove us to wait just a little while to see if we can get a better spin on the story?"

"Are you nuts?" The phone almost exploded with the vibration of Ted's laughter. "No, I don't want to wait. What, you mean hold off? Okay, you might have an angle here. Why the rush? Yes, let's see what else the two of you can dig up. After all, the video isn't going anywhere." Ted mulled the scenario over out loud.

"Okay, Ted, we agree. I'll contact you on Monday morning. We'll use this time to look for all the angles and put together one hell of a story."

BLOOD MOON

"It better be the best." Ted scoffed. "I'm counting on a twist that'll rock the journalistic world."

A frown crossed Alex's forehead, "Yes, goodbye, Ted." The phone snapped like punctuation in the dark. Alex flipped her hair from her eyes and flopped onto the bed, *the best indeed.*

The floor creaked against Alex's footsteps; each squeak announced her path toward the table lamp. She fumbled for the light switch; the beam fell across the floor to illuminate the warm antiques positioned corner to corner in the room.

She auditioned various hiding places. *No, that's too obvious..., under the bed? No, that's the first place anyone would look.* Alex peeked behind the dresser, placed her hand on the wall, and felt the indention. With one push of the furniture, it revealed itself; she squealed with enthusiasm. *Oh, yeah, that's great. No one could ever figure that out.* She positioned the camera in the perfect wedge, between the wall and the antique cabinet.

A smile of confidence lay across Alex's face to animate her feeling of accomplishment. Her sigh escaped into the room with a labored breath.

Hmm, what I need is a long hot shower. That's the ticket, yeah, something to wash away the darkness of my day.

The faucet proved a challenge, a modern fixture in the shadow of the past. Alex tugged to the right and then the left, releasing the warm water, watching it flow and fill the cracks of the ancient stones that covered the shower floor.

***

A cloaked figure hovered outside Alex's room, with a hand against the wooden door to sense the atmosphere of the surroundings. The sound of the shower flowed through the wall, echoing in the hall, like soft rain, while a knife picked the old-time lock. The door left open wide enough to aid in a quick escape.

The dark figure's reflection danced in the mirror, its shadow cast across the wall. It stood and traced the memory of Alex's steps through the room, with little pulses vibrating from the floor, hints to the location of the prize. Even its telepathy could not reveal the cameras' hiding place.

Ringing cut the air like a blade. One ring, two rings. The familiar cell ringtone assigned to Sara. "Oh, hi…, no, just getting out of the shower. Yep, everything's okay." Alex reached up to wipe the steam from the mirror. "Are you kidding? I wouldn't leave the video lying around. It's in a safe place."

The thief slinked to the bathroom door anticipating the reveal of the cameras' hiding place.

"No, under the bed, don't you think that's way too obvious? I did much better than that." Alex stomped her foot. "Really, Sara, if you must know, I hid it between the dresser and the wall. There's a deep crevice, and it fits into the indention perfectly."

"Yeah, I spoke with Ted and bought us some time." The cool air gave Alex a chill. She reached for the towel draped across the basin, moved her wet hair to the side, and answered, "Look, I'm freezing standing here dripping wet. I'll fill you in tomorrow morning. Try and get some rest. Okay, the same to you, and don't forget you owe me one!"

Like a flash, the being quietly moved the dresser to reveal the camera's hiding place. Its gloved hand removed the SD card, replaced the camera into the crevice, and escaped through the open door, closing it ever so gently. Its mission accomplished.

BLOOD MOON

Alex fluffed her hair, pulled on her sweatshirt, threw the blankets back, and dove into the soft, white bed. The nagging was relentless. She moved to turn the light off, but the camera called to her. She needed to see it, tucked in for the night in its hiding place, sheltered by the dresser and the wall.

She braved the cold floor and gently pulled the dresser out until she could peer between it and the wall. The darkness obscured the object, but Alex felt the cold plastic of the camera, false security that all was safe and well.

SARAH KAGE
Chapter 10 Deeds of Good and Evil

Outside the cabin window, moonbeams reflected across the porch. The light accented the small tornado of dried brush and twigs, the small vortex seamed to skip down the steps. Breezes swept the banister to dislodge a group of leaves held hostage by the wooden slats.

Jarrid didn't make a move. He wanted this moment to last forever, here with Sara folded into his chest, safe and sound, ignorant to the deeds that pulled at his heart. But he must tell her.

Sara's hair lay against his cheek; the smell of lavender filled his senses. He reached for a lock of the silky strands, feeling the fullness of her curls. He touched her chin and pulled her mouth to his lips. His kiss lingered, taking time to reveal the smoldering emotions that ebbed and flowed just under his skin.

The warm affection gave way to soft butterfly kisses trailing down the length of Sara's neck. Jarrid buried his face into her shoulder. He whispered, "You are my soul." Seconds passed before he lifted his head to her ear and proclaimed, "But we must talk. I have something to tell you. We can take a walk; I don't want to disturb Mom."

The urgency in his voice broke the spell. "Jarrid, is everything alright?"

He lowered his head once more into the comfort of her shoulder. "Yes, I just wanted to tell you some things that were revealed to me tonight, revelations that affect us both."

"Okay," Sara cupped his head in her hands and brought his face to hers. "Just let me make a quick phone call to Alex. I want to make sure she is settled in, and find out if she contacted Ted."

The open door invited the night breeze to swirl and collect in the middle of the room. Sara slipped out onto the porch without a sound, while Jarrid watched through the window. Her hair flowed in the moon's glow like dancing flames that kissed the darkness. A shiver ran up his spine—a reaction to the impending necessity of telling her about the medallion.

Sara raised her phone toward the sky, searching for bars and dialed the number. "Alex, were you away from your room? Are you settled in for the night?" Sara turned just in time to see Jarrid step onto the porch. She moved to the steps expecting him to follow and turned her attention back to the phone. "Did you think to hide the video?"

The phone crackled in her hand. "Darn reception…" She stepped down the stairs to get more bars and continued her questions, "You didn't hide it under the bed, did you?"

"Oh. Well, that was using your head. No one will think to look there. Did you speak to Ted?" Sara gasped. "Hey, did you check out the video? Did we get that thing on film?"

She heard the chatter of Alex's teeth. "Okay then, we'll meet in the morning. Yes, sleep well. We have a long day ahead of us tomorrow. Yes, I do owe you a massive one." Sara ended the call just as Jarrid brushed past her and down the steps.

His footsteps caused the dust to rise into the night air. He turned to offer Sara his hand, an invitation to walk with him in the moonlight. "We must talk."

Darkness emerged between them, in the softly lit forms of the trees. The animals protested with various sounds and calls, disturbed by their presence.

The moon fell upon Jarrid's face and revealed a hard, cold truth yet to be spoken.

"You're so quiet and distant, Jarrid. Didn't you want to talk?"

The agony on his face grew visible with each syllable spoken under his breath, "I can avoid it no longer; the truth must be told no matter the consequence."

The tall oak bent and yielded to the stiff breeze blowing down the hill from the Fortress. It coaxed Jarrid to spill the truth from deep in his being. "When I was young, my mother would tell me stories of distant times, fables of counsel men and elders who protected our village." The words stuck in his throat, he paused for a moment and looked for a distraction.

He stared down at their hands, intertwined in the darkness. He moved to place one on top of the other, a small ritual to bind Sara to him and prevent his tale from splitting them apart. "I will do everything in my power to honor our love and be loyal and true to only you."

"You're starting to scare me, Jarrid." Sara pulled her hands free and asked. "Has something happened?"

He turned quickly to hide his eyes from her stare, ran his fingers through his hair in the act of desperation, and shouted, "Yes, no, I don't know. I'm so confused."

Sara took his arm and confronted him. "Are you having nightmares again?"

"If only it were that simple." Jarrid's face crinkled in a tiny smile, a sort of relief. "These dark revelations are worse than any nightmare."

He moved to envelop her, to protect her from the truth of the events that tortured his soul. Her breath

BLOOD MOON

lingered on his shoulder. It penetrated the cotton fabric of his shirt and warmed the coldness of the night. He swallowed hard, gathered his courage, and proclaimed, "Sara, I have . . ."

The voice interrupted low at first, like musical notes that rushed down from the treetops. Jarrid moved Sara to the side and whispered, "Did you hear that?"

"No," Sara stepped back to secure her footing and answered. "You didn't finish your thought."

Jarrid stood in the tree line, silent and still, listening to the song of angels. *Jarrid, we will give you strength.* The voices played like a symphony, with each note falling on his soul. *These revelations are part of Sara's destiny. She must know.*

A strong wind blew down the trail and whisked the voice up and into the Fortress. "Okay, now I'm confused." Sara inquired, "What's wrong?" She confronted Jarrid and shook his shoulders. "Snap out of it," her voice heavy with frustration.

"It is okay." Jarrid took her hand and headed up the trail. "I am just trying to come to grips with all of the night's events. The thought of losing you shatters my mind."

"You have to understand that my job can be dangerous. . ." Sara's heart fluttered with each step. She pulled at his arm and tried to make her point. "But, I promise that my goal will always be to return to you." She had spoken these words to ease the pain that flooded across his blue eyes. *But was he telling me everything?*

"Look," Jarrid pulled her toward the end of the clearing and continued, "I respect your career, and I support you in your work. That is not the only reason for my fear." The words poured from Jarrid's mouth with no restraint. He waited in the dark for her reaction.

SARAH KAGE

Sara crossed her arms and pushed the pebbles under her feet to the side of the trail and surmised out loud, "So let me get this straight. You had a medallion that protects your family and the village. Your father died when you were young and left Mary head of the council until you became of age. But tonight, you lost that medallion to your childhood friend Anuk."

"Yes," Jarrid's face grimaced, her conclusions washing over him. "That about sums it up."

"Wait," Sara paused to find the right words to form her next question. "Are you telling me that a woman overpowered you and took the medallion from your neck? How's that possible?"

This fact was the nucleus of Jarrid's shame. *How indeed?* The words flew from his mouth in an attempt to explain. "She is evil and possesses some sort of mind control; she had me at a disadvantage." Jarrid searched Sara's face for a glimmer of understanding.

"So she took advantage of the fact that she's a woman, and you're a man?" Sara's words paved a path of her understanding. "There's only one tool that I know of where a woman can physically dominate a man, and that's seduction."

"So," Sara's heart fluttered in her chest. She felt the words rise in her throat and heard herself conclude. "She seduced you and took the medallion?"

"No. Of course not," Jarrid grabbed Sara's arm before she ran off, fleeing from the truth. He forced her to hear his story. "She did not . . . I did not . . . Even in my trance, I avoided her advances. It took all of my power to resist, but in that weakened state, she managed to accomplish one of her goals, and now she possesses the medallion."

BLOOD MOON

"So, you were tempted?" Sara proclaimed her cheeks moist with tears.

"Sara, I am a mortal man." He couldn't look into her eyes. "I have denied my sexual impulses all of my adult life. What do you want from me? I would hope the important part is that I resisted."

Was I unfair? After all, he had resisted. Sara's face softened in the moonlight. She put her arms around his waist and whispered, "I'm sorry. These revelations are so surreal. I need a moment to process all of it." She hugged him, his body melted into her embrace, and her forgiveness poured down like rain.

Once again, the angelic voice spoke to Jarrid. *The gift of unconditional love is your reward. It has been bestowed upon you by the woman you love. It's a tool you will use to defeat the Dark Army.*

Crickets chirped in a slow rhythm; their serenade orchestrated the couples walk through the trees. The afterglow of their feelings rang through the air and paved the way for the sweet moments to follow.

The soft moonlight descended through the trees to fall upon their silhouette. Jarrid pushed a red lock from Sara's cheek, stopping only briefly to stare into the pools of green and gold flecks. Her eyes, shining in the light to tell the story of love and forgiveness that only fueled Jarrid's desires.

"I love you, Sara, and I commit myself to only you." Jarrid's fingers ran across the curve of Sara's lips, and a small sigh pushed past his hand. He stroked her cheek, barely touching her rosy skin before he lowered his lips to seal his commitment.

"And I commit to only you," she whispered. Her heart opened to receive Jarrid's pledge, his kiss, fueled by intimacy, softened Sara's heart, helping her to pledge herself to him.

The night air fell cooler, the couple's words echoed off into the distance. Sara noticed that Jarrid was distracted, his stare pointed in the direction of the trees. She looked deep into his eyes. There a movement reflected, mirrored in the pool of blue, a figure in a black cloak standing beside the trees.

"Jarrid, did you see that?" Sara turned just in time to see the last shadows of the figure disappear into the darkness. "Someone's in the trees."

"Is anyone there?" Jarrid called out, "State your business." Only silence answered.

"Oh, I guess it was just my imagination." Sara touched his sleeve, not sure of what she'd seen. "I have a very active one, as of late." Yearning for a distraction, she pulled Jarrid closer and suggested, "Why don't we start up right where we left off?"

***

Anuk stood just inside the grove of trees and watched every move that Jarrid made. She was in his head and heard every gentle phrase of love that oozed from his lips. Her rage was uncontrollable. "How dare he confess his love for Sara? He should have been mine." The failure to seduce Jarrid earlier in the evening still stung Anuk's heart.

She circled the grove spinning incantations, invoking the Evil One's help. "Oh, Dark Prince, grant me the power to possess his soul." Garble expelled from her lips. She recognized the ancient tongue, the language of the Dark One. Her face twisted with the revelation, *I must come up with a plan, something to sully Sara and prevent her from fulfilling her destiny.*

BLOOD MOON

A black swirl cut into the night and engulfed Anuk with the revelation. "Yes, that's brilliant. I think that might work." She fell to her knees to give homage to the Prince of Darkness, for it was Satan's plan.

Anuk had been caught up in her incantations when the mirth crossed the night air and assaulted her ears. It was the words of intimacy that directed her attention toward the lovers. Each confession enraged her spirit and prompted her to initiate her plan.

One more invocation, the spell of mind control, tangled and dark, to creep into Jarrid's soul, "Yes, slowly at first, not too fast, we must wait for the right moment to strike."

The air of seduction blew through the trees and down the gray stones. Anuk's spell began gradually, with just a hint of things to come. She disguised her voice to orchestrate Jarrid's inner thoughts. She taunted him to feel the surge of sexual tension building in the depth of his loins.

Anuk orchestrated the dance, her thoughts as his own, *Yes, Jarrid, slow at first, she is but a flower.*

The kiss soft at first with only the cold, stone wall to resist against Sara's body, an ally in the evil dance dictated by Anuk's own devilish will. His passion ignited by the forceful, evil desires of a demonic spirit, flaming and taunting the surges of lust just below his control.

Jarrid's hands feverishly igniting the sexual taboo's etched into Sara's mind. Little sighs released into the air, her response to his urgency; the rise of her breast, like the ocean waves to cascade over her control. Sara's innocence hung in the balance between mind and body.

"Sara, I cannot fight any longer." Jarrid's words whispered between the rhythmic dances of their bodies pressed against the wall of no return. He searched for the moistness of her mouth, pouring all of his inhibitions into the depth of her soul. His words fueled her desires and she was lost.

The wind blew and carried the hem of Sara's dress up her thigh. The sound of scattering leaves echoed in the darkness, the wind forcing them one after the other up and over the fortress wall. Jarrid's chest heaved to reveal muscles that rose like islands in troubled waters of an endless sea. His breath mimicked her breathing—both rising and falling in unison, dancing to a distant beat.

Rhythmic beats drifted along on the breeze with a low rumble. Sara thought it was the beating of her own heart. She pulled away from Jarrid and stretched her neck in the wind, listening to the chants mimicking her heartbeat. "Do you hear it? Listen, there, just on the other side of the trees."

Whispers meandered in the breeze, faint at first. Jarrid looked to the trees on the edge of the clearing and listened. "Yes, I hear it now, like someone is chanting." Jarrid turned Sara loose and walked toward the haunting echoes just beyond the clearing.

He stood at the edge and waited for the source of the chanting to show itself, expecting it to leap from the trees and consume him. The hum rattled the leaves blowing in the night breeze. The sound circled him with intensity and pulled at his desires. The blood coursing through his veins, the sound beat in his ears. His heartbeat seemed to mimic the chants. Anuk consumed the inner corners of his mind, their thoughts as one she prompted. *Do it now, Jarrid!*

Darkness, deep and consuming, rose through his eyes. It caused his head to lower toward the ground to avoid Sara's stare while he stormed toward her with evil intent. The memory of the sweet moments shared by the lovers,

BLOOD MOON

were thrown to the ground, replaced with the urgency of lust and rage.

"Sara, I need you now!" Jarrid engulfed Sara; his arms tightened to bring her body into his grip. He didn't wait for her approval. He grabbed her hair, pulled her head back, and sunk his kiss deep into her open mouth.

Years of desire and passion, combined to fuel his lust, she gave no resistance, helpless to his advances. He cupped her buttocks and clutched her hard against his yearning body.

He released her head and stared into her eyes. Sara saw a small shadow dancing in his pupils. It was the vision of a woman cloaked in black, gyrating, and whirling in the moonlight. The chanting became louder and erased the image. Jarrid secured his grip and pinned her against the fortress wall.

"Jarrid, stop, you're hurting me! What's wrong with you?" Sara was helpless. She was no match for his strength, fueled by the chanting, driven by the wind.

His hands knew no limit; they continued to obey the rhythmic chant that grew louder with every lustful attack. Each fevered kiss and forbidden touch fueled Sara's soul, and her resistance ebbed away like the receding tide.

With a deep groan, Jarrid pressed his body hard against her tiny frame. He was a slave to the desire, guided by his growing need. He continued to have his way, only conscious of his lust, without concern or shame.

"Jarrid, please..." She didn't know if it was a command to stop or a plea to continue. Her desires rose from the depths of her stomach, regions of desire filled with warm blood to enhance his touch. She rose to meet his body, mimicking each hard push against her willing virginity.

SARAH KAGE

Then he pulled away. It was just enough to put a sliver of space between them. The chanting was relentless. It resounded in the background driving Jarrid to stare into Sara's eyes. Then with cat-like reflexes, he made his move. He reached for her hands, restrained them above her head to rest against the brick wall.

Grunts of lust and rage escaped his lips with every labored breath. Sara was confused, her thoughts jumbled. *Why does he feel the need to restrain me?* The thought vanished like smoke in the wind, fueled by the kiss, laid heavy and moist upon her lips.

His hand repositioned, anchoring Sara's wrists against the stones. He reached around and pulled her buttocks firm and hard against his loins.

Sara, what are you doing? Stop this now! The words rose from the depths of her soul. They climbed the flow of passion, rising to the surface of her consciousness. *Don't you think you've had quite enough?*

"Yes, enough." her words started low and then broke the night air. "Stop!"

Sara's pleas fell on deaf ears and fueled Jarrid's desire to push Anuk's will further into his soul. Every chant fueled his attack and instructed him to finish it.

One maniacal effort and Sara was on her back, restrained and helpless. Jarrid lay upon her, hands above her head. He lifted her dress above her waist to reveal the object of his madness.

She tried to resist, knew she must, but yes, yes. Jarrid's hand reached under her buttocks to raise her into his waiting ecstasy. He searched for the waistband, pushed hard against her, and with skill tore the barrier off and threw it into the wind.

"No!" Sara screamed, the word echoed against the wall and vanished into the night. She opened her eyes.

BLOOD MOON

The shadow of a figure floated above Jarrid's head. The same cloaked woman hovered like a hologram above their bodies and spoke directly to her. "You must give in, Sara. It is your destiny; my 'will' be done."

Jarrid raised his head to disturb the misty vision. The movement distorted the words, and they vanished to rise like smoke on the wind.

For a moment, Sara saw his face soften. "What, where...?" A moment of relief flowed through her heart. "Oh, Jarrid, please stop." But the words were wasted upon the return of the fevered and possessed man.

The pull of Anuk's evil grew stronger and forced Jarrid to bring the deed to a final climax. He rolled to one side and pushed his knee hard between her clenched legs. Her resistance was futile, no match for his strength. He spread her thighs and lowered himself into position.

Sara's body betrayed her; it rose to invite his advances, to match his lust pound for pound. He slid his hand under the front of her dress until he felt her breast tremble in his hand. He pushed the fullness toward her neck, cupped it hard, and rolled her nipple between his fingers. Once again, her spirit responded. A whimper escaped her lips, with uncontrollable desires racking her body.

Sara, get a grip. What am I doing? This man is raping me. Stop or the Spirited Sword of Purity will be lost forever. The words floated in the air. A ghostly projection of her inner thoughts, just below the surface, bubbled up from her childhood, placed there for this exact moment in time.

"Please stop, Jarrid," Sara made one last plea, "This isn't you. Resist her. I love you."

The chanting reached a fevered pitch and forced Jarrid to ignore her words. He bore down hard on her body and whispered in her ear, in a low guttural groan, "My monster is onto you."

Once more, Sara pleaded, "Jarrid, fight her! Don't let her win."

The words didn't faze Jarrid. He gave a tight tug on her wrist, repositioned her dress above her waist, and raised his body to reveal her soft virgin mound, exposed and vulnerable.

He tugged at his pants, fighting with the resisting zipper to release his throbbing staff. Its fullness emerged in a thunderous threat, to probe the darkness for its intended mark.

Carnal urges rose to the top of Sara's will. Her resistance faltered, every cell, molecular or otherwise, ached for him to fill her with his seed. She was lost.

The wind moaned and carried Anuk's words through the night. "Now, Jarrid, do it now!" The chanting, louder and louder, circled the clearing. "Take her, strip her title, and be one with me."

One with Anuk, over my dead body, Sara fought her way through the lust with Anuk's words rising like stepping stones through her tangled mind.

She struggled, only to encourage Jarrid to tighten his grip. He raised his leg to anchor his assault. In his heat, he released her hands to grab her buttocks and force her toward his pulsating staff, to bury himself into the forbidden fruit; virgins no more.

Jarrid's face contorted, consumed by his need, his entire being longing for that one explosive release. Sara seized the moment and used her legs to move away from his grip. She kicked him squarely in the groin to escape the final attack. It was a move her grandfather had taught her when she was a child, another tool in her arsenal.

BLOOD MOON

His longing for ecstasy and release, replaced with a searing pain that started low in his stomach. It gathered in the pit of his loins, twisted and dark.

Jarrid's pain fell upon him like a rock. He lay on the ground in a fetal position and called after Sara, "Wait, please come back. Why? What?" He watched her run down the path, her cries in the night like daggers through his heart.

"No! I will not be defeated." Anuk threw her hands toward the moon; her screech echoed through the night. Her mind intertwined with Jarrid's thoughts, the kick to the groin brought Anuk to her knees. She'd felt every inch of his pain. She fought through the ache and rose to her feet and called out, "Oh, Dark Prince, our plan has been crushed, and the Righteous One still has her power."

She fell back to the ground, the weight of her lust and evil smothering her, in her despair, she prayed to her master. The medallion dangled from her neck, resting on the ground, her prayers to the dark horse, breaking the silence of the night.

"Do not fear my child." Anuk's agony formed in the shape of tears that rolled down her cheeks. Each drop fell on the medallion and caused it to ring out with clarity, a backdrop for the evil words spilled into the night. "We will be victorious."

She brought the cloak to her tear stained face, wiped away her sorrow, letting the words wash over her in all their evil. "Yes, master. I will defeat the Righteous One. I hear, and I obey."

SARAH KAGE
Chapter 11 Night Visions

Limbs hung heavy across the path. The animals scurried from their hiding places. Moonbeams twisted around the trees with shadows morphing into monstrous shapes, but Sara didn't notice. Her cries echoed through the night, giving the silhouettes life.

Sobs echoed from the bottom of Sara's lungs and left her spent, the energy gone from the depths of her soul. She fell into the shadow of a large root, huddled in the darkness, with the thoughts of betrayal lapping at her heart.

Twigs snapped, the sound echoed against the trees, its announcement loud and clear. "Sara, is that you?" Anuk circled the old oak and bent down peering, at the woman crouched at the base of the tree. "My name is Anuk, a friend of Jarrid's. Do you need help?"

Anuk shifted her weight, leaned against one knee, and lifted her hand. In a quick movement, she removed her cloak's black hood. It fell to her shoulders and revealed mounds of ebony hair that glistened in the moonlight.

Her dark eyes were illuminated by the moon's glow, dancing, consuming every speck of light in the darkness. Silence lay on the forest floor like a spell snuffing out time and space.

"You are the one! I knew it was you." Sara's strength flowed from her gut; it caused her to bolt from her crouched position, to confront the woman in black. "I know Jarrid was under your spell. Somehow you controlled his actions. He would never harm me."

The crunch of leaves, disturbed by Sara's steps, broke the silence of the night. The two women stood face-to-face on the path, with Sara circling the strange woman, her voice ringing out with clarity. "What are you? How do you possess the ability of mind control? Are you a witch?" She demanded. "Well…?" Sara took another step toward Anuk, a move of dominance, punctuating her question.

"A witch, you say." Anuk grabbed her cloak in frustration, flicked it to the side, and stepped backward, a ploy putting space between her and Sara in the darkness. "Oh, I think you can do better than that." Anuk turned her back and stepped away from Sara. "You ask the wrong question. It isn't what I am. The correct question is why?"

Sara rushed Anuk, grabbed her arm, and twisted her around until their eyes locked. The medallion burst from its hiding place and rested on the rise of Anuk's breast, catching just enough moonlight to cast an eerie glow. The witch shook Sara off and stood her ground.

"Okay," Sara circled Anuk and confronted her with her question. "Let's start with that. Why did you steal the medallion? And while we're at it, why would you want Jarrid to rape me?"

Anuk turned to make her way up the path, a move of defiance dismissing Sara and her questions, but instead, she stopped, grabbed the medallion, and brought it to her lips. Her voice was soft, almost nurturing, "You really are naive in all of this." She turned just as Sara confronted her.

"You're an elusive little twit, aren't you? I've had enough of these games." Sara quipped, frustration rising in her voice. "What do you have to gain by forcing Jarrid to rape me?" Sara's eyes glowed with anger and defiance; she placed fisted hands on her hips and took a stance of dominance.

SARAH KAGE

A shrill laugh rose from Anuk's throat, "Oh, you are quite the warrior, but calm down sunshine. I feel the only answer I can give you, about the attempted rape, is to deny you *The Spirited Sword of Purity*, as foretold by your grandmother."

Anuk's words ended in a clap of thunder that echoed through the trees. It shook the ground and forced Sara's words into the air. "How could you possibly know about the importance of my virginity? My grandmother could never tell me the reason, only that I must stay pure. That my very life depended upon it."

"Okay, I get it." Anuk placed her hand on Sara's arm, only to be met with an act of defiance, her message loud and clear. "You think I'm your enemy. There's much more at stake here than you can imagine."

"Enemy," Sara stomped the ground and emphasized her response, "Let's see, you forced Jarrid to attack me. You confronted him, tried to seduce him, and stole the family heirloom. I think that falls under the definition of an enemy."

A gust of wind swirled between the women as if summoned by Anuk's will. The witch's low growl followed the sound of the leaves, whirling and scattering down the path. "Sara, you are really starting to annoy me." Anuk said in frustration, "Look, friend or enemy, these titles do not matter. We are all pawns in the destiny of good and evil."

All of Sara's nightmares played across her mind in a flash, each one taking its place, telling the story of the battle to come. They forced her voice from deep inside, "Witch! You speak in riddles and wield your intentions for your purposes. You will stay away from Jarrid." Sara's words spilled into the night, fueled by the anger that rose from the depths of her memories. "This is not a request, but a demand."

"Yeah," Anuk's frustration rose from under her cloak, its power fueled by Sara's words. She pushed the fullness of the garment off her arms, releasing the restraints on her response. "Like that's ever going to happen."

Calmness rolled over Anuk's face, controlling her emotions and gathering her wit. She leaned against a large tree, her cloak flapped in the wind and snapped like a whip, cracking and popping like embers in a dying fire.

"It is a shame that your grandmother did not tell you the reason for your purity." Anuk's words rose through the air between them. "It is one of many tools given to you by the heavens, tools you will need for the upcoming battle."

"Enough witch. Don't pretend that you know anything about me." Sara rushed up into Anuk's face, their breath intertwined in the cold night air. "Who do you think you are?" Sara's angry words flowed across her lips and fueled her to grab Anuk by the shoulders, shaking the very truth from her existence, but her grip met only air, causing her to fall against the hard bark of the tree.

"You know that anger will not serve you well in the coming days." Anuk proclaimed, escaping Sara's grip and moving across the path. "A clear mind will be a greater tool if you plan on defeating me."

"Witch, there's no battle for Jarrid's love, I have already defeated you." Sara's red hair waved in the breeze and framed the defiance that rose in her cheeks, an emotion that prompted her to back Anuk into the trunk of the large oak.

One second she was there and the next gone, only a fine mist swirled the trunk of the old tree and foiled

Sara's attempt at confronting her opponent. "Oops, you missed." It was the evil laugh that broke across the mist, causing Sara to turn just as Anuk came up from behind.

Her breath cascaded hot upon Sara's face, melting the last of the smoky mist to vanish into the night. Sara was backed up against the mighty oak, sequestered to hear Anuk's words, "This medallion..." she reached in between the space of their bosoms and brought the glowing disk in front of her eyes, gave it a shake, and proclaimed, "It is a curse. The power of the medallion is neutral. It only enhances the good or evil of the person who possesses it."

"My master demanded that I steal the medallion." Anuk backed away, letting Sara catch her breath. "He knew the lust in my heart would prevent me from delivering *The Book of Souls* to Jarrid, but the medallion would give me no choice."

Sara sucked in gulps of cold air, bringing back the life in her lungs and the energy to ask, "What are you—"

The sound of large, flapping wings came through the boughs of the trees. They pushed the air down, between the women, with Sara's words bouncing off the trunks of the trees. With each downward stroke, the dirt and leaves circled and engulfed the atmosphere of the confrontation that played out just below the branches of the trees. The shrill scream cracked through the branches and caused Sara to protect her ears from the onslaught of the relentless sound.

Its last screeching cry filled the air, and the sound of soaring wings slowly vanished, giving way to silence.

Sara lowered her hands from her ears with the memory of her last words still echoing in her thoughts. She focused in the dark just in time, hearing the answer to her question.

BLOOD MOON

Anuk grabbed the hem of her cloak and pulled it around her body before she vanished in the night air with her words ringing through the forest, "I am the Evil One." A strong wind blew dust across the path and caused Sara to cover her eyes, a distraction used to accomplish Anuk's disappearance into the darkness.

***

Only the echoes of the chanting rang in Jarrid's ears. The sounds mingled with the agonizing ache that forced him to clear his mind. The smell of the damp earth rose through his nostrils; it encircled his face and obstructed his labored breaths.

His belt buckle dug against the dirt and hindered his attempt at gathering his trousers from around his thighs. *What did I do?* He stood and collected himself, but his zipper fought against the attempt to brush away all evidence of the attack. His conscience fought him; confused and disoriented, he pushed the bushes aside, ignoring their intrusion upon his face. His forehead stung with the evidence of a wayward branch that didn't bend to his will. Pure frustration caused him to call out into the darkness, "Sara, where are you?"

Anuk stood just behind the line of trees in the clearing. She watched Jarrid fight the realization of his attack on Sara. A smile formed across her red lips. She gathered strength from the mere agony flowing from his very being. "Jarrid, its Anuk. Are you alright?"

She seemed to float through the darkness and stood directly in his path. "It was you!" Jarrid rushed the dark-haired beauty and grabbed her arm, bringing her closer. "You are responsible for my actions. I remember feeling your control. Your, I mean my attempted rape!"

"Yes," Anuk shook off Jarrid's hold on her arm and moved away, straightening her cloak, "until you didn't. I

148

never expected Sara's strength strong enough to fight you off." Anuk turned to walk away, leaving Jarrid pondering the importance of her revelation.

She second-guessed her retreat, turned back toward him, and spoke the words he yearned to hear, "No, Jarrid, you didn't succeed in taking her virginity, and she is aware that you were under my influence."

Her move calculated Anuk touched Jarrid's arm, assuring him that Sara didn't hold him responsible. He couldn't remove her hand quickly enough with the sound of disgust rising in his voice, "What could you possibly gain from me raping Sara? You are pure evil."

"I think Sara would agree with you." Anuk left Jarrid with his question falling from his lips, but decided she'd give him a clue about the battle looming in the distance. "I believe the word she used was 'witch.'"

"Yes, an evil witch," Jarrid yelled. His feet caused the gravel on the path to engulf Anuk. He circled her and crushed her attempt to slink away. He thrust his hands into the darkness, acting as a deterrent to her escape. She had no choice and yielded to his will.

She stood in the night with her cloak billowing out like a sail in the breeze, her escape thwarted. "We will be one, Jarrid, ruling over the evil invading this plane of existence. My master will demand it."

"Woman," Jarrid heard the laugh rise from the depths of his inner core, ringing out in defiance to Anuk's words. "The only master you bow down to is your selfish wants and desires. If you are conjuring spells to win my love or even lust, you are already defeated."

Anuk puffed up with rage, the ugliness rose from her heart, distorted her beauty, and morphed her features into something of pure evil. "I will be victorious with or without you!" She rushed Jarrid, standing in his shadow,

BLOOD MOON

and confronted his naiveté. "I am the Evil One, and my reign will be absolute."

A rush of the air fell upon the path with urgency. First, the wind pushed down, and then the air was sucked back up, causing the tree branches to sway up and down. The sound of large wings cut the air just as Anuk's last word left her lips, and she disappeared into the night. The scream, so shrill it threatened to erase reality.

Jarrid's unconscious ducking from the onslaught of the wings was met with the slap of Anuk's cloak against his cheek. The wailing scream echoed in his ears and caused him to search the trees for the approaching beast.

"What the hell…" But no one was there to hear his question. A swoosh of air pushed across his face, with a scream echoing from the clearing.

A voice came from just beyond the trees, low at first. "Jarrid, are you there? Where are you?" Sara pushed the low branches of the trees out of her way and called into the forest. Jarrid ran toward her, closing the space between them. He thrust his hands forward, and Sara fell into his arms.

The shadow of their crouched form draped across the path then rippled across the rock formations that kissed the fortress wall. The sharp scream echoed against the gray wall, dirt and leaves tore at the couple huddled in the darkness. Once again, the large wings drove the air up and over the stone wall, enhancing the screech; and then there was silence.

"Are you alright?" Jarrid took Sara's arms, helping her to rise, bringing her close against his chest. He picked the leaves from her hair and brushed the dirt from her face.

She was dazed and confused but buried her head deep into his chest, trying to escape the invisible foe. He took her face in his hands and whispered, "It's alright. Whatever that was is gone."

"No," Sara moved from his embrace, shaking her head. "That's the second time tonight I've had the same experience. Anuk…"

She turned, leaving him standing in the dark with the word echoing through his head. "What do you mean? Anuk, where…?"

Before he could finish the sentence, Sara ran back to him and threw her arms around his waist. She spoke her words through the cotton fabric of his shirt, "It's alright. I know it was Anuk and her evil spell that caused the attempted rape."

"I thought I'd lost you forever." Jarrid welcomed her embrace and pulled her closer, sequestering her to hear his words. "I couldn't stand the thought of you running off in the darkness, thinking I had attacked you."

Sara touched his cheek, bringing his face closer. She placed a soft kiss on his mouth, lingering for a moment, underscoring her forgiveness; and then she remembered the kick. "Jarrid, are you okay? I kicked you pretty hard."

"I am fine, just glad that you were able to protect yourself." The corner of his mouth rose, forming a slight grin, a ploy to avert her from his bruised ego.

The smirk quickly changed to a frown. Before Jarrid could form his words, the breeze circled the path and pushed the cold wind between them. Sara moved away, leaving a space for the circle of leaves rising against the wall.

The small vortex of dried debris towered above Sara's head with the light of the moon focused on a colorful object suspended in the middle of the leafy cyclone. She stared into the shape, the moonlight beamed and bounced off the shape of an eye. Each revolution grew brighter, exposing the bright purple and blue feather-like vision.

Without a sound, the tower of leaves dropped, and the object floated to rest in the curls of Sara's hair. Jarrid picked the jeweled feather from its resting place and examined it. "What? Where did this come from?"

"Here, let me see." Sara grabbed it from Jarrid's hand and turned, keeping him from retrieving it. "Wait. I think it's a peacock feather."

"Yes, that's exactly what it is," Jarrid grabbed the feather from her grip. "But peacocks are not indigenous to this area. I've never seen any evidence of this species in these parts."

Sara touched his hand admiring the green and purple feather. "Do you think that's what was flying around in the treetops before?"

"I'm, not sure? Whatever it was seemed a lot larger than a peacock." Jarrid continued examining the feather and remembered. "You said you heard the wings before. Did you mean when you were in the woods with Anuk?"

"Yes," Sara watched Jarrid's face twist into an agonizing expression. "She came to me right after... well, you know."

"You can say it, my attack," Jarrid finished her sentence.

"She wanted me to know that it was her influence that prompted your attack." Sara squeezed his hand and smiled. "That seemed rather strange to me. I questioned her intentions, and she spouted some nonsense about the medallion forcing her to deliver *The Book of Souls* to you. Do you know what she was talking about?"

"No, never heard of such a thing." Jarrid draped his arm around Sara's shoulder and kissed the top of her head. "Did she tell you anything else?"

SARAH KAGE

"Yes, as a matter of fact, she did." Sara's frown accompanied her words. "You know, she's pretty full of herself. She was taunting me, and her last words before she disappeared, still chill my soul."

"So, what did she say?" Jarrid took the peacock feather from Sara and placed it in her hair just behind her ear.

Each of Anuk's words spilled from Sara's mouth into the night, "I am the Evil One!"

***

The brick tower stood tall in the middle of the village courtyard. The worn and weathered clock-face glowed in the light of the full moon. Each second noted by the black second hand that seemed to skip through time, making its way around the old clock, ticking off each moment.

Moonlight flooded the night, gathered up against the clock tower, shooting around the hard corners, focusing into sharp beams that poured into the hotel windows. Thin rays of light honed through the sheer curtains draped across the window into Alex's hotel room.

She tossed and turned beneath the coverlet, causing the moonbeams to disperse and diffuse, only to mingle with dust particles that seemed to die a slow shadowy death in the darkness.

The moans of a troubled dream echoed against the walls, each sound louder than the last. Alex grabbed the sheets and gathered them around her neck. She tossed and turned her feverish attempt at escaping the nightmare. "No, it has to be here. I know I hid it right..." Her arm rose to point toward the ceiling, showing the hiding place of the camera, the direction distorted by the dream.

BLOOD MOON

Alex sat up in the bed with the sheets still clenched in her hands. The bells of the clock tower rang once, then twice, with the ring of the last chime echoing through the night. Alex's brain focused on the fact that the clock had struck two, but then a different ring broke her thoughts. The cell phone light bounced off the ceiling to interrupt the moment.

She untangled the sheets, reached across the bed, and grabbed the vibrating phone. "Hello, Mom, is that you? What, the kids? Mom, turn out the lights and don't answer the door; I'm on my way."

Alex fumbled for her pants in the dark, searching her pockets for the keys. The dresser offered no resistance. She pushed it away from the wall and pulled the camera from its hiding place. She tucked it inside the backpack and hurried down the hall.

The heavy stairwell door squeaked and shoved against her backpack. It held Alex momentarily until she tugged it away from the door's entrapment. She attacked the staircase, skipping two stairs at a time until she reached the exit and spilled into the hotel courtyard.

She ignored the night sounds and darkness that picked at her soul. She threw the backpack onto the car seat, jumped in, then started the car and pointed it in the direction of town.

The drive down the mountain pass was frantic. Alex's childhood neighborhood filled the car windshield with the alleyway behind her mother's house looming, dark and narrow. Alex turned the engine off and coasted toward the back of the old fence surrounding her mother's property. The windows of the house were dark, with no signs of movement around the perimeter of the building.

SARAH KAGE

She unwound the wire from the old gate lock and slinked into the back yard. Her foot hit the wooden box that surrounded the pump house. "Ouch, damn thing." *As many times as I've snuck into this house in the dark, I ought to remember the location of the old pump house.* She shook off the pain and crouched down to make her way across the yard toward the basement window.

"Great, it's still open." She mumbled, slinking through the narrow opening and sliding into the dark and dank basement. She stepped forward, landing squarely in an open cardboard box overflowing with this or that until she righted herself in the middle of the basement floor.

The light scored Alex's eyes with the vision of her mother appearing at the top of the cellar stairs. "Mom, turn the lights out, now," she whispered.

The darkness once again engulfed her as she stumbled up the old wooden stairs. "Alex, I didn't know what to do. They showed up right after I put the kids to bed."

"Mom, did you talk to any of them?" She grabbed her mother and guided her into the middle of the dark kitchen. She sat her mother down in one of the chairs.

"No, Alex. Give me a break. I know the drill." Alex stumbled through the dark room and peered through the living room windows.

The police and journalist gathered on the lawn with their cameras, microphones, sound equipment, and blue and red lights camped out for the duration. Alex turned back to see her mother close the distance between them in the dark. "What do they want, Alex? What've you done this time?"

"Really, Mom," She rolled her eyes in the darkness, glad that the lack of light hid this from her mother's inquiry. "This is nothing for you to worry about. I need to get the kids and sneak out the back. Can you help me wake them?"

"Mom, please." Alex put her arms around her mother and pleaded, "You have to trust me. I'll tell you everything when I can. The less you know the better. Now, are you going to help me or not?" Her mother slowly nodded.

Alex gathered the children at the bottom of the stairs. She tucked the long pajama legs into the tops of Lizzy's shoes and tried reasoning with her sleepy daughter, "Lizzy, please put your jacket on. We have to leave."

The curious girl was having none of it. "Mommy, I am too tired. You woke us up." Tears flowed from her eyes, and she complained, "Chad is too sleepy to go. We want to go back to bed."

"We're going on an adventure, a pretend trip." Alex corralled the sleepy babes toward the back door. "You're a princess, and Chad's a knight. Doesn't that sound like fun?"

Lizzy's lips couldn't have protruded any further from her tiny cheeks with a pout the size of Texas. "Okay, Mommy. Let's get this over with. I want to go back to sleep."

"Are you sure you know what you're doing. Alex?" Her mother kissed the kids and hustled them toward the backdoor.

"Mom," Alex laid her hand on her mother's shoulder and squeezed. "I have no choice."

"Okay, Chad, take Mommy's hand." She turned to face her mother waiting, in the darkness. "Remember, Mom, don't talk to anyone."

Alex rushed Chad out the door when she realized that Lizzy had gone on down the sidewalk and out past the old gate. "Chad, we must be very quiet until we reach the car." The small boy nodded his head and clenched her hand.

"Where are you, Lizzy?" She pulled Chad close and hurried through the backyard, whispering in the darkness.

The old gate loomed in the distance with the sounds of Lizzy's whispers spilling over the fence. "Who are you? Can I see your pretty feather?"

The street light in the alley shone down the road and illuminated the man squatting down in front of Lizzy. She was talking to him in low whispers, "What's your name?"

The stranger saw Alex approaching and stood, meeting her gaze. "Whoa, I mean you no harm. My name is Dax." Alex grabbed Lizzy's hand and pulled her toward the car.

Beams of light from the street lamp shone across his face, his intense green eyes danced with electricity. He leaned forward and opened the door. "I'm your mother's neighbor; I mean, friend. She asked for my help in getting you guys safely away from the reporters." He moved away from the open door, giving her some room.

He was tall and slim, his forehead wrinkled and worn. His eyes seemed much older than his face. Alex hurried the children into their car seats. She stopped briefly and addressed the green-eyed man. "Look, Dax, was it? I appreciate your help, but we can manage."

"Oh, please," Lizzy peered around her mother and put her hand out with tiny fingers reaching toward Dax. "May I see your pretty feather again?"

"Not now, Lizzy," Alex shoved her tiny hand back into the car, pushed the blankets out of the door, and closed it. "Dax, again, I appreciate your kindness, but I must get the kids away from this situation. I hope you understand."

BLOOD MOON

"Yes, and if I can be of further assistance, just let your mother know." He put his hand over his heart, bowed, and backed into the shadows.

She motioned through the windshield. "Okay, Lizzy, Mommy's coming." Alex ignored his exit and rushed around the front of the car. The driver's door complained and resisted her will then shut loudly. She started the car, drove down the alley, and turned onto the street heading in the opposite direction of the camped out reporters.

"Mommy," Chad was already snoring when Lizzy spoke, "Did you see his beautiful feather?"

"What's this feather you keep talking about?" Alex's heart stopped pounding for the moment. She took a breath and asked her daughter. "Was it on his hat or something?"

"No, Mommy." Lizzy giggled in a sleepy tone and answered, "It was painted on his neck. It had purple and green colors that glowed in the light. Right in the middle was this huge eye, like it was staring at me; all painted up like Aunt Minnie's eyes." Lizzy ended her observation with a yawn and drifted off to sleep.

The silence left Alex with the thought circling her mind. *What like a peacock feather?*

SARAH KAGE
Chapter 12 It is Written

The smell of bacon drifted from the kitchen and into the tiny parlor. Sara's eyes squinted, peered out across the landscape of the quaint living room, and then closed tight. She was not quite ready to face the morning; even the smell of a country breakfast could not budge her from the comfy couch.

Mary pushed the bacon around in the pan with the hum of an old-fashioned Scottish jingle escaping her lips,

"Cope sent a challenge frae Dunbar Sayin, Charlie meet me an' ye daur An' I'll learn ye the airt o' war If ye'll meet me in the morning."

She took in a deep breath to aid in the next verse but lost it to a giggle when Jarrid came from behind with a cup of black coffee. "Oh, Mom, be careful. I do believe your Scottish is showing." He placed the cup on the drain board, bent down and kissed the cheek of the cherub-like woman.

"Pish posh," Mary giggled and picked up a plate to retrieve the bacon from the pan. "You might want to wake our sleeping beauty. Breakfast is almost ready."

"Oh, give her a few more winks." Jarrid smiled and replied, "She deserves it."

The biscuits rose in the oven with an aroma of buttery enchantment. "These still have a few minutes to bake," Mary exclaimed with a sniff. She turned to face Jarrid and placed her hand in the center of his chest. "Now might be a good time to tell me about last night."

"You know I do not have the medallion!" Jarrid moved out from under her touch and walked to the sink.

"Jarrid, I have always known the destiny of the medallion," Mary spoke, her suspicions verified. "It was

159

the timing of the event that was elusive to my visions. I also know Anuk is the one who stole it."

"Did your visions show you how she managed to steal it?" Jarrid's guilt rose to the surface and marked his face in waves of red.

"No, they come to me in bits and pieces. It's not relevant how Anuk did it. The only thing that matters now is the sequence of events set into motion." Mary reached up to push the locks of hair from her son's face. The jagged edges of the cut on his forehead scraped her fingers. "Not, you too, how did this happen?"

"It is just a scratch, Mom." Jarrid grabbed her hand from his face and let his mouth run away with him, "It happened last night after the police shooting."

"What police shooting?" Mary confronted him, "Is that what was going on in the clearing last night? What were they shooting at?"

"You're not going to believe this, Mom." Jarrid placed his hands on her shoulders as if to lessen the blow of his proclamation. "Alex got it on video. The police had it cornered in the clearing and wound up shooting at it. Mom, I think it was a troll."

"Oh, Jarrid, what are you saying?" Mary's shoulders slumped, and her face turned ashen. "Those creatures have not been seen for hundreds of years. Are you sure?"

"There is more." Jarrid stood tall and continued.

"Go ahead. I am listening." Mary felt for the back of the chair and lowered herself into the seat. She brought her handkerchief to her face and dabbed the beads of sweat that rolled down her forehead.

"There was a young boy." Jarrid sat down beside her, took her hands, and said, "He was torn apart and left to die just outside the fortress wall."

SARAH KAGE

The words scraped at Mary's ears and caused her to ask, "Was it someone from the village?"

"I don't think so, but I do believe the troll was responsible. The village is in great danger."

Mary retrieved her hands and stood to rescue the biscuits from the oven. The pan resounded as she tossed it onto the stovetop, her knees weak with his revelations. She placed the towel on the handle of the oven and lingered, trying to regain her composure. "Jarrid, this news does not surprise me. It is the beginning!" Before Jarrid could answer, the screen door burst open, and Joshua spilled into the kitchen.

"Could you be any louder? Sara's still sleeping." Jarrid whispered, his eyes bulging.

The mere mention of her name caused Joshua to shudder. His face screwed into a frown, each word coming louder, "Did you tell Mom... about the wall?"

"Enough!" Jarrid pulled his brother toward the back porch and used his hand to muffle his words. Jarrid put his forearm across Joshua's throat, pinning him to the wall. "You will say no more."

A small nod let Jarrid know his brother would honor his command. He backed away to allow his brother to collect himself.

"Is there something you are not telling me, Jarrid?" Mary stood in the porch doorway and waited for an explanation. "What about the wall?" She folded her arms and filled the entrance, waiting for an answer.

Jarrid pulled Mary onto the porch. "What are you doing?" she asked.

"Look, Mom, I don't want Sara to hear." He corralled Mary and Joshua into the far corner and then started to pace in circles. "Okay, there is no easy way to say this, yes, it is true!" Jarrid's face was overwhelmed with

161

sorrow. "I followed Joshua into the Fortress, late last night, and found him standing in front of the wall, mesmerized by her image." Jarrid brought his eyes up to gaze into their faces.

Joshua interrupted his brother. "Mom, she is evil." He maneuvered himself in front of Mary and spoke the words fueled by pure fear. "I am sure of it. The picture is proof."

"No," Mary draped her arms around her youngest son and held him close, trying to comfort him. "No, Joshua, Sara is not evil."

"You did not see it, Mom." Joshua pulled away from her embrace. He calmed himself and turned toward Jarrid. "Tell her, Jarrid. You saw it for yourself."

Jarrid could not refute the fact that it was Sara's face on the wall, but he could not bring himself to think her evil.

"Sara is not evil. I am sure of it." Mary stood in the doorway and watched Sara as she slept. She turned toward Jarrid and spoke her words with conviction, "She is the one we will look to for solace in the coming days. Enough of this, breakfast is getting cold." Mary proclaimed, shaking off the revelation. She scurried off the porch and mumbled to herself, "No doubt, this will come to pass."

"You will be responsible for her." Joshua exclaimed, pointing his finger in his brother's face and shooting a stare of discontentment into his eyes. "I hope your trust is well placed." He turned abruptly, his anger raging and left the porch.

A rush of air flew past Jarrid's face, and the screen door slammed. "Are you not staying for breakfast?"

"No!" echoed from the steps. "Not on your life." Joshua raised his hand and dismissed his brother's question leaving him with his thoughts and doubts.

The dishes clanked, and the silverware rattled with each place setting arranged on the small kitchen table. Jarrid was placing the last fork when a movement from the parlor caught his eye.

Sara's toes stretched out into the air with her leg draped over the couch. An arm raised, each finger pointed toward the ceiling in a lengthy stretch accompanied by little grunts and groans.

"So," Jarrid stood at the edge of the couch, waiting for her eyes to open. "You are awake."

"Yep, sure enough," She opened one eye, grabbed his leg, and smiled. She sat up and pulled a nest of curls out of her face. "Is that breakfast I smell?"

"Mom's famous breakfast," Jarrid offered his hand and pulled her up into his chest. "Good morning. Did you sleep well?"

"Yes, I did," Sara answered, peering around Jarrid to see Mary busying herself with the biscuits placed on a large platter in the middle of the table.

"Okay, you two." Mary cleared her throat. "Everything is ready."

Sara skipped past Jarrid, flashed Mary a smile, and scooped a biscuit from the table, held it in her mouth, and collected her unruly curls into a bun, then removed the buttery concoction to proclaim, "Mary, this biscuit is divine. You guys start without me. I'll be right back." Sara turned on her heels and disappeared down the hall.

"Well, come on and dig in. The food is getting cold." Mary piled heaping portions of the hearty breakfast onto Jarrid's plate.

BLOOD MOON

Sara returned to a generous serving of eggs, bacon, and gravy. "You must think I'm starving."

"Just wanted to make sure you had enough," Mary added.

"This breakfast is amazing, Mary." Sara collected her second biscuit and dabbed at the buttermilk gravy on her plate. "I now see how your boys came to be so robust."

"Oh, I bet that's Alex." Mary's answer was interrupted by the ping from Sara's phone, the announcement of a text-message bounced off the parlor walls. Sara pushed the chair from the table and hurried to collect the phone. Alex's number displayed across the screen with the words in all caps,

MEET ME IN THE CLEARING IN TEN MINUTES.

That was it, a sort of cryptic message with no elaboration.

"Okay, Jarrid, I guess I need to meet Alex in the clearing, like right now. I don't know what could be so urgent, but it doesn't sound like I have a choice. Mary, please excuse me, but I think this must be work-related."

Jarrid gathered the dishes and put them in the sink. "Do you want me to come with you?"

"Do you mind?" Sara turned and asked Mary, "Sorry for leaving you with the cleanup."

"You go on now," Mary flicked her towel in the air and motioned for the two to join Alex. "Don't worry one second about me."

***

Alex and the children walked to the clearing, from the hotel and were standing in the middle when Jarrid and Sara's heads bobbed into view. The children sat behind Alex playing in the grass.

SARAH KAGE

"Oh, Auntie Sara, is that you?" Lizzy called out. The enthusiastic girl raced across the meadow with her arms outstretched. "Oh, Auntie, I've missed you so much."

"Lizzy, what are you and Chad doing here?" Sara knelt to her level and asked, "I thought you were with your grandmother."

"Why," Lizzy threw her arms around Sara's neck and shouted in her ear, "We miss you, Aunt Sara."

"I see she has recovered," Alex passed the reunion and made her way to Jarrid. "Bet you had something to do with that."

"Okay, Alex," Jarrid replied. "Enough of the small talk, do you have it?" He made the implication of a clicking camera, hoping Alex would get the hint.

"Oh, you want to know about the…" Before she finished her sentence, Jarrid shushed her.

"Yes, that is right. I want to know about the party." He winked, and she got his meaning.

"Well, the answer is yes. I got photos of the… party. They turned out better than I'd hoped. Got everything clear and precise; the star of the party is especially riveting." Jarrid nodded just as Sara joined their conversation.

"Hey, what was so urgent? And, by the way, what in the world are the children doing here? I thought they were with your mother." Alex yanked Sara's arm and pulled her away from the children's ears.

"Well, what's up?" Sara asked steadying herself on the unlevel ground. She peered around Alex watching Jarrid play with the kids.

"I had to rescue them in the wee hours of the morning." Alex moved to the side, pushed the leaves around with her foot, and explained, "Reporters and police surrounded Mom's house. She called me, and I

165

went and snuck the kids out the back and brought them to the hotel."

"I had no choice, Sara." Alex turned to watch Jarrid chasing the kids and taking his turn to be it. "The decision was the lesser of two evils."

"How'd you manage to get them out?" Before Alex could answer, Lizzy interrupted. She pulled Sara's arm and coaxed her to kneel.

"Mommy, look, it's just like Dax's feather." Lizzy raised her tiny hand to touch the green and purple feather tucked behind Sara's ear. "Where did you get it, Aunt Sara?"

"I found it in the forest." Sara shot Alex a puzzled look and answered, "Isn't it pretty? I think it's a peacock feather." Sara pulled it from her hair and gave it to the small girl.

"Look, Chad, I have a pea feather." Lizzy skipped and jumped toward Jarrid and Chad, jumbling up her words as she went, "It is just like the one painted on Dax's neck."

Jarrid heard the words and shot a glance at Sara, asking, "Who is Dax, and why is it important that he has a peacock feather tattooed on his neck?" He turned to Sara with the underlying question pasted across his face. *What was the coincidence of the feather?*

"Come on, sweetie. We're going to Mary's house." Alex slung the backpack over her shoulder and took Chad's hand.

"Oh, will there be cookies? I hope. I hope." Chad wasted no time and ran ahead, tugging on his mother's arm.

"Let's go, guys." Alex gathered the lad in her arms and proceeded to walk through the space between Jarrid and

Sara. "Whatever this is can wait. Sara, we've got a story to put together."

Alex trudged up the hill with the backpack slapping at her side. Chad was riding her hip and grabbing the straps to hang on. He wrapped his legs around his mother's waist while they made their way up the steep path.

"Where are you, Lizzy?" Alex called ahead, she mumbled under her breath, "That girl can never stay put." Once again, she called out, "Lizzy, you answer me right this minute." Alex stopped and let Chad slide down her side, lowering him to the ground.

Just a few feet, dead ahead, Lizzy stood motionless, staring into the woods. Alex took Chad's hand and called to her daughter, "Didn't you hear me call you?"

"Is there something wrong, Lizzy?" Sara came from behind and put her hand on Alex's shoulder. She called to the child, "Are you okay?"

"What do you see?" Jarrid stepped past the women and knelt behind Lizzy. He looked deep into the forest in the direction of her stare.

Sara closed the distance between her and the girl. She positioned herself directly behind her and tried to pinpoint the object that had captured the girl's attention.

Chad was trying to pick up a bottle cap, but Alex coaxed him to join her. She pulled him up the path and stood on the other side of Jarrid. She stretched her neck, looking for some clue as to what had demanded her daughter's full attention.

The group was silent; no one made a move. Even Chad mimicked the adults and stood perfectly still. Then, Lizzy's head abruptly turned to the left, as if something or somebody moved.

It was like someone pushed play. Lizzy's eyes danced, and her hands became animated. She turned her attention

BLOOD MOON

to Sara with the words bubbling from her mouth, "Oh, Auntie Sara, it was an angel. Prettiest angel you ever saw."

"What did she look like?" Alex knelt by her daughter, not wanting to show her disbelief, and spoke words of comfort, "How do you know it was an angel?"

"She was so pretty, Mommy." Lizzy's face lit up, and she went into the most childlike description, "Little like me, with long brown hair and pretty eyes. Her smile reminded me of puppies and kittens. Oh, I want to play with her. May I please?"

"Sweetie," Alex stood behind Lizzy and peered through the trees, almost hoping that she could see her daughter's angel, but the adult in her looked for a more logical approach. "It may have been one of the village children playing in the forest."

"No, Mommy," Lizzy shouted. "I saw her wings, they were folded behind her back, and her halo was on top of her head. Just like mine on Halloween, remember Mommy?"

"Alright, dear," Alex saw the passion in her daughter's eyes and decided to support her fantasy. "I believe you." She took the children by their hands and made her way up the path.

Chad dropped his mother's hand, fell back, and walked beside Jarrid. Sara slowed her pace to let them trudge the path together. He placed his large hand on Chad's small shoulder and guided him up the hill.

Sara's problems melted away in the warmth of the autumn sun. The birds sang, and the trees swayed in the breeze, rushing up the hill. Her movements slowed as if time paused. She could not move, only to stand on the path staring into the greenery of the deep forest.

SARAH KAGE

The movement was quick; Sara's eyes almost missed the blur that danced between the tree trunks. Then, her attention focused on the figure of a small child standing between two large oaks.

Lizzy was right. Sara's feet made short strides, and she moved closer. *She is a true miracle.* The little girl took a few steps backward. She ran her hand through her long hair, with each strand falling into place to rest on the top of her shoulders.

Before the last strand fell in place, another movement demanded Sara's gaze. The brilliance of white surrounded the small girl; each feather shuddered and brought life to the beautiful wings, the wings of an angel. Sara could do no more than watch.

Each wing worked together like a dance and rose above the halo, stretching outward to touch the sun. Once fully extended, they shimmied, each feather dancing to a silent tune. Then, the feathers quietly gave way, folded, and tucked against her tiny back.

The angel stepped forward, her eyes surrounded by an expression of yearning, her mouth slightly opened to form the words. Then lines of frustration formed across her forehead. She could not speak.

"Wait, please," Sara called out in desperation, taking a few steps forward, showing her desire to know this small angel. "I won't hurt you. I only want to talk." The being retreated farther behind the trees and ignored Sara.

The angel burst into flight and was gone in a flash. "Don't go. I want to know your name." Sara searched behind each tree and slumped against the last trunk with frustration ringing into the forest. "Please, I just want to know your name." Sara pleaded; her tears flowed down her cheeks, a symptom of the desperation to connect with this heavenly being.

BLOOD MOON

Sara's tears waned, and the wind blew across her cheeks. A strong gust blew through the treetops, and a small voice intermingled with the shaking leaves. She wiped her face and strained to listen. The muffled sounds rang through the air, the angel's cries of desperation, "What? I can't make it out. What're you trying to say?"

The first syllables rang true, "Angel…"

Sara cried out, "Yes, Angel. Please, can you tell me your name?"

The rest of the syllables bounced off the trees, low at first, "Angeli…" and then louder, "Angelica… My name is Angelica."

Then Alex's voice broke through and past the wind, "Sara, where are you?" she protested, "Quit fooling around. You better show yourself."

Alex hurried down the path to match Jarrid's brisk run and called out, "Sara, answer me."

"Guys, I'm right here, geez. I'm not a child, you know. I think it's safe to say that I can take care of myself." Sara paused on the path with the group running to join her.

"Mommy, slow down." The young boy complained. Alex released Chad's hand and met Sara on the path.

Trying to catch her breath, she scolded Sara, "You know, it would be better for your friends if you didn't run off into the forest. We need to stick together."

Sara started to apologize, but Lizzy darted around Alex's legs and rushed straight into Sara, who almost toppled to the ground. "Oh, did you see her, my angel?"

"Yes, I saw your angel, and she told me her name was Angelica." Sara cuddled Lizzy and gave her a big squeeze.

"Oh, my angel spoke to you? I told you she was real." The rambunctious girl proclaimed, "See, Mommy, I told you she was an angel."

SARAH KAGE

"Angelica," Alex shot a confused look in Sara's direction. "Did she speak to you? Is there something in the air that's causing your delusions?"

Lizzy shot an attitudinal glare at her mother and with the authority of a grown woman, said, "Mother, please! I am telling you it was an angel!"

The confident girl turned and dismissed her mother's reaction. She naturally migrated toward the one person who believed her. She grabbed Sara's hand, tugged on it, and spoke, "I knew you would believe me, Auntie. I think Mommy doesn't have enough faith."

"Faith indeed," Alex was a little agitated at her daughter's scolding and pushed past everyone on the path, mumbling, "I seem to be the only one here with any sense."

Chad stopped, knelt, and extended a chunky finger toward a very interesting green frog that jumped into his path. "Look, Mommy, its Kermit, the frog." He was so excited that he almost toppled over when he reached for the slimy creature.

"Come on, Chad." Alex turned just in time and saw him almost land face-first into the dirt. "Quit mucking around. Don't you want cookies?"

The promise of a sweet treat washed away all the Froggy excitement and Chad bounded up the hill, passing everyone along the way.

Lizzy, being a child, had already forgotten her mother's obtrusive reaction to her angel. The only thing she heard was 'cookie.' She dropped Sara's hand and chased after her brother, yelling, "You better wait for me, Chad. Don't you dare eat cookies without me?"

BLOOD MOON
Chapter 13 Stranger Beware

The gingerbread trim that lined the roof of the cabin porch was painted pink. A strange color for a cabin, set in a simple village, but the detail seemed to match Mary's personality. Her colorful mannerisms evident as the robust woman spilled out the front door and shrieked at the sight of the two children heading straight for her, screaming "cookies" all the way up the garden path.

"Oh, yes, my dears, and cookies you shall have, with some milk." Mary grabbed them both and squeezed so hard that Lizzy mumbled, "Oh, please, if you don't mind. I could use just one less hug to go with my three cookies."

The boy wiggled out from under Mary's arm and followed Lizzy toward the kitchen. The old woman was still giggling when Alex came up on the porch. "Your Lizzy is going to be a real handful very soon."

Alex answered Mary sarcastically, "Soon? I think that ship has already sailed. In a few years, I plan on sending her out to work while I stay home and eat bonbons."

Mary's chuckle resounded through the forest and bounced back against the porch walls. She headed into the kitchen behind Alex, her duty of Cookie Queen fulfilled. Lizzy and Chad were standing by the sink, each one looking very angelic, although Lizzy's halo seemed a little lop-sided.

The old woman's chuckle carried into the garden and caused a smile to rise on Sara's face. Jarrid took her hand and guided her up the stairs toward the porch swing. It creaked as they sat on the gingham-clad pillows that had been placed for comfort. Sara turned and peered into his eyes. "What's that? A question mark I see bubbling up on your face?"

He put his arm around her shoulders and pulled her close. "Angel, really, were you playing to Lizzy's fantasies?"

"No!" Sara pulled away, stopped the forward motion of the swing, and proclaimed, "You don't believe me? After everything we've been through in the past few months, you of all people…"

She bolted off the ruffled pillow, causing the swing's backward motion. "Jarrid, I'm telling you it was an angel… and not only that, but she'll be instrumental in the coming days."

Sara stood her ground even though every muscle in her body shook in the cool afternoon air. Jarrid jumped from the swing and held her trembling body in his massive embrace. "I do believe you." They stood huddled together on the porch, against the railing, lost to everything but the beating of their hearts.

A voice cleared itself once and then twice. "Um, excuse me, Jarrid. Pardon me for the interruption." Sara peeked around Jarrid and saw Mr. Choate standing on the bottom stair with his hat in his hand. "I would not bother you if it was not an urgent matter." He lowered his eyes in respect for the head councilman, then climbed the stairs and met Jarrid's stare across the porch. "And you, Miss Sara, so sorry. Please forgive me." He hung his head and spun the straw hat sheepishly in his hands.

"It's alright, Mr. Choate. It must be about what happened at the wall. I know you must discuss this with him. I'll excuse myself to the kitchen." Sara slipped through the door and joined the festivities inside the cabin.

BLOOD MOON

"You see, right there." Mr. Choate slapped his hat on his head and stomped his foot. "That is my point exactly. Why is she involved in the village business?"

Jarrid took him by the arm and directed him off the porch, almost pushing him down the stairs. His anger rose; he twirled the old man around to face his rage. "You know nothing about the importance of that woman in all of our destinies.

I am head councilman, and that gives me the power of leadership." Jarrid ran back up the stairs, onto the porch, turned and confronted Mr. Choate. "You and the others must afford me the ability to do that."

"And we shall." Mr. Choate gathered himself, tugged at the brim of his hat, grumbled, and said, "That is why we have called an emergency meeting; the assault on the Fortress must be dealt with. The meeting is not negotiable!" Mr. Choate followed Jarrid onto the porch and pleaded his case, "The council is demanding it. I was sent here to tell you to meet us in the church in an hour."

Jarrid faced the old man, the previous rage spent, and he agreed. The elder touched the brim of his hat and started down the stairs, then turned back and spoke, "The council has made it very clear. Do not bring those women to the meeting." Mr. Choate didn't wait for an answer; the cadence of his footsteps down the stairs matched the anger that rose in Jarrid's face.

Sara stood just inside the door and heard every word spoken. She swung it open and called toward the old man, "I'll honor Jarrid's wishes, and do whatever he asks of me, Mr. Choate." He pulled his hat further down on his face and bowed his head, acknowledging her proclamation.

"Tell the council I will be there in an hour." Jarrid called out to Mr. Choate. He didn't wait for an answer. It had all been said.

Jarrid sat next to Sara on the parlor couch. He took her hand and asked, "Why did you back down so easily about the meeting? I did not think it was in your nature."

"I pick my battles carefully." Sara retrieved her hand, stood up, and towered over Jarrid. "And this didn't feel like one worth fighting."

Chocolate framed Lizzy's tiny mouth, still clutching the remaining treat she asked, "Do you want a cookie, Jarrid?" With love, she held out the half-eaten sweetie and waited for his response.

Gobbling sounds filled the room, his pretense of eating the small morsel. He scooped Lizzy up and ran through the parlor, making airplane noises that competed with her girlish giggles.

Mary's keen Scottish ears picked up on the conversation. She came to the parlor with her apron bunched in her hands, wiping them against the patchwork material.

She paused and asked, "What meeting? Jarrid, is it about the…?" Mary followed her son into the kitchen. He pulled the chair away from the table and sat down, offering a knee to Lizzy, who was bouncing around like a spinning top.

"Yes, Mom," Jarrid answered, "They are going into the walls. They plan on investigating the sighting of the…" Lizzy looked up into Jarrid's eyes; not one word escaped her attention.

"I agree," Mary caught Jarrid's direction and added, "I believe that might be a plan of action." She enticed Lizzy from Jarrid's lap with the promise of still another cookie.

BLOOD MOON

"I am not sure that is the best approach, Mom." Mary brushed Jarrid aside, ignoring his opinion. "I am going to tell the council that Alex, Sara, and I are investigating the inner walls tonight." His words were final.

The co-workers almost dropped their cookies in unison. Sara spoke first, "What? The inner walls tonight, just the three of us?"

Alex could not speak; she stared at Jarrid, nibbling her cookie, but then she uttered, "I don't think..." Sara grabbed her arm and glared into her eyes, sending a subliminal message. "Ah, okay, I guess..." Alex answered with her cheeks turning a curious color of gray.

"Whatever you think is best." Sara offered, following Jarrid toward the door and taking his arm. "We'll stand with you." She squeezed his hand and gave him a gentle shove out the door. He turned quickly and stole a kiss before the door closed in between them.

The late afternoon sun had gone behind the trees with hues of blue and pink, flooding the garden path. Jarrid walked in and out of the sunbeams that washed over each step. Sara stood on the porch and watched the dim light dance across his shoulders. She noticed his frame seemed larger than usual; each manly step demanded the light and dust, bow to his royal stride.

He turned at the garden gate and gave one final wave before he continued with the grace of a king. Sara couldn't put her finger on the uneasiness of the image. Dusk took on an almost magical atmosphere; fairies and gnomes seemed to materialize in the garden, following this magical king on his almost impossible task.

A cold wind blew across Sara's face and she felt Alex's hand on her shoulder. She jumped back to feel Alex grab both of her shoulders. "What the hell? Are we really going into the Fortress tonight?" Alex's eyes flashed with fear. She turned loose of Sara's shoulders and waited for her answer.

"Um, we're journalists, right." Her demeanor softened. "We told Ted we'd have one hell of a story. Well, what better way than to investigate the Fortress?"

"Go get your camera." Sara waved her finger toward the parlor and stated, "I want to see the creature again for a better idea of what we're up against."

"Okay, fine," Sara kept waving her finger in the air until Alex shuddered in frustration and moved toward the screen door. "But you better prepare yourself. It's not any less intense on film." Alex disappeared through the screen door, mumbling, "I hope you know what you're getting us into!"

Alex plopped down on the porch swing, next to Sara, and tugged at the camera draped around her neck. She scooted back into the seat, letting her legs dangle in the air. "Do you think the council is going to let us go with Jarrid?"

"He's head of council." Sara watched her tug on the camera, removing the lens cover, and answered, "He is the rule, the final declaration. The leaders will have no choice."

"Well," Alex flipped the side viewer out, pulled the strap from around her neck, and answered, "I guess we're going to deliver one hell of a story, or not..." Alex kept pushing the play button with swear words tumbling from her mouth, "Damn it! What's wrong with this frigging thing?"

"Here, let me try." Sara reached for the camera taking matters into her own hands.

"Oh, frig, no." Alex's knee-jerk reaction pulled the camera out of Sara's reach with a few choice words spilling into the air, "I think not, Missy. After all, I'm the photographer in this duo." One last push of the button and all the color drained from her face. She turned the camera over to access the memory card.

A gasp sucked past Alex's lips with such intensity that Sara jumped from her seat. "What're you doing? What's wrong?" Alex slumped into the porch swing, almost becoming one with the cushions. The camera dropped into her lap, the memory card slot open and empty.

"You better snap to and tell me what happened to the memory card? Did you leave it in the backpack?" Sara reached out with her foot and nudged Alex's leg. "Say something."

All Alex could muster was to shake her head with a resounding "No..." One more nudge and Alex jumped to her feet. "Sara, it was in the camera. I never let the backpack out of my sight. I hid it in the wall behind the dresser when I was in the room. No one had access to it."

"Well, someone took it." Sara paced back and forth on the old porch; she stopped to stare directly at Alex. "Think back. Was anyone in your room?"

"Joshua!" Alex exclaimed. "He brought me to the hotel, but I had the camera in my lap the entire time. The only time I was out of the room without it was to take a shower."

The women's eyes directed into a pinpoint stare, and they both shouted out simultaneously, "Someone broke into the room."

"But who, besides the obvious people, even knew that the video existed?" Sara questioned.

All the color left Alex's face. She almost whispered, "Do you think it could've been Ted?"

"What would be his motive?" Sara thought for a moment. "He knows that we're out in the field with the video, putting together the rest of the story. He's the one who gave us until Monday to come up with the scoop."

"That makes sense," Alex pushed her hair out of her eyes, "but if not Ted, then who?" Both women sat down on the swing with the revelation of the missing memory card, twisting their guts.

"What in the world has gotten the two of you into such a tizzy?" Mary bounded through the screen door. "You look like you've just seen a ghost."

She bounced across the porch floor and prodded the two women. "Come on, join us in the kitchen. Lizzy's helping me make another batch of cookies. We could use your help."

Mary was confident that the two women were honoring her request as she headed for the kitchen without a care in the world; she had a natural knack for such things. Sara paused before she reached the door and asked, "What're we going to do?" Alex shook her head and walked into the parlor, following Mary's example.

***

Jarrid reached for the purple robe that hung in the old choir room, feeling the softness of the velvet, covering his back and draping around his shoulders. The texture of the material was a stark contrast to the commotion that riffled through his stomach.

The headdress of jewels felt heavy upon his head, a weight to match the responsibility he carried, the people's leader. He took the gavel into his hand and touched the smoothness of the wooden handle, stroking it until the top stopped his motion; the weight of the square head matched his heavy soul.

The loud cries of his fellow councilmen flowed across the staircase that led down to the church stage. Each

BLOOD MOON

man's voice rang clear with the fear and anxiety of the previous day's murderous events.

"With all due respect, has he lost his mind?" Someone shouted. Jarrid recognized the voice as one of the elders.

"I think he is letting his Maypole do the thinking for him!" One of the councilmen added.

The laughter and the comments piled up in Jarrid's ears. Each one stoked the fire that burned in the pit of his stomach. He could take no more.

He bounded down the stairs, two at a time, and thundered across the stage to the throne-like chair. His grip on the gavel was so intense it could've splintered in his hand.

With a mighty toss, he swept the robe up and across his shoulders, relieving his arms of their entrapment. He raised the mallet and brought it down heavy on the table. "There will be silence!"

The echo of the demand resounded through the broad beams of the church and fell on every ear. Jarrid stood slumped over the table with his head hung, his robe now coming together in front of his chest and his long hair covering the bulging blood vessels coursing up his neck.

The silence was deafening. Jarrid's breathing rang loud across every pew of the church. He slowly rose and brought his massive body up to stand with his feet apart, like a mighty oak. It was not a request, not a simple statement that poured from his tight lips, "Sit down and hear me!"

No man protested but dropped into the nearest seat at his command. Jarrid stood and stared at each of his fellow councilmen and waited for the anger to subside.

He laid the gavel on the table, removed his headdress, and ran his hands through his hair, an attempt at containing the rage that gripped his heart. He sat back in the throne and gazed out at the silence that now engulfed the room.

"You may approach me with your concerns, one at a time, and with respect." Jarrid loosened the grip of the robe around his neck and cleared his throat.

Mr. Choate spoke first, "Jarrid, I have informed the others about my suspicions that you plan to involve the journalists in your assault on the Fortress. As you can see, they haven't reacted well."

The eldest councilman raised his hand, and Jarrid acknowledged him. "These women have no business here, and I am sorry, but what could you be thinking?"

Fierce anger welled up on Jarrid's face. He moved forward and shoved the table toward the crowd, charging at the edge of the stage, where he stopped and shouted, "I am your leader. My decision is based on knowledge you do not have. You are all naive to the evil that surrounds us."

"Who is Sara, you ask?" Jarrid pointed his finger toward the crowd and proclaimed, "She is your salvation." The men took offense to his words, and an ocean of complaints and comments rushed up into his face.

"She is irrelevant," was the taunt. The statement rose above the pews without an indication of its author.

The group agreed while one man slowly walked to the front of the stage and addressed Jarrid. "How dare you choose 'this woman' over the elders of the village?"

"This woman... you know nothing." Jarrid jumped into mid-air, out to the front of the crowd, and pushed the villager back into the huddle of angry men. His words bellowed across the pews, "You stand here in front of me, in fear for your lives, not knowing that Sara, 'this woman' as you call her, will be your deliverer."

BLOOD MOON

A hush fell over the crowd; the air sucked from their lungs. The silence was a backdrop to the loud squeak that echoed from the large wooden doors of the church. All heads turned zombie-like in unison and stared at the black-cloaked woman who entered the room.

"Gentlemen," Anuk stopped just short of the first row of pews, reached up and pushed the hood of her cloak off her raven hair, "please take a seat. We have much to discuss."

She sauntered toward Jarrid, bowing her head, passing each pew, hearing their comments and smirks, closing the distance between her and their leader.

"What is Anuk doing here? She knows there are no women allowed in these meetings." The crowd once again rose up and voiced their complaints.

One of the elders from the back offered his impression, "She is loony, the black sheep of the village. Do not listen to anything she has to say."

Jarrid rushed the aisle and met Anuk in the middle of the church, but she seductively brushed past him on her way to the stage, took the stairs, and stood facing the audience.

"Do you not feel the power, Jarrid, even now swirling under your skin? It has always been there. You have tried to ignore it, but still, it conjures." Anuk circled the stage and stood at its edge, looking down at the mealy men below.

"Good or evil, Yin, or Yang. So confusing to a small boy." she looked down the aisle and addressed Jarrid. "But, you know the darkness of the Fortress better than any man in this room." She pulled one of the chairs on the stage to the front and placed her slender body onto the wooden seat.

SARAH KAGE

"Woman," Jarrid rushed the stage in a fit of anger, "you are what they say. Crazy."

"No, no, you naughty boy," Anuk stood, raised her finger in the air and waved it back and forth, "you must listen to my words." Anuk's eyes caught Jarrid's leap into the air as he landed right in front of her on the stage. She pulled her cloak around her body and scampered off just in time to avoid his grip.

"Jarrid's knowledge should be followed." She spoke, ascending the stairs of the stage, standing in front of the pews, and once again addressing the audience, "He has no other choice but to take Sara and Alex into the inner walls of the Fortress. It is his destiny."

The angry men taunted, "She is a witch. Her words are poison!"

"Let her talk," Jarrid spoke his curiosity getting the better of him. He threw his hand in the air with a motion of restraint and demanded, "I need to know more about this destiny of which she speaks. Continue, woman." He walked to the stairs and motioned for her to join him on the stage.

Deep, dark powers fought for position in Jarrid's soul. They mingled with the allure of the woman standing in front of him. Anuk circled Jarrid, close enough to stir the embers of the darkness, enticing him with her powers of seduction.

She rose up on tiptoes and whispered in his ear, "Crazy indeed." Anuk slid her body down the length of his side, turned slowly, and addressed the crowd, "Stop with your constant complaints! You men, with your war cries and dominance, you think women are not your equal. This ignorance will be your undoing." She walked to the edge of the chancel and pulled the large, leather-bound book from under her robe.

BLOOD MOON

One of the men stepped out into the aisle and raised his fist. "Oh, are you going to enchant us with an old book?"

Another man pushed past and rushed the stage. "I still say you are crazy."

The group chanted in unison until Jarrid's mighty roar filled the old church, "Enough!" He charged the group, stopping at the edge of the wooden stage. "If you value my leadership, you will sit down and come to order." He turned to retrieve the gavel and brought it down hard on the wooden ceremonial table. The sound echoed beyond the walls into the courtyard.

Anuk clutched the leather book to her chest, stood by Jarrid's side, and laid her hand on his shoulder. His reaction was explosive. "Do not think that you have control. The council is my domain!" He walked past her and adjusted the velvet robe to accompany him as he turned to address Anuk once more. "What is this book? Evil incantations delivered by your master?"

The cloaked woman dismissed his angry words and continued with her speech. She thrust the book out toward the angry crowd and proclaimed, "This is *The Book of Souls*."

She cradled the old relic in her arms and wove a child's tale, "My mother gave me this book when I was very young. It was not much use to a small child because it is written in Latin."

Incoherent mumbles started low and increased with intensity. "Has Anuk taken this meeting over completely?" Jarrid pointed his cloaked finger straight at the accuser and shook it violently.

Not another word was spoken; only the sound of frustration rose through the crowd like smoke.

SARAH KAGE

Jarrid looked down his outstretched hand, past the accusation, pointing toward the back of the church.

There, in the corner, stood a tall man. His voice rose above the noise of the crowd. "This book has ruled our existence for many centuries." The man touched the hood of his cloak, and it slid down and off his silver hair.

The years rose from his cheeks—each one acknowledged by the wrinkles that covered his face and forehead. A somber look framed his crystal blue eyes. The weight of his words hung in the air, and he stepped back into the shadows.

All eyes were directed at the stranger until Jarrid's voice rang out, "Who are you?"

Before the silver-haired stranger could answer Anuk whined, "Yes, Jarrid, you must take the ancient book back to its origins behind the inner walls."

"What trickery is this?" Jarrid reached for the large book, and Anuk offered no resistance. He stood in the middle of the stage, turning each yellowed page, thumbing past words written in Latin. He opened the book wider and shoved it in front of Anuk's face.

Her hands encircled and caressed the weathered book, its pages folded from Jarrid's massive hands. "Yes, the book is in Latin. My mother tried to understand, but she didn't know the language."

Jarrid became more agitated with each word she spoke. He moved toward her to take the book, but this time she resisted.

She opened it and fumbled for a page, a reference of great importance. "Here it is; the only part that is in English." The page yellowed, but the words rose from the parchment with great vibrancy. She pointed to the last two sentences of a poem and spoke the words aloud,

185

BLOOD MOON

"Look to the walls, her face to frame. The Righteous One will be the same."

"Smoke and mirrors, have we not had enough. Banish this woman and let us get on with the task at hand."

The motion came from the second elder, and the others chimed in, "We need to attack the Fortress tonight, there's no other way." The cries of the men filled the church.

Anuk felt the atmosphere of the room take a negative turn, her cue to leave, but first, she handed the book to Jarrid and spoke words for his ears only, "This book will be the key you will need to open the mysteries of the inner walls."

She slipped off the stage and made her way to the door, looking back at the angry mob seething in their discontent.

The hem of Anuk's cloak floated upward and grazed the cheek of the stranger who stood just inside the church doors. She paused briefly to stare into his blue eyes before she clutched the cold metal doorknob and slithered through the opening into the night.

Each man yelled out his concern, "Have the women completely taken over?" Jarrid followed Anuk to the back of the church. The voices became louder, rising toward the old beams, scattering across the ceiling.

One man's voice echoed through the crowd. "We will attack the Fortress ourselves." Jarrid's control over the meeting waned, the evidence slammed across his eardrums. The angry man continued, "Gather your weapons, and we will defend our homes." The men started to file out of the pews, beating down Jarrid's authority, agreeing in unison. "We will defend the village at all costs."

SARAH KAGE

Jarrid stood tall; the purple robe rolled down the length of his arms. The thrust of his up stretched hands forced velvet folds of material to gather around the top of his shoulders. The ancient book held over the heads of the angry men. He searched the eyes of the crowd for signs of submission, letting his words form in his throat and pour from his lips, "I will defend the village!"

Feeling the pressure, the men shrunk from his words, each one bowing to his authority with the respect of silence and acknowledgment. They gathered close and honored his demands. "You will not attack the Fortress tonight! Go to your families and gather your weapons to protect your homes.

"Leave this meeting with prayers on your lips, for the gift of strength to assault the evil that threatens our very lives." Jarrid pulled the worn book into his chest and bowed his head.

The silver-haired man touched Jarrid's shoulder and leaned in to whisper, "Please, we must talk."

Jarrid ignored the old man and shouted to the others, "Go now!" He lifted his head, opened his eyes, and made his last demand upon the councilmen. Jarrid brushed past the stranger and burst through the doors with a heavy heart. The cold night air collected in his lungs rushed out past his lips and gathered in billows of mist as he let out his ancient battle cry.

BLOOD MOON
Chapter 14 Unlikely Companions

Jarrid stood on the outside steps of the church and clutched the tattered and worn book to his chest. His robe blew in the wind and encircled the last sound of his warrior cry that escaped into the night.

Councilmen poured out from the mouth of the church, obeying Jarrid's demand, each one moving past their leader in silence. The last man to leave the sanctuary closed the old wooden doors and followed Jarrid into the courtyard.

The slamming noise disturbed a large hoot owl and rustled it from the trees just above the tall steeple. It landed on the eaves of the roof, seeming curious to the movement below.

It flapped its wings and ruffled them into place to rest against its down-covered shoulders. The owl's head turned from left to right, surveying the ground below with the occasional, "hoo... hoo..." seeming to ask its question of the two men. Were their destinies intertwined in the circle of the courtyard?

The purple robe gathered on the ground around Jarrid, where he knelt, like a river of velvet. Each fold of material rose with his acknowledgment of the man's footsteps that echoed and bounced off the walls of the old church cemetery. Jarrid turned just as the silver-haired stranger approached and addressed him, "Jarrid, please. We must talk."

"Look, I do not know who you are." Jarrid rushed past the tall man with piercing blue eyes and declared, "I do not have time for this right now."

The old man's hand lay strong on Jarrid's arm; with little effort, his forward momentum thwarted, his attention demanded with no escape. He locked eyes with the stranger, forced to listen, mesmerized by the eyes.

"Who are you?" Jarrid jerked his arm from the firm grip and demanded, "And what is so important?" He didn't wait for an answer, but continued, "You know what I am planning this very night, so please leave me to it."

Jarrid burst into the church, past the empty pews. He clutched the robe and folded it as he walked. He reached the front row of the church and turned, realizing he had been followed. "Wait, you asked my name," declared the man. "At least let me introduce myself."

He approached Jarrid and thrust his large hand into the air, which was promptly ignored. Jarrid turned toward the staircase to the choir room, with the folded robe in one hand and the book in the other. Something in his being caused him to stop dead. Anchored to the stair, he gave in and listened.

"My name is Nikko, and I have come back to my home to help you in your crusade against evil."

It started slowly, Jarrid's control of his wits. He faced the man letting the words of his revelation fall across his mind. "Your home, I do not recognize you, sir?"

The old man pushed past him, onto the top of the stairs and into the choir room, took the robe from Jarrid, and hung it on the hook before he addressed him once more. "My last name is Mardi. I am Jim Mardi's father."

Deep in thought, Jarrid answered, "I am not familiar with the Mardi family, at least not on a personal level, but I have not seen you in the village." Jarrid crossed the room to the back door and secured the lock. "How long were you gone?"

"Too long indeed," Nikko bowed his head, and with a look of regret, answered, "I went to the city to seek my fortune..." he raised his eyes and continued, "but that was a Fool's Folly, I know that now."

"I was compelled to return," Nikko walked toward the window, clenched his hands in distress, and continued, "but I did not know why, until you started to speak at the meeting."

"What could you possibly have to do with the Fortress?" Jarrid was confused. "You left your life behind. What could you have to offer to something you walked away from?"

Nikko retrieved a lantern from the shelf, started down the staircase toward the stage, and turned to ask, "Will you walk with me so I can explain myself?"

"Sure." Jarrid rushed past the silver-haired man and down the stairs, determined to dismiss the conversation, and added, "Why not. It is a free country."

Together the two men walked up the dirt path, with the light from the lantern rushing ahead in the darkness; neither one spoke of the evil that surrounded the very existence of the village. Jarrid stopped, waited for Nikko to catch up, and asked, "Do you know about the murder?" He shifted the heavy book and clutched it to his side, then continued up the path.

"Yes, it was on the news." Nikko hastened his stride and caught up to walk beside Jarrid. "It was the moment I knew my destiny lay in the walls of the Fortress."

Jarrid opened his mouth to respond, but the wind poured down through the trees and took his words up and over the fortress wall. Neither man could hear the other as the gust drove them against the bricks.

The fortress gate slammed against the lock, back and forth, the sound beckoned in the wind. Jarrid raised his hand in the stiff gale and motioned for Nikko to follow.

SARAH KAGE

Both men grabbed the gate and struggled to gain entrance into the Fortress. The walls sucked them in, and they lay against the gate in silence, leaving the angry gusts to subside and whistle off into the distance.

Jarrid retrieved the book from the ground and offered a hand to Nikko with the cold silence passing through the gate. "Hurry," Nikko whispered, "someone is coming."

The lamplight aided Jarrid's search. He knelt in front of a rock pile, and stated, "I need to hide the book until I can understand its significance to the Fortress. I will retrieve it later tonight." He moved the bricks to make a hole and buried the book deep into the crevice, then covered it with rocks.

The eerie sound of scraping bricks assaulted their ears. Nikko relit the lantern, cradled it to protect its light, and waited for the wind to subside. He shoved the light forward in the darkness to let its beam bathe the old hall in light.

"It sounds like someone has come past the gate!" Nikko slipped past Jarrid and followed the beam of light.

"Nikko, wait…," Jarrid's words were interrupted by the sound of footsteps echoing off the brick wall. "I know that sound. It is the sliding of the brick, the key that gives access to the inner chamber." Nikko lowered the lantern, his attention distracted by Jarrid's words. The light beam no longer raced down the corridor but pooled in a small circle around the men's legs.

Pebbles bounced off the metal base of the oil lamp with dirt and dust exploding into the air. Footsteps stopped just short of the light. Nikko raised the lantern, illuminating Joshua's face.

BLOOD MOON

"What are you doing here?" Jarrid grabbed his brother by both arms and continued, "You are the last person I ever expected to see in the Fortress tonight."

"I had to see her face again, framed by the wall, to settle my mind that she is evil." Joshua shook off his brother and stepped away from his anger. His voice broke with frustration, "My fear is all-consuming, not something I am proud of, but I will protect our family from her impending doom. Now let me pass."

"You are not going anywhere, little brother." Jarrid and Nikko locked shoulders and filled the narrow passageway in an attempt to stop Joshua. He shoved and pushed against the massive union of muscles and strength, until Jarrid spoke, "Fear, you say? Well, I suggest we face that fright now."

Joshua bristled up to confront his brother, but Nikko interrupted, "Whose face is on the wall?"

The words hung suspended in the air with the sound of bubbles popping; each syllable followed the last to burst upon their ears. The men stood frozen in time, their destinies intertwined for all eternity.

"Okay, little brother." Jarrid moved forward to push Joshua in the direction of the wall. "Let us settle this once and for all."

"Fine, we will do this indeed." Joshua swallowed hard, turned, and marched down the narrow hall.

"Whose face is on the wall, Jarrid?" Determined, Nikko persisted in having his answer.

"Not now. It is no one you know, but you will see for yourself." Jarrid rushed ahead, just as Joshua pulled the brick from its resting place.

The wall swiveled on its axis to give entrance to the inner chamber. The lantern's beam infused the darkness and announced Nikko into the inner sanctum of the Fortress.

Shadows danced in the flickering light, painting dark forms, beaming up the height of the walls. Nikko raised the lantern and surveyed each wall, looking for the face.

"Here," Jarrid took the light and spoke, "on this wall. Come, Joshua, it is time to face your fear." The wall existed in the back corner, framed by bricks in the shape of an arch. Jarrid pulled the light up to let the yellow glow wash across the wall.

"You see," Joshua's anxiety filled the darkness and spilled from his mouth, "you cannot deny the evil. It pours from her eyes."

"No, you don't understand." Nikko turned in the shadows and confronted Joshua. "Sara is not evil. The darkness lies behind her eyes because they are the entrance into the Fortress. Joshua, you are mistaken."

"How do you know her name?" Jarrid stepped into the light and confronted Nikko. "You speak as if she is someone important to you."

"She is very important to me," Nikko took the lantern from Jarrid's hand and raised it to illuminate the image of Sara's face. "But in truth, she is crucial to the world."

Lines of anger formed on Jarrid's face, and he pressed for answers, "You speak in riddles old man. I grow weary of your elusive manner."

"I am sorry, but this is surreal to me also. It was just last week that the vision of this woman invaded my dreams." Nikko stepped back to take in the beauty of the face that towered over the three men. "She is the reason I felt compelled to return to the village, the realization that the assault on the Fortress foreshadows my destiny."

"Your dream… Did it reveal any other clues?" Jarrid waited for Nikko to respond.

BLOOD MOON

"At first, it was hard to understand," Nikko answered. "The low voice whispered one phrase over and over again; 'through her eyes,' all souls will enter the Fortress through Sara's eyes.'"

"I have had enough for one night." Joshua listened to Nikko's tale, with distrust for the stranger. "I leave the two of you to admire the woman. I am going home with my opinions, uncompromised." He pushed through the wall opening and headed toward the old gate. The moonlight now poured through its slats to show the way out.

"You know, he will want to accompany you into the Fortress, but his destiny does not follow that plan," Nikko said and nodded goodnight. "I must talk to him before he leaves. I will meet you later to gather our supplies for the assault."

Jarrid was not in the mood to argue the fact of Joshua's entrance into the Fortress and waved Nikko off into the night.

"Wait, I need to speak with you," Nikko called from behind. "It is urgent." Joshua pushed through the old gate and stepped into the world beyond the Fortress wall, ignoring the stranger's request.

"Did you not hear me say I have had enough?" Joshua turned and bellowed. "I am not interested in your opinions or your premonitions, old man." The young man rolled his eyes and dismissed the gray-haired nuisance.

"Where are your manners? I am your elder, and you better damn well listen to what I have to say." Nikko circled Joshua and stopped his forward motion.

"Okay, get it off your chest. I can see you are hell-bent on doing so." Joshua crossed his arms in defiance to Nikko's words.

SARAH KAGE

"You will do well to accept Sara as an ally." Nikko had his attention, but would the anger let his words sink in? Joshua bristled, folding and unfolding his arms in response to his words.

"Your youth is a hindrance to my warnings, and that might be your demise." Nikko laid his hand on Joshua's shoulder to punctuate the importance of his words, but Joshua shuddered under the touch and stormed in the direction of home.

"Manners indeed, what we need now is hope." Joshua replied. He climbed the hill with his opinions still intact, mumbling into the night, putting space between him and the wizard of lies.

***

Jarrid stood in the confines of the inner walls with the lamp light pulsing across the face of the woman he loved. The stillness only emphasized her beauty with Nikko's spoken words rolling across his mind, *through her eyes.* Jarrid bowed his head, the weight of the riddle pounded in his ears.

The light started dimly at first, but soon a brilliant white glow consumed the yellow beam of the oil lamp. The pounding in Jarrid's ears being replaced with the soft ruffle of feathers.

Jarrid followed the sound to the front corner of the room; the bright light caressed the form of a small girl. The words spilled over Jarrid's tongue, "It is Lizzy's angel."

"Why is Sara's face on the wall?" Jarrid eagerly confronted the angel. "Can you tell me the importance of this miracle?" The angelic creature put her finger to her mouth and motioned for silence.

The room vibrated with an ethereal presence, and her white-feathered wings broke the darkness with beams of light. Each feather shuddered and danced to make the light shimmer like diamonds. The wings stilled, sheltering and encircling the small, heavenly being, hiding every attribute of her face and body until the burst of light revealed the metamorphosis.

Once again, the feathers quivered in the light to reveal a beautiful, young woman encased in the heavenly glow, her transformation complete. She reached out her hand toward Jarrid and spoke, "Yes, I am Angelica, and my sole purpose is to guide the Righteous One to her destiny."

"Is Sara the Righteous One?" Jarrid's emotions ruled his mind, and he blurted out, "Is that why her face consumes the wall?"

"Yes, she is the main piece of the puzzle," Angelica floated across the room to stand by the wall. She touched the face and continued to speak, "but you also have a role in the battle of good and evil that will play out this very night."

"You will take gifts beyond these walls." She left the shadows, her white light washing over Jarrid. "Sara's love and her virginity, which I believe she refers to as *The Spirited Sword of Purity*, together with your chastity and abstinence. These tools must not be sullied."

She took a moment to acknowledge the disappointment that flooded Jarrid's face. "Take solace, my fine man, in Sara's love and be true to her. Never doubt her ability to rise to the occasion and fight the battles that lay ahead."

"How do we obtain entrance into the inner walls?" Jarrid broke in with his impatience, "The riddle says 'through her eyes.' This meaning is not clear."

"Be still and have faith, is the answer I can give you. Believe in the power of love, and you will know the way."

"Riddles are not what I need to battle the evil." Jarrid's frustration pulsated through the white light. "Why can you not give me a straight answer?"

"Once you gain entrance inside the perimeter," Angelica moved toward the opening in the wall and turned to reply, "Take time to learn who you can trust." Her words rode the wind caused by the wings folding around her body, disappearing in a ball of light that raced down the corridor toward the gated entrance.

Jarrid rushed down the hall following the glow of white light and ran squarely into Nikko. "What was that?" Nikko asked. "The light washed over me, and it was blinding."

"Just more riddles." Jarrid offered in the dark. "Our group is on its own tonight. I will meet you back at the gate in three hours. Only bring the bare essentials; we must travel light." Nikko nodded in agreement, opened the gate, and watched Jarrid trudge off into the moonlit night.

***

The anxiety was palpable on the cabin porch. Not even the soft breeze cooled the frustration that poured into the night air. "Ted is going to kill us!" Alex gathered the camera from her lap and bolted from the porch swing. "How do we tell him we don't have the video?"

"We aren't going to tell him." Sara tugged on Alex's arm and pulled her back down onto the gingham cushion. "Let's think about this. Maybe we can get more video of the creature tonight when we enter the Fortress."

"Yeah, sure," Alex buried her back into the wooden slats of the swing and huffed, "there's an abundance of gray trolls running around behind the Fortress walls just waiting for a cameo appearance." She stopped, her

BLOOD MOON

forehead folded into massive lines of what could only be described as complete and total fear. "Sara, I think we're in over our heads. We're journalists, not heroes."

Alex's words filled the night and overpowered all other sounds. It left the silence to circle the porch and emphasize the danger that mounted with each passing second.

"Sara…"

The voice came from behind the swing, and through the wooden slats, so close Sara felt her hair move from the breath that fueled the word. Alex screamed, jumped from the swing, and dumped the camera onto the wooden deck.

"Sorry, I didn't mean to scare you two." Jarrid stifled the laugh that unconsciously sprung from his mouth.

"What were you thinking, or not thinking?" Alex curled her fist toward him, bent down, retrieved the camera, and scolded, "Really, Jarrid, things are a little tense around here, if you haven't noticed. We don't need people sneaking up on us. Geez," her indignation poured from her mouth, with a deep breath and a proclamation, "I'm going inside to help Mary. I can guarantee the mood is much lighter, besides I smell pot roast."

Jarrid called out across the porch swing, "Alex, I am sorry." His apology fell on her last nerve.

She felt for the screen door handle, stared him down with a look of intolerance, and proclaimed, "Yeah, whatever."

"Alex will be okay." Sara gathered her wits and stood up with her hands on her hips. "Just let her get some dinner. She'll forgive you soon enough."

"And what about you," Jarrid placed both hands on the top of the porch rail, peered between the slats, and asked, "Do you forgive me?"

198

SARAH KAGE

Her hands lowered in a gesture of forgiveness, and she replied, "Yes, this time."

She watched the wind blow Jarrid's long hair away from his face as he came around the porch to the steps.

He reached out an open palm, his invitation to join him. "Please, come take a walk. I need to talk to you."

His words sparked embers of the flame she had come to know too well. No hesitations guarded her reaction. She bolted down the stairs, taking his hand. "Okay, but dinner is almost ready. We don't want Mary feeling the need to send a search party out after us."

"She is a little intense," Jarrid smiled and proclaimed. "But we will not be gone long." He wrapped his arm around Sara's shoulders, and they walked into the woods behind the cabin.

The leaves crunched under their footsteps, each stride in unison, coupled together under the moonlit sky. An owl, just in the trees ahead, hooted down, asking its age-old question. "Who indeed...?" Jarrid mocked. He stopped and pulled Sara around and leaned her against the bark of an old oak.

She ran her fingertips across Jarrid's lips and felt his stubble resist her touch. Her hand captured against his mouth; he buried his nose deep between her fingers. "Hmm, you smell."

The indignant sigh spilled across the air, and she gasped, "I beg your pardon!" She tugged at her hand, instinctively, a reaction to his words.

He persisted, "onions and garlic?" Again he buried his nose while resting her curled hand against his cheek. "And just here," he pressed his mouth against the top of her curled hand, his lips drug across her skin while his tongue flicked to taste the residue of rosemary and thyme, "hints of dinner, I presume?"

BLOOD MOON

"Why, that's forward of you, sir." A short giggle escaped her lips.

He cupped her elbow and took her hand to place his mouth just above her wrist, the delicate hairs disturbed by his breath. "And here, a musky smell of sweat and lavender."

Her heartbeat hastened with each breath placed upon her skin. Jarrid ran his hand up the length of her arm to rest just below her shoulder and traced the beads of sweat that ran down her skin. She shivered and let her head fall into his embrace. Her red curls enveloped his face, and he buried his sigh into her neck.

Warm air expelled from his lips and gathered like a breeze against her pale skin, to penetrate and burst through to the cells below, igniting a chain reaction of lust and passion, only to be forbidden.

The weight of chastity fell upon them like a rock. She took his hand and placed it on her face, caressed his fingers against her cheek. "I know this is not easy." She pulled his palm toward her lips and planted a soft kiss upon its center.

He cupped her face in both hands and kissed her forehead with his words floating down to rest on her ears, "Not easy, but necessary."

He pulled her close, grasping for a distraction and announced, "I met a man tonight. He insisted that he accompany us into the Fortress."

Curls framed Sara's face, restrained by the sweat of her brow, then loosened by the night breeze. She took solace in the ringlet's freedom and embraced the coolness of the wind, a force of nature rising in the night, separating their bodies ever so slightly. She placed her hands on his chest to anchor the distance between them and asked, "Does he mean anything to you or the village?"

"No," Jarrid stared directly into her eyes, "he is a deserter to our way of life." He lowered his head and his voice, "but our destinies are bound, I cannot deny it. His information will assist our entry into the inner walls."

Jarrid didn't wait for her reaction, feeling the remaining desires well up in his body, combined with the night's impending doom; he broke free from all restrictions and kissed her. His mouth hard and fast, searching for the beginning of the end. Her resistance was weak; she responded and remained there within his arms.

The twig snapped and combined with a low hum, breaking the spell of lust. The medallion projected an eerie glow of green, Anuk's face only inches away from the tortured lovers. "Oh, my, am I interrupting?"

The green light magnified Jarrid's taut face and underlined his rage. "Anuk, what the hell…!"

"You again," Sara brushed away the steamy cobwebs, stood by Jarrid, and confronted the woman in black. "Can't you be witchy somewhere else and leave us alone?"

Jarrid put his body between the two women and roared, "Anuk, what do you want?"

She maneuvered herself in front of Sara and asked, "Did you show her? Tell of the part she plays in our world."

The medallion demanded Sara's attention. She watched it rise and fall on Anuk's breast only inches from her grasp, her attempt foiled with the witch's taunting words, "Oh, she does know!"

"But does she know it all?" Anuk swung around and confronted Jarrid. "The secrets that you carry will they be salvation or doom? Will she know your secrets tonight before we attack the Fortress?"

Sara stepped between them, to confront the witch's accusations. The roar of Jarrid's voice flooded over her shoulders, and he demanded, "You will not accompany us into the Fortress this night!" he screamed, "Do you hear me, Anuk?"

The anger from Jarrid's body pulsed in waves. Anuk bristled and answered, "You're not my master. His instructions are clear. You cannot stop me."

The voice echoed down the path and mingled with Anuk's defiant words. "Sara, Jarrid, where are you? Dinner is…" Alex came upon the trio in the dark.

Anuk stepped out from behind a tree, just in time to hear Alex's last word. She paused for a moment, flicked the hem of her cloak, and retreated into the darkness.

"Okay…" Alex saw the shadow, her eye catching the movement in the trees. She peered down the path and called out to the woman in black, but only the breeze echoed her words.

"Yes, Alex, we are here." Distracted, Jarrid replied, "Tell Mom to go ahead and start serving dinner."

"Go on." Sara turned toward Alex and added, "We'll be right there."

The pair looked for Anuk in unison with the words falling from Jarrid's tight lips into the night, he called to the witch. "You will…" But, she was gone, like a mist in the wind, with her voice still ringing in Jarrid's ears.

Sara grabbed Jarrid by the arm and demanded, "What secrets?"

He headed toward the cabin, but stopped and proclaimed, "Not secrets Sara, tools of battle. Now, unless we want Mary and all of her anger to rain down upon us, I suggest we go to dinner."

SARAH KAGE

"Jarrid," Sara stomped her foot, determined to get to the bottom of Anuk's words. "Wait…"

"Come on, you two." Mary swung the screen door wide and scolded the duo, "Dinner is getting cold." Jarrid shot Sara a look and rushed past Mary onto the dimly lit porch.

"Save it for after dinner, Sara. The natives are getting restless." Mary corralled her through the screen door and pushed her toward the waiting dinner.

She knew better than to argue with the matriarch of the family, Sara bundled her questions and stuffed them deep down below the terror of her uncertain fate and the shadows behind Jarrid's eyes.

BLOOD MOON
Chapter 15 Into the Walls

The flickering candles lit the warmth of the small kitchen; the sound of clinking dishes intermingled with the laughter of children. Lizzy ran between Sara's legs and the sink, she taunted Chad, "You can't catch me..." She scurried off just as Chad dove in and bumped his head against the cabinet door.

Alex jumped to his rescue, scooped the boy up, and cuddled him as she cooed, "Oh, baby, are you alright?"

He wiggled and squirmed, turning his head this way and that, trying to see Lizzy, pleading with his mother, "Mommy, let go. She's getting away!"

Lizzy opened the porch door, stuck her thumbs in her ears, waved her hands, and giggled the words out loud, "Catch me, catch me, you can't catch me."

Zigging and zagging, Chad hit the floor running between the kitchen chairs and bouncing off the couch arm, reaching the door just as Lizzy shot through to the porch, the door slamming to punctuate the chase.

"Sara, are you about finished, it's getting late?" Alex grabbed her backpack and sat down to the table.

"You know, this could've gone a lot faster if you'd helped?" Sara looked over her shoulder to see Alex jump from the chair. "No way, I helped with dinner."

The argument rose from the porch, "No, Chad, Mommy is taking me with her. I am going to bring my camera and help. We can take pretty pictures of the Fortress."

Chad wailed at the news of being left behind, his cries magnified off the acoustics of the porch. "Great, just what I need." Alex charged the door. "Lizzy, who told you I was taking you to the Fortress?"

"She's mistaken." Alex gathered her wee ones to the swing and pulled Chad into her lap. "Lizzy isn't going, sweetie."

"Oh, Mommy, please, I want to go." Lizzy curled up under her mother's arm and sniffled. "I can help you." She wiggled her butt to the edge of the swing, hopped off, ran to the screen door, and pulled her small see-through backpack onto the porch. She wiped her tears with one hand and shuffled around the crayons and hair bows with the other until her fingers grasped the pink and green toy camera.

She posed in front of the swing, brought the camera up to her face, and said, "Cheese," her voice cracking from the strain of her tears.

The screen door burst open, and Mary stepped onto the porch just in time to see Lizzy take a snapshot of her frustrated mother and a distraught brother.

"Oh Lizzy, you have your very own camera. May I see it, please?" Mary held out her hand and smiled down as she winked at Alex.

Her shoulders slumped, and her head hung, Lizzy stood defeated, nothing more to do but cry and hand it to Mary.

"Oh, what a pretty camera," Mary sat down next to Alex and chirped, "Lizzy, do you think we could take some pictures of the roses in my garden? I would love to have a picture for my table."

"I suppose." Lizzy wiped her tears and shrugged her shoulders. "What color are your roses?" She shuffled her Mary Jane's across the floor and slid up and onto the swing.

"Yes, you and Chad can stay here tonight, and first thing in the morning, we can get the picture before the

BLOOD MOON

dew dries on the roses. The red ones are my favorite. What is your favorite?"

"Pink is the prettiest. Do you have pink roses?" Lizzy bubbled up, and her eyes danced.

"The pinkest you have ever seen." Mary giggled, her belly bounced, so her apron bobbed up and down.

The swing shook with Lizzy's exuberance, as she coaxed her brother, "I did not want to go to the old Fortress anyway. We can play in the garden. I think that sounds funner, huh Chad?"

"See, sweetie, you'll have more fun here with Lizzy and Mary." Alex hugged the reluctant lad and prompted him to follow his sister.

"And cookies, Mommy, can I have cookies, please," Alex assured her tiny prince with a nod. His puffy eyes danced with contentment, and he surrendered to follow his sister inside.

***

The last plate was rinsed and placed in the drainer. Sara folded the dry cloth and put it on the stove handle. The kitchen was quieter now, the proverbial calm before the storm. A movement caught her eye just on the other side of the kitchen table.

The door frame looked oddly small, as the width of his shoulders filled its opening; his masculine, muscular frame was a distinct asset to the kitchen décor. His hair fell in waves to adorn his head with the royalty of the mighty beast. He had the aura of a warrior, his weapons honed and ready for battle. She was glad he was hers.

Mary broke the shadow of the candles and came toward her, their eyes met, and a sudden sting filled Sara's cheeks. *How long had she been watching me?*

SARAH KAGE

"A penny for your thoughts, son," Mary flashed a wink at Sara and moved toward the doorway. She placed her hand on Jarrid's shoulder,

He patted it without a word and stepped down onto the porch. Sara made a move to follow, but Mary gestured to discourage the idea. A moment alone with her son before his duty to protect the village is the message Sara received loud and clear.

"I have seen tonight's outcome in a vision." Mary's voice called from across the porch. Jarrid's fingers laced together to rest on the top of his head, his thoughts interrupted by his mother's voice.

"You will be victorious in bringing your chosen few through the veil and into the inner walls." Jarrid turned to face her words.

He walked toward her and asked, "Yes, but will I be able to bring them home?"

The dimness of the soft light touched Mary's face, and she added, "This vision did not elaborate, but I have faith in your abilities and your destiny."

His head bent toward the floor. Jarrid's frame waivered with the weight of the responsibility that lay upon his soul

"What has you so troubled?" Mary touched her son's face.

He turned his back, an attempt to hide the guilt and shame of the strain in his mind. "You would think that my thoughts would be filled with the impossible task of breaching the fortress wall, but it is much darker than that."

"Tell me what troubles you." Mary offered her hands to soothe the apparent pain that riddled his face.

"The darkness swirls under my skin. It picks and tears, trying to undermine the love I feel for Sara." He lifted his eyes to confront Mary's look of surprise. He saw the concern and lightened his words, "Anuk is insisting that she be included in the group tonight. I have told her that would not be possible."

Mary hesitated before asking, "Is Anuk the source of the darkness? Is she the one who taunts you?"

"She controls my dreams with lustful, demonic possession, invading my nightmares, and sometimes my waking thoughts. She is hell-bent on fulfilling some crazy pact with the Devil." Jarrid turned and walked toward the back of the porch, out of the light, to hide his shame.

"You must be strong and resist." She took Jarrid's hand to console him, but instead, the illusion crashed across her mind. A vision of the medallion loomed large just between their faces. It's intention clear to only her.

"You must listen to me. Anuk must go with you into the Fortress. It is the only way that you will be victorious." She stared straight ahead and waited for his reaction.

"Are you crazy? Did you not hear a word I have said? She is a threat." Jarrid paced across the width of the porch. "What possible reason would I have to bring the darkness with me into the battle?"

"There will be no victory without the medallion." Mary crossed the porch, took off her apron and sat down, her face cold and stern.

Her words forceful, stopping Jarrid in mid-pace, asking, "Where does the medallion fit in all of this?"

"It is the material key, the end game, the light in the darkness." Mary stood and placed herself in Jarrid's face. "It's the enlightenment of God's grace and the future of the world as we know it."

There would be no argument; Jarrid nodded his head in agreement. Anuk would accompany him into the Fortress. Jarrid trusted his mother's visions.

The statement, unavoidable, Sara stood in the doorway, she recognized her timing stunk, but spoke anyway; "Jarrid, it's time."

"Okay, good, I'll gather the children for their goodbyes." Mary interrupted with animated hands, rushing toward the door. She flashed Jarrid a look and hurried into the kitchen.

"I'll meet you out front," Jarrid stated, acknowledging Sara's words with a nod, but standing his ground, not willing to follow her into the house. His mother's visions weighed heavy on his soul, and now he had to tell Sara that Anuk would be part of their group.

***

The silence in the forest made the night seem darker. The moonlight skipped and bounced between the tree limbs to orchestrate the shadows that raced up the path, silhouettes of the three unlucky companions. Single file each one walked with the weight of the night's adventure heavy upon their souls.

"Hey, Alex…" Sara called as she shortened the distance between them. "How did you get away from the kids without a scene?"

Alex switched shoulders and gave the backpack a gentle squeeze. "Mary, she has a way with them. They were so excited about their garden adventure; Lizzy practically pushed me out the door."

Sara reached for the backpack, placed it on her shoulder and felt for the camera. "Don't worry…" Alex said, nervously, "I've checked for it at least ten times already."

BLOOD MOON

The backpack rode low on Sara's back as she called to Jarrid, "Hey, wait up." She took his arm and tugged on his sleeve. "Would now be a good time to talk about your secrets?"

The sarcasm in her voice jolted Jarrid, and he snapped, "Really, Sara, you pick this moment."

He lengthened his stride to put distance between them, rounded the corner, stopped in front of the wall, and addressed Nikko, "are you ready?"

The old man's face stonewalled, his words stolen, the lantern's light cascaded across Sara's face, and all he could see were the eyes. Nikko could not answer.

"Hello, my name is Alex." Jarrid rose from his inspection of the supplies and interjected, "Alex, Sara, this is Nikko. He will be accompanying us into the Fortress."

Nikko dropped his gaze and answered, "Oh, pardon me. Yes, please to meet you both."

"Yeah, she has that effect on men." Alex quipped with a mumble.

Sara's anger had passed the point of politeness, and she bellowed, "Jarrid, a word… now!" She marched up into the tree line, her red hair blazing in the moonlight.

"Oh boy, looks like you've gone and done it now, Jarrid, meet Sara's dragon." Alex giggled nervously and helped Nikko with the supplies.

Jarrid followed Sara into a small clearing; he pushed through the low hanging tree limbs just in time to see her standing in the shadows, her red hair blowing like the crest of a mighty fire lizard. He stood before her and offered his hand in a gesture of peace.

"No… this is not how it goes, you and your manliness or dominance. It's my turn to dominate." She charged toward him and stood up in his face. "How is it that

Anuk, who means nothing to you, knows your secrets and taunts me with this knowledge?"

She circled in front of him, her anger making it difficult to stand in one place with the last revolution ending up closer in Jarrid's face. "How can we face this task with the barrier of this mystery between us?" She turned away before her anger consumed her.

Jarrid had never seen Sara in such a rage, didn't know she was capable of such anger. He pooled his words wisely before he spoke, "I never intended to keep these things from you. I promise that before we enter the inner walls tonight, you will know everything that is between us."

The power to maintain the rage ebbed and flowed until Sara felt it leave her with only tears to fall down her cheeks. She turned to face his surrender, spent from the powerful emotions that forced her to confront him; the dragon chained.

Only traces of the dark, red anger flowed from her fingertips, thrown to the ground as she shook her hands to release their hold on her troubled heart. She moved forward with only one thought in mind, to feel Jarrid's familiar embrace and to trust once more.

She walked forward and buried her face into the coolness of his shirt. Jarrid's arms wrapped around her, and he hung his head in reverence, to feel the trust given to him freely.

He breathed in the fragrance of her hair and felt his mind still, and thoughtless, void of all impressions and words, the gray tones faded in and out until the void sucked him into the illusion. There in the darker corners of his mind a vision of naked dark skin, caressed by jet black hair. Its length bounced just above the curve of rounded flesh that ended on the tops of long silky legs.

BLOOD MOON

The vision focused in and out with gray static interfering with his mind's eye. Each time the forest came into view, the image once more demanded his attention. A few seconds of clarity allowed him the opportunity to push Sara aside and seek the assistance of a tree to steady his body against the next image.

Sara took offense to being shoved but soon realized that he was in distress. "Jarrid, what's wrong?"

She moved to his side as his trembling body convulsed in waves, the fits coming in rhythms of violent order.

Jarrid's mind danced to the beat, correlated with the next revelation. Her dark bosom filled his hand, and he reached to feel the fullness of her firm buttocks, round, and firm to his touch.

Then just a few seconds of reality crossed his mind, hearing Sara's words echo in his ears, "Jarrid, snap out of it. You're scaring me."

He had no control; the vision demanded his presence. The picture stabilized in his mind and distorted reality. The next image took his breath, and he physically collapsed onto both knees with his hands limp by his side. The hallucination found him standing. The grayness framed his tall, naked body shining in the light, Anuk's hands, from behind searched low for the object of her desires.

He heard an inner voice cry out, *get a grip*! His mind came to him in the form of questions. *Is this real or a dream? Do I have the power of vision?*

No answers for the analytical mind, only the heat poured upon him by Anuk's touch, bringing his questions to a dead halt.

"Jarrid…" Sara shook his shoulder until every ounce of strength poured from her tiny frame. It was no use.

"Jarrid, no…" she jumped to her feet and screamed out, "Alex, Nikko, please help."

His conscience heard her screams, but still, the hallucination continued. He was lost now consumed by the desire that throbbed and drained the blood from his power of resistance.

The hallucination was now Jarrid's reality. Anuk stood close, pressed her naked body hard against him, and kissed his chest to ignite the flame higher. He pulled her head back, forced her bosom from his chest, and looked down the length of his torso to watch her dark mound surround the ache of his desire.

Fully involved, vision, or reality made no matter. Inner desires ruled all. They lay naked, Anuk's body straddled across his lust. She restrained his hands over his head, her strength conquered him, and her will drove the illusion. His body arched toward his lust, the need all-consuming. Her legs spread wide above his pelvis, she reached down, spread her mound, and positioned his length to slide between her full lips, bearing down and teasing with strokes just outside the realm of consummation.

Each pulse coming closer to the point of no return, the blood rising through the length of his desire, his body arched for the climax.

"What's wrong?" Alex and Nikko clawed their way through the thick brush and came upon Sara as she reached the edge of the clearing.

"It's Jarrid; he's having an episode." She grabbed Nikko's arm and directed him to the other side of the trees. "Hurry, please."

She ran ahead and came upon Jarrid slumped on his knees. "Jarrid…" She called out before she reached him and extended her hand to touch the extreme arch of his back, feeling each spasm flow from his body.

BLOOD MOON

Nikko and Alex rushed the scene with a brilliant, blue light overpowering the night. Its flash blinded the duo and caused them to cower to the ground. The static electricity filled the air and crackled with the light pulsating around Jarrid and Sara. Her hand melted to Jarrid's shoulder with branches of blue lightning shooting from her fingertips. The light blinding, Nikko covered his eyes and shouted out to Sara, "No..."

The bolt shot back into Sara's arms to leave Jarrid in a pile against the tree; each branch of the light traced its path back into Sara's body.

She gathered him into her arms and cradled his head. "Jarrid, please..." He raised his hand to her face and started to cough.

Nikko pulled out his canteen and offered small sips of water. His eyes never left Sara's face. "What the hell happened?"

"I am alright!" Jarrid refused the water and tried to find his footing. He skimmed off the concerns by pushing everyone away.

"Just give me a moment." He ran his fingers through his hair and tugged on his shirt to cover his body, remembering his nakedness in the visions.

Looking at the tips of her fingers, Sara stood silent like a pillar. "Did you see it? The lightning was coming from your hands." Alex grabbed Sara's wrist and touched the end of her fingertips. "How did you do that?"

"It wasn't me." Sara yanked her hands free and offered her solution, "Must have been part of his seizure, or he did it, or this place, damn."

Nikko was guiding Jarrid back to the gate, slow and easy. "Come on. You need to gather yourself before we go inside the walls."

Alex pushed for the answer, "I don't know, Sara. It looked pretty witchy to me. Is there something you need to tell me?"

Sara took offense to her statement and declared, "Anuk is the only witchy one in these parts, and that's one witch too many for me; must have been a fluke."

Her friend shrugged her shoulders and added, "Yeah, but that sure could come in handy. Feel free to protect me anytime with your light, my fairy friend."

"Fairy friend, indeed, maybe you can protect us with your vivid imagination."

Alex dropped the humor. "Wait, Anuk. Who, what? Is that the woman I saw on the path tonight when I called you guys for dinner?"

Sara smirked, "Oh, you mean the black-cloaked, raven-haired beauty, with a killer body? Yeah, that's Anuk, the Village Witch."

She didn't wait for a response. "This has been a great start to our night. Hopefully, Jarrid's fit will be the worst thing we encounter."

Absolutely, and what was that *thing* we encountered? Alex wondered out loud, realizing that Sara was leaving her alone in the dark clearing.

***

The cabin was strangely quiet, the lingering scent of pot roast mixed with the smell of the candle wax dripping onto the kitchen table. "Okay, Chad, ask Lizzy if she has any three's." Mary prompted with the lad sitting on her lap, his cards spread in his tiny hands.

"Do you, Lizzy… have any three's?"

"Go fish," Lizzy demanded, slapping her hand on the table.

BLOOD MOON

Joshua stood on the porch, peering into the dimly lit rooms, feeling Chad's frustration with each of Lizzy's turns.

"Do you have a king?" Chad sheepishly asked. He watched the small boy pull the card from his hand and relinquish it over to his sister; the matched cards lay in a straight line in front of her. She clutched her last card in both hands and asked, "Do you have a four?"

It was too much. Chad looked up at Mary as if to ask, do I have to give it to her? Must she always win?

Mary's heart broke, and she squeezed him. "Okay, I think it's time for a bedtime snack." Chad shoved the cards in Lizzy's direction and hopped down to follow Mary to the cookie jar.

Mary gave Lizzy a cookie and a teacup for pretending. The girl propped her king and queen up against the flower vase and carried on a conversation with the royalty, "King Ralph, would you like some tea?"

"Come on, Chad, we'll leave Lizzy to her tea party." Chad stuck his cookie covered tongue out at Lizzy and followed Mary to the porch.

Joshua opened the screen door and escorted them to the swing. "Don't worry, Chad. We can have a pretend sword fight when you've finished your cookie."

"Well, I can see Chad has cheered up, but what is bothering you, son?" Mary handed Chad another cookie and turned her attention back to her question.

"I wanted to go, face the battle with Jarrid, but instead, he took her." He walked to the stairs and then quickly turned back. "He asked me to stay behind and protect you, and I agree with that, but…"

Mary handed a napkin to Chad and left the swing to sway in the night air. "Jarrid is following my instructions.

216

My visions dictate who accompanies him into the Fortress."

Joshua stood on the bottom step and watched Chad appear from behind the skirt of Mary's dress, his tiny chocolate-covered finger pointed toward the garden gate.

Mary stared over the top of Joshua's head and bellowed, "What is she doing here?"

Her raven hair blew in the breeze; she stood motionless in the dark shadows of the garden. Joshua rushed her from the steps, "Woman, you have no business here, be gone."

Mary gasped and spoke, "Anuk, why are you not with Jarrid and the group at the Fortress?" She stepped down into the garden with her forward motion halted in mid-step, her tongue stymied. Chad lowered his cookie to his side, his tiny frame anchored to the porch, frozen in the moment.

Lizzy burst through the screen door, still babbling to her imaginary royalty, "Yes, we shall take a walk in the garden." She stopped short, ran to Chad, and shook him. "What is wrong?"

Chad's eyes blinked, he shook off the spell and pointed toward the women once more.

Anuk raced past Joshua, stood before Mary, who was still captured by her spell, and addressed the children, "Oh my, what pretty little angels."

She reached her hand out to Lizzy and guided her down the stairs. "I would like to walk with you and your king into the garden."

Lizzy ran past the dark-haired woman and straight into Joshua's legs, where she surveyed the situation and shook her head vigorously.

BLOOD MOON

Anuk turned to Chad. "Come, little one. I will take you to your mother." Hearing her words, Chad shuffled down the stairs and took the stranger's hand.

Joshua felt his mind swirl; his feet felt like heavy stones. He watched Anuk walk into the forest with both children in tow, their destinies foretold in the ancient *Book of Souls*.

SARAH KAGE
Chapter 16 The Book of Souls

The girls' voices echoed through the trees and swirled around Jarrid's head. He leaned against the stone wall with both palms planted against the rough exterior, his body still shaken by the seductive hallucination.

His canteen ready to assist Jarrid, Nikko stood beside him with his back to the coldness, "Quick, tell me. What the hell was that back there? Were you in some trance or possession?"

Jarrid turned and placed his back against the wall; he hung his head and spoke one word, "Evil."

"Jarrid, are you…" Sara stepped forward, touching his arm, but the image of the blue lightning caused her to retreat and stumble on her words, "What was going on back there?"

He bolted from the wall, shook his head, and yelled, "Do not want to talk about it now. We have to approach the inner chamber before dawn." He bent down to help Nikko gather the supplies and left Sara standing with no resolve.

"Hey guys," Alex flew up from behind, still electrified by the sight of Sara's newfound superpower. "Did you know Sara was a freak? I mean, really…" She slapped her friend on the back, "Ole lightning bolt here, stole the show."

"Okay, well," The men turned at the same time to shoot a stare right through the overzealous sidekick. "I guess we better get started."

The gate offered no resistance as the small group entered the inner hallway. Nikko busied himself, lighting the lanterns and passed them around. "You girls stay here

BLOOD MOON

in the alcove, and we'll scope out the wall and find the entrance."

Sara started to open her fiery mouth, and all Jarrid had to do was look down his stone, cold face at her, and she reluctantly surrendered. "Okay, I guess the less noise, the better. We'll wait here until you find the entrance."

"It is closer to the top and right in this area." Jarrid quipped. He and Nikko slowly surveyed the corridor, running their hands up and down, feeling each brick as they followed the wall down to a dead-end and started back to retrace their steps.

"Are you sure the brick is the key?" Nikko rested his shoulder against the wall and watched Jarrid methodically search for the slightest protrusion, but the sound of falling rocks flowed down the corridor with 'Sara' written all over it.

"Why do we have to wait and let the men be the heroes?" Alex whispered, Sara stomped her foot to scold her, but instead, the vibration caused rocks to cascade to the floor and gather at their feet. The dust flew up and choked their every breath.

A pile of small rubble gathered in the corner. Sara shined the lantern in the direction of the noise. She kicked the loose rocks and stood over the disheveled pile.

The lantern caught something in the light. Sara bent down to get a closer look. A corner of brown leather peeked out from between the fissures with a satin ribbon cascading down to encircle a row of smaller rocks. She knelt, reached out into the shadows, and moved to retrieve the hidden treasure.

"No, do not touch it!" Alex had been peering over Sara's shoulder and almost swung the lantern into the alcove wall, toward Jarrid's voice, gasping and reeling to recover the light.

SARAH KAGE

"Alright, Jarrid," Sara kept her surprise to herself and jumped to her feet. "If we're going to be a team, you have to start trusting us."

He ignored her complaint and moved to retrieve the leather book from its hiding place. He gathered the relic and stuffed it into his satchel. "Let us gather as a team and plan our next move."

He didn't wait for an answer but sat in the middle of the corridor with his legs crossed and motioned for them to join him.

They sat in a circle; the hum of the lanterns broke the silence and lit their faces. Jarrid stared straight into Sara's eyes. "You want to know my secrets; the truth be told this is their moment." He stirred and brought the satchel to his chest, dug in between the folds of material, and retrieved *The Book of Souls*.

"I told you, Sara, before the night was over, you would know my inner soul and all of its darkness." With that, he opened the book and proclaimed, "This is the first of three secrets."

"This book was brought to my attention tonight at the council meeting. Anuk stormed the church, disrupted the proceedings, and made a spectacle of the importance of me possessing this ancient relic."

Alex repositioned her legs and offered her observation, "Yeah, the Village Witch." Sara pinched her leg and burned the image of her disapproval deep in the recesses of her friend's mind.

'Witch' Jarrid's mouth turned up into a smirk, hearing the word, probably Sara's pet name, spoken as her tongue painted the picture of the woman in black.

He cleared his throat and continued, "She told me it was *The Book of Souls*, and that it would be instrumental in the battle rising between good and evil. The only problem, Latin is the written language."

Sara plunged across Jarrid's lap and grabbed the book. She could contain herself no more; his surprise allowed her to maneuver the large relic into her lap. "Okay, let's check out this secret of yours." She turned the pages faster and faster than complained, "Hey, it's not Latin. Looks like English to me."

He returned the action and procured the book with a show of strength. The force landed it squarely in his lap, and it opened to the page with the words of the poem spilling across the yellow parchment.

Jarrid flipped the pages, one after the other, as the words came across clearly in English. Not only the poem, but every page now translated in a modern tongue. "Most have something to do with the Fortress," he puzzled.

He turned the pages back to the poem, hesitated, and read,

> *"Into the walls, the walls of pain, two who are pure must remain."*

Sara jumped to her feet and speculated, "So that's what *The Spirited Sword of Purity* is, like a weapon to defeat evil." She sat back down. "Keep going, don't stop."

Jarrid lowered his head to focus on the next stanza,

> *"Love and hope, innocence and wisdom, will conquer the evil and reclaim the kingdom."*

"I thought we were looking for ways to save the village, not a kingdom." Alex spouted.

"Hush Alex," Sara scolded, glancing toward Jarrid, "Continue."

He placed his pointer finger on the next words,

> *"With walls in light the darkness to pierce, your hearts and souls and many tears."*

"Hearts, souls and tears, boy, they aren't joking around. It sounds like the test will be fierce." Alex blurted out.

"What comes next?" Sara placed her hand on Alex's arm and prompted Jarrid to continue.

The book weighed heavy on Jarrid's lap, and he pulled it up closer to his face, the words flickered in the light and became clear,

> *"After the feast, no one will remain. But the sacrificial lamb will be the same."*

"A sacrifice demanded." Nikko rose from the circle, the words raining down upon his destiny; he knew this in his heart. He brought his lantern higher in the air to shed light on the poem of eternity.

Jarrid read the next words in silence. He lowered the book and looked directly at Sara. "This is the revelation of the second secret."

She took in a deep breath and waited for the words to flow over her. "Go ahead. I'm ready."

He moved closer to her and whispered the last verse,

> *"Look to the wall her face to frame; the Righteous One will be the same."*

Jarrid broke the tension and stood to deliver his words, "Joshua and I have been to the inner wall. We have seen the meaning of the last verse. The Righteous One's face consumes the wall."

Sara jumped to her feet and confronted Jarrid, "Who's face is on the wall?"

He felt the need to embrace her. His arms circled broad and strong. "Angelica came to me while I was alone in the chamber and verified that the woman's face on the wall would be the deliverer."

Sara pulled away and spoke with her voice cracking, "Who is she, Jarrid?"

He didn't answer except to say, "Come, I have found the brick, the key to the entrance. We must go now, Sara, you will see for yourself the importance of the second secret."

Nikko protected the group from behind, while Jarrid directed Sara straight toward the inner chamber, revealing his brightest secret.

Jarrid reached the brick, and Nikko raised the lantern, shining the light on the beginning of the rest of their lives.

It protruded out from the wall and beckoned to be pulled. Jarrid grasped the coldness and yanked the brick to life. It started as a low rumble, raising the wall a couple of inches, swiveling on some hidden hinge.

As soon as there was the smallest of openings, Jarrid took Sara's hand. He waited for the wall to offer up its doorway and lifted his lantern to invite her in.

They walked across the threshold together with Nikko and Alex following close behind. The four lanterns swung and cast shadows on the walls. Alex ran from one side to the other with her light cascading down, searching for the face. "Where, Jarrid, I don't see anything."

SARAH KAGE

Nikko started to walk toward the back of the room, paving the way for the reveal. Jarrid stopped Sara, turned her, and asked, "Are you ready to face your fate?"

All she could do was nod her head in an attempt to be brave. Alex rushed past Nikko and lifted the oil lamp. The face surrounded her; the sheer magnitude of the eyes caused her breath to escape with a gasp, and she yelled, "Sara, it's you. Your face is on the wall."

Sara took small steps toward the focus of the oil lamps. Curls of red hair filled the wall from side to side; there was no denying it. Her eyes, on the wall, shot through the dark and filled her heart with dread. The vision too much, her knees buckled, and the weight of the revelation took its toll; she sunk to the ground.

Jarrid caught her just before she pooled onto the cold floor. He gathered her and tasted her lips, an offer of support, he kissed her tenderly.

In the brief kiss, the visions of the past and the possible future flooded Sara's thoughts. A veil lifted between their souls, and she saw what lay ahead, a glimpse of Jarrid's heart, and she heard distant thunder.

Alex had one hand, and Jarrid the other, lowering Sara against the corner of the wall. She gathered her faculties, threw back her head, and grabbed Jarrid's arm for the leverage to stand in front of the wall.

He came from behind and steadied her feet. "Jarrid..." she reached back to take his arm, never letting her eyes off of the wall's image. " The Righteous One, what does that mean?"

"I am not sure." Nikko stepped in front and motioned to Jarrid, not wanting to overwhelm the lass. Then, he took his queue and answered, "But it is clear, you are meant to be part of this providence, the main character seems to be your role."

BLOOD MOON

She turned and buried her head in Jarrid's embrace. She raised her chin, stared deep into his eyes, and wondered what exactly he wasn't telling her.

He felt her question and answered, "Sara, I must tell you the third and last secret that stands between us." He moved to look up into the large green eyes pouring down from the wall. "This is the hardest secret to confess. Please understand I had no choice. Anuk possesses the medallion."

"Please don't start the confession of your darkest secret with the name Anuk attached to its outcome." She moved away and folded her arms around herself as a defense mechanism to any secret that involved the witch.

His embrace folded back around her, and his words spilled from his heart with fear and dread, "Anuk must accompany us into the Fortress!"

The words circled her head and intermingled with voices coming down the corridor. Nikko rushed the wall opening, shining the light from the lantern out into the hall. Sara heard Jarrid's confession ride the walls and mingle with the voices of children.

Alex pushed past Sara, perplexed and blurted out, "Is that Lizzy's voice?"

"I don't believe it." Nikko backed into the room and shouted to Jarrid, "Why would she bring them here?"

The voices, louder now, echoed down the hall and bounced off the inner chamber walls. Lizzy pushed through the wall opening and flew straight into Alex and grabbed her legs. "Mommy, I am so glad to see you. Please do not be mad. She made us do it."

All eyes fell on Anuk as she entered the chamber and put Chad down to run to his mother. "Mommy, Mommy..." the small boy jumped into Alex's arms. " Are you mad, Mommy?"

"No, my sweet," Alex took Lizzy's hand and moved away from the Village Witch.

Anuk caught a glimpse of the wall. She stood small and insignificant against the portraits awe. "So I was right; you are the missing piece."

She turned, gazed upon Sara, and strolled up to the wall. "Don't think just because your face pours from the entrance to the Fortress; you have won. The Evil One will win this battle." Anuk circled Jarrid and flashed a smile as if she knew something between them that no one else knew, the fourth secret.

Jarrid slid to Sara's side, the weight of the vision heavy across his face. She pushed him away and demanded, "So your big secret, Anuk is part of our group?"

He moved to embrace her, but her fiery heat would not allow it, "Why Jarrid? Remember my dream; she will put you in danger."

Her lantern scraped the ground, the metal base grinding against the floor. She pointed the light toward the noise and stopped cold. Joshua pushed his leg into the opening, and squeezed through the barrier, with his fingers gripped around the swiveled wall, forcing the entrance wider.

Jarrid rushed to his brother with the anger seething through his teeth, "Joshua! What are you doing here?" He grabbed him by the arm and forced him into the middle of the room. "Explain yourself, little brother."

"I was protecting the children. Anuk took them." He stood tall and tugged on his shirt, looking away from Jarrid's accusing stare.

Before Anuk could pardon herself, Jarrid continued, "Okay, now go back, take the children to Mom, and protect our home, leave this very second." Jarrid grabbed his brother and shoved him toward the hall.

BLOOD MOON

Lizzy ran and put herself between the two brothers. She grabbed Jarrid's leg and screamed, "Listen! Don't you hear it?"

She jumped around their legs and stopped just shy of the wall opening. "There, in the hall. It sounds like a kitten."

The faint meow purged through the opening muffled with a small scraping sound. Lizzy strained to listen. "Be quiet, do you hear it?" She looked up into Jarrid's face. "It is crying."

Alex instinctively knew what her daughter's next move would be and lunged toward her, trying to avoid the inevitable. Lizzy shot through the opening as she called out, "Here, kitty. I will help you."

Joshua caught Jarrid's look and disappeared after the small girl. "Lizzy, wait, come back."

The massive wall responded to Joshua's voice and moved ever so slightly to close the opening to the hall. "Joshua, the wall is closing. Quick, take Chad." Alex begged.

Her words, a key, the wall moaned, dropped down off of its hinge, and started to close. Alex rushed the wall, trying to hold the cold lock on their tomb and pushed the frightened boy toward the hall. "Chad, go to Joshua."

The screams echoed through the room with the wall only feet away from closing them off from the outside world, and Lizzy's attempt to save a kitten.

Joshua's voice mingled with the groans of the closing wall, "Lizzy, stop!"

The wall moved faster. It's opening only a few feet from closing the only known portal to the outside world. Just before the dust swirled around the last few particles of escape, the kids were shoved into the inner chamber, by Joshua's unseen hand. Lizzy fell into the room with her arms full of the tiny black kitten; she had risked all to save. The wall's last assault, to close the group off from the world and force them into their future, its ritual spent to open no more.

Jarrid clawed at the wall and called out, "Joshua, are you alright?"

A faint voice slowly answered from the other side, "Yes…" and faded off into the silence which filled the dank air of their tomb.

Jarrid bowed his head to Joshua, in reverence to his fate written in the wind and the fact that he would not stand beside his brother to protect the village.

"Oh, is my kitty, okay?" Lizzy sat up and unfolded her arms to see the small black-face peering into her eyes. She stroked its ebony coat with tears falling down her cheeks. "You are okay. I saved you."

Jarrid bent down to pet Lizzy's new friend. "You are a brave one." The kitten meowed as if to introduce himself.

He motioned to take the kitten from her arms, and she hesitated. "Oh, please, Jarrid, he is very scared." Lizzy jumped to her feet, crossed the room and sat down in the corner with Alex, as Chad reached across his mother to pet the small feline.

"Okay, everyone," bellowed Jarrid, "please gather round. We have to find the way into the Fortress. Let's start with the book." Anuk pulled on Jarrid's arm to coax him to sit, but Sara intercepted her charm and moved between them.

"Yes, Jarrid, the book could give some other clues now that it is in English."

The book made no complaint to being retrieved from the satchel; Jarrid laid the heavy relic between his crossed legs and opened it to the beginning.

BLOOD MOON

There was pushing and shoving one shoulder against the other, the two women jockeying for the best position to gain Jarrid's attention. Anuk reached across Sara, batted her black eyes, and suggested, "Read out loud, Jarrid. Start at the beginning." She wiggled back into her cross-legged position, wrapped her cloak around her legs, and waited.

"Oh, yes," giggle, giggle, flash, flash, "Please Jarrid…" the mocking evident to everyone in the group.

The kitten escaped Lizzy's death grip and pranced toward the group to lie in Alex's lap. The young girl squeezed herself between her mom and Jarrid and clumsily scooped the black fur-ball into her lap, poured her relentless affection upon the tiny beast, and cooed, "Saved you. Yes, I did. You are my kitty now." Alex flashed a look of '*oh, no you don't*' that was interrupted by Jarrid's loud voice.

"Yes, the words will give us the truth." He flashed a grin at Sara to acknowledge her rightful place by his side.

He bent his head and started to read,

"*The time of intolerance, evil and hate, one man for another, rules the face of the earth. When Satan gathers his forces together, and many battles have been waged and won, then the last crusade will begin.*

"*Two, who are pure, from different worlds, will unite in love and wage the final conflict. The future of the*

230

world will be in their hands."

"You…" Anuk shoved Sara into Jarrid as she jumped up and pointed to the wall. She stood in the grace of the Righteous One's image and addressed Sara, "Your innocence and love are the tools, but it will be no use. My master will be victorious."

Jarrid bellowed, "You are so dramatic, sit down and listen, woman." She shuffled her feet and rejoined the circle.

He lowered his eyes and read louder,

"Their allies will sacrifice much. Lives and loves will be lost, but the Righteous One will not falter."

Alex broke in, "So, are we to believe that Sara's face, framed by the wall, makes her the Righteous One of whom the book keeps referring to?"

"Angelica hinted to that fact in her riddles," Jarrid replied. "For now, we will have to keep the faith and believe that in some way, we will come to understand the truth."

He turned his attention back to the book,

"Once the darkness falls upon the Righteous One,"

Jarrid's eyes focused on the page.

"It will be a night without end. The story foretold, and nothing will change the beginning, only the end will be determined by the

BLOOD MOON

choices that are made by the Army of Light."

"Oh, please," Anuk snorted, "some army, a couple of virgins, an old deserter, a half-wit photographer, and a couple of kids. Oh, and don't forget the black cat." Anuk's evil laughter filled the chamber. She rose up, circled the floor, and bent down to pet the mouthy feline. "And a pretty little mouse chaser you are."

The kitten jumped from Lizzy's arms, hunched its back and hissed, its claws slashing at the taunting words.

The wave of Jarrid's hand to dismiss Anuk's theatrics brought attention to his words,

"There will be a reveal of great evil. Temptation and seduction will pour out of the demon. Be wise in your choices, think with your souls, and not the flesh, for it is weak and will fail you. Choose your allies wisely and always know that once a choice is made, there is no turning back."

The black cloak moved back and forth with Anuk's stride, her pacing grated on Jarrid's last raw nerve. "Blah, blah, blah, this is getting really boring." She knelt toward his ear and taunted, "Get to the good stuff and try and condense it. We are not getting any younger."

Sara's green eyes pierced the dark and glared upon Anuk, her vocal cords rattled and gave pause to the words spilling from her mouth, "Anuk, take a seat and keep your opinions to yourself."

"Hmm, sounds like someone is jealous." Anuk turned to Jarrid and teased, "Why is she jealous? Jarrid, do you have any clue?"

"Enough, you will sit down and be quiet. I have had it with your disruptive behavior." Jarrid bellowed.

Nikko piped in, "Look. We are all in this together. Whatever happens to one of us happens to the group." He paused, offering his opinion.

"Anuk does have a point. We need to find a way out. I will read ahead and summarize the words." Jarrid studied the text for a few moments, gathered the information, and enlightened the group,

> *"The undead will rule the evil. A greater book foretells of death and destruction, which will invade the world in the last days."*

Nikko rose to his feet and started to circle the room. All eyes followed him as they listened to Jarrid read the book's revelations.

> *"Those who will die by evil will not render their flesh to the ground. For there will be no death, in the days of turmoil, much violence, and many casualties, but no death. Your brother will be as dead but still walk, all of the pain and agony*

BLOOD MOON

*to endure. Fear for your life
but safeguard your soul, at
all cost."*

"No…no," Nikko walked the parameter of the room, casting his lantern's light along the bottom of the walls. "Jarrid, quick, the room is closing in."

Each wall pushed toward them in unison. The room surrendered, closed in faster, and forced the group to huddle in the center of the chamber. Jarrid joined Nikko in searching for a way out. They stood at the portrait, watching the eyes close in; the scraping sound of the walls overpowered their voices.

"Did Angelica tell you anything that would help us get out?" Nikko yelled, still watching the eyes coming closer.

"Riddles, poems, the same as your dream, she said through Sara's eyes."

"Are you sure those were her exact words?" Nikko's question sparked Jarrid's attention. He ran to Sara, turned her around, and stared into the pool of green and gold.

A vision of the angel pooled in Sara's eyes and Angelica's words spilled into the air, above the sound of the impending walls, they heard her words, "Through the eyes."

The kiss was quick but powerful; he lifted his lips from her ruby mouth and proclaimed, "I know how to reach the other side."

The walls closed in and forced the group to huddle closer together. Alex gathered the kids. "Jarrid, whatever, just get us out of here, quick."

Still lost in Sara's gaze, he commanded, "Everyone, follow us through the eyes."

"Are you mad?" Nikko rushed up into Jarrid's face. "What sorcery convinced you to walk through the wall?" Nikko shot Anuk an accusing glare.

"We can do this, Sara. Take my hand and follow me into our destiny." He held her close and faced the wall, one last look, and they leaped into the wall, straight into the eyes.

A ripple of sound and light shot through the room, and the wall closed around the couple, vanishing as one form, into the inner-walls.

"Nikko, help me with the children." Alex shoved Lizzy into his arms and knelt to gather Chad.

Lizzy screamed, "No, Mommy, kitty is too scared to walk into the wall." Nikko grabbed her, feline and all, looked back at Alex and jumped into the eyes.

"Unless you want to face this alone, I suggest you follow me." Anuk gathered her cloak to engulf Mother and Son, "Hold him tight, we are going through."

The hem of the black cloak resisted, lingering for a moment before being sucked through the wall to the other side.

The room stood in stillness, a witness to the group crossing the veil into the Fortress. The walls continued marching toward one another, closing the chamber room, ending the age of reality.

PART TWO THE FORTRESS

SARAH KAGE
Chapter 17 The Fortress Speaks

I am forever, the veil between Heaven and Hell. I have stood since the beginning of time. High walls and turrets stand on three sides, the fourth invisible and swallowed by the rock, a mighty mountain. My presence obscured from the human eye, only brought forward by the evil deeds of man; memories erased from all who knew the truth.

The dungeons dark with the stains of the battle for good and evil, the blood memory courses through my hallways, and intermingles with the roots that invade my walls. Still, I stand, waiting for the last crusade.

It was not always so. Laughter and righteousness prevailed; all my halls adorned with merriment. The worlds' planes coexisted within these walls, neutral to good or evil, all realms of reality worked together for the betterment of the universe. The ancient fables brought to life with the existence of werewolf, vampire, Fae, and other creatures now referred to as fantasy, but I know the truth.

Before I get too deep into my story, let me introduce myself. Castle Kur is my given name. Although known as the entrance to Hades, my purpose is to join the planes of the worlds. Human, spirit, and entity they all reside within these walls.

Oh, you're not a believer. Just because you don't believe it doesn't make it not so. Humans have proven that point over and over again. Hear me and know, you have broken bread with an immortal many times, and rest assured fairies have buzzed in your ear, or a werewolf has sniffed the night air, taking in your essence.

BLOOD MOON

But, to make you believe is not my plight in this story. If you find your way into my inner walls, there will be no doubt.

On a lighter note, if you walk this way, you can see the Great Hall; it flows down and around. The small cubicles nestled in the high walls were homes to the entities trapped here in between the worlds.

The architectural beauty still flows and gives the shadows life. The ornate wall carvings still encased in wooden scaffolding, as if waiting for the Avalonian elves, masters of rock carving and bladesmithing, to finish the faces that stare down upon all who enter. Sadly, they will have to wait longer. The Avalonian bloodline ended with Excalibur. Oh, you didn't know? I'm afraid that tale will have to wait.

Now, if you will join me in continuing down the hall, please be very stealth minded. I do not want to catch the attention of the undead that use this walk-way to enter the courtyard. They see all.

Oh, the face of doubt has once again forged a frown. Hmm, never mind, the truth always reveals itself. The undead or the Army of Darkness, whichever you prefer, does their masters bidding.

They march around the Fortress in their decaying bodies; shoulders slumped, heads hung, arms limp by their rotting torsos. The entities huddle together, almost as one unit of terror. Slowly they walk toward no particular destination, with no directive until the onslaught begins. I cannot pinpoint what sets them off, scent, or movement. There is no rhyme or reason, but when it does occur, no human is safe.

My best description is a feeding frenzy. No longer are the undead sluggish and undirected, but fierce and focused. There only task to rip away the souls of the humans and offer their trophies to the Dark Prince. I shudder every time they attack, but the worst part is the transformation of the soulless humans; they become another soldier in the Army of Darkness. It is a frightful sight, but enough of that. Alright, the hall is clear, let's proceed.

Okay, just around the bend in the courtyard, you can feel the breeze flow down the hall. It is deep in the inner walls, and although this garden is open to the sky, it is hidden behind the veil and not visible to the village below. The Great Wall rises, standing tall but invisible.

We shan't stop to smell the roses. There is much more to see. Please, this way, follow me. This arched doorway leads down to the underbelly of the Great Fortress. Many fables and fantasies got their start in these dark and dank rooms.

At the bottom of the long, winding stairs is the armory. Although quiet and shadowy, there was a time when fire, water, and ice came together to forge many legendary weapons; there were also tales of swords smithed with dragon fire. You see here, the long tunneled tube that rises to the courtyard, an avenue for the breath of the beasty.

Again, I know, humans have to see to believe, but haven't you been challenged with that concept? I mean, you are asked to have faith in God. Hmm, alright, apples and oranges, but still the stories of old have their truths.

The opportunity has arisen to give you a glimpse into the story of a famous sword, forged in this very room. It has many names, Calad-Bolg, which means hand lightning, or the more famous Excalibur. Oh, I see by the look on your face it is familiar. Your hand gesture and facial animation tell me that you have heard the story. But do you know who made the sword for King Arthur?

BLOOD MOON

Yes, a bloodline of Avalonian elves worked the ancient art of bladesmithing, honed it so well that the blade was legendary. So powerful and meant for the hand of only one king and at his demise was thrown into the deep dark pool. Possessed by the Lady of the Lake and taken down to her watery home, the famous Excalibur, never to rise again.

I seem to have captured your attention. Good, let's continue. Up to the courtyard once more and if you look to the east, just there between the low clouds, it rises like a painted lady in the sky. The church's stained glass window glows with the colors of round Christmas candy. The ornate door covered with carved faces of the righteous, framed with the columns of wooden sculptures of angels and demons.

Just beneath the sanctuary, standing above the maze of walls are the tall turrets, bathed in the fog like soldiers, bearing their secrets to all who enter. Their rooms, small bits of solace and comfort, the refuge given to the tortured souls of the Realm of Darkness; this repose, of course, is false hope.

Yes, the voices coming from the Great Room offer an introduction to its lost souls. Follow me down the hall, just a few paces and around this bend. If you haven't guessed already, you are in observation mode, and the human residents cannot see or hear you. It is also hard for the non-humans to detect you, although not impossible. I will try to predict your questions and offer up the rule-of-thumb here in the fortress walls. Let's take a moment to observe the group.

The first thing you notice about this massive meeting room is the large wooden cross in front of the columned insets that circle the perimeter — each alcove occupied by the remains of a mummified corpse or the bones of some unlucky victim. The décor, the Dark Prince's evil style, is consistent throughout the castle.

As you can see, there are about forty or so people and entities gathered into, what can only be described as cliques. Observation leaves no doubt as to who is in charge and the hierarchy of the individual groups.

Of course, I know these leaders well. You see the man there in the corner with the largest group. His name is Caleb Grimewulfe. Indeed he is followed by the cream of the crop, the elite of the cliques.

His hazel eyes pierce through the black shroud tattooed across his sight to disappear under his long black hair. His face and neck, down to his navel, also tattooed with symbols of the Ancient Lykoan War, his Wolfen bloodline immortal and alien. No, he is not human, but humanoid in appearance.

By the door, a smaller group huddles around the table in reverence to the man sitting at the head, deep in thought. His body frame smaller than most of the leaders, with porcelain blue, ashen skin, and yellow eyes. Fingertips shrouded in long pointed nails, not necessarily an attractive quality, but attracted you are.

Sebastian is by nature, the consumer of blood. The ancestors of his bloodline also fought in the Lykoan War of 1348 B.C. set to defeat the Wolfen Aliens, but more about that when we visit the Sun Dome.

Now, if you will direct your attention toward the back wall, you will see the iridescent green feathers encompass the shoulders of a small-statured figure. The fairy's black hair and piercing green eyes could only mean the presence of Tank, the leader of a smaller group, which includes the Fae of the castle, one of the oldest entities in the Fortress.

BLOOD MOON

It looks as though Tank is sensing our presence, an advantage of his magic; let's hurry with the other introductions. You see the two men standing with Tank? Their groups wane, people coming and going with the wind. The cloaked gray-haired man is Vincent. He is the keeper of the flame. All of my lanterns burn into infinity because of his magic.

He is the resident warlock. His magic makes time standstill. In these walls, there is no need for food, water, umm facilities, every function frozen in time. The only exception to this magic is sleep. Not even his incantations can overpower the need for rest.

The other man, or should I say, giant, is Thadeous. No last name, but we call him the rock, for apparent reasons. His dress and gear are a dead giveaway to his origin. Iceland, Scandinavian, mighty warrior, his massive chest, arms like steel, and monstrous legs bare proof to his victorious battles and demand respect from all.

I think Tank has detected us. We have stayed too long. Quick, out to the hall and fast like the wind to the east just before the church; okay, I think we lost him. Yes, here we are, now for the most evil and notorious structure within these walls.

Please follow your eyes up to the tallest building inside the Fortress. It is known as the Sun Dome. It's sinister past and purpose has seen many transgressions. We will take the back stairs, winding and steep, to the central sun chamber.

The round room lends itself to the observation of the Sun Ritual. If you look to the ceiling of the tower, you can see the golden dome that retracts to receive the full rays of the noon sun. The large cross with its chains' is constructed directly under the retractable opening, to assure a swift execution to all vampires.

SARAH KAGE

This demise was the fate of the Pendas bloodline; yes, Sebastian's ancestors met their end in this very room, almost ending the Pendas royalty.

The Lykoan War raged for centuries with the alien species, both Vampire and Wolfen, battling for the domination of the human race. To win the right to seed the planet with their kind and create the hybrid that would rule the planet. Some scholars speculate that these DNA manipulations resulted in some of the oldest Egyptian kings.

If you direct your attention here on the etched ceremonial cross, you will see the hieroglyphics that have been translated to tell the story of the Star people who reigned in the time of the Egyptian King Akhenaton. Said to have been of alien blood himself, but never proven, always speculated upon, I wonder which bloodline flowed through his veins.

Oh, and here close to the bottom of the cross. This particular etching speaks of the Red-Headed One, the Righteous One who will reign and defeat the Dark Prince. I have heard it said through the centuries that red hair was a sign of royalty and the mingling of human and supernatural bloodlines, something about their Rh factors. Well, this is undoubtedly Greek to me. However, prophecy tells of the one who will deliver mankind and lends itself to interpretation, but I have seen her face on my wall and felt her red hair consume its boundaries.

Am I rambling? It seems you are losing interest in my speculations, very well then, let us continue. Do you see that tower across the courtyard? Right there with the cobblestone roof. Yes! That is the Tower of Souls. I am forbidden to talk about the tower until the fulfillment of prophecy. I can tell you it is where the last battle for good and evil will be fought, but not until the Righteous One crosses the veil.

Quickly, down the stairs, across the courtyard and back into the Great Hall. Just here, down this smaller hall, is the Throne Room. It got its name because it is the royal chamber of the World Council. Seven thrones perched upon raised floors encircle the perimeter of the ornate room. Each alcove embraces a massive jeweled stone chair, with its back walls draped in the skulls and bones of the leaders who came before.

Oh, we are here just in time the councilmen are starting the meeting. It looks like we have a few absentees, there are three thrones empty. Let's listen in and observe the proceedings. Caleb has brought the meeting to order.

The dark-haired, tattooed warrior slid to the edge of his throne. "We'll start even though Dax is not present."

"It is hard to expect a peacock to be reliable." Sebastian slumped back into the hard stone of his ornate perch. "Shapeshifters', what do you expect?"

The green feathers ruffled across Tank's back as he bolted from his stone chair. "Yeah, he's out, probably saving the world. You know I never understood why he's the only entity who can cross the veil."

Metal disks of battle jewelry clanked together with Caleb's movement from his throne. "We'll proceed without him. We need to make our preparations for the arrival of Jarrid and Sara. Have you felt the trembling of the fortress walls?"

Well, bless my stones. It has started. Yes, Caleb speaks the truth. I have felt the tremors rattle my corridors and hallways, but prophecy fulfilled. I am not sure. I have waited so long for Sara to breach the veil and come into her rightful place among the councilmen. Will her throne be filled and prophecy engaged?

Wait, what did Tank say? My magic is waning a little; I am struggling to hear.

"Her throne has sat empty for too long." Tank's green feathers once more smoothed into place, as he rose from his throne and stated. "I can feel her presence. She has indeed breached the veil."

Oh look, do my eyes deceive me? Its Dax, he enters the chamber. We must listen to what information he brings to the council.

A few peacock feathers floated into the air, riding the gust of wind that preceded Dax, leaving a trail as he took his throne among the other councilmen. "I see you've started without me. A shame really since I've seen her. We rode the spiral wind that connects our worlds. I made sure the group came through the veil."

"What do you mean group?" Caleb's hazel eyes pierced through the black shroud and glared at the shapeshifter. "It should have only been Jarrid and Sara."

"Yes, the two who will fill the empty thrones, but fate has dictated other souls to fulfill prophecy. Don't you remember the words, the Evil One? She also comes to face her fate." Dax jumped to his feet and confronted Caleb. "It doesn't matter who or what, it is accomplished." He turned toward the door and demanded, "We need to gather everyone and let them know what's happening. Sara, Jarrid, and their group will reach the Great Room momentarily."

Oh, bless my hearth. It has come to pass. Okay, tour over, I must return to the Great Room and await her arrival. It is the beginning, the time to end all time. So, allow me to bid you adieu. You are on your own. It has begun!

BLOOD MOON
Chapter 18 United

Purple haze covered the cold stone walls. A ghostly green mist ebbed and flowed down the hall toward the Great Room and hovered close to the floor. Voices bounced off the jetted stones, the sounds pooled in small puddles gathered on the uneven floor.

Small streams of water flowed through the wall's nooks and crannies and dripped down into the crevasses to add their contributions to the ever-growing murky pools of water that dotted the stone floor.

The puddles echoed the rumbling coming from inside the walls. Each wave caused the water to ripple and bounce with a rhythmic dance, faster and faster to announce the parting of the veil. Events set in motion millennium ago, prophecy fulfilled, fate sealed by her passage through the castle wall.

No one, human or spirit, was present in the shadowy hall, to witness her fall to grace. The air morphed to erase all sound and light, leaving only void and darkness. No eyes to see the black, cold slice of time, the beginning of the end.

The feeling of falling brought up tides of nausea, deep in Sara's throat, the sensation waned and circled just under her breath. Jarrid held her as they fell, wrapped in his massive arms falling further and further into the void. He whispered close in her ear, "Sara, do not let go. I have you," his words served as the only anchor in this sea of nothingness.

His embrace made it difficult to raise her head, to look over his shoulder, their hair mingled together and tangled. Bolts of lightning struck and lit the vortex giant and swirling, its funnel rotating and collapsing. Each time the bolt cracked, the light focused on Nikko, Chad, and the rest of Anuk's group, their bodies just out of Sara's reach.

And then there was nothing.

"Auntie Sara, are you alright?" Lizzy's tears streamed down her face and fell on Sara's cheek. The kitten's cry fell upon Sara's ears like a symbol causing the ringing and the dull aches to echo with the beat of her heart.

Lizzy sat on the floor with the kitten wrapped tightly in her arms and waited for Sara to respond.

Alex and Nikko crawled to the corner and fell in a heap with Chad draped across their laps.

Jarrid lay on his side, scrunched up in the fetal position, and coughed violently. He called out, "Sara," his coughs stealing the very breath to fuel his words, "are you alright? Say something."

"Yes, I'm okay." Sara pulled herself up and crawled to Jarrid. She helped him sit to catch his breath.

Being a child, Lizzy ignored the bleak circumstances and joined Chad in the corner. "See, Kitty is okay, so we are okay, right, Mommy?"

"Yes, dear, we're fine, for the moment." She added under her breath. Nikko helped her up, and they turned their attention to Jarrid and Sara.

The kids accepted their mother's assurance and turned their attention to the black kitten, who was purring, head butting, and turning somersaults to land on his back in front of the two sprites.

They rubbed his ears and neck, spreading his black fur and letting it fall hair by hair, watching his blue-black skin reveal itself with each stroke. His shiny hair and dull skin was a backdrop for the blues and purples that seemed to jump right off his neck and out between the separated strands.

BLOOD MOON

"It's like Dax, Mommy." Lizzy jumped to her feet, spilling the kitten on the ground in the process. She screamed out to her mom, "The kitten has a pea bird feather on his neck, just like Dax."

The cry came from nowhere and consumed the hall; its bleak and dark tone caused shattering pain, the group cringed and covered their ears for protection from the loud sound. A vortex of wind circled the tiny kitten with a combination of dirt and peacock feathers to hide the nakedness of the tall stranger that rose from the form of Lizzy's feline friend.

Jarrid and Sara scrambled to their feet and backed up against the wall. Alex ran to gather the children and hid them from the man's reveal, as Nikko stepped up to confront the shapeshifter.

"Sorry, guys," Dax shot a smile in Alex's direction and gathered the peacock feathers together as a covering until Nikko offered him his cloak. "Guess I didn't think this through."

"Oh, it's Dax, the pea-bird man." Lizzy snuck out from Alex's grip and exclaimed. The entire group broke into uncontrollable laughter.

"Yes, Dax," Alex muffled the smirk and grin as she addressed the familiar man. "I remember. You helped me the night I took the children from my mother's house."

"Sorry about the theatrics," Dax added, "but I was trying to coax the children into the hall without them being afraid, but the doors closed before..." He shot Alex a look of defeat. She placed her hand over her heart in a gesture of understanding.

"So you are Dax, a shapeshifter?" Jarrid pushed forward to acknowledge the strange man and offered his handshake.

"Ah, yeah, just one of many freaks..." Alex shot him a glare and nodded toward the children. "Umm... I mean friends that will welcome you to this side of the Fortress." He lowered his voice and continued, "Our leader Caleb is the resident...alien Wolfen, and we even have our very own Sanguinarian, Sebastian, whom you are about to meet."

A question mark flooded Sara's face, and she mouthed the word 'vampire' to Alex making sure Lizzy didn't get her drift.

"Wait..." Jarrid looked around at the group, searching for the familiar raven hair and black cloak. "Did Anuk come through the wall?"

"Yes, the Village's Witch? She was hell-bent on following you two, but she protected Alex and Chad through the vortex." Dax shot a puzzled look in Jarrid's direction. "I can't imagine what that was all about?"

"Where is she now?" Jarrid reached out for Sara's hand, feeling the need to have her close in Anuk's absence.

A breeze floated through the group and caused Dax's cloak to fill like the bellow of a ship. He quickly gathered it and pointed down the hall toward the Great Room. "The vortex didn't affect her; she headed down the corridor toward the voices that rise on the wind. Do you hear them? They are waiting for you, Sara..." Dax reached down and took Lizzy's hand as he continued, "The woman from the wall, the Righteous One, sent to fulfill prophecy."

There was no argument to this fact; Sara had become accustomed to the title, and her inner Warrior Princess screamed in her soul, rising to the challenge.

BLOOD MOON

The small group led by the shapeshifter walked toward the Great Room. Lizzy tugged on Dax's hand and asked, "When will my kitty come back? I will miss him."

"If you are good, and listen to the adults, then maybe he can come and play with you, but you know I think he needs a name. Don't you?" Dax swung her hand and skipped down the hall, giggling like a schoolgirl at Lizzy's name choices.

"I know," quipped Dax, "How about Daxter?" The shapeshifter's contribution to the name game, the laughter filled the hall.

Excitement oozed from Lizzy's face. She dropped Dax's hand and ran back to greet Alex. "I'm going to be really good, Mommy, so I can play with my kitten, Daxter."

"Oh, Lizzy," Alex scooped her up, gave Dax a nod, and proclaimed, "You are such an optimistic child."

***

Thadeous looked up from scolding the teenage boy just as Caleb and Sebastian cleared the doorway of the Great Room. "Don't you have anything better to do? You should pick on someone your equal."

"Everyone, please settle down. I know that you are upset." Caleb slapped the giant on the back hard enough to make his battle gear sing and continued to address the room.

One of the men from the back addressed the leader, "Felt like an earthquake."

"It's nothing to concern your selves with." Caleb jumped on the table. "Your leaders are aware of the disturbance and understand its significance." Caleb squatted down and surveyed the room.

SARAH KAGE

"He is correct." Sebastian jumped up and stood over Caleb. "Our guest will be arriving soon. Please, do not be afraid."

The room was chaotic, the people spoke all at once, but one voice cracked like thunder to silence the crowd, "Guest indeed, who speaks of my presence so informally?"

All eyes focused on the voice coming from the door way. Caleb jumped down into her path and stared at the raven beauty, her body seeming to glide through the crowd; each person parted like the red sea.

Caleb's eyes fixated on the woman, her beauty captivated his soul, but the medallion that hung from her neck broke the spell, and he demanded, "How is it, woman, that you possess the sacred medallion?"

Before she could answer, Vincent jumped between them, raised his staff in the air, and called her out, "Witch, be gone!" The air circled her with the magic dying at her feet.

"So many questions," she raised her hand to dismiss Vincent's futile attempt at magic and brushed him away to disappear into the crowd, then focused her attention on the tall stranger now only inches from her face.

Tension physically gathered between the beauty and the beast. Its fury released as a ball of light that rushed toward the ceiling and dispersed in silver beams, like the ends of a child's sparkler.

The crowd backed away to leave the pair alone in the center of the room. Vincent shouted out, "Look the medallion." It floated, suspended in air, just between the adversaries. Its green glow pulsated and bounced off Caleb's shrouded eyes.

In a split-second decision, he lunged for the relic only to grab thin air and taste the dust gather in his throat, his face finding its place lodged up against Anuk's black pointed boot.

Laughter and giggles poured from the door opening, and every eye turned to see Dax, barefoot, hair tussled, pawing at folds of black material with one hand, and escorting Lizzy into the room with the other.

"I will deal with you later." Caleb mumbled at the witch. He gathered himself, wiped the dust from his pants, adjusted his pride, and parted the group to address Dax.

Lizzy hid behind Dax's cloak, still clutching the shapeshifter's hand. He dropped his grip and directed her to stand behind him, her wild-eyed stare peeked out from the folds of black material, and she gasped.

The dust rose and enveloped Caleb's feet as he rushed his fellow councilman, his eyes bursting with amber and gold, a sign of his wolf tendencies. Dax's hand fell sturdy on Lizzy's shoulder, moving her further behind his cloak, to increase the distance of the Wolfen's stare.

"Hey... cool your fleas." Dax bent his stare to the floor, not wanting to confront the Wolfen councilman.

Not lifting his eyes, Dax exclaimed, "I'd planned on introducing a rather less dominant leader to our queen."

"Wait..." Sara led her group and reached the door first. Jarrid pushed the others to beat her to the room.

"Sara, it's me, stop." Dax shouted. Lizzy turned just in time, her voice flowed up from the bottom of Dax's cloak, and she slid in front of him to avoid the impending collision.

Sara could not stop. She plowed into Dax and became tangled in a combination of him and his cloak, as he gathered Lizzy and jumped to avoid the inevitable storm. Her blazing red hair the thunder and Caleb's Wolfen eyes the lightning.

SARAH KAGE

The air seemed thin and inadequate. Time slowed, each blurred second filled with ancient memories. Caleb could resist no more; he reached out toward the red haired beauty and took her hand. "Raven is it... I feel your spirit. I..."

Sara wrenched her hand from his grip with little webs of lightning snapping to break the connection. Like the choreography of a practiced dance, the onlookers reacted to the event, their movements in unison to the commotion.

"Oh, no, this isn't going to end well." Alex's words were heard across the doorway just as Jarrid entered the room.

The statement rang in his ears as he shoved and confronted Caleb, starring into his Wolfen eyes, "Freak... back down."

"Wow, this is no way to treat our guests. Caleb, watch your manners." Dax positioned himself in between the two, man and beast. Jarrid backed down first and turned to Sara. "Did he hurt you?"

"I think you might want to ask Caleb that question, looked to me like she was handling the dog just fine until you burst in." Alex flashed a wink in Sara's direction and joined Dax in gathering the group together.

"Really Jarrid, she's right. I can handle myself." Sara laid her hand on his chest and moved to join the others. Jarrid caught Caleb's stare from across the room. His eyes focused on every move she made, ammunition for the jealous fire that raged just beneath his skin.

The low rattle of Jarrid's contention rolled across his face. He listened to Caleb, introduce himself to the group, and then there she was. Anuk stood close and teased Jarrid. "Well, it looks like Sara has quite the connection with the wolf."

BLOOD MOON

His fingers gripped around her neck as he pulled her feet off the ground and brought her face closer to his words, "Wolf, witch or prophecy makes no matter, Sara is mine!"

The words echoed and fell on Sara's ears just as he dropped Anuk back down and released his grip. "Oh, I would say that is not a look of approval on the queen's face." He shoved her away and headed toward Sara's stare, but she slinked away into the crowd to leave him with his doubt.

"Witch, you overstep your authority. You have a lot to learn." Vincent commanded and motioned for her to join him in a personal conversation.

Under her breath, the words formed, "Learn indeed. My reign will teach you just how hard it will be to endure your private hell." She flashed an arrogant smile and followed him into the shadows.

Two sets of eyes connected, Nikko's demeanor directed Jarrid to focus his attention on their mission. The old man gathered the kids and corralled the girls, his stance between Jarrid and Sara, a physical boundary to the discontent of the royal pair.

The crowd had been distracted with all of the chaos, but now became animated with their calls for explanations. "Who are these people? How can we trust them?"

"Prophecy..." Caleb reclaimed his position of authority and spoke out, "is how we trust these people."

A couple of the men of the group shook their fist in a rebellious gesture. "What makes you so sure these are the chosen ones?" The group agreed and seconded the question. "Bring us your truths so that we can decide for ourselves." The crowd agreed vigorously.

SARAH KAGE

Jarrid's feet rushed the crowd, pushed them back and toward the wall, he circled and pulled the satchel from behind his back, thrust the leather book into the air and proclaimed, "This book has withstood the ages to be delivered and known, to recognize and proclaim the truth you seek."

"*The Book of Souls*..." Caleb stood to confirm Jarrid's words, "Prophecy in written form."

Suddenly the weight of the book overtook Jarrid, and he lowered it to his side. The two men stood in a moment of brotherhood united by the truth of prophecy and the protection of their queen.

Still, the group was unsure and pushed for answers. "More magic, seems like that is what has gotten us into this mess." Shouts of agreement filled the chamber

The tug came from behind; Alex pushed through the crowd and pulled on Sara's arm. "How should I address you, my queen?"

Such force, the recoil surprised Alex, the gesture intense and brutal. Her face distorted to show her disapproval. "Knock it off, Alex. Don't you think you should be getting pictures of this? I'm sure Caleb would be more than happy to show his teeth."

It was like a clap of thunder, the realization between both professionals. "Sara, where is the backpack?"

The words spilled into the air with Alex's declaration, "Don't even joke about it; you brought it through the wall."

"No..." Sara reached her hands around to her back even though she knew it wasn't there.

"Wow, I think the backpack is the least of our worries." Alex declared with her fingers grabbing Sara's face and pointing it in the direction of the ceiling.

BLOOD MOON

There, perched on one of the insets of the wall, he crouched. Ashen skin, black hair, and sunken yellow eyes, Sebastian watched as the two women sunk behind the table.

"Is he gone?" Alex rose up to search for his face among the crowd. "Do you see him?"

The question needed no answer, with the vampire's cold breath tunneling down the length of Alex's neck, his closeness, now undeniable. He buried his face into her shoulder and inhaled her essence

"Hey, bloodsucker..." Sara grabbed his arm and twisted him away. "You need to get a grip. We're not your dinner."

"Oh, ladies, you misinterpret my intent. There's no thirst in this place. You are in no danger." He raised a dark eyebrow and added, "I was only admiring your... beauty."

"Indeed..." Sara stepped in front of Alex and willed the sanguinarian away, the bellow of his sleeve covered his eyes, and the hiss rolled off his tongue. He was gone in a flash.

"This book was written to accompany prophecy." Caleb reached and relieved Jarrid of its weight. The dirt rose up from the floor and circled the form of Sebastian as he materialized right between the two men.

"Hey, what gives?" Caleb cradled the book in his arms and shoved the dark form squarely into Jarrid.

The frustration seeped from Jarrid's eyes. He grabbed the vampire and removed him to the side, while releasing the wrath of his torment firmly in Caleb's direction, his hand thrust forward with its demand. "You will return the book."

The cold stare caught Caleb's attention. He turned toward the vampire and commanded, "Sebastian, be of some use and gather the councilmen to the Throne Room." His tone left no room for argument, Sebastian's yellow eyes flashed, and he was gone.

"I am the interpreter..." Caleb moved beside Jarrid, opened the book, and pointed to the phrase.

> *"The poisoned angel will lead the fold into slaughter with the dragon."*

All resistance fell from Jarrid's demeanor, and he accepted Caleb's words as prophecy fulfilled.

> *"The Evil One will lead the undead in their war against the righteous, to win the evil battle her transformation born of the frenzy that will take many sheep."*

Caleb searched Jarrid's eyes for understanding.

A small breeze blew down upon the book and turned the yellow parchment pages to reveal the answers. Jarrid met Caleb's stare and spoke, "Its Anuk. She is the Poisoned Angel."

"Yes, and she wants you to reign with her, to be her dark mate." Caleb waited for this revelation to sink into the depths of Jarrid's soul.

"She tortures my mind and seduces me with her evil; your words are true." Jarrid's eyes rose to meet Caleb's stare with the embers of Anuk's fire glowing in his mind's eye, the scene of his transgression.

"It is time." Dax moved from the shadows and into the space occupied by *The Book of Souls*. He locked eyes with Caleb and then disappeared into the crowd.

BLOOD MOON

"Time for... what is this trickery?" Caleb didn't answer but closed the book and surveyed the room for his queen.

"No deceit, just Sara's rise to her station as our leader." Caleb left Jarrid to contemplate his words and moved toward the center of the room.

"Everyone gather around. The time has come to grant your six councilmen the right to coronate Sara as your leader against the undead." Caleb jumped on the table and searched the room for her red hair.

"This place gets creepier every second." Alex slumped into the chair, but the thought of the missing camera interrupted her posture, and she bolted forward to ask, "The backpack didn't make it through the wall, huh?"

"Doesn't appear that it did...," Sara shrugged her shoulders, "guess fate dictated that outcome. I'm not sure our lives beyond these walls even exist anymore. Kind of makes the camera irrelevant." Sara never dropped her eyes from the fact that Caleb was standing on top of a table and staring intently in her direction.

He recognized her stare and shouted across the room, "Sara, are you ready to meet your destiny?" The crowd cheered, now content to follow their leaders, but Sara only heard some of Caleb's words.

"What's he talking about, am I ready?" Jarrid pushed through the sea of people and pulled Sara to the side. "We are summoned to the Throne Room, something about your coronation as their leader."

All she heard was leader, something inside rose up, an emotion buried for all eternity, to burst through and ignite her Warrior-Princess battle cry. "And lead, I shall."

***

The large wooden doors responded to Dax's demand and opened to reveal the large room with its ornate battle symbols and ancient artifacts. A light from some unknown source, shown on the main throne and illuminated its jeweled arms and stone carved legs. Five councilmen adorned their places of leadership; Caleb sat on the edge of the largest stone chair. He pointed toward the empty throne between Sebastian and Dax, just to his right. "This has been reserved for the head councilman of the village, Jarrid, your rightful place in our world."

"These symbols of leadership..." Sebastian's voice filled the chamber, "they have stood since the beginning, even before the Lykoan War." He moved from under the symbol of his Pendas crest and continued, "Each bloodline represented by the stone chairs that circle this chamber."

The fairy councilman took his cue, "My Fae ancestors used the Fortress as the entrance to the human realm." Tank moved to escort Jarrid to his throne, "Before the time of the tribulation that separated the two realms."

Dax offered his hand to escort Sara to her throne and explained, "From the beginning, the shapeshifters of the worlds were granted the ability to cross the veil and influence the human race, a kind of gift between the worlds of fantasy and reality."

His staff clicked each time it met the floor. "Your coronation will bring evil to the surface, put in motion prophecy, and unite the realms..." Vincent touched the staff to the leg of the royal throne, and it vibrated to life, "its battle rages in these walls as we speak."

"This debt that I owe, a promise from my ancestor Uther Pendas, to the Dark Prince..." Sebastian slid into his place under the crest of the Pendas bloodline, "the battle of the Righteous One, my burden to bear."

The vibration coming from the seat of power pulled at Sara's soul. Caleb took her hand, persuaded her to take her place among the six heads of state, to reign as their queen and the deliverer of prophecy.

"You are our destiny and true salvation. We pledge our loyalty and protection to you, Sara." Six men now knelt, their heads bowed with reverence and hope.

The arms of the hard stone chair caressed her skin; her back pressed against the ancient chair as the vibration pulsed through her entire being. The six bowed heads fueled the electricity pulsing through her veins, gathering where her fingertips touched the stone. Her stare caused Jarrid to raise his eyes, to see the electricity flow from her hands, just as Tank rose to his feet and spoke out loud, "Sara, you are fairy!"

SARAH KAGE
Chapter 19 The Dragon Slumbers

S tatic electricity hung in the air and rained down, bouncing off the thrones, only to dissipate into the cold stone floor. Each council member stood lifeless and void, no reactions to Tank's words, left to stare at their queen, and ponder the realization of her Fae birthright.

Two men with different agenda's approached her throne. "No, Jarrid, stay back." Sara folded her arms against her body to corral the unruly lightning and continued. "I can't control it. I don't want to hurt you."

"Please, let me help." Jarrid stepped forward, ignoring her fear. "You won't hurt me."

Her stare rose up like an ocean wave, breaking against his words, the force causing him to pause, her question haunting, she asked, "How can you be sure?"

"Did your family speak of its fairy lineage?" Tank placed his hand in the middle of Jarrid's chest, and gestured for his patience, "I can teach you, Sara, how to control the light." Tank turned from Jarrid, offering his help.

"Fairy…" Jarrid ignored Tank and rushed Sara pushing him aside. "Really, you believe this freak?" His question directed into Sara's eyes.

"No… I don't know." Her shoulder brushed against Jarrid, leaving the sting of a crackle, the left-over electricity that still surrounded her body.

"Tank, do you think she is a fairy?" Caleb stood in the shadow of the thrones, "How could she not know this?"

"Sara, stop," Tank's grasp prevented her from leaving, immune to the lightning bolt running down the length of his arm. "This is a gift handed down from your fairy

BLOOD MOON

bloodline." He addressed Caleb's question, "I think it was activated when she came through the veil."

"Gift…, fairy…" she stopped, tilted her head, and realized, "Tank, you're immune. How is that possible?"

"We are kindred and impervious to each other's gifts." Tank took her hand to prove his statement. "How do you not know of your heritage?"

"Enough of your interrogation," Jarrid reached for Sara and once again came face-to-face with her gift; its fury surrounded his body and left him limp to kneel in front of his queen.

"Are you going to continue being a stubborn ass?" Tank shouted as Jarrid rose to his feet and stepped back. "Or maybe you'll listen to me now?"

"Please, Jarrid," Sara reached out to close the distance between them but pulled back her touch. "I have to deal with this. Let Tank help."

A silence fell over the room; each man offered their support in a show of unity and stood their ground to place confidence in Tank's abilities. Jarrid reluctantly followed suit, knowing he could not live without her touch; he surrendered to Tank's will.

"Do you trust me?" Tank guided Sara back to her throne; her electricity enveloped him with no effect. "You must center yourself." He gently placed her in the cold seat and knelt beside her.

"I am Fae?" She brought her hands together, watching the bright branches of light dance between her fingertips. She dropped her hands into her lap; her surrender caused Tank to rise.

"Yes," He moved closer and looked into her eyes. "Fae lineage from somewhere in your ancestry, buried by the millenniums. From the strength of the gift, I would say you have royal fairy blood in your family."

SARAH KAGE

A gasp filled the chamber with the men speaking one to the other, "Royal bloodline, the prophecy didn't predict that outcome."

"This gift will surely help defeat the Evil One." Caleb stepped forward with his observation.

"Wait," Sara rose and stomped her foot. "It's all so overwhelming. This so-called gift is starting to feel like a curse." She dropped back down to sit with her words ringing out into the chamber. "I can't touch the man I love for fear of inflicting great pain, and now you say I must battle the Evil One with these lightning bolts from Hell."

"Sara, it is not a curse..." Tanks feathers ruffled loudly. "If the truth be known, the lightning won't affect most of our enemies. Some entities are immune." Sara started to rise again to protest his words. He confronted her to stop and listen. "I'll teach you to control it."

"Wait, it won't affect the freaks, but inflicts pain on the man I love. What good is it? I need to give this back to whoever; I denounce its existence. Control it! Oh no, I want it gone." Sara slumped back into her throne and moaned with frustration.

"Look," Jarrid rose and confronted Tank. "It is of no value. You must do something."

"Wait, hold on just a minute." Caleb rushed the throne and spoke, "How can you be so sure that this talent is not of some significance? We may not be able to understand its true capacity; let us not be hasty."

"Can't you put a governor on her," Sebastian added his opinion and pressed the matter, "or suppress it somehow?"

"No," Sara's temper emphasized her words. "I want no part of it." She glared at Jarrid, remembering the look of pain; his face grimaced with each of her touches. "It must be banished forever."

"There is one thing I can do." Tank paused and continued, "Sebastian is correct. I can cap it off, force it to reside deep in her psyche, but it won't last, its force will be released."

"Yes," Caleb stepped up to her throne and petitioned the queen. "Sara, what if it's a gift from God? The one tool to save the world and fulfill your destiny, it's too valuable to snuff out altogether."

"You know better than anyone here, Caleb..." Sara clutched at her heart, a motion of empathy. "The agony of not being able to touch the one you love. It is your life every day." Sara hung her head and spoke the words softly, "I am not willing to do that on purpose."

"Please..." Caleb paused to puzzle for a moment, then looked into Tank's eyes as he pleaded with Sara, "Give him a chance to bury it, at least until you can learn to command it."

The scraping of the wooden doors against the stone floor echoed through the chamber, announcing her entrance, like rolling thunder. Caleb rushed the intruder and placed his body between the witch and his queen. Jarrid joined him seconds later to form the base of the triangle, a formation to protect Sara from the witch's powers enhanced by the glowing medallion hanging from her neck.

Green iridescent feathers ruffled to reveal Tank's fairy wings, engaged to anchor his feet at the point of the triangular formation, but Sara brushed him aside, having no part of his brave gesture, her Warrior Princess now in full battle mode.

The other councilmen formed an arch behind Sara and stood to confront the witch, compelled to use whatever force necessary to protect and honor the Righteous One. Tank retracted his wings and pushed his way to the center of the semicircle, hell-bent on assisting her whether she needed it or not.

"Oh my, such a show of force, really, guys, I only want to talk to her." Anuk moved closer, causing Jarrid and Caleb to close ranks, preventing her approach.

"You are not welcome. This ritual is for royalty only." Vincent left the formation and pointed his staff directly at the witch. "You have no business here."

"Oh contraire," she shifted her weight to gaze into Jarrid's eyes. "I think the Village Councilman would disagree with that statement." She rose on tippy-toes, whispered in Jarrid's ear, and kissed him on the cheek.

The air sucked out of the chamber, a reaction to the anger flowing through Sara, the lightning striking with multiple bolts to scatter the men to the farthest corners of the chamber.

Static air rose and directed the blue lights to form a web of electricity, with its force pinning the men to the inner walls. Sara engaged her hand to shoot a large bolt in Anuk's direction; it caught her just as the evil laughter left her throat and prevented her from any further taunts.

Breezes from the force of the electricity circled the room, Sara's red hair flowed like fiery flames, licking and kissing her cheeks, spurring her on. Each moment that passed fueled Sara's confidence, giving her the strength to continue her attack.

The power of the large bolt lifted Anuk into the air. Her eyes rolled back in her head, raven hair floated in the air, weightless and untamed. The councilmen helpless, witnesses to the intensity of this unbridled power now uncontrollable, loose in the chamber.

BLOOD MOON

The raven-haired witch trembled, forcing her arms to wave in the air to banish the fairy magic. She lowered her head, sucked in the bolt and broke the connection, falling to the floor in a crumpled heap.

Air once again enveloped the room and allowed the men to recover their will. Sara's voice blew like a trumpet, "Oh, no, you don't." She tried once more to restrain the witch. But her anger was spent with the manifestation of the lightning bolts.

Each councilmember acted with hive mentality and circled Sara to protect their queen, the gesture only infuriated her, and she broke through their protection just in time to see Anuk recover.

Even Sara's uncontrollable trembling could not induce the bolts to flow from her fingertips, her anger spent. Anuk straightened her cloak and brushed her hair out of her eyes. "Well, that was quite a show, but is that all you've got." She walked closer and spouted her words for all to hear. "So you are Fae, but as you can see, it will take a lot more than mere electricity to stop me."

"Oh, there's more..." Sara stepped closer to emphasize her words. "That was just the tip of the magic. I was holding back." She separated her feet and stood to confront the witch, "I will defeat you."

"This medallion, which I confiscated from Jarrid, oh, and you should press him for those details. I think you will find them—a bit juicy." She confronted Jarrid, brushing his body as she turned to continue, "The magic of this ancient relic will assure my success in defeating you, besides I don't think you can control your newfound powers."

"Jarrid has told me how you mesmerized him and stole the medallion. Witch be gone! You have no power over me." Sara rushed Anuk and stood her ground.

SARAH KAGE

"So Jarrid, you told her the whole story?" The look poured over Jarrid's face, a look of complete fear, the one secret not yet divulged, the one Jarrid knew he could never admit. "Is that a yes? I am sure there are no secrets between you."

"The medallion hangs from your neck," Caleb pushed forward and confronted Anuk. "But you will never win, I can guarantee it."

"Wolf, leave me. I still have tricks up my sleeve, things you know nothing about."

Anuk turned to leave the chamber, Caleb's Wolfen eyes shown amber with the promise of his transformation and he stepped between her and the door. "Your promises, the change you are seeking, it is close upon you, but mark my words, you will not have Jarrid as your dark mate."

Her black eyes flashed with the swish of her cloak, and she addressed Sara, "Oh, I wouldn't count on that. We will have to wait and see."

"Where... What," Sara's mouth opened to form the words, to argue Anuk's point, but she was gone, vanished from the Throne Room with only the wooden doors slamming shut to announce her exit.

"She is the most annoying woman I have ever met!" Sara stood in the middle of the chamber with her fist rolled up, banging against her thighs. "She has a nasty habit of disappearing just when I figure out some perfect comebacks."

"Anuk is a witch..." Vincent paced toward the doors and shoved his staff in their direction, "she was born that way."

"Born indeed..." Caleb stepped in front of Sara and offered his hand, "are you sure she wasn't hatched?" He guided Sara toward the hall and looked back over his

BLOOD MOON

shoulder, "My brothers, join me, we must gather our people and prepare to move them to safer accommodations further inside the Fortress."

The sight of the Wolfen taking Sara's hand bubbled up in Jarrid's gut and colored his response, "Born is too human, I think Anuk was vomited up from the bowels of Hell."

The rush from behind took Sara by surprise. Jarrid's authority evident in the abrupt way he encouraged her to hurry toward the hall. He walked beside her and whispered in her ear, "Must not get too friendly with the dog!"

Vincent pulled Jarrid's shoulder from behind before he could finish his sarcasm, separating him from Sara and Caleb. "You have much to learn about women." Vincent's large hand lay heavy on Jarrid's shoulder, forcing him to walk ten paces behind the others.

"Hey..." Jarrid rolled out from under his grasp and bellowed, "Watch it old man. How is it you are giving me pointers on women. I do not see a female warming your bed." Vincent let out a heartfelt laugh and continued to offer his words of wisdom.

***

The crowd cheered as the councilmen filled the Great Room. "Three cheers for our leaders and our newly anointed queen." Fists beat on the wooden tables, the substitution for a cold mug of beer; animated gestures welcomed Sara into her new role.

Not to be one-upped, Lizzy parted the crowd and shouted from clear across the room, "Auntie Queen..." her curls bounced, fingers laced with Chad's hand, she dragged him through the mob as her ever-present sidekick.

SARAH KAGE

She stopped just short of Sara and pulled Chad, front and center. "Auntie Queen, were there kings and horses at your party?" She fussed with Chad and prompted him to stand still and at attention. "This is our queen, Chad. You must bow." She tossed her curls and attempted to curtsy, spreading her shirt out by her side.

The smirk was not containable, and Sara giggled, "Oh, Lizzy. Nothing has changed; you may still call me Auntie."

"Oh, I do not know," she pulled on Chad's hand and forced him to stand still, "I think we shall call you Queenie."

"Must I also call you Queenie?" Alex stood next to Sara and watched her kids skip away to rub shoulders with the other children of the group. "You know, without a doubt, my daughter is name-dropping as we speak."

"Have you noticed?" Sara tilted her head toward Sebastian, "He can't keep his eyes off you, girl." The vampire threw Alex a wink while he mingled among the group, spoke with the leaders, and prepared for the move.

"How could I not feel that stare, it's intense, but really, he's a vampire." Alex mouthed the words, but her body betrayed the very statement.

"And when has the fact that a man's a bad boy, ever stopped you before?" Sara dropped the zinger, shot Alex a sarcastic look, and made her way to join Caleb and Jarrid.

"Sara…" Jarrid reached out his hand as she approached, but she hesitated. He ignored her reaction. "No, do not… I need you to touch me."

BLOOD MOON

Tank offered his hand as a barrier, "You must allow me to bury the lightning. Please, Sara, there's no other way."

"I cannot..." Jarrid moved to take Sara's hand as he proclaimed, "I will not live without your touch. Do it, let Caleb and Tank help you control this gift."

Flashes of always recoiling from Jarrid's touch scoured her face and carved deep lines into her forehead. "Okay, just make sure it stays hidden. I don't want to know it exists."

"Do you trust me?" Caleb tugged on Sara's hand but looked deep into Jarrid's eyes. "Sara, come to my room tonight."

"Alone with you..." Jarrid shouted through his gritted teeth, "No way in Hell!"

"Oh, I see the green-eyed monster raises its ugly head." Caleb declared, "Tank will perform the magic, but my wolfness will intensify his power?" Caleb backed away to give his words some space.

"Wait, Tank can be there, and I can't?" Jarrid's anger morphed into a childlike question.

"Look, this won't be an easy procedure. We need all of Sara's concentration on the task at hand. Not looking at you to see if you're upset or jealous. Do you get my drift?" Caleb offered his up-turned palms as a gesture of understanding.

The words stuck in Jarrid's throat gathered just before his tongue and nearly choked the life out of the statement, "Yes... I agree. Whatever you think is best, Caleb."

"Do you agree to these conditions, Sara?" Caleb waited for what seemed like an eternity.

"Yes... just make it go away." She fell into Jarrid's arms, no hesitation, the lightning momentarily exhausted, needing to feel his strength flow through her body and to assure him that she was still his, body and soul.

"Everyone, please gather round." Caleb assumed his usual position on the tabletop and addressed the group. "We need to retire and rest; I plan on moving the group further up the hall and past the courtyard toward the towers." The councilmen gathered around the table to add their support to Caleb's words. "We feel it will be safer and provide a better vantage point against the attack of the Army of Darkness."

"Undead?" Alex's question spilled into the room just as Sebastian circled her and jumped up to join Caleb on his lofty stage.

"Yes..." He crouched down and looked into Alex's eyes as if she were the only person in the room. His stare relentless he continued, "The Army of Darkness, the Devil's Zombies, they have many names."

He slowly motioned with his outstretched finger for her to come closer. The choice was not hers, and she obeyed. Her face was only inches away from the vampire, the sharpened fingernail sprung from his fingertip, and he slowly moved her hair back behind her ear, bent forward and whispered, "They will suck the very life from you..." his breath tunneled in her ear. " And take your soul for the Dark Prince."

"Come on..." Sara grabbed Alex's arm and removed her from the trance of the hypnotist. "You need to keep your charm to yourself, vampire!"

The laugh started deep in his chest and rang out as he proclaimed, "Oh, but it oozes out to be captured by the night; I can't help it." Again the laughter rang out with Sebastian jumping from the table to follow the women through the crowd.

BLOOD MOON

"Walk faster, Alex." Sara dragged her, dodging the curious eyes, trying to put space between them and the vampire. She took a second to peer over her shoulder, hoping against hope that he would have lost the desire for the chase.

"Hey, what gives?" Sara had stopped—dead. Alex collided into her just as she turned and planted her feet on the floor. "Have you changed your mind about Sebastian?"

The words were muffled by Sara's hand, crumpling Alex's face, fingers pressed against her cheek, turning her in the direction of the bright light that filled every corner of the Great Room.

Screams echoed each one louder than the next. The light centered in the room and shone down, dispersing across the floor to push the people back. Sara fought her way to stand in the light-beam and addressed the room, "Please, do not be afraid!"

There was a disturbance in the crowd, their stances separated by some unseen entity. "Queenie, is it my angel?" Lizzy burst through and ran to Sara, grabbing her legs with her head pointed up toward the ceiling. "Is it Angelica?"

"Everyone, she will not harm you." Sara embraced Lizzy and stepped back to the edge of the crowd. "She is our guardian."

The screams of the people vanished into the air, replaced by the wonderment of words with praise and adornment. The entity floated down on a beam of light with her wings folded around her soul, her feet touched the floor, and the light dispersed through the room to extend out and down the long corridor.

It started slowly at first, the ruffling of her feathers, the pearlescent white blinding as each wing gradually unfolded to reveal the beautiful angel. Her smile beamed and foreshadowed her message. "Good people, please do not fear one another, you are the Army of Light. Look around and memorize the faces in this room."

Caleb pushed through the crowd and spoke, "Who are you? What are your intentions?" The angel stepped toward the Wolfen and touched his shoulder, "My fellow being, I am called Angelica, and your name is Caleb; one of God's creatures." The fight left Caleb's body, her words a confirmation of his place in the coming battle.

Her voice rose, and she spoke, the words filled the room. "These faces will be your salvation and your only allies. In the coming days, know each other well and learn to rely on one another."

The features on her face distorted slightly to match the foreboding words that followed, "These tidings I bring in joy, but I say to you, like the evil in the world, this is not a perfect group. Like the lamb before, one among you will be a betrayer."

Angelica moved closer to Sara and Lizzy, her words rolled across the floor and burst into dark phrases, "The metamorphosis will take place, and the demonic throne claimed. Take refuge in the fact that in mortal form, the Evil One cannot harm you."

The angel turned her attention to the leaders. "Jarrid trust Caleb. Invite him to teach you the things that you will need from *The Book of Souls*, to survive the coming assault."

The slightest movement of her wings lifted her to tower over the Army of Light, her words punctuated by the pulsing beams of light, "And I say to you, this is the last battle of good and evil. Your actions will determine the fate of humanity and whether good or evil will reign on this earth." The wings started to envelop her light; she bowed her head to the leaders and started her ascent.

"Angelica, please do not go!" Lizzy's fingers reached out to caress her glowing robe. The illumination touched the small girl and kissed her soul.

The angel looked down into her eyes and declared, "My little Lizzy, you were the first to believe in me." The entity touched the girls glowing curls and continued, "Through your love, I was able to fulfill my duty. You will always be blessed. Just remember the Father, and I love you." She touched Lizzy on the top of her head, folded her wings, and disappeared into the darkness.

"Imagine that; we are God's creatures…" Sebastian confronted Caleb and mocked the angel's words. "Do you think there is a heaven for us, brother?"

"So who do you attribute our creation to, but God. Aliens and freaks have a creator. God does not make mistakes." His words offered with passion.

Sebastian stared off into the distance with his yellow eyes searching for the woman he would cross eternity for, a human woman and a vampire, surely not a union sanctioned by God. His words slipped across his glistening fangs, "Oh, but to be mortal!"

The people slowly regained their wits and mingled about gathering their belongings for the move. Jarrid had stopped to help a gaggle of young girls who had dropped their satchels. "I bet they dropped those on purpose just to watch his muscles ripple in the candlelight." Alex grabbed Sara and pointed her in the direction of the spectacle.

"Could they be any more obvious, on purpose, indeed?" Sara's eyebrows rose as she snorted, "listen to the insidious giggles. It's humiliating to watch." She turned her head, not wanting to witness the girlish flirting.

"Come on, Sara. You've got to admit the man is fine. Can you blame them?" Sara's gaze was directed to watch one of the girls lay her hand on Jarrid's shoulder and flash her eyes, relentlessly, as she snickered, "Oh, Jarrid, you are so strong."

"I think those girls could use some more help. Don't you agree, Alex?" Sara's fire rose on her face, she moved Alex to the side and stomped off to enlighten the young girls on the art of; 'he is mine!'

The shove landed Alex directly into the arms of the resident vampire. A loud gasp crossed her lips. His hands wound tight around her arms; he stared into her eyes and asked, "Would you be willing to escort me to my chambers? I need you. There is something I would like to discuss."

"Stop pulling that glamour-crap on me!" She shook him off like a bad dream. "Really, if you need something, just ask, okay?" She pointed toward the door and motioned for him to lead the way. Before following the sanguinarian out the door, she searched the corner for Sara and shouted the words across the room, "I'm going with him."

The argument filled the air. A profane 'No,' Sara's disagreement of Alex's distinct lack of common sense; flooded above the crowd. The form of the syllables struck Alex's eye, but their sound fell on a deaf ear.

BLOOD MOON
Chapter 20 Mortal Dreams

The atmosphere lay heavy and gray, so saturated with foreboding that Sara half expected a storm to gather in the corner and rain down on the few people still gathered in the Great Room.

A small corner was carved out and fitted with a make-shift bed. Jarrid tucked Lizzy and Chad under the dreary covering and sat on the floor, waiting for their eyes to close from the heaviness of the day.

Jarrid's last statement to Sara floated across his mind. *You must rid yourself of this thing that threatens our union,* his eyes cloudy with the fear of 'never touching her again,' he hurried the children to sleep, his distraction for the night.

"I'm leaving now…" Sara instinctively reached to touch Jarrid's shoulder but second-guessed the gesture, raised her hand to her lips, and blew him a kiss instead.

"Are you ready?" Tank's face appeared at the door. "Didn't want you to be in the hall alone, Caleb sent me to escort you." He bowed and pointed toward the hall.

He could feel her cold stare penetrating his back; he turned to witness her angry face as she proclaimed. "An escort, for the queen, the one you have all laid your bets upon, wagering she will defeat the Evil One." Sara rushed past Tank, exercising her ability to protect herself, her words filling the dark hall. "Gah, I give up!"

"Do you even know where you're going?" Tank rushed ahead to corral the headstrong, dominant queen, now stopped dead in her tracks.

"Sure…" She grunted her face redder than the curls that hung in her eyes. "To meet up with Caleb, who is in his…?" Softness draped across her features, and she admitted. "Okay, I might need a little help. Lead the way."

The doorway branched off the hall, its entrance curved to conceal the fact of the vast, cold room decorated with shelves of books and war artifacts. Caleb stood in the dim light with a weathered book, its pages bathed in candlelight.

"I see you're still angry, probably a good thing." Caleb lifted his eyes toward his queen. "Your power will be closer to the surface and easier to deal with." He closed the book and motioned for her to take a seat.

"You can thank Tank for my anger, although I hear it was your idea to have me escorted." Caleb brought his eyes up and stared into her fairy gaze.

"I think standing will be a better vantage point," Tank insisted, "Here Sara, up against this wall." Caleb was right. The anger ignited the blue lightning to flow through her body and conduct into Tank's hands as he pulled her under the light, pushing her against the wall.

"Good thing you're immune, huh?" Sara jammed her back against the wall and proclaimed, "Let's get this over with!"

"Are you sure this is what you want?" Caleb touched her arm and watched the spider web of electricity travel up toward his shoulder, raising the tiny hairs, a symptom of the heightened sensation of her power.

"Would you want to touch Raven again?" Sara asked. The question caused Caleb to fall back; his mind raced with the revelation of her name.

"Okay, we need to do this now while her powers are flowing." Tank stood in front of Sara and steadied himself against her shoulders. "Caleb, are you going to help or what?"

BLOOD MOON

"Sorry…" he stared into Sara's eyes for understanding. " Tank, what do you need me to do?"

"Once I get the connection to her power, I need you to put your hands on my shoulders and pull as much of your wolfness forward as you can." He faced Sara and instructed. "I need you to go down deep, try to find the source of the power, feel it in your gut." Sara scrunched her face and reached inside with her heart pounding. Tank spoke his next command, "Let your mind go blank, call to it."

"Keep vigilant, Caleb. It will happen in the blink of an eye. Be ready." Tank placed his hands on her stomach as if to will the power out into the open. His hands cupped against her skin, her mid-drift exposed. "The electricity is crossing my barrier." Tank anchored his grip.

"I can feel its intensity." Caleb steadied his feet, waiting for Tank's instructions.

The ohms flowed and circled the room, growing louder with each passing second. Tank yelled out, "Now, Caleb, grab my shoulders."

The blue light followed the path of least resistance and encased Caleb from his hands to his feet. "Tank, I can feel it too, is that suppose to happen?"

"Hang on and do your wolf thing, concentrate. I need your power to connect to the other side." Sara's body trembled, and Tank struggled to keep his hands pressed hard against her. "I'm starting to break through, amp it up a little." Sweat poured from Caleb's forehead, his face contorted, with his transformation just under his skin.

Tank's head fell forward just as the room exploded with the exit of all power. He fell against Sara, and they slid together onto the floor in a pile.

"Are you guys, okay?" Caleb shook off the effects of the ritual and approached Sara. "Say something. Are you alive?"

He pushed her hair from her face and used his sleeve to wipe the sweat away. "Jarrid…" she whispered. Tank pulled himself to the wall and propped his weary body against the stones.

"Caleb…" Sara pushed away and scurried toward the other wall. "What… What happened? Is it done?"

"Who the hell is Raven…?" Tank blurted out, "Damn, girl! You have a Royal Fairy Grandmother!" Tank's face glowed, and his eyes were as big as saucers.

"How is it you speak of Raven? What did you see?" Caleb addressed Tank and pushed the matter fiercely.

"Cool your fleas; give me a second to gather myself." Tank's first concern was to assure Sara, and he spoke directly to the queen. "Your Fairy Grandmother, Lucinda, came across the barrier and enlightened me to your lineage. She was a high Fairy Priestess, which explains your power."

"That's great, and all, but is it controlled?" Sara rose to her feet and pressed for the answer to her question. "Is it buried?"

"Raven, you called her name…" Caleb pulled on Tank's shoulder to get his attention. "Why did that name come out of the ritual?"

"I think I can explain." Sara crossed the room and approached Caleb. "Do you remember in the Throne Room when everyone was telling me to keep the power, and I spoke of your longing to touch a loved one every day?"

"Yes, I remember pausing because the statement was so personal and strange. What did it mean?"

BLOOD MOON

Her head lowered, and she continued, "The first time we met, and you took my hand, do you remember my reaction?"

"Yes…" Caleb pondered the encounter as he spoke, "I felt something in your touch, the essence of my dead wife, Raven, flowed through you." Caleb searched Sara's face for understanding. "I could feel her spirit pouring from your touch."

"Do I look like her, Caleb?" Sara circled the room to stand in front of the Wolfen.

"No, not at all, but Raven's spirit fell upon me and washed away hundreds of years of yearning and loss; I could not help myself."

"Sara, you speak as if you know her." Caleb's curiosity piqued; he rushed her for more information. "How is that possible?"

"Her spirit came through the portal, just like Lucinda." Tank spoke, trying to lighten the mood. "Girl, it's pretty crowded in there."

"Do you think…?" Caleb lowered his head, a little ashamed even to ask the question. "Could we do it again; maybe I can communicate with her."

"We cannot risk it!" Tank shouted the words without thinking. "I'm so sorry, Caleb, but the attempt would be at Sara's risk."

"Your pain is my pain, Caleb. I've endured your sorrow for only a day, and my heart aches for you." She melted into his embrace, a token of her understanding. "With all the magic around us, maybe there's another way. I promise you we'll try." Sara backed away to let him come to grips with his grief.

"Sara…" Tank guided her toward the door. "Your gift is buried. I don't know for how long, but you should get a warning before it comes back to full strength."

SARAH KAGE

"Thank you, Tank, for honoring my wishes." A smirk rolled across her lips, "Lucinda, huh? A Fairy Priestess, no doubt, that should make for some interesting late-night conversations." She turned to leave with her hand in the air to discourage Tank from accompanying her, "I will be fine; I think Caleb could use a strong fairy friend right about now." She slipped out the door, her heart racing with anticipation of once again touching the man she loved.

***

It was a cave, with its cold stone walls, hanging stalactites, large cracks, and deep crevices. Carved out from a smaller hole that branched off the hall and tunneled into the mountain, backed up against the Fortress.

Alex followed Sebastian down the corridor watching his stride, telling herself it would just be a conversation between acquaintances. But her arguments faded with the allure of his swagger.

She watched him stop just in front of the cave opening. He gestured for her to enter; his yellow eyes flashed and sparkled. *Would it be of her own free will the obedience to this alien creature?* Her question answered with the opening of her heart while she passed into the massive cave.

"I'm not surprised you accepted my invitation." Sebastian removed his shirt and hung it on one of the stones that jutted out from the cave wall. "I've seen your heart; it's adventurous."

Her eyes, naughty and disobedient, drank him in. His chest rippled, the muscles accentuated by the ashen skin tone. His long black hair fell on his shoulders, reflective like a mirror, to frame his yellow eyes that danced in the light.

BLOOD MOON

"You're a little cocky, wouldn't you say?" Alex backed against the stone wall; her voice squeaked with sarcasm.

A laugh conjured in his throat. "Cocky, what a fitting word." he walked toward her, positioned his hand on the wall above her head, leaned into his arm, buried his face into her hair and sucked in her very essence.

"I knew there was more on your mind than just a conversation." She leaned under his arm and slipped away from his stance.

The whirlwind surprised her; a flash and his body pushed hard against her, forcing her back into the indented cave wall. "I do believe you read between my lines, Alex. I can smell that you're here of your own free will."

He anchored his legs, pushed hard against her, searched for her mouth, and unleashed a thousand years of pent up frustrations.

She responded, every molecule of her being broke open in surrender. Still, she hesitated, her hands the only thing still under her control; she shoved the alien back, escaping his lustful manner.

"Hmm, you resist, but I know the truth, felt your desire, tasted your need." He followed her into the center of the cave.

"Your face..." Alex peered into his eyes; the light from the lanterns shone the pinkness gathered in his cheeks. She moved closer and touched his skin, now almost red. "You are warm... How...?"

He moved a little closer, just enough to make his answer intimate. "I'm not a folklore vampire, Alex." He reached for her hand. "You can feel the warmth flow through my veins. When I'm aroused, my blood flows stronger and raises my body temperature."

SARAH KAGE

"So, I guess you don't sparkle." A little giggle escaped into the cave, a sign she was trying to lighten the moment. "So, what other unique attributes do you possess?" She resisted his charm and backed away.

Once again, she was against the wall; Sebastian's hands smoothed her hair from her face, and he whispered, "I would rather show you."

He kept the pressure on her body, leaned against her, and breathed short warm breaths down her neck.

His sigh fell on her skin and caused her head to tilt, an offering of her submission to his alien desires. The blood coursed just below her skin, his thirst irrelevant. Beads of sweat burst under the pressure of his lips, with each kiss tattooed by his sharp fangs.

Small trembles erupted from her shoulders; she gasped and stated, "I can feel your heartbeat."

He didn't acknowledge her words, his passion rising; he continued his reveal. He placed his hand across her eyes and threw his head back. The visions played out in the air of the cave, holograms of his alien world, and the Lykoan war between the alien races of Vampire and Wolfen. Her eyes filled with the revelations of his alien bloodline, the union of Drakoids giving birth to pure Vampires, his ancestral beginnings. His memories were flooding her mind.

Her body limp, Sebastian braced her, lifting her arms over his shoulders. "You are now part of me to see what I've seen. We will always be connected."

She raised her head to welcome his kiss, fell into it with all the fever of denial and temptation that flowed between them.

The warmth of his body caressed her, his movements slow and powerful her resistance a distant memory. Little moans escaped her lips; with every touch, he awakened

BLOOD MOON

her fire. She grabbed for his belt buckle, not willing to wait for his next reveal. He touched her hand to slow the pace, savoring every second of her desire.

The momentary pause brought her clarity, and she asked, "Wait, are you...," she hesitated then raised her hand to her face to hide her embarrassment and continued. "I mean, do we need protection?"

"I've taken care of it, I promise you." His words strong and convincing; she surrendered her concerns.

Her desire peeked out from the light cotton fabric covering her breast. His fingers felt the small mounds, hard and rounded, rising to meet his touch. He pulled his torso away, just enough to reveal her bosoms. His touch light, to rub against the rounded flesh, the back of his fingernail slowly raked across her nipple, with gasps of her desire filling the air.

It was more than they could bear, evident by the frantic dance to relieve their bodies of their encumbrances, yearning to be naked and consumed.

Alex offered no resistance to the cold, hard floor, no matter as she guided his hands to explore her waiting body. Sebastian reached between her legs and whispered in her ear. "Alex, I am... unique!"

Before she could inquire about the meaning of his words, it became apparent. It started as a slow vibration. His hand searched for her moistness, with the pulse coming stronger. His fingers warm and tingly like the buzzing of bees, the sensation compelling, driving her to rise against his touch, and then she paused.

"What the hell..." her eyes flashed with excitement. " How'd you do that?"

He only smirked and continued to stir her passion. The words rolled across her ears, whispered as a proclamation, "Alex. There's something else you need to know."

Primal need colored her words. "No, it doesn't matter. Whatever it is, don't stop." She reached down to caress his warm shaft pulsing against her leg. He moved to stop her hand and guided it up above her head.

He used his leg to coax her surrender, prompting her to reveal her approval. "Alex, are you sure…?"

There was no hesitation, only her words rushed and desperate, "Sebastian, take me now."

He filled her, paused, and watched her face dance with the realization of his vibrating attribute, then savored each stroke, his passion rising to the surface. The intense pulsation filled her womb and rose up to explode into her very soul.

Her heat pulled at his seed, he placed his hand across her face and their minds united, their moment of ecstasy combined, the pulses rising and falling together into the connection of their minds.

His cold hand lay across her hip, a stark contrast to the heat they had shared only moments before. Alex lay with her eyes shut, curled up under his arm, fighting the urge to examine every part of this magnificent alien male specimen.

Moisture in the cave formed a mist that hovered just above their bodies, obscuring the reveal of Sebastian's greatest attribute. Alex stared; a blush covered her moist cheeks.

Her fingers reached below the mist, hesitant, she pulled back but second-guessed her reaction and continued.

The reveal was familiar, nothing out of the ordinary, her memory confirming his maleness. Maybe slightly larger than what she was used to, but that could not account for the mind-blowing, earth-shattering, electric sex, that had just rocked her world.

"Find what you were looking for?" His voice rose to part the mist. He rolled to his side, grinning from ear-to-ear.

His voice startled her, and she retreated, grabbed his face, dove into his eyes, and asked, "How did you…? What was that…? Damn never mine, can we do it again?"

***

The room was small but functional. Just one of many that lay inside the perimeter of the Great Room. Sara stood in the doorway and watched the rise and fall of Jarrid's chest, resisting the urge to wake him with uncontrollable kisses.

The hard floor comforting, any place to lay her weary head. She slid in behind his massive body, hugged him gently, and offered her words into the night. "I love you, Jarrid." The intimate moment stirred him, her words stored in the recess of his mind. He patted her arm, and they drifted off to welcome the end of the day.

Dreams invaded Sara's sleep. Two hands held the ritual knife, its blade shimmering in the light. Black hair entangled, laced through the witch's fingers, weaved around the jeweled handle. A stiff breeze blew the tresses away just as the downward force plunged the knife toward his chest.

Driven awake by pure will, Sara rose up, screaming, "Jarrid, no…" But he was not there. Her hands felt for his warm body with the sleep falling from her eyes, the dream eating at her heart. She stumbled toward the Great Room, following the voices that echoed on the other side of the door.

SARAH KAGE

The air was thick, laden with the concerns of everyone's safety and the upcoming move. Sara paused a few moments and took inventory of the situation. Alex spotted her, dropped Sebastian's hand, and charged forward, hell-bent on spilling her words before Sara was even in earshot. "Well, you slept long enough. We must talk."

Alex dragged her friend across the room, sweeping her away from prying eyes, bursting with her news. Sara resisted, turning her head to find Jarrid among the elders, his eyes locked on her bending to Alex's will.

"What's so important that you feel the need to drag me across the room? Did Hell freeze over?" Sara folded her arms and impatiently waited for her comeback.

"Funny you should mention Hell…" Alex paced back and forth in front of the wall "because last night, I went to Heaven." Sara's eyes flashed, her curiosity peaked by Alex's statement.

The group's activities faded in the background with Alex's claim ringing in her ear, "To Heaven, with a vampire?"

"Sara…" Jarrid's voice was commanding, rising over the heads of the group, "we need to talk." His eyes locked onto her red hair.

"This will have to wait," Sara reluctantly said, turning away from Alex, "but believe me; we'll talk about it, my promiscuous friend." She turned toward Jarrid, as he marched toward her with his agonizing question rolled up in the creases of his forehead.

He didn't give breath to his question, but tested his theory, lifting her above his head. "Yes…" He reveled in her touch and lowered her body, kissing her with all the passion denied the previous day.

BLOOD MOON

She cupped his face in her hands, looked into his eyes with tears collecting and trickling down her cheeks.

His words flowed from his heart, and he responded to her declaration, offered in the still of their night. "Sara, I love you too." He touched her tears and wiped them away.

The union of these two people anchored the center of the room, oblivious to the other people mingling and scurrying around.

The tug on Sara's shirt, hard and commanding, broke the tender moment. "Sara, I am called Arianna." The small woman pushed Jarrid and wedged herself between them. "Please do not be sad!"

Arianna cooed and giggled with the antics of a small child. "Don't listen to her." Thadeous walked up behind Jarrid. His massive warrior-body towered over the young woman. With the charm of a barbarian, he offered his opinion. "She is just a half-wit and would not know sadness if it bit her on the ass."

Forgetting her thoughts for the moment, Sara called out, "Who spoke such cruel words?" Her face had been buried in Jarrid's shoulder so she couldn't tell which of the men had spoken with such malice of thought, and she wanted to memorize his face.

The group parted, wanting no part of the chastising glare that Sara was shooting in Thadeous's direction. She was taken back a bit by the greatness of the man that stood in front of her. Composing herself, she asked, "Are you the one with the cruel mouth?"

A smile slid across his lips, and he answered, "Yes, it was I. What is it to you, oh Righteous One!"

This comment caught Sara off guard, enticing her to ask. "And what might your name be?" she stepped closer to the tall, muscular man.

He tossed his black hair from his shoulder and roared, "Thadeous, and you will do well to remember it, woman."

From the manner of his speech and adornment, Sara could tell that he must have been one of the people lost inside the Fortress for many years. He had an arrogance of a mighty warrior, and the way he'd addressed her, she could tell that he didn't have much use for women.

Almost seven feet tall, he had the brawn to be a mighty warrior, indeed. Sara turned her head to see if Jarrid was going to step into this verbal confrontation, "Oh no, you started this. It is your battle." He made a gesture to egg her on and folded his arms, content to leave his queen to her subject.

"Look, I don't know what time you come from, but I do know that your insults to Arianna are barbaric. Was compassion not part of your world?"

Thadeous made his move, grabbed Sara around the waist, and pulled her up into his chest. Jarrid's eyes shot toward the barbarian with his strides removing the space between them, rushing the brute, his fist raised in the air.

"Jarrid, forgive me," his words left his mouth faster than he could drop Sara to the floor. "I sometimes forget this is not my world, and that this time is not my own. I will apologize to Arianna for the words."

The barbarian confessed. "Sara is right." He turned his attention to the child-like woman and offered his apology. "I am a barbarian. I humbly apologize to you, Arianna."

"You are a mean man, Thadeous!" The woman grabbed her skirt and ran out into the hall, her sobs muffled, Sara running after her.

Anuk stepped into Sara's path and taunted, "My, my, what a calming effect you have on men, quite an

BLOOD MOON

inconvenience if you ask me." Sara stepped around her, but the witch matched her move, forcing her to listen, "You see, I like a man who will not back down from a woman."

"Witch, you are infuriating!" Sara's temper rose to the surface, forcing her to stand and confront Anuk, but the dark woman turned her attention to Jarrid. She circled him, touched his shoulder, and asked, "Remember Jarrid, how you were raised to treat women, or has she tamed you as well?"

"Oh, what is wrong?" The witch's question infuriated Jarrid. He grabbed Anuk and shook her with great force, with her words fueling his anger. "Are you afraid that Sara would not love the real you, the boy with the dark secrets!"

"Enough of your lies, Anuk," Jarrid screamed and released the witch. His temper drove his actions, and he proclaimed, "I will tolerate no more."

The rage caused his body to shake, her smirk the fuel to every wave that flowed across his face.

"This is rather boring, Anuk," Sara stated. She raised her hand in the air, turned, and headed toward the hall. "I'm going after Arianna. I think she needs a friend." His objection stuck in his throat, Jarrid's voice stymied.

Alex came up from behind and questioned. "Where are you off to now, Sara?" she whined, "We need to…"

"Look…" Sara turned and confronted Alex, spilling her words, dripping in sarcasm. "We will talk, Alex, about your so-called night in Heaven." Anuk stepped forward, but before she could open her mouth, Sara made the universal sign for 'I'm watching you' and slipped out the door.

"Damn! You need to control your woman, Jarrid." Anuk pulled her cloak around her body and disappeared into the group.

"Aren't you going after her?" Alex moved toward the door and turned back. "Well, are you?"

"And miff the Red-Headed Queen? Not on your life!" He dismissed Alex and mumbled under his breath. "That would be the biggest mistake of my day."

BLOOD MOON
Chapter 21 Luna

The scent of Sara's red hair floated under Thadeous and Caleb's noses as she rushed by them on her way to soothe Arianna. The barbarian lowered his eyes in response to her relentless, stone-cold, and unforgiving glare. Jarrid's hard gaze, a silent demand for the two warriors to follow Sara into the hall, obeyed.

"She's a stubborn queen." Alex stood next to Jarrid and stated, "But, isn't that what you love about her?"

"Yes, it is." He declared, stroking his chin, his words profound. "My breath is hers to command. She anchors my soul to this material world." He bowed his head and left Alex reveling in his romantic prose.

"Sonnets of love, is that what you crave, woman?" Sebastian came from behind and wrapped his arms around Alex's waist. She turned to watch the color flow through his face and down to his chest.

"Poetry is nice," she said. "But, your touch is electric and all that I crave." Alex surrendered, feeling the need to gaze into his yellow eyes. The kiss soft, his lips trembling, their slow vibration reminded Alex of the bees, and she melted into his warm embrace.

***

"Where are you?" Sara whispered, entering the room. Sobs came through the doorway betraying the woman's hiding place. Arianna sniffled and moved further into the shadows.

"Don't be afraid." Sara's footsteps echoed and mingled with the soft whimpers coming from the shadows in the corner. "Please, can we talk?"

"Don't want to talk. Go away." Arianna's words flowed from the corner. Sara's eyes grew accustomed to the dark; the woman's movement betrayed her hiding place and showed her small frame huddled against the wall.

"I'm here to apologize for Thadeous." Sara knelt and spoke softly, "He's from another time. He can't help himself any more than you can help being small." Sara stood and stepped closer to the corner.

"I am small, no matter, though." Her body broke the shadows, and she came out of the dark, stood in front of Sara, reached up, and touched her face. "You are so beautiful." Arianna wiped her tears with her sleeve. "Angelica told me our protector would be kind."

"You know, Angelica?" Sara shifted her weight, looked into Arianna's eyes, and touched her tear-stained face.

"Oh yes," Arianna's demeanor changed, and she twirled around until she flopped on the floor and continued. "The angel has been with me for a long time." Her dizziness gone, she jumped to her feet. "Angelica protects me."

Moans from the other room, interrupted Arianna's words. "What's wrong?" She approached Sara and pressed for an answer.

"Shh," Sara stood up, raised her finger to Arianna's mouth and nodded her head. She pointed to the window on the far wall and motioned for her to follow. The sounds came across the sill in groups of moans, cries, and inaudible syllables.

Arianna stood on tippy toes with her eyes just above the window's ledge. Once again, Sara whispered, "Be very quiet, Arianna. It is important." Basic verbal commands were easy for her to understand, and Arianna tipped her head to show she understood.

BLOOD MOON

One heavy moan racked Sara's ears and demanded her eyes to fall upon the group gathered just across the hall. Figures moved in front of the room's doorway, casting shadows of demonic, possessed entities.

"Arianna," Sara whispered, "take my hand, we must leave, but move quietly." Sara's glimpse into the other room portrayed the nature of the demons and prompted her to pause. Brief glimpses of flesh falling from the bone, black eyes sunk into skulls, with patches of hair hanging from rotting flesh, the vision seared into her conscience.

The demon's movements were hypnotic, lifeless motivation, their strides short, without purpose or drive. Heads hung, shoulders drooped to emphasize their grotesque hands that swung with the rhythm of a slow march.

Each entity moved to the same beat, each step in unison, driven by the same directive and in the same direction, like watching a flock of geese flying north for the winter, one single mind in control.

Then the spell broke, Sara's fog cleared to see one of the undead stop. It turned in her direction, its grotesque finger raised in the air to single her out, the shrill scream a call to action for its brethren.

The attack was very different, no longer slow and unmotivated but pushing forward with only one thing in mind, to rip the souls from the humans unfortunate enough to cross their path.

"I am scared." Arianna tugged on Sara's arm. "Let's go now." Sara dropped her hand and stared frozen. The screams assaulted their ears and demanded attention. The undead's mission now seemed to be singular and selfish. They scratched and clawed at one another, each one tearing through the flesh of the one unlucky enough to be in its way. Unity replaced with a singular mentality and the lust for human souls.

Their screams echoed across the hall and broke Sara's stare. She turned and ran directly into Caleb. "What are you waiting for?" he screamed. Arianna flew past Thadeous, shooting a glare up and into his eyes, not waiting for anything she raced toward the safety of the Great Room.

"Go now!" Caleb screamed. He stood and looked into the eyes of the demon; it was only inches from entering the room. It honed in on Sara, the intention clear.

"Help, anyone, please." Arianna rushed into the Great Room, hands flailing in the air and uncontrollable fear bursting from her small frame. "We are all going to die!" She ran to the back of the room and into the darkest corner she could find, buried her head in her hands and sobbed.

"What is it?" Jarrid approached Arianna and demanded, "Where is Sara?" He grabbed the woman and brought her to her feet. "Tell me…"

"Jarrid, a little compassion…" Alex turned to Arianna, gathered her into her arms, and rocked her back and forth. "It's okay, I've got you." Alex glared at Jarrid and opened her mouth to scold him, but Caleb's voice boomed from the door and overpowered her words.

"Everyone gather whatever you can carry." Caleb rushed into the room with Sara following close behind. Chaos overtook the group; each leader gathered their followers and hurried them toward the door to move up the hall to the towers.

"Sara, over here…" Jarrid pushed through the chaotic flow of people trying to reach the door. "Quick, help Alex gather the children."

BLOOD MOON

"Auntie… Mommy, where are you?" Sebastian gathered Chad into his arms and hurried Lizzy toward the door. "No, not without Mommy," Alex suddenly appeared at Sebastian's side, took Lizzy's hand, and followed the vampire toward the hall.

"Look, quick the door…" Nikko pushed his way to the front of the group, spread out his arms, and commanded, "Stop! Move to the back of the room, away from the door."

They marched into the room as soldiers, stepping to a cadence that no one else could hear, slowly pushing inward toward the middle of the room. Gasp escaped the women's mouths as they covered their noses against the stench.

The first few demons crossed the threshold to stop and stand just inside the door, frozen like statues, as if waiting for some demonic command. The silence was profound, only the labored breathing of fear rose above the group, and then it began.

The whimpering echoed against the walls, "Lizzy, Chad, you must be quiet." Jarrid bent down and picked Lizzy up into his arms. She buried her head into his shoulder, still whimpering. "Lizzy…" Jarrid stood her in front of Alex and offered words of encouragement, "Be a brave girl, Lizzy. Close your eyes and hold my hand, do not open them for any reason, no matter what you hear. Can you do that?"

Before Jarrid had finished his statement, Lizzy grabbed his hand and closed her eyes so tight they wrinkled up into her forehead. "Okay… they are closed."

The demons methodic movement pushed everyone closer and closer to the back of the room, huddled together for protection. Twenty or more demonic zombies stood just inside the doorway, filed in a line down the length of the wall. Silent and motionless, they stared at the terrified group.

"Just be quiet and don't move." Caleb's voice, low and calm, trickled through the room. Sara searched his face, her eyes wide with questions. His head shook, and his shoulders shrugged, he had no answers to give.

The scream, loud and shrill, echoed across the air, a battle cry to unite the entities in their quest. Again the singular mentality prevailed, and the undead became agitated, frantic to sniff out and capture the human soul.

"I cannot... I have to..." The woman's feet scratched for traction, running headfirst into the path of the demons, escape the only thing she could fathom, pushing through to the hall on the other side.

The attack swift and merciless, the woman's body thrown to the floor, affording the undead the power of devouring her flesh, with the last piece of her humanity ripped from her lifeless body, soulless, she arose as undead.

This scene played out over and over. The people were stricken down; their numbers added to the undead's army, one soul at a time.

"Jarrid..." Caleb grabbed his arm and motioned his hand toward the back of the room. "Take your group and huddle up against the sidewall." Sara grabbed Alex and Chad and directed them to follow Jarrid, with Sebastian following close behind.

"Jarrid, go, I have Lizzy." Anuk took the girl's hand and prompted her to follow.

"Keep your eyes closed, Lizzy." Jarrid reminded the small girl. He joined Sebastian in the chaos, directing the people away from the slaughter, in the front of the room.

BLOOD MOON

"Lizzy, it's Mommy," Alex glared at Anuk, snatched her daughter's hand, and stared the witch down until she turned and walked away.

Before Anuk turned her head, the demon was there. It stood in front of her, blood and saliva dripping from its fangs, slowly streaming onto the floor.

There was no stopping him. "Jarrid…" Sara's words flowed across time in slow motion; she watched his body fly between the demon and Anuk. Its claw-like hand rose in the air to make its mark on the black witch, but Jarrid took the intended blow and fell to the floor, lifeless.

"Sara, get the others back." Sebastian and Nikko grabbed Jarrid's feet and pulled him to safety with the demon's full attention, now, directed toward Anuk.

"Bring him here." Sara motioned for the group to give them room. "Here, against the wall."

"I am okay…" Jarrid resisted help. Then, the silence crept across the room with an eerie tone, chaos, and voices snuffed out by the black deed done, the birth of the Evil One.

The slaughtered took their place among the undead to walk the halls and do their masters biddings. They turned their backs and methodically walked through the door, never to be human again.

"Come on…" Caleb prompted Jarrid, "Let's gather everyone and start for the tower before they decide to finish us off."

"I did it, Jarrid. Just like you told me, kept my eyes shut hard." Lizzy pushed her way through the group, so proud that she had kept her word.

"You are a brave one, little Lizzy." Jarrid motioned for Alex. "Now go and take care of your mom and Chad. Keep them safe while I help Caleb." The strong-willed little girl skipped off, such an uncanny gift for survival.

SARAH KAGE

A scream interrupted Caleb's words. "Where is Anuk?" Jarrid rushed toward the doors, the Army of Darkness had gathered its forces and marched down the hall to celebrate the coronation of their Dark Queen.

"Look…" Caleb grabbed Jarrid and turned him around and pointed down the hall, "its Anuk."

Anuk's body lay crumpled and bloody. The frenzy ended just as Jarrid turned to enter the hall. He watched the demons remove themselves from her corpse. "There…" Caleb gasped and pointed toward the sounds. Everyone in the room gathered in the hall behind them to witness the metamorphosis.

Her legs, twisted, broken, and mangled. Her arms covered in blood with pieces of flesh torn and hanging. The first movement, her tangled limbs, righted themselves to bring her body into a crouched position. The injuries healed, the change begun.

"Hey, what gives?" Caleb took Jarrid's arm to stop him from going toward Anuk.

"What do you think you are…?" Sara demanded. She pushed the crowd aside and slid in beside Jarrid just as Anuk turned and addressed her audience.

Her clothes, torn and revealing, skin like mocha and dark eyes the color of the raven, black hair shimmering in the dim lantern light. Her beauty enhanced by the Devil himself. "Look upon me, Jarrid." She paused and took a few steps forward, pulled her tattered shirt from her bosom, and licked her full lips.

She tossed her hair and changed her approach. "Sara, unless you have not guessed, I am the realization of your worst nightmare. Yes, I am the woman of your dreams, the Evil One."

"Anuk, I knew it…" Sara proclaimed.

BLOOD MOON

The Demonic Queen floated across the floor and stopped just inches from Sara's face. "My name is Luna, the daughter of the Devil." She didn't wait for Sara's reaction but placed her hand on Jarrid's chest and spoke her words for all to hear. "There will be a battle of good and evil, and the Righteous One will be defeated. Yes, Sara will die, and Jarrid will give up his soul to reign with me as my dark mate."

The Evil Queen didn't wait for an answer or notice that Sara had shoved Jarrid aside and was planning for the battle to start that very moment. Luna's army waited for their queen to direct their next move. She let a smirk crinkle across her lips, her excitement evident; she gathered her forces and slinked into the darkness.

"I shouldn't have to prod anyone to leave the Great Room." Sebastian stared at Sara and continued. "We will go now."

***

The bend in the hall circled to end in the courtyard, "This is a good place to stop before we make the final attempt to reach the tower." Caleb's words fell hard upon the weary group.

"I'll take the first watch." Sebastian second-guessed his proposal. Alex's smoldering eyes caught his attention, punctuating her disappointment. The pout across her lips, the realization of his absence in her bed and her arms.

"Sara, are you alright?" Jarrid witnessed the panic and fear roll off her shoulders with her words spoken, said out loud for courage, "I'll be fine. Let's get these people to safety."

The courtyard lay hidden behind the mist, a sanctuary for the retreat of the group on their way to the towers. The giant oaks stood at attention, like soldiers standing in the moonlight, their casted shadows lent to the eeriness of the surroundings.

"Everyone gather close..." Caleb stood in the circle of trees surrounded by a brick wall. "Seek out the rooms that are obscured by the mighty oaks. These hidden accommodations will offer shelter for a time." No objections rose to meet his words, too weary for questions the group dispersed.

"This way, behind this hibiscus bush..." Jarrid took Sara's arm and gently guided her toward the opening that appeared with the sweep of his strong hand.

Grass grew along the floor, like a patchy green rug, an extension of the courtyard's landscape. Its fertile fingers marched across the floor to form a bed of grass, soft and inviting in the middle of the room.

Sheer exhaustion hung in the air; Sara stood in the small space idle, no emotions flooded from her being. She lifted her eyes and stared into Jarrid's face, bathed in the pools of blue, a moment to form her demand, "Tell me your secret, now!"

She anchored her feet in the green mound of grass, placed her hands on her hips, and demanded once more, "Your secret, tell me now!"

"Dark truths of a young boy, to innocent to know their meanings, pushed down into the recesses of my mind." Jarrid turned from her gaze, tore his fingers through his hair, and turned back to show her the agony that tormented his soul.

"These secrets will be our undoing." She commanded, "The one thing that will eat away at our trust and love," Sara stepped forward to close the space between them, her words profound, her gesture meant to close the emotional gap as well.

BLOOD MOON

"You must let this go? Luna puts far too much importance on these tales of childhood games." Jarrid's eyes pleaded, but Sara would not relent.

"Once again…" Sara's will resided somewhere beneath her fear. "You need to tell me your secret!" She held her ground and waited for his answer.

"Since you are hell-bent, I will confess, but it is of no relevance to our love, trust, or ability to fight this war with Luna and her army."

"Power is a strong word for the games I played as a boy." Jarrid crossed the room, touched the cold, stone wall, and leaned against it for strength. "Silly really, even to speak of it out loud. It worried Mary enough for her to forbid me to call upon it, rebuked it as the tool of the Devil." He turned to see Sara's eyes soften, her hard stare now, more curious than judgmental.

"Mary knew of it?" She confronted him, "Why'd she assume it was a dark power?"

"Her ancestors were known to dabble in the ways of the Wicken, not really considered evil powers, but someone took them too far, wielded the control to worship the Dark Prince." He stopped to analyze her reaction and declared, "It was only a game."

"I find Mary to be pretty level headed." She moved closer to Jarrid, her manner softer and more open. "She wouldn't have been concerned without good reason."

"Yeah…" Jarrid scoffed, "I do not think she told me the complete truth, but none the less, I obeyed."

The grass surrendered to Sara's footsteps, which correlated with the cadence of her fingers tapping on her face. She stopped, rubbed her chin, and continued, "You still haven't told me what it is. Are you stalling?"

"This power is locked somewhere in my mind. Luna seems to think I can still call upon it." Jarrid stood in the middle of the room, his forehead wrinkled, *is it even possible that I am capable of pulling it forward from my mind's eye?*

"I won't wait another moment..." Sara stood up into his face and demanded, "Reveal it now, Jarrid."

"Oh, for God's sake, woman, *telekinesis*; I could move things with my mind." Jarrid could not believe his eyes. It was not the response he had expected, not even.

"What..." Sara's uncontrollable laughter filled the room, her snorts and laughter contorted her mouth. "That's your deep dark secret; the one the witch was so determined to enlighten me with."

She wrapped her arms around her stomach and tightened their grip to control the bouts of hilarity ringing out across the room.

"It could be dark, moving things with your mind." The words were even sillier when spoken out loud. "Well, okay, maybe not." His laughter spilled into the room.

"I guess it would depend on what you were moving." Sara's relief flooded her face, her amusement quieted, and she cupped Jarrid's face in her hands. "Now, there is one less secret between us."

"People's demons are not so dismissible. You demand my secrets, but not all monsters are connected to devilish desires, or reside close to the surface." Jarrid moved to envelop her with every ounce of his being. "Every evil thought or devilish transformation hides in the eyes, the resting place for what resides behind the mask."

He slid his cheek against her face, grabbed her hair from behind and whispered in her ear, "Never look into their eyes, your opponent's stare; the connection to what resides in the dark recesses of the mind."

"Who do I think I am?" Sara repelled Jarrid's touch and moved away. "Why do I think I'll be victorious, nothing in my past has prepared me for this battle." She shuttered and moved closer. "The Righteous One, it's all so overwhelming."

"It only means that you are pure of heart." Jarrid buried her face into his shoulder. "This you have carried all your life. Now it is a tool to help you face whatever looms before us."

His kiss was like an old pair of pajamas, waiting for you at the end of a long, hard day. Passionate but not fiery, his lips touched softly, erasing her fears and melting away her doubts. Hands lifted to move the tiniest lock of hair, his finger tracing the shape of her ear to anchor the strand, its curl obedient to his touch.

Her eyes closed, drinking in the comfort of his manner, her kiss gentle, matching his intent, sweet and innocent. She opened her eyes and bit down softly, pulling his lip, testing the waters of passion, to feel the hidden heat flowing beneath his touch.

The heart wants what the heart wants, an old saying, its words written on the edge of Sara's lips, the kiss pulsating to push her concerns deeper into the corners of her mind. Her eyes popped open, *had Mary told him the whole truth?*

Jarrid flashed his blue eyes, pulled her close, and whispered, "We will be victorious; you should have no doubt."

Her hesitation ran deep, not a reaction to his words, but the uncertainty of a darker secret swirling in the background of Jarrid's past.

SARAH KAGE
Chapter 22 Blood Moon Rises

The open-air room lay in waiting, its architecture steeped in mystery and ancient formalities. Circular and ornate with stone tables and chairs positioned around the edge of the space. Large vines intermingled with the stones and crept into the openings, with small alcoves sprinkled around the perimeter.

"Keep moving. Hurry, just a little further." Caleb and the other leaders guided their followers down the hall, herding them toward the space Caleb had sought out on his investigation of the Fortress Towers.

"Okay, Caleb, which way now?" The men stood at the back of the circular room, staring into three open hallways, two well lit and inviting, the other dark, dank and foreboding.

"Tell me you're not wasting time trying to make an educated decision. You know which one it'll be; you couldn't possibly have a doubt." Sara taunted with sarcasm in her voice, "It's always the darkest, coldest, most uninviting choice. That's your answer every time." She left the men to ponder her words and joined Alex and the kids in the center of the room.

"You know she's right." Caleb stared into the dark hall and mumbled, "Whatever it takes 'ole wolf warrior.'" The Wolfen grumbled to himself and continued, "Yes, and as our queen has deciphered gentlemen, this will be our way to the towers."

The group settled down and claimed small spaces of the room for themselves, filling the nooks scattered around the circular wall. Jarrid motioned for Sara to find a moment of seclusion, away from prying, curious eyes.

BLOOD MOON

She pointed her finger at him and motioned her best come-hither gesture.

"There is seduction in your eyes, my queen." She grabbed his arm and directed him down into the shadows, to stop just in front of the wooden door, a most curious anomaly in the ancient Fortress. "Do you require seclusion, my queen?"

She pulled his head down, tasted his lips, and opened the door in unison, their bodies crashing through the doorway, bursting into the tiny room, disturbing the table and chairs just inside the threshold.

Most of the furniture in the Fortress had met its death many centuries before. "Wow!" Sara exclaimed, falling into the chair. "Don't see many of these around." Her eyes scoured the room and took in its charm.

"It's a bed. Well, in the loosest sense of the word." Sara moved across the room and sat on the boards anchored across slats with a ragged covering thrown across makeshift pillows.

The magical lanterns cast shadows across the floor, to flow like honey across Jarrid's muscles shining in the dim light. Sweat and skin joined together to shine like diamonds. Her desire fell upon her like the exploding of fireworks, the scene like the old-time black and whites, the dashing hero to take the damsel in his arms, and kiss her.

"Sara?" Jarrid waved his hand in front of her face, her blushing cheeks the telling sign. He leaned down to stare into the mystery of her blush.

"Oh…" she murmured, "just daydreaming of something I can't have, at least not yet." She glanced into his eyes and quickly changed the subject. "It looks like someone lives here."

SARAH KAGE

Their eyes honed in on the doorknob, the brass-finish shining in the glow of the lanterns, not even a second to think about the outcome before the door swung open. Ticking of metal, like gears in a clock, preceded the woman, the sounds muffled by the closing of the door.

Surprised to see visitors, she cleared her throat and asked, "Do you make a habit of entering someone else's accommodations?" Her strawberry colored hair, braided, and held in place by clock gears and gizmos; her chest was heavily laden with chains of gold, dripping to a point with industrial nuts and bolts. Leather folded and curved to form her apparel, worn and soft from years of service.

"Please excuse us." Jarrid stepped forward to offer his hand. "We did not know that this part of the Fortress was inhabited."

The handshake ignored, the strange woman quipped, "Yes, indeed, this is my home, for the short term." She walked to the table and placed a collection of industrial salvage in a pile.

"I've been waiting for you, Jarrid." She raised her head and looked deep into his blue eyes and proclaimed, "Watched you take your place as head councilman, second-guessed your every move, I have come to know your soul and your desires."

"Hmm," The queen positioned her body between the strange woman and the silly grin on Jarrid's face. "My name is Sara, and you are?"

"My name is Anastasia." The glimmer in her eyes reflected and bounced off the shiny metal discs hanging from her neck. Jealousy rose from the top of Sara's head like steam from a tea kettle.

"Oh, Sara, there's no threat here." She pulled a chair out from the table and motioned for the two to join her. "Your possessiveness always colored my observations;

you wore it like an old coat. It will serve you well in the coming battle." The bracelet of old keys dragged across the table and clanked together, the moisture of her hand tracing a path as she pointed in Sara's direction. "Please, sit, and I will explain."

Jarrid slid the other chair away from the table, and positioned his large body in the seat, copping a position to stare at the strange woman. "Really, Jarrid," Sara scoffed at his antics, mimicked the move and joined the conversation. "So, what kind of entity are you?"

Her laughter caused the many pieces of steam punk bobbles to jingle and chime. The woman composed herself and answered, "I knew you were Fae from the day you drew your first breath. I'm a kindred spirit, known by the name of Seglind, a fairy that tells the future and becomes one with her wards."

"Wards," Jarrid slid back into the chair, looking puzzled?

"Yes, the subjects that are assigned to me by my ancestors." She stood up and circled Jarrid stopping behind his chair and reaching for the bulge against his back. "Oh, I see you have '*The Book of Souls*' in your possession.'"

"How is it that you speak of this book?" Jarrid jumped up and confronted her, grabbing the relic to bring it around to his chest.

The instinct automatic Sara's chair pushed back, her body between her kindred and her man. "Hey," Sara shouted, "those sudden moves could put you in a world of hurt." The queen's body flushed with adrenaline to accentuate her statement.

"May I?" Anastasia dismissed Sara and pointed to the book. Jarrid didn't take his eyes off Sara, only hesitating for a moment; he pulled it from his satchel and reluctantly handed it to Anastasia.

"Yes. Here it is." Sitting down, she lifted her head to make sure she had their attention and started to read,

> *"The betrayer will try many times to stop the Army of Light. She will pursue until she is successful in her attempt to consummate her entanglement with her dark mate."*

Pausing only a moment, she continued,

> *"Her birthright is to reign on the earth as Queen of Darkness."*

Anastasia's audience seemed to be lulled into complacency, her words familiar to the duo. Then the declaration that pulled the couple from the depths of their minds. Their eyes glazed and dull suddenly were burning crystal clear; her words a gift given to spring hope in their hearts and give strength for the battle.

> *"There will be a union of love: consummated on holy ground by two who are pure."*

Suddenly the words were new, brimming with the promise of the lifted curse, the promise of love. Anastasia glanced at her audience and continued to read,

> *"This will not be an immoral union, but one blessed and recognized by*

BLOOD MOON

God, a true marriage that will bring forbidden passion, to a sweet climactic unification. Beware the beast will use seduction to prevent this union."

Then Anastasia's face went blank as she continued to read,

"The betrayer, denied of the one she lusts after, will use her evil ways to seduce the one she wants. Only his love for another will keep him safe from the evil, but this is not written in blood for the betrayer is very powerful and her persuasion irresistible."

"Yes," Sara moved to circle Jarrid. "The betrayer's name is Luna. Her black coronation happened only hours ago." Jarrid's face turned red, Anastasia peered in his eyes, he could feel her judgment, knew she could see the truth.

"You're the one she wants." Anastasia directed her words at Jarrid, needing to make her declaration sink into his mind. She took a deep breath to fuel her proclamation and continued, "She wants you to rule beside her, darkness your destiny, forced upon you, accomplished by her steely knife."

The air pulled from Sara's lungs, Anastasia's comment landed across her mind and conjured the image of the dreadful nightmare, so real the light in the room seemed to bounce off the image of the blade, flashing in Sara's memory.

"When the time comes, Jarrid," Anastasia ignored Sara's empty stare and continued to speak, "Protect your soul and carry Sara's love in your heart. It'll be the weapon that you'll use against this evil."

As she finished, Jarrid asked, "Anastasia, will you be able to join our group and give us direction?" Sara had gained her composure and stood next to Jarrid.

"No, I regret that I can be of little help to you. My capacity is only advice. I have waited many years for you to fulfill your destiny, but this is the extent of my assistance. You must go now and prepare, the battle is coming and the next days will prove to be the most difficult of your life.

"Oh, I want to show you one more thing before you go." Anastasia sat back down and turned the pages of the book. Her fingers maneuvered, and she wielded the book like a weapon, turning to a place that seemed familiar to her.

A puzzled look came over Jarrid's face, and he asked, "How is it that you are so familiar with this book?"

Her eyes lifted, she folded her hands over the ancient text and declared, "I am the author of this book, and it has been one of my duties to prepare for this battle! My true purpose is at hand, my sacrifice for the battle, but enough of that."

No time passed between her last word and the reading of the revelations that were seared into the pages before her.

"The Feast of Souls will take many lives. Once the undead claims the soul; it

BLOOD MOON
will be enslaved forever to walk in death."

"These words, we know to be true." Sara reached for Jarrid's hand, "The evil ritual happened right before our eyes."

"Fear for your soul, not your life," Anastasia acknowledged Sara's comment and continued, "the ones who refuse the mark of the beast, who make a stand for purity, their soul will rise to meet the heavens and become one with the universe, to live in the light."

She closed the book, ran her fingers across the leather cover, and once again emphasized, "You must not worry about death, for in this place it's inevitable. You must protect your soul, and this is the single most important thing I will tell you."

"We will heed your words, Anastasia." Sara reached across the table, took her hand, and sealed her vow with a slight squeeze, a show of commitment to the Seglind.

"Now go children, take the book, it will be your salvation." She looked into Jarrid's eyes and suggested, "You should take the group and move toward the high grounds of the Fortress." She made her way to the door as she spoke, "There's a tower located at the back. Behind it is a place that is very difficult for the evil army to access. Try to get the group there before it's too late."

The silence enhanced Anastasia's hand gesture, a directive to move the two young people out into the hall. "Yes, thank you for your guidance," Sara prompted Jarrid to take the hint and walked him past the table and toward the door. "We will heed your words."

Jarrid brushed past the woman and gathered the book. "It was a pleasure to meet you." He flashed Sara an 'alright, already' glare and followed her out into the hall.

"No, Caleb, I need to talk to her first." Sara's face rounded the door frame just in time to hear Alex's words. "You need to wait your turn."

Then the group collided, Alex, Caleb, Tank, and Thadeous piled upon one another, their bodies like a pile driver pushing Sara against the wall.

"Hey, guys. Lighten up, seriously." The shove a response to their actions, Sara pushed through, grabbed Jarrid's hand to right herself and let out a huff.

The argument ensued, "I have business with the queen." Caleb stood royally, his Wolfen chest puffed out.

"Haven't you heard the saying, ladies before wolves?" Alex stood her ground and insisted. "Besides, I was here first."

"I think you're going to lose this one, Caleb." Tank laughed and positioned his wings to rest on his back.

Sara quipped, "I suppose you and Thadeous want a word with me as well." She motioned for Jarrid to walk with her down the hall.

"Na," Thadeous shoved Tank down the corridor. "We go where the action is. Figured Caleb was looking for trouble."

"Well, looks like he found it." Jarrid laughed and joined the giant, "In the form of a redhead."

The men's voices bounced off the corridor walls and rushed forward to empty into the circular room. Alex stood in front of Caleb, not budging, her intention to speak with Sara, not negotiable.

"Women," Caleb kicked the dirt and turned to join the men. He turned back and growled, "You must seek me out, Sara, before we move toward the tower; we must speak. Do not hesitate to find me." Defeated, he left the two women to their idle gossip.

BLOOD MOON

They sat cross-legged in a small alcove in the wall. Alex just stared at Sara, not knowing where to begin. "Well, it's your nickel. What's so important that you would stand up against Caleb?" Sara's eyes popped, "Oh wait, is this about the 'night in Heaven'?"

The redness started in Alex's cheeks and rose to ignite her answer, "I had sex with the vampire." Alex jumped to her feet as if the sound of her confession set off an alarm. She focused her attention on her friend's face.

"You think this is a revelation. I knew it was going to happen when you followed him out the door." She stood to leave, curious about Caleb's pressing matter. "I don't have time for idle girl talk about your night with a demon."

"Oh, I think you're going to want to hear this." Alex cocked her head to the side and spilled her secret, "Sara, he vibrates."

"What vibrates?" Sara asked with a certain air of innocence.

The silly laugh started low and colored Alex's cheeks, "Oh, everything. Just use your imagination."

"Really?" First, Sara's face gleamed in awe, then a smile from ear to ear, her exclamation profound, "Lucky girl!"

"I've changed my mind. Give me every juicy detail." She settled down on the hard floor to revel in Alex's tingling girl talk.

"Sara, have you ever wondered, I mean, thought about how they feel at the moment of ecstasy? Is it comparable, more sexually heightened then ours?"

"You know, Yes, I have." Sara's curiosity peaking she asked, "What are you saying?"

"I know firsthand." Alex paused, "He is capable of a kind of mind-meld and right at, well you know, our

314

climax, he joined our minds, and I could feel every contraction, pulse and sensory-driven release that ran the length of his desire."

"Oh my," Sara's pulse rose with each descriptive adjective that Alex spoke into the cold stone space. "What kind of vampire is he?"

"He showed me with his mind, where he originates from, his bloodline, and the unique qualities of his heritage. Sara, he can control his seed, make it fertile or sterile at the moment of release." Sara's face froze as Alex proclaimed, "That's the kind of vampire he is."

"Hey," Caleb stuck his head inside the small space and demanded, "I knew it, just idle gossip. Sara, we must speak now!"

A small sigh of frustration escaped her lips, "Okay, Caleb, gees. What is it Tank says, 'cool your fleas.'" She stood, turned to Alex, and whispered, "Hold that thought," Sara chirped, shooing her friend out of the space.

Alex had given Sara just enough information to wet her curiosity. "Okay, we can finish this later." She brushed past Caleb with a smirk on her face. "She's all yours, wolf."

The corner of the alcove stood in dark shadows. Caleb sunk into its darkness and hid his face. "It's Raven. I want to talk about my wife."

"Raven is a beautiful name." Sara reached out and took Caleb's hand to coax him out of the shadows. His face somber, the pain visible, "its okay, Caleb, ask me anything."

"There's so much, how is it..." The Wolfen moved away, wringing his hands, bringing them to his face and blurting out, "Tell me everything you feel of her."

BLOOD MOON

His pleading eyes burned in Sara's heart, her answer void of substance, "I only caught a glimpse of her during the ritual. She floated across my mind in her attempt to get to you, such a well of sorrow, Caleb, how did she die?"

His eyes rose to stare at the ceiling, the memory a distinct tale of regret, "Impaled in a sea of corpses, left for days to rot in the sun, her murderer Vlad the Impaler, her sin to defeat his army."

"She was a Vampire Warrior?" Sara surmised, prompting him to continue, "How long were you married?"

"We were promised from birth." His eyes clouded over, and he slumped against the wall. "As our traditions mandated, but I loved her fiercely."

"Take my hand, Caleb." Sara slowly moved closer and offered her touch. "I know she is here with me."

The Wolfen hesitated, even the possibility of Raven's touch too much to bear. Sara sensed his reluctance and pushed the matter. She cupped his face in her hands; tears fell down her cheeks, the passion flowing from the other side to unite the Wolfen and his beloved.

The assault came from the doorway without warning. Jarrid approached the room just as Caleb's head flew back, and he called her name, "Raven…"

"Jarrid, stop," Sara's words filled the room just as his body crushed Caleb to the wall.

"This conversation is over!" Jarrid shoved his arm into Caleb's neck, fire in his eyes, and spit spewing from his tight lips.

"Enough. You don't understand." Sara pulled on Jarrid's shirt to stop the assault. "I'm a channel for his dead wife. It's not his fault."

SARAH KAGE

"It's true," Caleb shoved the angry man to the floor. "I felt it from the first day I took her hand." He reached out to help Jarrid stand.

"During the ritual," Caleb grabbed Jarrid's shoulder to get his attention, "my wife, Raven crossed the veil and reached out to me."

"It's the truth, Jarrid." Sara coaxed him to relax. "I'm but a vessel for her communication."

"Great…" Jarrid spouted, brushed the dust from his pants, and stared at the Wolfen with contempt, his words directed at Sara. "Now, I have to deal with your connection to his dead wife. You ask much of me, woman."

"Jarrid, stop, control yourself." Sara grabbed at his arm and pulled it down, her frustration evident. "Really, this is so petty. Why must you look for smoke when there is no fire?" He pulled away and stared across the room, his intent to stake his claim. She crossed in front of him and declared. "Please try to focus on Anastasia's words. Remember the hope she has given us."

"Yes, hope is the reason I fight so fiercely for what is mine." Caleb must understand we are as one.

"I would've done no less, Sara, to protect my wife." Caleb bowed his head to Jarrid, a symbol of respect, given by the Wolfen leader.

The tension faded, and Sara added, "We're a team. Nothing will deter us from our destiny." She bowed her head to the two men. "We must go back and prepare for the move to the tower." She turned to lead; reluctantly, Jarrid and Caleb followed their queen.

***

The group gathered in the center of the room with their meager possessions, ready for whatever lay at the other end of the hall. Sara wanted to finish her

317

BLOOD MOON

conversation with Alex but realized she was more than involved with her vampire lover and the kids. Sara watched as a man approached Jarrid.

"A word please," The man placed himself in Jarrid's path and spoke, "my name is Nathaniel Clark." The stranger shoved his hand out to introduce himself.

A quick manly handshake ensued. "Clark, that name seems familiar." Jarrid puzzled. "Are you from the village?"

"Yes," Sara had joined them, and he acknowledged her briefly. "I was a young man when I crossed the path of one of the gray trolls of the Fortress. I do not remember how I came to be here, but I have been here since that day."

"So, you were part of the village when it was young?" Jarrid acknowledged Alex and Sebastian as they approached the conversation. "Did you know my parents?" Jarrid queried.

"Your father was the one I remember best; he was an honorable man. I was but a teenager and worked with him on a barn build." Nathaniel tipped his head to Sebastian and continued, "Your mother Mary would bring us food during the day. I always admired how much they loved one another."

"That must have been just before my father died." Jarrid sighed.

Jarrid's face forlorn, Nathaniel's face confused, the words breaking the tension, "Sebastian, stop." The commotion came from behind and cut through their words.

"Nathaniel, I apologize." Sara took his hand and made light of the rude interruption. "Young love, what can I say?" Laughter broke out, and Sara stepped between Alex and her vampire and added, "He is a beast."

SARAH KAGE

"No matter, I just wanted to meet you, the head councilman of my village." Nathaniel bowed his head and left the conversation.

***

The journey down the dark and dank hall was uneventful. "See, Caleb, I told you." Sara prodded, "We would probably have encountered the Devil himself in one of the other inviting halls; just a little psychology, works every time."

"It's just the way of the girl." Jarrid laughed and followed Sara to the end of the hall. "No rhyme or reason, just do not fight it."

The large room introduced itself, with high vaulted ceilings and ornate stain glass windows. The group filed in one by one to admire the beauty of the architecture and vastness of the surroundings.

"Now this is more like it." Thadeous pushed his way to the front, "reminds me of home." The giant looked small in the vastness of the room—a wide staircase against the sidewall, with two platforms. The middle landing led to the stage, and the other to a large wooden door, on the second floor.

The warrior bent down and picked up the small boy, climbing up his legs. Chad had taken a liking to Thadeous and followed him everywhere. Just as he reached the stairs, Alex called out, "Chad, come here." The boy complained, "Oh, Mommy, you never let me have any fun." Thadeous lowered the boy, and Chad stomped off mumbling.

"This is a pretty good room for defense." Jarrid offered as the councilmen were getting ready to explore what lay past the door at the top of the stairs, "only two ways in and out." He stopped at the top of the stairway, turned to wave at Sara, and followed the other men through the door.

Everyone busied themselves, preparing to rest before their next move. Sara looked for Alex, but she was preoccupied with the kids. She decided to find the most secluded spot in the room. Her eyes glanced past the stage. There in the corner, a room with a shrouded curtain caught her attention.

It was small but functional, not a castle but secluded. Sara hummed as she worked to make the room as inviting as possible. A little hay and a discarded piece of material fashioned a bed. She stood with a smile on her face, the promise of Jarrid's body lying close to hers made the room bearable.

A hand appeared and pushed the tattered curtain aside. Arianna skipped into the room without an announcement. "Oh," Sara chirped, "It's you. Is there something you need?"

"Have you seen Angelica?" Sara figured she was just lonely and wanted to talk.

"No, Arianna." Sara waited for her to continue.

The small woman stood and pondered her next words. She stared intently into Sara's eyes and blurted out, "Are you and Jarrid in love?"

"Yes," Sara smiled and gave the truest answer. "We share a deep and profound love for one another." Sara could not imagine what her next question would be, but to her surprise, Arianna smiled a huge smile and disappeared through the curtain.

Hmm, that was strange. Sara brushed off the encounter and finished arranging the room. Her fingers touched the makeshift bed with Anastasia's words ringing in her ears. She took a breath and spoke them out into the room. "A true marriage recognized by God." The thought was more than she could bear, her joy all-consuming, she wept.

BLOOD MOON
Chapter 23 Escape

The staircase rose wide and circular, like an ornate piece of jewelry to compliment the wooden stage, topped by the royal stained glass window. The sounds of slumber echoed through the room, the stillness an illusion to the tragedy of the situation.

Her vision cloudy, Sara fought to wipe Luna's nightmarish ritual from her mind. Jarrid had lingered too long; she didn't like for him to be out of sight, fearful that the demon woman would accomplish her mission.

Winding steps offered themselves as distractions; each one slowly accomplished, bringing Sara to the top of the stairs. The square indentions of the wood door like picture frames. She touched them deep in thought, a vision of Jarrid's strong face materialized filling the space. She smiled and stepped down to the lower landing, waiting for Jarrid to return.

The door burst open, sending a whirlwind down the stairs and across Sara's cheeks. Her heart fluttered, and she waited for the men to emerge. A sigh of relief, her thoughts directed to the loud belly laughs echoing down the stairs. Thadeous bolted through the door with the other men chanting and joking. "Hey, did you guys ever see a giant move so fast?" Tank taunted.

Caleb pushed past the mountain of a man and slapped him playfully. "Don't you think the sword was a little overkill, Thadeous?" He laughed uncontrollably.

"It was just a rat." Tank exclaimed and pushed past the warrior.

"Don't like rats!" Thadeous yelled, his head hung in disgrace.

SARAH KAGE

Sara stood in front of his shame and offered him words of encouragement. "They would be singing a different tune, Thadeous if the rat would have suddenly turned into a demon." The smile peeked out from his reddish beard, his hand clutched his heart, and he declared, "The protection of my queen at all cost."

The steps absorbed the sound of the taunts and laughter. Sara stood concerned and called out to Thadeous, her voice cracking. "Where's Jarrid?" Before the warrior could answer, the door opened wider, and Jarrid appeared cooing to the small black kitten cuddled up to his massive chest.

"Is that Dax?" Sara reached for the tiny kitten and buried its head into her neck. "How... I don't understand."

"It was Thadeous' unwarranted scream, just before he pulled his sword and conquered the mighty beast." The smirk colored Jarrid's face, his laughter eased Sara's concerns, and he added. "Next thing you know, Dax morphed into the kitten; go figure."

Little growls rumbled in Sara's ears, the beginnings of Dax's complaints that would no doubt come to life when he transformed to challenge Jarrid's humor. "Might as well make the best of the situation," Sara laughed. "He can spend the night with Lizzy. I'm sure she'll be glad to see Daxter."

The men settled down to rest, Daxter curled up into Lizzy's arms and squeaked a small complaint before he closed his eyes, content to be Lizzy's kitten for a time.

There was no movement as Jarrid's soft footsteps fell strategically around the sleeping group. He pulled back the torn curtain to reveal her handiwork. "Hmm, you have been busy." He lowered his head and entered the bedchamber. "Your bedding suggests that we sleep

BLOOD MOON

together, woman." He sat down and pulled off his boots. "Are you not afraid I will take advantage of your choice?"

No time for an answer, Jarrid pulled her down into the hay and laid her back, no resistance to his touch. The kiss warm and sweet, just this side of uncontrollable passion, her fire flamed by his lips. His touch tender but all-consuming, she responded to his need, their lust dancing just this side of surrender.

Sheer will broke the spell, and Sara gasped with her words giving strength to resist the urgent pull on her virginity. "Jarrid…" her hands coming between them, she slowly pushed him away. " I have the same need as you. I don't want to cross the line." She sat up and buried her face into her knees.

"Where does that come from?" Jarrid embraced her, folded his arms around her, and gently rocked his question to life. "How can you find the strength?"

"Anastasia…" She pulled away from his embrace and continued, "her words from the book; they give me hope for our future." She rose to her feet, stood over Jarrid, and pleaded. "Have faith with me; it won't be long, I know this in my soul."

The gentle tug brought her back down on the hay. Jarrid's loving arms told the story with his words to follow. "Your faith gives me hope, lay with me, and know my intentions are honorable." They curled up one to the other, under the blanket of faith and the hope to dream of the reality of Anastasia's words.

***

"Everyone, your attention, please." Caleb paced across the stage; his shrouded eyes flashed his stride frantic, he stopped. "We must make our approach to the corridor and make our way to the tower. Take this opportunity to prepare; we will plan to meet at the hall in two hours."

"How do we measure time, brother?" A voice demanded.

"Yeah, sorry, um…" He looked up to a hole in the roof as sunlight poured across the floor. "When the sunbeam reaches the hall, we will gather to make our way."

"Daxter, no," Lizzy chased after her kitten and called to him, "please, come back."

"Sweetie," Alex bent down to her daughter and tried to comfort her, "Dax needs to be with the other men to get ready for our move." Lizzy folded her arms to stifle the grumbling in her throat. "Why don't you and Chad go with Aunt Sara? I'm sure she could use your help in the preparations to leave." Alex winked at Sara and continued. "Sebastian and I need to make some adult arrangements. Could you do that for Mommy?"

The wink, a non-verbal gesture, and a kind of shorthand that Sara understood from years of practice; translation, we want to be alone, please watch the kids. "Come, Lizzy, I think Jarrid needs our help." Sara tugged on Lizzy's reluctant mood and coaxed her to follow.

"Shh…" Sebastian's hot breath touched Alex's ear, an indication of what he had on his mind. "Follow me, quietly." He led her to the lower landing on the stairs, everyone below too engaged to notice their escape.

In a flash, they were on the other side of the door, Alex whispered, shy and innocent, "where are you taking me? Whatever do you have on your mind?"

The vampire's cheeks flushed with no answer. He guided her to a secluded room, the silence only adding to the intrigue, leading her back into the shadows. "No one will bother us here. We are alone." He pulled her hard against him. His need rose from his heat, unleashed upon her skin.

BLOOD MOON

His taste almost sweet, Alex gave in to his will and was lost to his desires. "You like to be in control." She pushed the hair away from his neck and kissed his flushed skin, her mouth open and lustful. "Your vampire nature warrants it so." She whispered in his ear. "Ever wondered what it would be like to surrender?"

Sebastian's yellow eyes flashed, the mere suggestion caught his attention. "What give you control?" His fingers traced her cheek on the way to her lips. His fingertips vibrated, oh so softly.

"No…" She grabbed his hand and forced it toward his back, "none of your tricks." His curiosity peaked, a moment of excitement, and he relaxed to give in to her will.

"You told me about your stamina, one of your vampire traits." She reached and guided his other hand behind his back, leaned harder into his body to anchor his wrists below his waist and against the wall. "Want to play a little game to test that theory?"

"Hmm…" his voice broke with a slight shiver, "and what is the name of this game?" He moved to free his hands, but Alex's body kept just enough pressure, enticing him to give in.

The cold stone raked against his hands, but she was in and owned his heart. "It's a silly little game I like to call Queen of Passion." She buried her face against his skin, gave his neck a light nip, and whispered in his ear. "Are you game?"

"Before you answer, you might want to inquire about the rules." She released her spell and moved to the center of the room.

He was smitten, embarrassed to let her know that he would follow her anywhere; to do anything. "You're correct. If I'm to submit to you, then you must lay down the rules beforehand."

Her laugh suppressed, she rushed to his arms, the kiss deep and hungry, she pulled away and proclaimed. "For this game to work, you have to follow all my rules. Do you agree?"

His warrior vampire screamed from somewhere deep inside, so against his nature to submit, but his desire won out, and he spoke the words. "Yes, I surrender."

The movement swift, Alex dropped to her knees, released his belt, and pulled his pants to the floor. She stood to face him and stated, "First rule," she looked into his face, making sure she had his attention. "You may not reciprocate anything that I do. I am the giver, you, the receiver."

She knelt once again. Her hand pulled at the bunched-up pants a signal for the vampire to raise his foot, an effortless motion, and his boots were scattered across the stone floor with his pants soon to follow.

Alex rose from the floor and seductively removed her shirt. "Second rule," she continued. "Once the game begins, you may not move any part of your body. You must remain still."

Playing along, Sebastian replied. "I understand." He moved to finish undressing; he stood, waiting for her command, naked and vulnerable.

"Third rule," Alex followed his lead and removed the last bits of her clothing, "you may not touch me."

"Wait…" He started to make his complaint, but she moved to stand behind him to envelop him with her hands, her touch driving him to relent.

Her body facing him once more, she reached down to caress his yearning alien arousal. Each movement, more intense, she whispered, "Fourth rule," his moans mingled with the shadows, his need apparent she stopped, completely still; agonizing seconds later, she demanded. "You may not climax."

"What…" he grabbed her shoulders to drive home his question. " No, then what's the point of this game of yours?"

"Oh, you will have to master it, and then you can tell me the answer." She slowly walked away and continued. "This game can become rather intense, so there's a built-in safety word, agreed upon before we begin."

His dominant will started to fill the room; Alex brought her body close and melted into his embrace. His resistance mellowed. She instructed him on the last of the rules. "You will be brought to the brink of your release many times. After all, it's a test of your stamina."

"Yes, and I've already agreed to the terms, so bring it on." He took her face in his hands and planted the kiss, his last show of dominance before the game began.

"And the last rule," Alex spread their shirts on the floor and sat down, enticing him to join her. "There's a time limit agreed upon before we start. I suggest we start with the equivalent of thirty minutes."

"You must remember, I'm alien," he proclaimed, sitting next to her. "I think we should start with an hour."

"I suggest you make that decision after you have mastered the game." Alex gently pushed on his shoulders, coaxing him to lay back. "If you disobey any rule during the time limit, and ignore my instructions to submit, you lose the game, all intimacy stops."

He rose up on his elbows and asked, "And what happens if I prove worthy and make it to the end?"

"Why you win, of course." She gathered the remaining clothes and positioned them under his knees to encourage him to relax and let his thighs fall open. "If you last until the end, then all rules are banished, you become dominant to take anything your heart desires. My submission guaranteed."

"Do you agree to all of the terms and stipulations, and if so, what is your safe word?" She waited in the dim light, excited for his answer.

He laid back and quipped, "Piece of cake and cake is my safe word."

She rose from the floor and slinked to one of the oil lanterns, tipped it, and pooled the oil in the palm of her hand. She sat back down and threaded her legs under the vampire's thighs, with her feet pointed toward his head. She slid her body to mold against his buttocks, drizzled the warm oil on his stomach, and instructed, "Sebastian, place your hands over your head and close your eyes. It begins."

"You must relax and surrender." Her hands rubbed the oil up and over his torso, down the length of his thighs with her thumbs pressed hard against his groin, to follow the creases of his inner legs. She watched as the passion rose in his face, his head turned from side to side with short moans escaping his lips.

"I am in control; my will, be done." She repositioned to kneel just inside his opened thighs, reached her hands up and around his neck to smooth the warm oil against his skin. She rubbed her naked breast down the length of his body to spread the oil between their bodies.

The touch of her bosoms' ignited his fire, and he rose to meet her body, she pulled away. "You must not move." She pushed his pelvis down and anchored it to the floor with her body.

"Yes, tell me your desires, instruct me on how to bring your heat." Her hands pooled around the base of his groin and cupped his maleness softly, to wind up circling the large protrusion of flesh mounded up around its tip, to reveal the protrusion, his alien anatomy revealed.

The moans, coming faster now, accompanied by his soft words, "Yes... yes."

Once again, his hips thrust into the air to meet her strokes pound for pound, and then she stopped. "No movement, remember." She waited for a time, letting his heat subside just enough to cool the intensity. She slid her body like a snake, circling his stomach, her hair and face touching but not, his length yearning for her attention.

Her hands continued the relentless game, the focus on his impending climax, her hands centered on his pleasure ring, to fuel the end game.

The urgency evident in his words shouted into the air. "Is... time up?"

With that said Alex slowed the rhythm and fell into a sort of cadence, backing down the dance of passion. She watched the rise and fall of his chest, an indication that his heat had momentarily cooled.

"I want you," she whispered, "to feel your release." Her words ignited his drive, and he reached down to pull her on top, but she pulled away and said, "Rule number three broken, you're almost there, the end comes in only moments."

Her rhythm now relentless, her technique overpowering with speed and focus, his proclamation shouted into the air with fever and desperation. "Now, it must be..."

"Your time is up." Alex moved away from his trembling body, the words his directive to take her and finish what she had started.

SARAH KAGE

No questions, statements or directives, her words the key to his release. No time for romance or sweet declarations of surrender. He jumped behind her, buried his climatic release into her waiting orgasm, magnified by the stillness of the cold room, and took the trophy, his winning title, the King of Passion.

***

A murmur fell across the group with questions and anxiety, anticipation for the task ahead. Five councilmen stood on stage, their backs to the group, in deep consultation. "It is time." Jarrid dropped Sara's hand, bent down to kiss Lizzy on the cheek, and approached the stairs to reach the lower landing.

The pacing seemed to fuel his nerve; he gathered his hair into his hands, turned his back to the crowd, dropped his hands, and turned back around to search for Sara's face.

Jarrid's mere presence demanded attention, as the councilmen relinquished the floor to his words. The quietness of the room only emphasized his personality. A smile caressed Sara's lips. Her body recognized just how damn attractive he was.

Jarrid's mouth opened, and his hand gestured to emphasize the first word. His speech was interrupted by the large wooden door at the top of the stairs, announcing itself with a loud bang. Laughter and robust opinions flowed from the crowd. Alex led the way, stepping down and past Jarrid she taunted, "Don't let me interrupt, by all means, continue."

Sebastian's ashen skin glistened in the light; his black hair lay wet and disheveled a dead giveaway to his antics behind the wooden door. "By all means, Jarrid, continue." He strolled past Sara, his tone non-apologetic, stared at Alex, and disappeared into the group.

BLOOD MOON

A whimper of a laugh escaped Jarrid's lips, and he gathered himself to speak. "Mine and Sara's destiny has intertwined to bring us to this place." He paused for a moment, collected his thoughts, and continued, "I pledge my loyalty to her and everyone here. I will lend my support to your leaders and unite with them with honor and integrity, the only outcome in mind, to win the battle and return home with my bride."

The room broke into chaos; Caleb rushed to the front of the stage and motioned for everyone to calm down. "Let him speak." He waited for their obedience and gestured for Jarrid to continue.

A gaggle of women stood around Sara with smiles and congratulations. "This is not the time for celebration." Jarrid took a few steps down and glared at the women. "There are insurmountable walls in our path. The first is the ascent to the tower."

Softness yielded his tone, and he took another tack. "Sara and I met an extraordinary woman earlier. She called herself Anastasia." Jarrid climbed back onto the landing and continued. "She told us she was the author of *The Book of Souls* and foretold of our marriage, consummated within these walls; man and wife in God's eyes."

The wooden door crept open, the squeaking like nails on a chalkboard. Jarrid rushed down the stairs to stand with Sara and Alex, the glow of red peeked around the door to spill down the stairs, the chanting emphasized, coming from the upper hallway. The crowd gasped and fell back into the corners of the room, shrinking from the red light.

A small group of undead slowly descended the stairs, gathering on the lower landing, waiting for their leader. The red light glowed stronger. Its beam reached down the stairs and out into the crowd. The chanting cut off like someone picked up the needle from an old vinyl record, the silence profound.

Its hand offered toward her escort, to precede her entrance, its rotting flesh swung, meeting her request. The undead accompanied the Dark Queen to the landing, bowed to show his loyalty, and relinquished the floor to her Dark Majesty.

The buzz from the crowd became deafening, an assault to the Dark One's ears. Luna threw her hands into the air and commanded that silence reign. "You need to listen; your very life and soul could depend upon it." She tossed her raven hair and stepped down to stop just before the end of the stairway. "Anastasia was correct, you must protect your soul, but her words were futile, I will be victorious."

Her beauty was undeniable. Sara cringed; she'd hoped that the Evil One would be hideous like her army of rotting flesh, but alas, the spell of her beauty was captivating.

"Well, Jarrid is that a look of surprise that I see on your face and you Sara, could that be a look of fear. I know that you expected me to be un-attractive, sorry to disappoint you." The newly transformed demon circled the pair.

Her eyes flashed with delight as she taunted, "Yes, I am the one whose coming was foretold to you. Anuk's death guaranteed my reign. I am the betrayer. My desires are quite simple."

Jarrid reached to push Sara behind him and stepped up to confront the demon, but she ignored him and continued. "You should have honed your powers when you were young, Jarrid. They might have come in handy in the battle to come."

BLOOD MOON

An evil aura filled the room, causing the crowd to retreat further into the shadows. The move was swift and calculated; Luna grabbed Sara by the throat, her icy fingers choking the very life from the Virgin Queen, her words heeded. Jarrid's movement was a thoughtless action. His attack met Luna's swift reaction, raising her hand, banishing him from protecting his betrothed. Sara's gasp for air demanded Luna's attention, the life oozing from Sara's face her breath stolen, the thrashing ceased.

A smile crossed Luna's face and her ego fueled her words. "Behold Jarrid, this was far too easy." She focused on the life leaving Sara's limp body. "Now, we will be one."

The growl started low at first. The rush of the sound cut the air, and Caleb charged. His Wolfen tendencies rising beneath his skin, he brought the demon woman to her knees.

Claws of surging anger slid across her mocha skin and sliced her beauty into shreds. Feeling the threat, she addressed Sara, "Look upon me and remember, my day is near, Jarrid will be mine."

A vacuum pulled the wooden door shut, sucking the Dark Queen and her army out and into the darkness. Caleb sat in a heap, held up by the wall, still reeling from the impossible transformation. Jarrid gathered Sara in his arms, rocked her, and whispered. "The Poison Angel did not win this battle, for I am and always will be yours."

The women rallied around Sara, offered her water, and soothed her mind from the assault. Jarrid stood helpless, overseeing their attention, feeling lost. Nikko came up from behind and placed his hand on Jarrid's shoulder, "You must keep the faith, son."

"I just do not feel that we are ready to fight this battle." Jarrid hung his head and called across the crowd.

"Sebastian, we must move now to the tower, Sara, and I need some time to prepare for what is to come."

"Yes…" Caleb gathered himself, reached past Jarrid, took Sara's hand, and continued. "We must reach the safety of the tower. Our survival depends upon it." Jarrid showed no jealousy but instead gave respect to Caleb for his selfless act of courage. The Wolfen slinked away to recover and join his fellow councilmen with their duty to protect the queen.

"Jarrid, I know this is not the time," Nikko stood in Jarrid's space and demanded, "but it is of utmost importance, we must speak." The old man motioned toward the door and pushed the curtain aside, coaxing Jarrid to follow.

Standing in the corner of the small room, he stated. "The night we met, Jarrid, that night at the council meeting; I told you I was the father of Lora and Jim Mardi." Nikko placed his hands against the wall and lowered his head. "I lied! I couldn't tell you the truth. I was afraid if you knew the whole story, you would prevent me from coming with you, and your life depends on me being here." He turned toward Jarrid, to face his demon straight on.

"I knew you when you were a baby; in fact, I was there the day you were born." Jarrid was very intrigued with the direction that this conversation was taking and prompted Nikko to continue. "It was a beautiful day. Mary was anxious for you to arrive. I can remember her getting up that morning singing a very cheerful tune."

Hearing this, Jarrid broke in, "You remember her getting up? Why were you there with her? Are you a relative?"

Nikko continued. "Please, Jarrid, listen, and I will tell you what you want to know. Yes, I am a relative. Your

BLOOD MOON

mother was very excited about having a baby. She planned for you to be a boy. I don't know if she knew or if it was wishful thinking, but that day when you came, she was thankful to see that her dream had come true." The old man's words flowed through Jarrid's thoughts, grateful for the distraction to the battle ahead.

"She had arduous labor with you," Nikko sensed his acceptance and continued, "and we wondered, for a while, if she would make it, but she is of good stock, and finally, the blessed event occurred."

"From the moment you were born," Nikko's face gleamed with joy as his story filled the small room, "we all felt that you were special, but I guess every parent feels that way about their child."

Nikko looked deep into Jarrid's eyes to see if he had guessed the truth, not sure he continued. "Your mother told you that your father died?"

An ashen tone flowed down Jarrid's face, a symptom of his mind protecting itself from the shock of a secret being revealed. The floor called to his knees, and he fell, slumping forward. He stared up at the old man looking right past him.

Nikko knelt in front of Jarrid and spoke the words that he'd hoped he'd never have to say. He confronted the demon that he never wanted to face. "Jarrid, I am your father."

These words rang in Jarrid's ears. His mind began to spin, and he felt the walls closing in. He jumped to his feet, screaming, "'No! No! You cannot be my father. My father is dead. Mother would not have lied to me!" Jarrid felt a weakness in his knees that he had never known before and giving in to the strange feeling he stumbled toward the wall and leaned against it for strength.

SARAH KAGE

"Please let me explain. I need to tell you the reason!" He moved to prevent his son from leaving.

"If this is your truth," Jarrid turned to him with great hate flowing from his eyes and replied, "then be damned. There could be no excuse for a father to leave his children and his wife; it would be unforgivable."

"Look, I'm not trying to justify what I did." Nikko still felt the need to explain the reason that he'd left. "Please let me speak."

Jarrid relented against his better judgment and leaned against the wall to hear the old man's ranting.

"I was a very wild child," Nikko circled and stood by the door, "my parents were of the village, but they were not good people. My family didn't function with love and compassion. Hate and petty jealousy were the prime ingredients in my childhood."

Jarrid moved across the room he wanted to jump out of his skin, to let this truth pass him by, but his feet betrayed him, forcing his respect for this man.

"I yearned for the city, for the excitement and the opportunities that were beyond my reach." Nikko spilled his truth with a compelling fever. "It was a burning desire to leave the village and make my way in a different world. I'd planned this through my teenage years, thinking nothing could change my mind, and then I met your mother.

My emotions were under her spell, and I fell deeply in love. A raging passion and she felt the same for me. In the back of my mind, I knew that the dream of the city wouldn't leave me, but I pushed it further and further into my sub-conscious.

As our relationship grew and we knew that we wanted to spend our lives together as man and wife, I told Mary of my dream of the city. I asked her to accompany me as my wife, but your mother couldn't find it in her heart to leave the village for it was her home. I loved her so much that I thought I could forget about my desire and stay, that her love would be strong enough to satisfy the need that had been growing in my soul for many years.

At first, things were grand, such a wife. She fulfilled all my needs; our love grew to greater depths than I'd ever dreamed possible. Every day was like the first. Our love took on such depth that it scared us."

Jarrid couldn't find the strength to interrupt Nikko's confession, so he let him unload his story, purge it all without interruption.

"Then you were born, I held you in my arms, what more could a man want?" Nikko was thankful for Jarrid's attention and continued, "With all my soul, I wanted what I had to be enough, but no matter how hard I fought, the inevitable came to pass. I became depressed. Your mother noticed the difference; it was after Joshua's birth that she prompted me to follow my dream. Her sacrifice was for my spirit.

Again I asked her to come with me. Still, she refused, except this time she told me that she knew I'd have to follow my heart and go without her. She loved me so much that she was willing to let me go.

As much as I loved your mother, it was still harder to leave behind children that I would never know. It was a sort of arrangement between Mary and me, an understanding that I needed to follow my heart. But how could I explain this to my sons? Mary decided that she would tell you and Joshua that I was dead." Nikko fell against the wall and steadied himself to finish the truth.

"We agreed this would be the easiest and least painful arrangement. I have thought about you and your brother many times, started to go back to the village and tell you, see what kind of men the sons of Mary would be, but I did not have the courage.

The words collected in Jarrid's mind and brought on the uncontrollable fears pooled in his thoughts, *was Nikko telling him the truth?* The wall was the only support against the demons cast in his direction.

A pause came across Nikko's lips, his acknowledgment of Jarrid's distress. "Please, bear with me, Jarrid." The nod, an incentive for the old man to proceed, he cleared his throat and continued. Then one night in a dream, I was shown that I'd be part of your future, I'm here to save you from premature death. I know that you cannot forgive me, but you must allow me to fulfill my task. I lost you once my son; I do not want to lose you forever."

Jarrid listened in awe to this imposter. He walked away from the wall. Great hate welled up in his voice, and he addressed the man who had revealed himself as his father. "I do not know what cruel joke you are playing old man, but my father is dead, and I will keep him buried in my heart and mind forever!"

Jarrid stormed out, removing himself from the stories of an imposter, and the illusion of his heritage, his heart closed to the truth that tore at his soul.

BLOOD MOON
Chapter 24 The Sacrifice

Sunlight flooded across the floor and touched the wooden walls of the dark and dank hallway. Caleb stood mesmerized by the beam's slow, fluid movement, each inch of floor kissed and lit with the sun's beam of light to point the way of their escape.

A Light popped through one of the windows, and the beam shot down the hall, an open invitation to the battle that lay ahead. Nikko slipped behind Caleb and touched his shoulder. "It is time. We must go now."

"Everyone," Caleb's voice bellowed over the old man's head, it was his intent to gather the Army of Light. "Come close. We must make our ascent to the tower."

"What's wrong?" Sara headed toward the stage just as Jarrid rushed past. "Wait, are you alright?" Her hand fell on his arm; he pushed by, his eyes anchored to the floor, his soul lost in torment.

"Jarrid…" Louder and more direct, she stepped into his path.

Evidence of pain dripped from every feature on his face, he recognized her concern and answered. "I am okay." He turned his body toward the stage, but doubled back and took her into his arms. "I will gather our things and meet you at the hall." He kissed her quickly and turned to accomplish the task.

The group gathered at the hall and followed Caleb into the twisting and turning corridor. "Hey Vincent, can you do something about the lanterns? I cannot see a thing." Caleb motioned for the group to continue. "Sebastian, take the lead, I will bring up the rear." He walked the hall to encourage the group to continue their journey.

SARAH KAGE

"Token of light, hear my plea. Brighter than the sun ye shall be." Vincent hurried in front of Sebastian, flicked his wand into a spiral and spoke his incantation down the dark hall. The lanterns obeyed and filled the space with light.

The chanting sounded and circled Jarrid's head. The familiar sound stopped his forward motion, leaving him to stand in the middle of the hall with his ears tuned in to their frequencies. Sara turned with the question forming in her mouth, but Jarrid motioned and commanded. "Shh... Do you hear it?" He lowered his gaze. "Never mind, it has stopped."

Frustrated, he hurried her down the hall. "Thought I heard chanting," He exclaimed, joining her to walk at the back of the group.

"Oh good," Caleb shouted, approaching the royal couple. "You have our backs. Vincent is working on better lighting ahead." He walked backward and voiced his concerns. "We should stay close as a group. I have no idea what is ahead." He gave a nod and hurried to help Sebastian lead them to the tower.

Time passed marked by the tiredness of the group. Everyone bunched together into a small round room with a ladder in the middle, the end of the hall, the entrance to the tower.

The headcount complete, Caleb climbed the first rungs of the ladder and spoke, "We will gather here and catch our breath before we make the climb to the tower."

A few of the older people in the group complained. "How will we ever be able to climb to the tower?" Their voices rang out across the room.

"We have plenty of strong men to help each and everyone make the climb." Sebastian walked through the crowd to offer his encouragement.

BLOOD MOON

"I need to talk to you." Jarrid took Sara's arm and coaxed her out from under the arched doorway. "Walk with me." He turned and headed back down the corridor and stopped under one of the lanterns.

Weary, he slid down the length of the wall and sat on the stone floor, his head in his hands, he waited for her to join him. "Something's wrong. Why can't you tell me?" Sara stood in the hall, frustrated, and concerned.

His palm extended upward an invitation to join him, wanting to unburden his heart. Sara slid next to him and cuddled up into his chest. "You can tell me anything, Jarrid."

He caressed her into his embrace and then folded into her lap like a child. "After Luna's attack, Nikko corralled me in our room and unloaded a deep, dark secret." He rolled closer into a ball and buried his face in her lap. "It rocked me to my core, and I may never be the same."

Her hands touched his face, bringing it up into her stare, but his resistance held fast, and he muttered the words into the space between her bosoms. "Nikko is my father!"

"Jarrid," her gasp audible, "you thought your father was dead. Isn't that what Mary told you?" She tried to look in his face, but he held his breath hard against her chest.

"Yes, Sara, but he is very much alive." He jumped to his feet and shouted in frustration. "I guess I should be happy, try to forgive him, to understand the reason that he left us, but the pain is too much; the scar too deep."

"You are the gentlest man I've ever known." Sara rose to face his torment. "I know that it is hard for you to accept the reason that he left, but I also know that you are a fair human being, despite the hurt you will find it in your heart to forgive him, to rise to the occasion and be the better man."

Their bodies spent, they sat back down, his movement swift, the embrace urgent, to surrender his forgiveness. He sought solace in the fact that she knew him almost better than he knew himself. The emotion consumed his soul, a son for the love of a father, the pardon offered, no matter the sin.

Emotional exhaustion flowed between their bodies, and sleep overtook the shadows in the hallway. The hard floor interrupted Sara's nap, and she stretched her arms to wake. Thadeous stood with his back to her, surveying the corridor, like a centurion. Her small sigh brought him forward. "My queen," he bowed and stepped closer. "Do you require my services?"

The sleep still caressed her eyes, and she rubbed them, her hands searched the wall, and she called out, "Jarrid..."

"He is gone." The giant's armor clanked with his steps. "Nikko has gone after him." He bowed and pointed down the hall in the opposite direction of the ladder room.

"What do you mean, gone? When...?" In a flash, she pointed her feet in the direction that was indicated, "How long ago?"

"Jarrid's instructions were clear, my queen." He followed her and moved to stand in her way. "You are to come with me to the tower."

The glare was not royal, her face distorted, but the scorn of a woman hell-bent on her way. "Either accompany me or get the hell out of my way."

"If you are determined to follow him," he moved in front of her. "I will escort you." His shadow towered down the hall, his sword drawn, he led the way.

BLOOD MOON

***

The obscured opening came into view; Jarrid hadn't noticed it before when the group walked the corridor. The chanting echoed from the narrow indention, a sliver between two walls. The cadence was familiar, the musical backdrop to the night he tried to rape Sara and the fevered chants that brought him and Nikko to the fortress wall, their meeting a divine intervention.

Once his body disappeared into the crevasse, the chanting became louder and directed him to drag himself through the sliver between the walls. He pushed his foot across the narrow floor and dragged his body to the end of the constricted corridor, making his way, closing the distance from the outer hall to the location of the chants.

Light shone into the large cavern, lighting the room, revealing the passageway. Jarrid aligned his body with the edge of the opening and peered into the massive room.

The two-story ceiling dripped with moss and vegetation. The chanting still occupied Jarrid's mind with the scene of an altar coming into view. He quickly scoped out the architecture looking for the best vantage place to view the undead, gathering around the altar.

Then she moved into his view, her body adorned with a black see-through gown. Her raven hair and mocha skin shone in the dim light from the lanterns. The evil ritual's curse caused a knot, forming in the pit of his stomach, the incantation forbidden to mortal eyes.

Again the chanting took front and center only to be disturbed by the occasional scream from one of the undead. The creatures busied themselves with the preparation for what Jarrid assumed to be a ceremony. A stone table pushed up against the back wall held the carcass of a lamb; its throat cut the blood ceremonial.

SARAH KAGE

The group of undead, gathered around the table, dispersed, leaving only one with the chore of filling a gold goblet with the lamb's blood. The other evil entities joined Luna at the altar to start the ritual.

Have to find a better vantage point. The boulders, scattered around the room, offered the best solution. Jarrid picked out the nearest one and slinked to hide behind its mass.

The chanting ceased, like a reset, no movement broke the shadows, demons silent and still with Luna standing in the center, waiting for some remote command. Each hand rose into the air in unison, still no sound as they lifted her body into the air above their heads, her arms reached up, she called to her Dark Prince.

With dramatic results, the chanting broke into the silence. They lowered Luna down and gathered around the altar. There was a rhythm to the chants, an ancient seductive beat. Luna gyrated and danced; she answered the demands of her body with her hands, searching for the fever that taunted her loins. She buried her fingers into her need and brought her free hand up to her chest, igniting a second fire centered on her breast.

Stones rattled against the boulder, Jarrid moved, repositioning himself against the rock, his arousal too uncomfortable to continue kneeling behind the barrier. Luna's fevered incantation stopped. The gasp left her throat, and she turned in the direction of the noise.

"Jarrid, I know you are there." Her head turned toward him, and she proclaimed. "This is for you, my love. I am ready to take you." She let the black material fall from her hand to gather at her feet. "Your desire betrays you. My body yearns for the release only you can provide," her final statement the beginning, "Come, be one with me."

BLOOD MOON

"Temptress, you will never know my love, not even my lust." He jolted up, stood with authority, his words a declaration. "You are not demon enough to make me take you."

She glided down to him and turned into his path. Her words like sugar; "Foolish man, you are powerless. Your lust for me began long before you were a man; we were meant to rule this place of horror as mates."

The lustful demon lowered her shoulder, allowing the material to fall and enhance the rise of her breast. She lowered her eyes to gaze upon Jarrid's approval. "Yes, you cannot deny the fire that burns in your soul." She moved closer to fuel the flames. "Your body betrays you, enhanced by your virginity and the call of my seduction."

She gyrated against him, His lust drew her to his body, with hands swift and forceful; he pushed her away and screamed. "Enough, you will not..."

Buttons flew across the room, her hand swift; she tore his shirt from his chest. His complaint lost in the hard lustful kiss driven by demonic desire, his resistance futile.

Her one tool which she wielded with expertise, his virginity left him powerless to the demands of his fully matured body, his fight abandoned. His pent up sexual frustration drove his hands to pull her into his surrender, his abstinence a fleeting idea, her pull too strong.

"Come, it is time." She took his hand and guided his tortured body toward the altar. Her evil now in control his resistance overpowered by his lust.

"My love, your surrender," Luna whispered into the room.

The chanting acted as a drug and clouded Jarrid's mind. The stone of the altar pressed cold against his bare leg, her magic seamless to strip him and place his naked body upon the sacrificial stone.

SARAH KAGE

Spinning images seemed to dance across his reality. Luna's hands unleashed, exploring forbidden places, his body rising to meet her touch. The thought of Sara, a distant memory, his lust, driven by Luna's dark magic, all restraint lost.

Like a gazelle, Luna leaped into the air and straddled her naked body across Jarrid's swollen desire. She leaned down to whisper in his ear. "Soon, your body will have its release, and your soul will be mine."

His moans filled the air, so lost in lust and desire, he didn't feel the ropes around his hands and ankles, the undead tying him to the stone, preparing him for the transformation.

"Occidere eum, occidere eum, occidere eum," The chant louder, each demon added his voice and gathered around the altar. Jarrid's lips repeated the words; the Latin translated with a whisper, "Kill him…"

Each syllable of the chant prompted Luna to move her buttocks further down Jarrid's body until she hovered directly over his swollen desire. She positioned her mound against his shaft and pushed down hard, careful not to gain penetration, for he must remain a virgin until his death. His moans came fast with great intensity, his release close at hand. "Quick…" Luna called to the demon, "bring me the goblet now."

"Oh, Dark Prince, your will be done." She buried her flesh against his pulsating staff and anchored his risen body to the cold stone altar. His fever now at the point of no return, she dipped her hand into the warm lamb's blood and ran her finger across his chest in the shape of a pentagram.

One of the demons came up behind her and started chanting an ancient spell, his demonic words, encouragement for her to finish the ritual. He straddled

BLOOD MOON

Jarrid's legs and positioned himself behind the temptress, eager to help his queen with her seduction and continued his chant. Luna slowed her pace to leave Jarrid's body trembling and grasping for the release only seconds away.

As the ceremony proceeded and the demon's chanting grew louder, Luna leaned forward and whispered once more into Jarrid's ear, "feel the lust grow stronger, know that you will reign with me. You will be an Evil Prince to rule forever."

The demon pulled the knife from a hole in the altar, his spell now placed upon the steely blade. Luna reached behind and took the ceremonial dagger, pulled it from its sheath, revealing its blade, and spoke the words out loud, "Give in to your dark side, Jarrid. Join me. You know it is your birthright."

Jarrid's hands fought the ropes, his consciousness cleared, and the fear apparent in his face. His eyes opened just as the undead chanted his final words, the ritual brought to its conclusion. Luna screamed her last command, "It is written," She raised the knife above Jarrid's chest and brought its spell-bound blade toward its mark, the offering of his soul to the Devil himself, her father, his promise of their evil matrimony. The scream echoed through the room and bounced off the altar; then there was darkness.

***

Nikko watched helplessly, hidden behind the large boulder in the Altar Room. His decision calculated; he knew there was only a short amount of time to go back and bring re-enforcements.

Thadeous filled up the chasm of the slim hallway, barely moving his fingers to motion for Sara to follow. His head turned toward her, buried against the stone wall. "Come on. It isn't much further."

SARAH KAGE

His body prevented most light from entering between the walls. The darkness cascaded down toward the Altar Room, only to peek around his legs in tiny bursts.

Nikko felt his way through the darkness his face and shoulders plastered into the wall; he shimmied toward the larger hall, frantic to get help. "Oh, thank God, Thadeous, I was coming to get you. Jarrid is in trouble." Nikko tugged on the barbarian's arm and pulled him toward the Altar Room.

Sara pushed the warrior, her tiny frame no match for his bulk, her words flaming, "Nikko, where is Jarrid?"

"At the end of the corridor, hurry," The urgency in his voice prompted them forward, to push their bodies down and out. "We are almost there. I will signal to stop. At that point, we will need to sneak out from between the walls and take cover behind the boulders in the room."

The large stone barely hid Thadeous; his armor betrayed him and announced their feeble attempt at hiding just as Luna rose up on her knees, lifted the blade as far as it would go and with a mighty yell, released all of her strength to bury the ritual blade deep into Jarrid's chest.

No thought or will stopped Thadeous' self-less act. Sara jumped to her feet just in time to witness the giant sail through the air; his sword rose to strike the steely blade from the demons' hand. His monstrous body rained down on Jarrid, protecting his friend from a soulless death. Luna had no time to react and plunged the blade deep into Thadeous' massive back, her mark true; he fell to the ground and pulled her with him, his last act of courage.

"No, Thadeous…" Sara rushed to Jarrid just as Luna fell to disappear behind the altar. The undead stood as statues awaiting their queen's instructions. Sara reached Jarrid and sobbed into his chest.

The sound of cracking bones and screams of agony rose from the floor. Sara lifted her head from Jarrid's chest. Her eyes fixed on the glistening red skin and the massive arch of Thadeous's back as it rose up from behind the altar. His spine ridged with hideous bone formations like the back of a mighty dragon.

"Jarrid... wake up!" Sara punched and prodded his lifeless body. Her eyes captivated by the evil transformation playing out on the other side of the altar. Thadeous's body twice its size, now forming before her eyes. His colossal neck, the stump for his head, its features hideous, the frame for the sharp, rounded horns that popped from his forehead, the sound nauseating, Sara hid her eyes.

"I love you, Jarrid. Please wake up." Her lips soft upon his face, his reaction slow at first, he started to stir.

"Son..." Nikko came up by Jarrid's side. "Please, you must wake up." He pulled at his shoulders and with Sara's help, managed to get him to his feet. She looked back over Jarrid's shoulder just as the Demon Prince stood for the first time. His massive body like an animal with a long, scaled tail, horns for a crown, and teeth sharpened to points.

The shake violent, the monster embraced his new body and addressed Sara, "Hmm..." he leaned across the altar and pawed at her, grabbed her arm, and spoke, "Are you the one that brought me forth?"

"Let go, you evil monster." She escaped his grasp and turned back to Jarrid.

The transformation too much for the Evil Queen, her body lay at the bottom of the altar. She came to just in time to see her dark mate pawing after Sara; her words screeched into the air, "No, no, Jarrid, I want you." She laid her trembling body across the altar. Great sobs filled the room, her agony released.

Sargon's massive hand reached for her raven hair and yanked it from behind, his monstrous voice bellowed out in anger, "He is not your mate. It is I, Sargon. Enough of this, we must unite." The demon didn't wait for Luna's reply. He dragged her past the altar with a devilish scream, pulling her into the darkness to consummate the unholy union.

"Come on, Sara. We need to get Jarrid back to the tower." Nikko slinked between the corridor walls, and Sara followed, helping Jarrid maneuver the narrow passage. Before she passed into the corridor's darkness, she heard Sargon's screams and turned to watch him drag Luna away to embrace her evil reign.

***

"Okay, everyone, when the rest of the group returns, we will start our climb. Please ready yourself." Caleb jumped off the ladder and approached Sebastian. "I hope they return soon. We need to…"

The chatter started at the door and filtered through to Caleb's ears. The group parted and made way for Nikko to carry Jarrid in to lay him in front of the ladder. Sara rushed to his side, fussing with the cape thrown across his body.

"What happened?" Caleb rushed to ask. "Is he okay?" He didn't wait for an answer but instructed the group. "Stand back, and give them some room."

"He will be fine." Nikko stood and offered his opinion. "But we have much bigger problems." He squatted back down to help Jarrid recover.

"Yes, we do, and the problem has a name, Sargon." Sara stood, folded her arms, and addressed the crowd.

BLOOD MOON

"Luna has managed to take a mate. Our friend Thadeous gave his life to protect Jarrid from that horrible fate." She turned back, reached out to take Jarrid's hand, and continued. "His selfless act, his life given in Jarrid's place, he transformed into Sargon, a hideous evil creature to reign by Luna's side."

A wretched scream pierced the air, and the group cringed, the demonic couple's scream like cats in heat, fighting through the night. "The loss of our friend saddens me, however," Caleb offered up what was really on his mind. "It does my heart good to know that Luna is getting what she deserves." Caleb stared at Sara, bowed his head, and continued. "Jarrid, are you well enough to make the climb?"

Before he could speak, the bright light filled the space and flooded up the ladder to light the way to the tower. Jarrid's memory returned to the flash of the steely blade and the vision of Thadeous right before the dagger sunk into his chest. "No, not Thadeous," Jarrid shot up and cried out!

The rustling of feathers caused the group to part; her white light preceded her to envelop Jarrid, her pearlescent wings circled round to caress him in her angelic embrace. She kissed him lightly on the cheek and spoke her blessing, "You are anointed my son, to be the Prince of Light. You will reign; your battle foretold, to seek her hand, the union of righteousness. Grieve for your friend, but know his sacrifice will aid in you being victorious over the Evil One."

Her wings softly collapsed toward her back, and she addressed the group, "We can't afford any more time for grief, my fine people. The undead gather, their queen and king will emerge from their union with only one thing on their minds, to kill Sara."

SARAH KAGE

The clanking of nuts and bolts and the ticking of clocks filled the room. Angelica's wings shuddered and added to the sounds that announced Anastasia, the tail of her brocade gown rubbing and catching on the stone floor. Jarrid acknowledged the peculiar woman. "Are you joining our retreat to the tower?"

"Oh, please do…" Sara contributed her thoughts. "Your presence would really be appreciated."

"That is not my purpose." Anastasia's eyes fell upon Angelica, and she continued. "I am an ally, but this will be the end of my journey."

The conversation between the two women was like a dance. Some unknown music choreographed before this moment, their intentions agreed upon with the outcome unanimous.

The screams of the undead broke the spell, their attack only moments away. "Start climbing now!" Caleb instructed the older people to go first. "Sebastian, Tank, help the weakest of the group to climb, now."

"Come on, kids…" Alex gathered the children and started to climb. Sebastian stood on the top rungs and guided them to the top of the ladder. Only Sara and Jarrid remained in the room with Angelica and Anastasia.

"Sara, what are you waiting for?" Alex called down from the top of the ladder.

The undead filed into the room in their usual slow-motion fashion. Jarrid once again petitioned Anastasia. "I wish you would reconsider and go with us."

"No time for that, Jarrid. You must go now." Anastasia positioned herself between Angelica and the undead, who gathered in a group just in front of the ladder.

"You are jeopardizing your soul and the battle, Jarrid. You must go now and get Sara to safety." Anastasia shoved the councilman toward the ladder and stood to face the undead.

In the chaos, no one noticed one of the undead sneaking around the back of the ladder. The demon's decaying hand reached through the rung and grabbed Sara's ankle.

The words of the ancient prayer flowed from Angelica's lips, her body rising, wings spread to touch each side of the room. The ladder began to vibrate and shake. Sara reached between the rungs and gouged at the lifeless eyes, while Jarrid pulled the demon around the ladder, slinging him into the middle of the room.

"Climb, Sara." They reached the upper rungs and turned just in time to watch one of the undead unleash his attack directed at Anastasia. She fell to the floor before he even touched her. Angelica's words, the ancient language, caused the air to leave the room, a vacuum of silence, all actions halted.

Voices of Cherubs hummed and sang the music to coax Anastasia's soul to join Angelica and make her journey to the bright light. Her spirit stopped momentarily to address Sara. "This is my wedding gift, my purpose to sacrifice my body as a sentry to protect you in the Days of Peace." Her spirit rose, her destiny fulfilled. She was finally free.

The undead cringed, the mere sight of Anastasia's body lying at the bottom of the ladder, acted like a collar of garlic to a vampire. They retreated with screams, pushing back to the evil shadows where they lived.

"Go now, my children..." Angelica floated to face Jarrid. "Anastasia's body will act as protection. The undead won't be able to follow you to the tower. The ladder is the only way in."

SARAH KAGE

"Really, you guys. Do you need a special invitation?" Alex's face poked across the opening at the top of the ladder and prompted. "You have to see this." Her face disappeared with only her hand shooting through the hole, emphasizing her impatience.

"We need to move, Sara." Jarrid pushed her through the opening, her words expelled from her lungs, his large hands moving her forward into their destiny.

Angelica pulled her wings against her body, floated through the opening, and gave thanks for Anastasia's sacrifice of love.

BLOOD MOON
Chapter 25 Days of Peace

Colored beams of light shot from the circle of stained-glass windows and surrounded the top of the tower. The wall held a circular staircase. Its landings scattered on each floor of the castle-like turret.

A large stage with rows of stone pews took up the back part of the room, with a staircase on the left that seemed to go nowhere. Light shone from the windows, lifting the mood of the group, with the promise of safety and relief from the undead.

Angelica's light parted the group on her way to the stage. A collective hush followed her until she reached the podium and began to speak with a voice of authority. "These will be your Days of Peace." Jarrid and Sara made their way to the front of the crowd, embraced each other, and let a sigh leave their lips, a second to breathe.

"Before we begin, I would like to have a moment of silence for the sacrifice given by Anastasia." Angelica bowed her head and gave thanks.

"Mommy…" Lizzy tugged on Alex's hand, tightened her arm around Chad's shoulders, and whispered her question. "Did Anastasia go to Heaven?" Her eyes were filled with tears, her thanks for the gift of love.

"Yes, sweetie…" Alex knelt and gathered her daughter close. "She is with the Father now."

Lizzy wrapped her arms around Alex's neck, sniffled, and declared. "She will keep us safe, Mommy. I will thank Father tonight when I say my prayers." Alex squeezed her daughter, pulled Chad close, and directed her attention to Angelica.

"I know that some of you suffered losses with the last attack. We mourn the soldiers of the Army of Light." She bowed her head in reverence and continued. "Anastasia's gift was substantial, and her sacrifice afforded this peace I speak of." She moved out from in front of the podium and pointed to the rooms scattered around the tower. "You will find refuge in these accommodations, a time to gather strength and prepare for the battle ahead. Anastasia's body at the bottom of the ladder will prevent any undead from reaching this chamber."

The angel motioned to the crowd an invitation to the councilmen and their queen to join her on stage. Sara stood by Jarrid's side with the others standing close. Angelica pointed toward Jarrid and Sara. "These are your protectors, the ones who will finish the battle started by Luna and her Evil Army."

Angelica took her hand and coaxed Sara to the front of the stage. "The weight of the world lies on your queen's shoulders." She embraced Sara and walked her toward Jarrid, offering him the Righteous One's hand and proclaimed. "Virtue has been their cross to bear, *The Spirited Sword of Purity* protected at all cost. They have proven themselves worthy."

"Yeah, love and purity, this stuff is relevant, but we are warriors and need to know what we're up against and how long this peace will last?" Caleb paced across the stage, stopped, and waited for the other councilmen to agree.

"You say, Days of Peace…" Sebastian crossed in front of Caleb and asked, "What exactly does that mean?"

"Well, I would assume…" interrupted Vincent, "some creature comforts will be in order." He walked up the stairs and stamped his staff against the floor. "There's a kitchen just on the other side of the stage, fully equipped with everything needed to feed an army."

BLOOD MOON

The group started to clamor, each one speculating about the return of hunger. "Is it true?" One of the men rushed the stage to wait for the answer.

The affirmation floated into the air, Angelica's acknowledgment swift. "Yes, this is true, but only one of the gifts given to enhance your strength and stamina needed for the confrontation."

All Sebastian heard was *hunger*; he dropped to his knees and stared out into the crowd with his fear falling upon Alex's stare.

Angelica could feel his terror and quickly confronted his concern. "Sebastian, we'll deal with it. I promise you." She bowed her head and helped him to his feet.

"As you have guessed, along with hunger comes the need for facilities, and those are located around the base of the tower." Laughter wafted above the crowd and lent an air of comedy in a room drenched in drama.

"I have a significant announcement to make concerning Jarrid and your queen." This statement raised the level of excitement in the group, with silence falling over the crowd.

"Anastasia prophesized that Jarrid and Sara's marriage would take place in this very chapel." Her declaration interrupted by the cheers and whistles that filled the room and rattled the windows. She waited for the celebration to subside, then continued, "The consummation achieved inside these very walls."

The councilmen gathered around Jarrid and began to congratulate him, the backslapping and shoving customary among warriors. He moved away from their comments and gathered Sara in his arms before he addressed the room. "Well, I have to ask her first, and of course, she must accept." Sara's face turned red, and she pushed him away with a smile.

SARAH KAGE

"Just a few more things before you seek out your accommodations." Angelica pulled Sara away from Jarrid's side and continued. "Food will be provided daily by the Father. Please go about your days with peace and seek out the things that bring you happiness. Your hope will be the armor that you'll carry into the battle." The group mingled and celebrated their freedom, then scattered off to find the first thing that made them happy, a place to call their own.

Angelica pulled Jarrid across the stage to rescue him from the exuberance of his fellow warriors. "Okay, you guys can celebrate with a beer later, right now; I must show them the wedding chamber."

The men's mouths watered at the mere mention of a beer, and they shot like little boys in the direction of the kitchen. "We will save you one, Jarrid." The laughter followed them off the stage, "or not!" Vincent shot back.

The staircase rounded to follow the wall; Angelica led the royal couple to the top landing and stood in front of the door. "This will be your wedding chamber. Jarrid, your room is on the lower level, your accommodations until the wedding." He nodded his head in agreement.

The door opened into a massive room decorated with red and gold oriental rugs and velvet drapes. An enormous bed draped in hues of gold with fringe and tassels, decorating the many pillows scattered at the headboard.

The fireplace stood on the other side of the room, its wooden mantle ornate, the hand carvings of angels and harps cascading down the sides and across the top. The fire roared to lend its warmth to the room and entice the lovers with its romance.

"I hope this meets with your approval." Angelica moved to the other side of the room, with a sitting area

BLOOD MOON

situated in front of the fireplace. "It should make for a romantic honeymoon."

"This is perfect." Sara reached for Jarrid's hand, pulled him close, and stated, "Much more than I expected. Thank you, Angelica."

"Your sacrifices have not gone unnoticed; you have earned the right of becoming man and wife." Angelica reached for the door, but turned back and continued. "Cherish your moments of peace and rest, to gain strength from each other's love." They didn't wait for her to leave, the joy overcoming their desires.

The fire crackled and popped, its warmth circled the room and fell upon Sara's back. Jarrid's slow breaths cascaded down her neck, his hands taking liberty's just this side of taboo.

The stubble of his beard raked across her skin, and her eyes opened to peer over his shoulder. "Look," she gently pushed Jarrid away and walked over to the door on the outer wall. "I wonder what's behind this door."

She made a sudden move to open it, but Jarrid quickly maneuvered himself in front and pushed it open to reveal a small bathroom.

"Oh, I don't believe it!" She brushed past him and stood in the middle of the Victorian style washroom, with a claw foot tub positioned on a platform, complemented by the water-closet toilet. In the corner was an old trunk with a large window just above it.

"Well, my queen, I think this will do quite well." Jarrid stepped in to inspect the small room.

She walked toward the tub with the hope welling up in her soul. She touched the faucet, gave it a spin, and waited, holding her breath, expecting nothing. The steaming water flowed from the ornate tap and swirled in the bottom of the tub. "No! It can't be. Hot water! Am I dreaming?"

The warm bath called to her, causing her to shoo Jarrid out, demanding her time to once again feel like a woman, instead of a hard calloused barbarian. "Go, do some man thing, have a beer, just let me have this time. I promise it'll be well worth the wait."

"I will be right outside the door." Jarrid backed away and slipped out into the bedchamber.

The tub filled with the sound of the soothing water, small waves lapped to cross each other and shine like diamonds. Sara turned her attention to the trunk and found some gauze material and a rope. The mirrored image clear, evidence of waged battles smudged across her face, hair matted, and tousled. Her inner-Warrior Princess revealed.

She lowered her tired aching body slowly into the warm liquid; its heat kissed her skin and embraced her with its warmth. Her eyes closed as she slipped her shoulders under the water, but the smell of lavender soon caused her eyes to peek and feel for the bar of soap resting on the rim of the tub.

"Hmm…" her reaction to the feel of the soft soap, its lather leaving the smell of fresh lavender upon her skin to wash away the hints of danger, her red hair submerged and washed to soak in the fragrance.

Each drip of the faucet lulled her into a false sense of security, lingering in the haze, steam, and scent of fresh flowers. So soothing, she almost fell asleep, sinking further down below the water.

A soft knock filled the room, and Jarrid inquired. "Are you okay?"

His voice startled Sara; she came up with the water reacting to her motion to spill over the tub. "Yes…" She wiped the suds from her face and assured him. "I'm almost done. You're next."

She hurried to rinse her clothes and hung them to dry. She wrapped her wet hair with a torn piece of the gauze material, separated two more pieces, dried herself with one, and fashioned the other as a make-shift robe, anchored with the rope. The mirror reflected her image. She lifted the material above her bosom, not wanting to be too enticing, tightened the rope, and took a deep breath.

The door slowly opened, Jarrid stirred from his twilight, blinking his eyes to adjust to her beauty. She stepped across the floor and met his strong embrace.

"Hmm, woman, you are nothing if not tempting." He slid the thin gauze up and under his touch.

"Excuse me. Pardon me. I think not." She guided his hands to his waist and slipped away. "I suggest you follow my lead. I ran your water, go before it cools." She rushed him into the bathroom and pulled the door shut, yearning for the comfort of the soft bed.

He made short work of the warm water, the lavender soap not his choice, but it was better than nothing. His ear was ever vigilant to the sounds coming from the other room, not wanting to leave Sara alone.

The gauze material wrapped double around Jarrid's waist to fall against his loins, tucked between his legs to anchor behind him and into the rope, tied and draped around his hips.

Reflections of an ancient warrior stared back at him from the mirror, suddenly shy and self-conscience of his mature body. His hair fell wet on his shoulders, tiny streams dripped down his chest, toward his waist, the water soaked up by the thin white material.

SARAH KAGE

The bedroom warm and inviting, he stood watching Sara's chest rise and fall with soft breaths, followed by tiny sighs; sleep overtook her body stretched out on the bed, her robe barely covering her curves. Jarrid's uncontrollable urges surged through his very being, his restraint waning.

A soft voice called his name. "I must speak with you." Angelica pushed the door open and motioned for him to join her on the landing. "Yes, let me put something on. I will be right there." The angel floated down the stairs to the floor of the chapel to stop in front of his bedchamber.

She stepped over to the stone pew and motioned for him to join her. Angelica waited for him to sit down and then proclaimed her joyful news. "You and Sara will be married in this very chapel in two days." Her face beamed with the joyous proclamation.

"Two days..." Jarrid jumped to his feet, turned, and sat back down. His face white, he touched the angel with clammy hands and gasped. "How..." He caught his breath and whispered as he remembered. "What about the medallion? It must be part of the ceremony; tradition demands it."

"First, the good news, this wedding will be a holy union, recognized by God. It will take place here in the chapel, and Vincent will preside, with you and Sara writing your vows." Angelica rose and contemplated her next revelation. "With the consummation of your wedding, Luna will have one less hold over you and Sara. This gift was given by God to help with the battle between good and evil."

The angel sat her pearlescent body back onto the stone pew; her face drooped with a frown. "What is wrong? Is it the medallion?" Jarrid's guilt spread across his face; if not for his lustfulness, he would still possess the medallion.

"Yes, the fact that Luna possesses the relic is a bit of a problem." She knew the reason for his guilt and tried to focus his attention on the future. "Luna will use the medallion to force you and Sara to sully your love, to consummate it before the wedding. Your very souls are at risk. If she succeeds, the battle will be over before it has begun."

Angelica moved to stand in front of Jarrid's bedchamber. "I have laid some fresh battle clothes and gear on your bed." She opened the door and gestured for him to follow. "You must retrieve the medallion from Luna and offer it to your bride as an engagement gift. Only with it securely in your possession can the wedding take place."

"It will not be easy? Sargon will be a formidable enemy." Jarrid's opinion filled the room. He stepped toward the bed, and picked up the leather pants. He touched the metal armor and embraced the sword. "But I will be victorious, and fight by the side of my wife, to stop the end of days."

Before Angelica left Jarrid, she offered one last piece of advice. "You will need strength, cunning, skills, and above all else, the power that resides deep in your soul, call upon it to conquer her magic and win the medallion back from her evil grip."

"Go now, Jarrid, with my blessing." Angelica watched as he sheathed his sword, swallowed his fear, and accepted his mission, the possession of the medallion the only thing standing in the way of his marriage.

Her light faded, leaving Jarrid alone with his fear and joy, Sara's love in jeopardy and his life on the line.

SARAH KAGE

Sleep had been elusive for Nikko; he slipped behind a column in the chapel and listened to every word between Angelica and Jarrid. The medallion was a part of his family since the beginning, its powers mighty. It had blessed the union of the head councilman and his bride through the ages.

So the medallion had been bestowed upon Mary, and now her son. Nikko's mission to help Jarrid retrieve the family heirloom, present its powers to Sara and bless their wedding. He followed the sound of Jarrid's sword clanking against his armor, its call to action, his fate now set in stone.

***

The rounded corridor poured out of the Altar Room and circled down to the pits of Hell. Roots entangled with bones and pieces of rotting flesh to hang down and mingle with the moisture collected in the décor, to drip onto the stone floor. The perfect atmosphere for Luna and Sargon's evil honeymoon, compliments of their Dark Prince.

Sargon's lust was mammalian, driven by his malignant transformation. He dragged Luna further down the corridor until he could wait no longer, slung her against the wall, and violated her. His animal physique mingled with her virginity to tear at her will. His demon screams followed the last powerful thrust, his evil desire, the union consummated on unholy grounds. "It is done!" Sargon pulled away from her body only to reposition her for his next assault.

She was lost, now giving in to her animal desires; she wrapped her legs around the red demon and surrendered her first orgasmic release, calling out as the last tings of pleasure flowed down her legs, "Jarrid..."

BLOOD MOON

The roar tore at her ears, his hand relentless across her face, bringing her against the wall. "My name is Sargon, your mate. I will make sure you remember this." He grabbed her again and threw her against the wall with his hand around her throat.

The smell of her blood riled his senses and prompted his evil lust to rise once more. His claw raked at her buttocks. Her position fixed to bury his final desire, his hand still around her throat; he surrendered to her pull and buried his demon seed deep into her womb.

Sargon released her and fell to the ground. His lust and anger satisfied; he drifted into a deep sleep. Luna huddled against his body, bruised and battered, the union brutal, but her ache for Jarrid consumed her thoughts. Sleep the only kindness afforded to the Queen of Darkness.

The searing pain disrupted her sleep; the Devil stood in the shadow of the corridor, his black wings folded against his body. Satan drifted across the floor, coming closer with every breath until his nostrils flared at the smell of blood and lust rising through the air.

He gathered his wings around his body and retreated from the stench. Luna bowed and hid her face, "I am your servant, you, my master."

"I've heard your cries, the sorrow in the outcome of your wedding." He moved to stand over the sleeping Sargon. "You didn't succeed in your attempt to take Jarrid for your mate." Luna rose and started to talk. He raised his finger to her mouth and continued. "But I think Sargon is a much better choice." His evil laughter filled the air.

Satan's wings extended, and he backed Luna against the wall. His teeth bared the words profound. "It is no matter. You will have a second chance to steal *The Spirited*

Sword of Purity from your adversaries." He stepped back to give Luna room to breathe. "The lovers are on their way, Jarrid, with his sword and soon Sara will follow to protect him from your assault."

Luna's passion for this fight was waning, but she must obey her master. "How would you have me serve you?"

"Oh, your job is straightforward." He slithered to the other side of the hall and spoke the words. "The lust consumes them, and all their God can say is 'No, my children.'" Again he rose up in her face. "You must use the medallion and tempt them, persuade them to give in to their animal desires, ignite their passions, and take away their control, push them into each other's lust."

She moved to open her mouth and complain. "But Jarrid's virginity is of no concern to me anymore." She cringed toward the ground and covered her face.

The Devil's wrath swift and wretched, his anger vomited from his mouth. "This is not about you, whore. Their virginity stops me from conquering the world, and threatens *The Feast of Souls*."

He rushed across the hall, pushed his demonic body against her, pinning her to the wall. "I will control their souls, the end of days accomplished." He moved away just as she slid down the wall, and fell in an obedient heap on the floor.

"Your victory, Luna, will guarantee the title as the Dark Queen to sit by my side with Sargon, to rule the new earth, draped in darkness, my thousand-year reign written in blood."

The Dark Prince raised his hand and caused Luna to fall into a deep sleep. He whispered in her ear. "Invade Sara's dreams and enlighten her to the fact that Jarrid is on his way to defeat you. Prompt her to join his fight. Do it now." His laughter haunting, the Prince of Darkness, took his leave.

***

The lavender scent rose through the air and drifted under Sara's nose each time she stirred to move the bed sheets. Her mind rolled in a dream state, watching Luna walking toward her to stand by the side of the bed. Not able to move, she watched as the witch shook the bedpost and demanded. "Acknowledge me; do you think you are sleeping beauty?"

Luna taunted, "Coward! Really, Sara, this is a dream, and everyone knows dreams can not hurt you." The sheets crumpled around Sara as she pulled away to sit against the headboard.

"Quickly now, you must go to him." Luna's demeanor changed, and she coaxed Sara. "Jarrid is outside the protection of Anastasia's body and is headed toward the Altar Room to battle Sargon; without you."

"No..." Sara grabbed, at the linens, twisted and contorted to restrain her violent lunge from the bed. The coldness of the floor centered her, and she realized it was a dream. She ran to the bathroom, grabbed her damp clothes, dressing as she bolted out the door, her intention to end Luna's hold on her once and for all.

Sargon moved to wake Luna from her dream, his intention clear, she pushed the thought of Jarrid far back into the dark corners of her mind, surrendered to her mate and the demands of her Dark God, the screams echoing through the halls of the mighty Fortress, their lust satisfied once more.

***

Nikko reached the narrow hallway and pushed himself toward the Altar Room. His eyes fought for just a glimpse of his son before he confronted the witch and her demonic mate. The sound of metal scraping on the wall told him Jarrid was close.

"Jarrid..." Nikko whispered into the darkness. "Is that you, son?" Jarrid halted his approach and turned his head toward the voice behind him in the narrow corridor. "Speak up, it's me, son."

"You should not have followed me, old man." Jarrid's breath fell hard against the stone wall. "Go back; I must do this alone." He reached the Altar Room and spoke his disapproval once more. "Turn back and make sure Sara does not follow me. This is not her fight."

"You are going after the medallion. I know you must present the wedding gift to Sara." The old man took Jarrid's arm and pleaded. "I have your back son, please."

Nikko's words played across Jarrid's mind like a musical key. Each syllable placed in just the right pitch to trigger the forgotten memory, the gift of a small boy playing in the Fortress.

"Listen to me, old man, and do as I say." Jarrid grabbed Nikko's arm to emphasize the importance of his words. "I know Sara has followed me. You must stop her."

"Yes, my leader." Nikko knew he had relinquished the title to his son many years ago. "I hear and obey." The father bowed to his son, the only option, to obey Jarrid and retreat.

BLOOD MOON
Chapter 26 The Medallion

Echoes of Jarrid's memories flooded the Altar Room. Sara's screams bounced off the wall to mingle with the coldness in the space; his body draped across its stone. The final second's right before Thadeous gave his life, the steely blade finding its mark, the ultimate sacrifice of a friend. The vision of the evil red glow to announce the birth of Sargon, Luna's demonic mate, the transformation erasing all traces of Thadeous and his selfless act.

The scream pulled Jarrid back into the present, his eyes staring upon the altar; he focused on his task, the medallion. The words remembered and their advice poignant, *the power you have buried for all of these years.*

Footsteps mingled with his thoughts, painting a picture of a small boy playing in the inner walls of the Fortress. Afternoons wiled away with saving princesses and battling dragons. It was a fine line between reality and the whims of a young knight, fantasy wielding the tools of battle, his life for his kingdom.

It moved, the stone obeyed his thought, pulling away from its resting place, only directed by pure will. "Hmm…" Jarrid remembered the elated feeling of having power over the rock, and then the shame when Mary announced it could only come from evil.

Never attempt that again! Mary had yelled when Jarrid so proudly announced his ability. *You must not play in the Fortress. It is an evil place.* Jarrid did play behind the walls of the Fortress, but never again attempted to summon the wicked gift, until now.

A slap of thunder rounded the room, ending in the hellish scream that poured from the corridor past the altar. Jarrid's thoughts scattered to the wind, only to fall upon his lips in a profound proclamation, "Of course, the buried gift."

The marching steps sounded through the corridor, the undead coming out ahead of their king and queen. They filled the Altar Room, surrounded its perimeter, and waited for the dark couple.

Jarrid dove in behind a boulder, undetected by the zombie creatures, and watched the evil pair enter the room. Sargon had Luna by the arm, an indication of his dominance over his queen. His red scales covered the demon from his head to the long forked tail that swung violently to match his apparent agitated mood.

Sargon looked exhausted. He pushed Luna to the ground and lay down beside her, his eyes yearning for sleep. The undead stood down, hung their heads as statues in the protection of the newlywed couple.

That could have been me. Jarrid took in every demonic detail of Luna's King. His face distorted and grotesque, with a body over nine-feet tall and shoulders to frame his massive chest like the mantel of a large stone fireplace.

The red devil moved to disturb Luna, with the medallion clanking against her skin. Jarrid summoned the feeling from his stomach, the single desire to possess the medallion and float it into his waiting hand. The sweat formed on his brow, the exertion of his will forcing the relic to rise and release itself from her neck, but alas, it merely shimmed against her mocha skin.

The knot in Jarrid's gut released and focused on the fact that he had only been able to disturb the medallion, just enough to raise Luna's suspicions. Her movement caused Sargon to rise and sniff the air, his senses filled with the intruder's essence.

BLOOD MOON

Jarrid's swift movement caught the eye of one of the undead, and without warning, they were on him, escorting him to bow in front of their queen, the sting of evil fists encouraging him to obey. "Should have stayed put, foolish man!" she laughed. "But you did not, and now you are my captive, the need for a mate, already satiated."

"Release him!" She raised his face to demand his attention. The command obeyed, leaving Jarrid slumped to the floor; his head hung in confusion. The undead meandered around the room, causing Luna to become agitated, and she screamed, "Leave me, away with your rotting corpses."

The sound scraped across her ears, Luna's last syllables shouted into the room. She turned just in time to see Sara leap for the concealment of the boulder, her hiding place offering protection while she contemplated her assault.

Nikko breached the narrow opening just as Sara rose to confront Luna. He had obeyed his leader and gone back, but his soul wouldn't let his son face Luna alone. "Sara…" he blew his cover and pushed into the room, "stay back, wait."

"Welcome, everyone, so glad you could join us, Nikko." Luna shot her finger in his direction and used her magic, placing him against the wall; he was helpless, left only to watch.

"Jarrid… snap out of it." Sara helped him to his feet and headed for the wall.

"Oh, I would really love it if you could stay a little longer." Luna spouted as she noticed Sargon had awakened from his slumber and moved between the lovers. The demon pushed Sara toward the altar, pressing against her body, anchoring his large claws down on the stone, on each side of her hips, pinning her beneath his weight.

"Well, Sargon, are you intrigued by her beauty?" Luna stood beside the altar and taunted her mate. "Do you wish to have her for your own, to take her virginity as you did mine?" She pulled at his shoulder to release his attack. "Sorry to disappoint you, my love, but Satan will not allow that."

Sara sprung from the demons release and joined Jarrid, slumped against the wall. Luna slinked toward them and whispered in Sara's ear. "It is such a shame that you do not know Jarrid's, physical love." She reached for the medallion and shone it into Jarrid's eyes while she pulled on Sara to join her in the middle of the room.

The medallion glowed green and pulsated with a lustful beat. Helpless against its pull, Jarrid and Sara gathered to hear the words. "You may have a seat," Luna instructed, moving the medallion back and forth in front of their faces.

"Lust is an emotion just this side of love; one complements the other." Luna placed Sara's hand on Jarrid's unwilling arousal. "The power of lust is all-consuming, give in, and let your sins combine."

Sara's soul screamed somewhere in the depths of her mind. The ache for control rose up and shook her very foundation. Luna reached for Jarrid's hand to place it against Sara's virgin mound, but instead was met with Sara's resistance, the strength of ten men rained down on the witch with the intensity of all the pent-up sexual frustration from years of abstinence. Sara pounced.

"You–will–not–sully–our–love," each word spoken with the force to back Luna against the altar, bent to Sara's will, the Evil One's face riddled with confusion.

BLOOD MOON

So swift was Sara's attack, the velocity so strong, it had missed Sargon's attention. He roared and jumped to save his queen, met by Jarrid's vigorous attack, bringing the demon to his knees, the blade just grazing his shoulder.

Luna's outstretched neck still dangled over the altar with the medallion exposed and vulnerable. Before Sara could loosen her grip to grab for the relic, Nikko jumped up from behind, and grabbed the medallion to release it from Luna's neck; its liberation caused him to fall backward and watch the round disk float into the air just in front of Jarrid. "Son, grab it!" he called as he landed violently against the wall.

Sargon's point of view led him to believe that Nikko had grasped the medallion before he fell and lunged with his outstretched claw to strike the old man down. Jarrid watched, in horror as the demon opened Nikko's chest, the gaping wound glistening in the dim light.

In one movement, Jarrid shoved the medallion in his pocket and leaped over the altar to push Sargon away. Sara pulled Luna from the chantry and drove her toward the corridor with her taunting words. "Be gone, evil witch. Take your demon mate and scurry off to the dark underworld where you belong." Sara shoved the witch down the corridor and turned to Sargon. "Take your evil wife and go from this place. You no longer possess the medallion; your powers are weak. You didn't win this battle. Go and lick your wounds."

"Nikko, hold on we're going to get you help." Sara turned her back on the insignificant pair and helped Nikko to his feet. "I think it looks worse than it is, Jarrid." Hearing her own words to bolster her assurance, they maneuvered Nikko's body through the crevasse and toward the tower.

"I'm okay, son." Nikko whispered his head under Jarrid's shoulder, "it's just a scratch."

"That's the spirit, Nikko." Sara chimed, "You'll be good as new." The old man passed out into a haze. "He will be fine," she whispered over Nikko's head.

Jarrid's face etched with hope, his mouth open to speak the words, "No, don't you understand? Luna did not do this. It was Sargon, but Nikko still has his soul, he is not dead. They did not succeed."

They quickly took Nikko to Jarrid's bedchamber. Angelica followed behind the group, "Bring him here and lay him on the bed," she ordered. Jarrid pushed aside his sheets and placed his father's head on the pillow. The angel went to the door and demanded. "Someone get water and clean cloths."

"Father, please forgive me." Jarrid clenched Nikko's hand and cried out. "I am a fool! Please don't die."

"Here, we must clean the wound." Sara took the cloth, motioned for Jarrid to move and knelt to take his place.

"He will be fine." Angelica embraced Jarrid, and he buried his sobs into her feathered shoulder; his tears enhanced the light and flowed down her white gown to fall on Nikko. Each tear a crystal-clear ring, sounding to enhance a glow that touched Nikko's body and surrounded it with a hum and pulse to heal the old man. Angelica's love multiplied by Jarrid's tears.

***

The roar was volcanic. It rose up the long corridor with its origin deep in the bowels of the earth, the anal highway to defecate the wrath of Satan and his miss-content, to spill into the Altar Room; rank and putrid.

The rock and dust preceded the dark entity, swirled and fell chasing Luna and Sargon from their resting place, forced to flee into the room to wait for his arrival. The opening of the corridor concealed with the dusty mist, disturbed by the flapping of the Devil's black wings.

"You have failed me!" The rush of Satan's wings blew the debris up and against Luna's skin. Sargon moved to protect his queen, but the talons of death scraped across his red-scaled skin, causing him to retreat. Satan's black wing raised, and twisted to land a blow across Sargon's chest to send him back down the corridor.

"Wait... it was not his fault." Luna scurried across the floor on her hands and knees, then stopped and rose to face her angry king. His grotesque features snarled, saliva dripped from his extended fangs. She placed her hands in front of her face, a symbol of surrender, and waited for his assault.

"You are a useless child," his words hissed through his clenched teeth. He stopped just in front of her crouched body, knelt with his wings folded behind him, softened his approach, and asked, "Now woman, tell me how you are going to accomplish *The Feast of Souls?*"

"It will be done, master!" The words poured from Sargon's reptilian mouth, his forward motion intent on confronting the Devil. Satan rose and turned his attention toward the author of the words he longed to hear. Sargon stopped dead in front of the winged devil, bowed, and offered his allegiance.

"Do you not wish to defeat God, to stop his thousand-year reign on the earth?" Satan spoke, acknowledging Sargon's alliance and changing his demeanor, his words offered as a father to his offspring. "We shall reign. Bring Hell to earth and banish good forever." Satin's teeth showed from behind his trembling lip as he spoke, "I will not be the fallen angel, but the rightful king."

His shout undermined his poise; he took a more subtle approach and asked, "Alright, my children enlighten me on how you plan to accomplish my wishes?" The Devil retracted his fangs and his wings, to present a softer side and waited for their response.

"My magic is strong, even without the medallion." Luna sheepishly approached her master. "Sargon is much stronger than Jarrid." She watched Satan's face, no clue she had convinced him. "Our army is capable of taking the villager's souls, leaving us to concentrate on Jarrid and Sara, it is achievable."

"Please tell me you are not going to rely on your wiles; lust is not the answer." The Devil pushed her against the wall, making his point. "You must take a different approach."

"I will rip them to pieces." Sargon moved to separate the winged one from his woman. "We will be victorious."

"Well, I think it will be in your best interest to accomplish my wishes." His black wings folded around Luna as he walked her toward the corridor. "Do you know what your fate will be if you lose?" His sleek wings closed in and flooded her mind with the image of her defeat. Her eyes filled with the vision of flames consuming her body, hanging on the cross, Sargon's one chore to heap the wood onto the flame. "Now you know, this will be your reward for failure, the never-ending death by fire."

He dropped Luna's trembling body, extended his wings, and disappeared down the corridor with the sounds of batwings screeching to punctuate his descent to Hell. Once he crossed the barrier, the air was sucked from the room to snap in their ears; Luna and Sargon crumpled to the floor, huddled together for protection.

BLOOD MOON

"Why does he not do it himself?" Luna whispered into Sargon's scaly chest.

"Blasphemy woman, have you not angered our master enough?" He pushed Luna away, huffed, and commanded. "You must obey!" His words echoed in the room as he secretly asked himself, *why does Satan need our help?*

Her hand ran down his scaly back. Luna turned him around and said, "Never mind, my love. We will be victorious." He wrapped his tail around her waist, pulled her in, and let all thought leave his mind, happy to share his lust once more.

***

The air in the room became stifled; the group huddled around Jarrid's bedchamber. The sound of relief flooded through the doorway. "He's okay," Caleb yelled as he pushed his way out into the chamber. Nikko sat up and sipped some water, looking a little worse for wear, but nonetheless recovered.

"Thank you, Angelica." Nikko squeezed her hand and continued. "It's a true miracle given by the grace of God." Jarrid smiled at his father and kissed Sara on the head.

Jarrid rose and made his way through the people, nodding his head to coax Angelica out of the room. "I need to ask you a favor." He took her arm and led her to the corner of the chapel. He reached into his pocket and brought the medallion out just enough for the green glow to encircle his hand. "I have the medallion."

"Oh, Jarrid, with all the fuss, I didn't want to inquire." Angelica bounced with enthusiasm. "Now, you can propose."

"And that is the favor." He looked around to make sure no one was listening. "Can you set up a romantic dinner in the garden? Nothing fancy, maybe cheese and meat, possibly wine?" His face beamed, the color rising in his cheeks.

"Oh, yes, that'll be wonderful." Angelica sensed a little imp in Jarrid's smile. "I have a list of flowers; they will be part of the surprise proposal." He handed the crumpled paper to the angel. "Is this too much to ask?"

"I would be honored to assist in the proposal." She took the paper from Jarrid, scanned the items, bubbled over and proclaimed, "This is a wonderful surprise." She started to leave to make the arrangements. "Everyone will help; I'll make quick work of it. Oh, and I shall gather some special clothes for the occasion..." She didn't finish but turned to rush along; her enthusiasm spilled over in the form of praise.

"How is Nikko?" Jarrid approached Sara, offering his hand in appreciation.

"He's resting, his wound completely healed. We dodged a bullet this time." She walked out into the chapel and sat on one of the stone pews. "I didn't dream it, right?" She pulled on his hand to guide him next to her.

"We have the medallion." The words spilled out with a ring that demanded a kiss. Soft and sweet, no lust or urgency, he nodded his head and asked. "Would you accompany me for dinner in the garden?"

"Oh, how lovely, almost like normal." She stood up and danced around like a ballerina. "Food, wow, I can't even remember the taste." She stopped, took his hand, and bowed. "Yes, my love, I will break bread with you."

He stood and scooped her up, swung her around, and gently lowered her to the ground. "Angelica has laid out clothes for us." He backed away, dropping her hand. "I need to check in on Nikko first, but I will meet you shortly, in the garden." Jarrid backed away from the stone pew, not wanting to take his eyes off of her beauty, knowing that in the coming days, they would be man and wife.

***

"Angelica, we must speak." Sebastian rushed up to the angel, her flowing gown swishing with the preparations for the proposal dinner. He followed her from one end of the kitchen to the other, trying to get her attention. "Please, the hunger…"

The words wrenched at her spirit, she handed the vase to one of the women and addressed the vampire. "Yes, Sebastian, let's go to the garden."

The fresh air of the terrace fell on Sebastian's senses and helped to curb the repulsive, uncontrollable thirst that racked his very being. Flowers dotted the small round courtyard with stone benches scattered among the bushes and trees. His thirst had driven him from the kitchen; the villagers crowded in the small space only tore at his blood curse.

"Please place the napkins on the table." Angelica directed as she approached the garden and hurried Arianna with the chore. "Now, go back and help the others." The angel coaxed the woman through the archway and turned to Sebastian.

"You promised you would help… the hunger is overpowering." Sebastian's face contorted with the agony of his thirst. He rushed the celestial woman with his emotions pouring from his eyes.

"Surely, you have come up against this before. How have you survived these millenniums with humans as companions?" She placed the utensils on the tables her back to the vampire.

"Control, practiced through the ages, but being in this place, being almost human, no blood lust or even pang to tempt me." He walked to the table, circled the angel, and continued. "I curse my alien blood; being mortal is the only mission I've ever sought. I'm tired and have lived many lifetimes; mortality is the cure for my disease." He fell to his knees, petitioned the angel, and pleaded. "Please, grant me the gift of mortality, take the blood curse from me, and allow me to walk as a man."

"Your humanity is evident..." She took his hand and prompted him to stand. "But alas, you ask me to perform a miracle." She guided him toward the door, patted his hand, and offered up her solution. "Let me talk to the Father. After all, I do have a little pull. But in the meantime, I will supply you with animals here in the garden."

She stopped at the door and stated, "Just feed when everyone is sleeping, you'll be better accepted if you don't subject the group to your alien ritual." She placed her hand on his face and left him with hope and glimpses of his humanity.

"Sebastian..." Alex lowered her head under the trellis. "Are you alright?" She moved into the garden, shrinking the space between her and the vampire.

"Stay back, Alex." Sebastian moved to hide behind a tree; his words compelling her. "It's not safe. I can't be trusted." He hid his face and backed into the shadows.

"No, Sebastian..." She moved to embrace his love, confident in his humanity. "You won't harm me." She touched his ashen skin and waited for the familiar blush, but the coldness only gave weight to his words.

"To harm you, Alex would be the true suicide. My life ended with the lance of the white oak, self-inflicted, no longer willing to exist." He walked out from the tree, stood paces away, and covered his fangs, struggling to retract them he stated, "Haven't you ever wanted to be something else, change who you are?" He turned to escape the breeze, floating her scent under his nose.

"Of course, there's not a person or entity in the universe who hasn't felt that way at some time in their life." She stepped clear, lessening the distance between them, his reaction swift.

"I want to be human!" The words roared from his mouth, the profound idea now given life, to hang between them in the garden air. "But my birthright, the very essence of who I am, dictates my hematophagy, the call of my ancestors." He reached toward her, motioned to take her hand, but then retreated. "Who am I to ask for a miracle, let alone expect my desire to be granted?"

"We will figure this out." She grabbed at his arm as he pushed past her, compelled to leave, a necessary action to curb his temptation. "Please, Sebastian, wait."

It couldn't happen fast enough, his will too strong to risk the possibility of sinking his fangs deep into the woman he loved. "I love you, Alex." He flew past her, his words still echoing through the garden, leaving her to wonder what their future held.

***

"Beers all around, my fine wench," Caleb lowered his fist onto the table. "Ah, Nikko, you must join us for a drink. I think you earned it, my man." The Wolfen councilman slid down the bench to make room for the man of the hour. "Jarrid, come, we owe you a beer." He motioned for his fellow councilman to join the merriment.

The beer flowed; the buxom beauty slammed the glasses in front of the men fending off the robust gestures of 'getting to know you better, my dear' pawed across the table, met with her evil eye and half-hearted slap. "Join us, Jarrid, there is much to discuss." Caleb winked at the lass, shot her an up-turned eyebrow, and stated, "So, Jarrid, a married man?" The chug of beer lasted for seconds until Caleb lowered his hand and waited for his response.

"Seems so, my friend, I plan on asking her tonight." Jarrid accepted the cheers of the men and chugged his beer before offering his smile, "That is if she will have me." The chuckles rounded the table.

"To Jarrid and Sara, may they find happiness in this place of sorrow?" Caleb raised his glass, offered his toast, and drowned his sadness until the glass surrendered its last drop.

"What's the purpose of all this merriment?" Tank was tipsy. "We'll never get out of this hellhole." His left-wing fluttered, leaving his right to droop and extend toward the floor.

"He's right, you know." Sebastian approached the table, his blood thirst satiated by the deer Angelica had provided. He motioned toward the woman with the beers and sat down in between Caleb and Jarrid. "Seems we're compelled to spend our remaining days running from the undead and fighting our inner demons for pastimes, the future is pretty bleak."

"Speak for yourself, vampire." Jarrid shoved his shoulder into the pessimist. "I am going to marry the woman I love to prove that there is a future." He raised his glass to stamp his belief. "We will go home; I know this in my bones."

"I agree..." Caleb rose to tower over the men, stroked his chin, and spoke directly to Jarrid. "There's only one thing standing in our way; *The Feast of Souls.*"

"From *The Book of Souls*, I remember." Jarrid almost choked on his beer. "What did it say?" He turned to Caleb and stumbled over his words, "So Satan can possess all the souls of the world, to stop God from sending the fallen angel to Hell during the thousand-year reign."

"Do not forget the mention of the spiritual world." Caleb proclaimed. "Satan wants to rule all supernatural entities, to have them join the fallen angels in conquering the human souls as soldiers in his evil army."

"What, be a solder for the Devil?" Tank raised his drunken head from the table, blinked his eyes, and mumbled as both wings drooped to the floor.

"Does the book tell how this will be accomplished?" Nikko asked, rubbing his chest, still not believing he was alive to ask the question.

"Sara is to confront Luna, her tools of righteousness, virginity, and anything else she can muster, to banish the Evil One to Hell, Luna's master's plans foiled." Jarrid ran his hand through his hair, his anguish evident across his face.

"You know I still say Sara's lightning could have saved the day, especially with the medallion boosting the intensity." Caleb continued and asked, "Speaking of the medallion, did you retrieve it from Luna?"

"Yes, I did, and I plan to present it at dinner, right before I pop the question." The group mumbled and chirped in a drunken language with cheers and approval circling the table.

"It is done." Angelica approached the rowdy men and touched Jarrid's shoulder. "Everything laid out to your specifications." She winked at the group and scurried off to the kitchen.

"Well, you best not keep her waiting." The glasses were raised with the clank of their toast, a symbol of hope, faith, and the dream of victory painted on their drunken faces.

The surprise must be tended to, Jarrid bid goodbye to his fellow man, turned toward his bedchamber to dress and planned every moment in his mind until he was dizzy. He reached in his pocket to feel the medallion, the promise of a wedding, the first step in going home.

BLOOD MOON
Chapter 27 The Queen's Proposal

The moon shone down into the tiny open-aired garden. Its beams draped across the trees and bushes, the lightning bugs placed like strings of lights, twinkling in the darkness.

Scents of flowers drifted in the air with the sound of a stream flowing just behind the wall. Its origin the waterfall, cascading down the mountain to cut a path through the courtyard. The cold mountain water fell down the cliff toward the village below.

The wine wedged between two rocks, chilled by the mountain stream, waiting for the moment of celebration to begin. Jarrid knelt and twisted the bottle to ensure just the right temperature, making sure not to splash his ornate clothing adorned for the occasion. Beads of sweat traced a path down his face and mingled with his hair, blowing in the cool breeze, his nerves rattled.

A table stood in the center of the courtyard lavished with a linen tablecloth and the careful placement of stone and wood, two settings with crude utensils to mark the festive occasion.

A vase of exotic flowers rose from the center of the table with a gold, jeweled box, the centerpiece, and a platter of meat and cheese accompanied by a large French loaf.

His turquoise-blue, buttoned-down, Victorian coat, cut around the waist with its tails draped down the back, falling past his knees. The black vest rode his chest like a second skin to reveal the white shirt, open at the neck, his maleness displayed in all its glory.

Jarrid bent down to smell a particularly beautiful blossom, his black leather pants yielding to the bulk of his legs, he lingered in the moment. It was perfect, just as he had instructed Angelica. The only thing left now was to propose to his queen, the woman he loved.

The rustling of petticoats broke the night air; Jarrid rose to his feet, his eyes honed in on the trellis, her arrival announced by the swish of her dress. Emerald satin gleamed in the moonlight, her red hair capturing his heart. She seemed to glide across the grass. He took her hand, spun her around, and tripped over his words, "M…, my I do believe that Angelica has outdone herself tonight. You are a vision."

Nervousness twinkled in Sara's eyes, a smirk crossed her face and she responded. "Thank you, my love. You look your part as well, a fine Victorian gentleman."

Dark green folds of material surrounded her bosom and bunched up to enhance her cleavage, surrounding her shoulders to frame her neck, the milkiest tones a contrast to the emerald earrings dripping from her ears. Jarrid bowed after seating her and moved to take his place.

One of his surprises shone down on the table. He had employed Tank to supply groups of tree fairies to assist with the romantic lighting. Their silky wings fluttered and diffused the light like millions of candles dancing in the wind.

"I see you have enlisted our friends." She smiled and raised her eyes to acknowledge the Fae ambiance scattered in the trees. "It is magical." She reached across the table and squeezed his hand.

"Oh, I almost forgot." Jarrid jumped from the table, his muscles rippling, and his physique mesmerizing. Sara watched him kneel and recover the wine.

He stood by the table and stared at the bottle, his eyes catching a reflection coming from Sara's hand. "You might need this." She handed him the corkscrew and bowed her head, "Unless you were planning on tearing it out with your teeth."

"Sarcasm, at this festive occasion," His belly laugh shook the black buttons on his vest, a release of nerves; he welcomed the distraction and poured her a glass of wine.

"These flowers are beautiful and so exotic. Some I don't recognize. The colors are vibrant," Sara ran her fingers over the delicate petals and bent to take in their scent.

"Walk with me," he answered, brushing her hand and guiding her to the outskirts of the garden under the twinkling trees. "These flowers tell the story of our lives, happiness, blessings, and tribulations."

He stood in front of the Lilacs, touched the light, purple blooms, and continued. "The subtle lavender hue of this particular flower stands for the first pangs of love, the fluttering and nerves of the promise of courtship."

Jarrid picked the bloom, turned to face her, and continued. "I remember the day when you stood in my mother's garden, strong, independent, and more beautiful than any woman I had ever seen." He reached to embrace her, the satin material of her gown complained with each caress.

He tickled the Lilac bloom across her face and under her nose. "Take a breath to remember this moment, a snapshot in time." His mouth lay upon her lips, crushing the flower between their cheeks; the seal of a memory formed.

"Close your eyes, my love." Jarrid pulled away and gathered the next flower. He took her hand and placed the bloom in her palm. "They say..." He moved away and directed her, "flowers can speak." He guided her hand and the petal to her ear and asked. "What does it say, Sara?"

"Don't be silly." She pulled on his shirt, closing the distance between them, bringing him closer. "What'd you mean?"

"Just trust me." He guided the bloom to her face, touching each petal across her cheek. "Tell me what you hear."

A little reluctant and shy, she humored him. "Hmm… well, it calls to me, pleads for me to linger in the moment, speaking of love and passion, the first kiss of a lover."

Redness in her cheeks matched the pink in the Peruvian Lilly. He took the flower, kissed her forehead, and directed. "You may open your eyes."

"Oh, Jarrid, it's beautiful." She brought the petals to her nose and breathed in the intoxicating aroma.

"This Lilly is the sign of friendship that grows into strong love and devotion." He took the flower and placed it behind her ear. "I did not know, that first day, how special you truly are, your friendship cherished to bloom into unconditional love offered so freely."

The flowers, his words of love, and the wine welled up in her soul, and she fell into his arms. "Jarrid, is this real? Please tell me it isn't a dream."

"Oh, but it is just that, a dream of wonderful things to come." He reached over her shoulder and picked the next flower bunched in a pot on the garden wall. "The Tulip, is a sturdy flower, and rightfully so, for it carries the meaning of beginnings, the start of something beautiful, our marriage as the threshold of our life."

"It's all too much." She grabbed him, wrapped her arms around his waist, and crushed the flowers between them. "I love you so much, and I cannot wait for the rest of our lives."

BLOOD MOON

Their embrace timely, Jarrid moved to the next reveal. He pushed past Sara, knelt and gathered a fragrant bouquet, strategically picked for his finale.

His stance tall and royal, he presented his offering. "You see, here in the middle, the Stargazer Lilly, the sign of wealth and prosperity. And here laced around the outside are the Jasmine for sensuality," He paused for a moment with a grin falling across his face.

The bouquet begged to be admired, the fragrance stimulating, floating past Sara's nose. She grabbed his hand, bunch and all, burying it into her face, the petals crushed against her senses. "Jarrid, will we be happy?"

"Oh, my love," he pulled her into his arms, fighting his tears of joy, he proclaimed. "Our love will pass the test of time; not even death will separate us."

His embrace lingered, the flowers offering their gifts to seal the commitment between this man and woman, their hopes and dreams unveiled in the garden of exotic flowers.

"I'm famished." Sara pulled away and headed for the table. She looked back at Jarrid and asked, "What..."

"Okay, wow, I guess it is always priorities with you." He smirked and joined her as a prelude to his last surprise. She piled her skirt under the table and embraced the material with as much ladylike charm as she could muster.

"I hope the village will not be a disappointment to you when we get home." He tore the bread and placed the meat and cheese together.

"What about the village?" She stopped chewing and tipped her head. "You mean when we get back?" Sara's thirst overtook her curiosity, and she sipped her wine.

"I suppose you can write for the Thornfell Village paper." He poured himself more spirit and assumed.

SARAH KAGE

"To be honest, Jarrid, I haven't let myself think past the battle and its outcome. But that wouldn't be a deal-breaker." She hesitantly proclaimed.

"And children, you do want them, right?" Jarrid sheepishly stared across the table.

"I would be proud to have your children, and yes, I'd always planned on being a mother." She leaned into the vase of flowers on the table and added. "I see our future, and I'm at peace with its possibilities."

It was time; Jarrid picked a select bunch of flowers from the vase to include red Roses, Orchids, and Camellias. Sara noticed the intenseness of his stare. He bunched the flowers together and cleared his throat. The sound of her gasp filled the garden, his hand steady; he opened the jeweled box in the center of the table.

He pulled the medallion from the bin with its usual green glow. He wrapped the gold chain around the flowers until the round disk lay like a necklace to adorn the bouquet.

Sara's fingertips started to tingle, the hint of the gesture dancing across her face. Jarrid placed the petals under his nose and took a breath, his hesitation to gain strength for his proposal.

"These flowers tell the tale of our future, the Rose, our everlasting love." Jarrid pushed the chair back and rounded the table, "the Orchids, my pledge to lavish you with luxurious attempts to honor your every need."

Tears started to fill Sara's eyes; she pushed her chair back and waited for him to continue. He took a knee, pulled the medallion up with a crack in his voice. "The most important flowers in this proposal bouquet are the Camellias, which represent a long and loving life. Sara, you are the most important person in my world, my home, and future."

BLOOD MOON

Her sobs lay upon his heart; he took her hand and offered the medallion with his words. "You are my match." He kissed her hand and pressed it to his cheek. "This moment in time seemed to be destined from the beginning." He lifted his head and stared into her eyes, "I promise to let you grow without borders and love you without end."

A look of doubt crossed his face. He unwound the medallion from the bouquet and offered the flowers with a trembling hand. "How this ends is completely in your hands." His eyes flashed, and the words flooded from his mouth. "Sara, will you marry me?"

The chair toppled over as Sara sprung from her seat. "Yes, yes." She grabbed his neck, forcing him to stand. "I love you with all my heart." The tree fairies clapped so hard that their lights amplified, mingling with the fireflies, the light pulsing to the rhythm of the couple's heartbeats.

"My love..." Jarrid pulled away only to unlock the chain of the engagement symbol. "This medallion, a family heirloom, will seal the commitment of our love." He moved to place the relic around her neck, to watch it fall upon her skin, and to marvel at its glow turned a royal blue. "This is my promise of love."

The symbol lay upon her chest, excitement bounded from her eyes. She buried her face into Jarrid's shoulder and wept. The garden fell silent, a sort of reverence to the sweet unconditional love shared by the betrothed.

"No, it's okay. They're done," Alex whispered.

"Shh..." Angelica tugged on her shoulder. "Give them a little more time. Geez, Alex," she pulled harder on her arm to encourage her counterpart, "this is a private moment."

SARAH KAGE

"Ah, pish posh, let's get on with it." Alex burst into the courtyard, with Angelica reluctantly following behind. "Well, from the looks of it, she said yes."

She approached the couple and barged in between them. "Come on. The group is waiting in the chapel to hear the good news." She stopped before leaving the garden and turned to Jarrid with a laugh. "Oh, and the men are planning a bachelor party. I think you better hold on to your hat." She winked at the groom and passed through the arbor into the chapel.

"Hmm," Sara cleared her throat. "Go on ahead." She pushed Jarrid out of the courtyard. "I just need a moment to collect myself." Angelica winked and coaxed Jarrid to follow her, gushing wedding advice, guiding him out of the garden, and onto the stage.

"Thank you, my kindred," Sara bowed to the trees, "for the most unforgettable night of my life." She backed through the arbor with her head still bent in admiration, turned, and headed toward the others gathered in the chapel.

"So, she said yes," Caleb called from the group gathered in front of the stage. "Don't get too comfortable, Jarrid, you still have to survive the bachelor party." The men raised their mugs and taunted. "Yeah, you still have some wild oats that need sowing."

Her glare rained down on the boisterous group. "I think you men have no good in mind." Sara flicked her gown and demanded. "You'll not sully my man." She pointed her finger to every culprit in the crowd, and they shrunk like violets.

"Okay, we've much to prepare and little time to do so." Angelica hurried the couple down the stairs. "The women have to gather in Sara's bedchamber to plan the wedding party." Alex led the women to corral and sequester the bride, chasing her up the stairs with giggles and taunts, preparing for the ceremony.

"Everyone else, come with me." Angelica started for the kitchen. "We'll prepare for the feast." Even the children skipped and pranced, offering to help with the festivities.

The men approached Jarrid and teased. "Are you ready?" They motioned to the kitchen. "Keep the beers flowing; there are games afoot." The hoard tugged and pulled until Jarrid relented and took the first of many beers to follow his party now in full force.

"Before things get too out of hand," Jarrid filled Nikko's mug, "I would like to make my choice for the wedding party." He topped off his stein, raised it in the air and motioned toward his father. "I would be honored if you would accompany me as my best man, Dad."

"It would be an honor." Nikko made a fist and pounded his chest. It was his son's gesture of forgiveness, rounding his heart, soothing his soul.

Cheers fell in a chorus with mugs pounding the table. "Okay, now that's out of the way, what do you say we start celebrating?" Dax made rounds and filled the mugs.

"Ah, virgins…" Caleb raised his glass to toast, "that should make for a rousing good roll in the hay." He lowered his beer to wait for Jarrid's response, "Nothing to say. Well, the first time is always awkward."

The smirks and grins pasted across the men's faces, caused Jarrid to blush. His third beer was dulling his senses and making him bold. "I know what to do. I have watched the farm animals enough, and it is all mechanics, right?"

The suds blew past Dax's lips, the uncontrollable laughter oozing from the corners of his mouth. "Well, knowing where to put it is certainly a plus, but women are a different breed, my friend."

"Leave the youngster alone," quipped Sebastian, "She will make sure he gets the hang of it." The mugs clanked on the table in unison with the men's celebration waning into the dark.

"To my son," Nikko stood up and demanded the attention of the group, "may he find happiness in his woman's arms and victory at the end of his sword?"

"And what would a father say to his virgin son the night before his wedding?" Caleb put his arm around Nikko and inquired.

"Well," the old man bent down to look past Caleb and directly into his son's eyes, "my best advice is to hold on tight, son, to whatever she offers up." He snickered loudly and continued. "The woman is the boss under the sheets, makes for a fucking good ride."

"Ah, there's a good man," Caleb shouted toward Nikko. Vincent approached the drunken conversation, gathered his cloak, and joined the celebration.

"A ride, you say. I would rather think of it as magical, love carried to its highest form." The wizard wiped the tears from his eyes. "Although I think Nikko is right, you better hold on with all your might."

Arguments filled the chapel, as not every man agreed with Vincent, something another round of beer cured in a timely fashion.

Cheers sounded, "Hey, let's play, *Never have I ever.*" Caleb tossed back the last of his beer, called for another, and suggested.

"Yeah, and since Jarrid is the guest of honor, he should go first." Tank sat down by the groom, stared in his face, and waited.

BLOOD MOON

"Okay…" The groom raised his hazy eyes and stated. "Never have I ever–been arrested." He put his chin in his hand to keep his head up and observed his fellow contestants take their licks.

"That was a hedged bet, for who among us hasn't been arrested?" Caleb interjected, his mug now half-full. The men chugged their beers, all except Jarrid.

The game lasted until the pitchers stood empty, and their heads waved heavy on their shoulders. More advice was given to the young buck to assure the consummation, and the pleasure of his virginal bride, combined with taunts and jokes of his stamina.

The flow of alcohol slowed, and the men gave in to melancholy thoughts. "This celebration is what we needed to distract us from the battle that looms in our future." Caleb turned his stein up to suck the last drop of bitter beer, a reminder of the evil that lurked just outside the chapel.

"Yeah," Sebastian offered. "What a way to spend a honeymoon." He shot Jarrid a look and pushed his empty mug to the middle of the table.

"Did you ever read about Armageddon in the bible?" Jarrid asked as he sat up and braced himself against the table. "The part about the undead walking the earth and God sending the Devil to Hell for a thousand years," He took a moment to brush the hair from his eyes. "I think we will all be adversaries in this very battle."

"Well, I get the undead, but how are we suppose to help God banish the Devil?" Tank slurred his words though his question was sincere.

"Sara is the key," Jarrid stood next to the table and continued, "my wife, our queen to battle the evil and save mankind." The words came from his mouth, the weight of their meaning too much, and he wavered to lean against Caleb.

"Okay, friend," Caleb braced the groom against his shoulder and spoke, "I think it is time for you to retire. You have a big day ahead."

The rabble-rousers escorted a drunken groom to his chambers, each man showing his respect to disperse for the time being; until the wedding.

***

The fire roared in the wedding chamber, hues of blue and purple colored the shadows and corners of the room. Sara sat crossed-legged on the bed with Alex sprawled on her stomach, her legs twisted and bouncing to and fro.

Sounds of drunken cheers floated up the stairs, the remnants of the celebration winding down in the chapel. The other women had retired to make preparations for their parts in the wedding, and the children were busy helping Angelica with the feast.

"So, Lizzy will be the flower girl," Alex rose on her arms and sat across from Sara on the bed, "and Chad the ring bearer, well I mean medallion."

"Angelica is bringing the wedding dress in the morning," Sara added, pushing off the bed and starting to pace, "also your bridesmaid dress and the corsages."

The fire crackled an invitation to stand in its warm embrace, Sara's face framed with a frown.

"Do you think your gown will be what you'd have selected?" Alex sat on the edge of the bed and swung her legs against the bed. "It must be sad having someone else pick out your dress, something you've dreamed of since you were a little girl."

"What's it like, Alex?" Sara had moved to stand in front of her friend to stop her antsy movements. The bride somber and flushed waited for the answer.

BLOOD MOON

"What's…?" Alex stopped and grinned widely. "Oh, you mean what, sex is like?" She stood to pace across the rug, stopped, and peered into her virgin friend's face. "Well, don't expect too much the first time." She flopped into the chair and twisted her hair. "I mean, you are both virgins, so even if you know how it's done, you can't compensate for experience." She rose from the chair, gathered Sara under her arm, and moved her to sit on the bed. "Look, everyone has been a virgin. It isn't a condition that lasts for long."

"I just want it to be perfect," Sara whined.

"How could it not be so, he is the man you love. You can see it in his eyes; there is no other for him." She moved from the bed and turned to say. "Trust in love, Sara. It will see you through." Alex yawned through her advice. "Okay, it's time for bed. You need your rest; you're going to need it for the ceremony."

Muffled sounds of the party rushed past the open door. Alex gave a wink and headed out to gather the children. She poked her head back into the room and stated. "Hold on tight, my dear. It will be a piece of cake."

The fireplace embers glowed, the light bouncing off the ceiling, casting shadows across Sara's body. The scent of flowers still drifted in the air and cradled the queen as she slept. Pinks and yellows of the Peruvian Lilly drifted across her dreams. Her sleeping thoughts honed in on the petals of a flower so close she could touch them.

A long slender thread of silk dropped down from the petal, with the tiny spider frantically making its way back up to the flower. Her dreamy eyes focused on the smallness of the insect and his monstrous determination to once again rest its body on the beautiful blossom.

"Hmm, quite determined, wouldn't you say?" Sara felt the presence of Luna bent beside her. "Such audacity, this tiny creature in a world of giants, it should just give up." A swift movement and Luna snuffed the life out of the tiny insect. "Better to end its suffering."

"I'm sick and tired of you invading my dreams." Sara's words directed in the witch's gaze, "Can't you face me on the plane of reality?"

"Oh, what has you so riled up?" Luna broadened the scope of the dream with the wave of her hand.

It was the garden, the scene of beauty with the proposal memories flooding Sara's thoughts. "Why did you pick the garden for the backdrop of your illusion?"

Luna seemed agitated, her answer sarcastic, "Just wanted to congratulate you on your proposal." Luna walked to the outskirts of the garden. "I heard it was a truly romantic event."

"What's it to you, witch?" Sara moved to end the dream by leaving the garden and willed her mind to wake.

"It was truly unique, Jarrid's attempt at romance." Luna walked to the table with the proposal bouquet front and center. "Although, a little mushy for my taste." She touched the flowers, and they wilted into dry twigs. "He only showed you the beauty of the garden."

"What do you know of beauty, you black-hearted bitch!" Sara followed her to the edge of the bushes, grabbed her arm, and made her listen. "You're just sore that Jarrid wouldn't fall for your evil temptations."

"Oh, really, that must be it." Luna bent down to smell the bush with the purple flowers and bright red berries. "The garden also holds many dangers." She picked a clump of the fruit and offered it to Sara. "This, for instance…" Sara refused the offer. "Hmm, good choice, you see these are the berries of the Deadly Nightshade, one of the most beautiful plants, its diversity a plague to rob its admirer of their very life. You are smart and cunning, Sara, I will give you that."

Luna rose to move across the garden. "We will meet in battle, and I shall pull the anchors of your soul from your body, an offering to my Dark Prince to drop the veil and bring Hell and earth together."

Fire rose in Sara's heart. She tore across the garden lawn to end the evil threats, tangled with the black witch until the satin sheets demanded their attention snarled and twisted in Sara's bed. Her face buried in the pillow, petals crushed into her face, and the taste of bitter berries in her mouth.

***

The chapel fell silent with the slumber of the soul's intertwined in this world between fantasy and reality. "Sleep, my angels." Alex brought the blanket over Lizzy's arms and tucked her in like a burrito. Chad turned with his arm thrown across his sister; slumber easy for ones so little.

The curtain, over the doorway, blew in the courtyard breeze, shifting the shadows into the form of a man. Alex rubbed her eyes and called out. "Sebastian, is that you?" He stepped into the room and leaned against the wall staring at Alex until she bolted toward him arms outstretched.

"Alex, no," he exclaimed with his yellow eyes wide and pleading. He moved to the corner of the room. "Give me a moment, my thirst is just below my control," His words desperate, he whispered. "Let me acclimate myself to your scent."

Distraction was her nervous response. "So, a wedding," She moved across the room toward the dresser, looked over her shoulder, and stated. "I never expected it, not under these circumstances." She retorted, fussing with the bottles of perfume, lined up on the shelf—a gift from Angelica for the women in the wedding party.

"Will this help?" She removed the stopper from the bottle and dabbed the dropper against her neck.

"Hmm," Sebastian moved across the room and stood close, taking in the soft fragrance of vanilla. "It is tolerable."

"Lavender," He brushed his arm over Alex's shoulder and acquired the bottle from the shelf, pulled the stopper, and drug it against the nape of her neck, "A scent to calm the beast."

Sebastian's rosy blush was the telling sign for the hunger both satiable and forbidden. He turned Alex around and pressed her body into the dresser causing the bottles to fall from the shelf, "Shh, the children."

The vampire buried his head into her shoulder, his face flushing with color, he professed. "I will find a way for us to be together, as human or vampire it makes no matter. You are my future."

BLOOD MOON
Chapter 28 The Wedding

Garlands of flowers draped across the stone pews. Fairies flitted in front of the stage, hanging puffs of chiffon material in cascades across the raised platform. Tank had enlisted his Fae family to help with the decorations.

Laughter and jokes spilled from Jarrid's bedchamber, the men of the village cheering him on and continuing the taunts of the night before. "Well, you make a fine groom, my son," Nikko straightened the boutonniere and brushed the dust from Jarrid's tuxedo.

The top hat sat on Jarrid's head, a fine piece for a wedding, his long hair tied behind with a small twig fashioned as a ribbon. "My hands are clammy." The groom's words pointed toward the floor, with each syllable he pulled at the bottom of the high-waisted coat, shaking his legs to encourage his muscles to take their perspective places.

"How are we going to know when it's time?" Dax, in his royal blue tux, stuck his head out the door, surveying the chapel and asked.

"Angelica will come and get us before the ceremony starts." Vincent responded, donning his most ceremonial cloak, he pushed past Dax and hurried to greet Tank's people.

"We need to vacate the room." Dax added, "It will be needed for the bride to dress and the rest of the bridal party to gather before the walk down the aisle."

The pews filled up with rainbow colors from the clothing handpicked by Angelica. The women in beautiful, colorful gowns and the men decked out in top hats and suits.

SARAH KAGE

Decorated pews had been positioned in rows, leaving an aisle down the middle, pointed in the direction of the stage. A trellis of exotic flowers, Roses, Stargazer Lilies, and of course, Camellias, stood at the end of the walkway with flower pots on both sides.

A small, holding area had been fashioned right outside Jarrid's room, to keep the reveal of the wedding dress and the vision of the bride hidden before the ceremony.

Candles and oil lanterns lit the large room with yellow and gold lights dancing across the faces of the attendees, to enhance the ambiance of the chapel. Illumineria flambeau lined the stairs to the wedding chamber with drapes of chiffon material twisted up the staircase.

"Isn't she ready yet?" Alex called out, running into the wedding chamber full blast, gathering the discarded clothes as she entered. "It's almost time. Has anyone spoken with her?" Alex pounded on the bathroom door. "Hey, did you get cold feet and drown yourself?"

The door swung open, and a radiant bride pushed past with the Victorian undergarments laced and procured. "How in the hell did you lace yourself up in that contraption?" Alex put her hand over her mouth to capture the laugh.

"Angelica insisted. I didn't have the heart to argue the fact before she stuffed me into this ridiculous piece of Victorian torture." Sara pulled at the bottom of the lingerie, trying to coax it to surrender.

"You know," Alex joined in to pull the laced apparel around and center it between Sara's bosoms, "it will take him a little longer to un-wrap his gift, which might give you the slightest amount of time to gather your wits." Both women chuckled.

"Quickly girls," Angelica burst through the door and gathered the wedding dress from the closet, "we must hurry to Jarrid's chamber, there's not much time before the ceremony begins."

"Wait, he can't see me!" Sara's eyes bulged. "The reveal is all I have to offer him as a gift." She approached Angelica to take the dress.

"I know, sweetie, this is not exactly the wedding you've had in mind, but the pomp and ceremony is not the point." The angel peered into Sara's eyes and nodded her head. "Besides, I ran the groom and his entourage off and sequestered them to the kitchen until we can get the bridal party safely behind the curtain."

"I shouldn't have doubted you, Angelica." Sara took the angel's arm and continued. "Thank you for all you've done for us." She hugged the winged entity as the group gathered the pieces for the ceremony and sleuthed off to Jarrid's chamber.

"Come on, Lizzy, don't dawdle." Alex gathered the children and headed out the door, looking back at Sara. "Aren't you coming?" She asked, gathering Chad to bring up the rear.

"Just give me a moment; I'll be right behind you." Sara gathered her robe and tied the belt around her waist. She looked up just in time to see Caleb walk through the door.

"Hey wolf, we don't have much time, make it quick." Alex stared at Caleb and prompted the children down the stairs with a curious look plastered across her face.

"We haven't had an opportunity to talk, the wedding has taken over," Sara said, moving to cross the room. She closed the robe tighter around her chest and sat in the overstuffed chair.

"I wanted to see you in private before the ceremony." The Wolfen guarded his mannerisms. "Just so you know, I asked Jarrid if it would be alright, wanted to be in his good graces." He sat in the matching chair opposite Sara and paused.

His eyes stared, looking right through her. "Are you okay, Caleb?" She moved from her chair to kneel in front of the Wolfen.

He took her hands and exclaimed. "Sara, you are so beautiful." He jumped from the chair, paced in front of the fireplace, and turned back to say, "I can't explain this uncontrollable feeling; it comes over me anytime you are near."

"Let me help you," She moved in front of the distraught alien and offered words to soothe his conscience. "It's not me you seek, but the connection to Raven."

"I want to believe that. It would be much easier to accept; my honor in tack, but the pull is so strong." He searched her face for a sign of understanding.

Her head fell back. "Sara, are you alright? Talk to me." Her eyes rolled to expose her white, milky orbs. Raven's voice filled the room. "Caleb, Sara is your destiny."

He brought Sara's head forward and asked. "Raven, don't go. Please explain yourself. She's promised to another. I have no right."

"Your future lies within her boundaries." The voice echoed off into the distance, leaving the alien with pains of guilt and shame.

"No, I will not act on my feelings. Honor is the way of the Wolfen." He steadied Sara's stance and pleaded. "Sara, please talk to me."

"Oh my, it must be this corset, did I faint?" She wiped her forehead and leaned against the wall. "I'm fine. I just need some air."

"It was Raven, she spoke to me." He walked across the room and continued. "Look, I'm sorry to bring this up now." His stride carried him toward the door. "We can talk after the wedding."

"Okay," she stated with a confused look. Caleb left her to her thoughts; she pulled herself together, and joined the others in Jarrid's chamber, with bits and pieces of Raven's conversation mingling in her mind.

The small room oozed with perfume and the swish of chiffon. Alex gathered Sara's unruly curls and piled them on top of her head with wisps of red ringlets escaping in all the right places, falling past her shoulders, down her back.

"Okay, so we have to put the dress on from the bottom," Alex fussed with the ringlets, reaching for the headdress on the shelf, burying her chest into Sara's face. "Let's go ahead and put the veil on and get your hair managed and secured."

The lavender material of Alex's dress rested against Sara's arm with her friend struggling to position the tiara that dripped with sparkling gems, and sheer chiffon. Suddenly, from nowhere, reminiscence flooded the bride's senses. The lavender hue of Alex's dress ignited the memory of her proposal bouquet, the remembrance a gift from her betrothed.

"There." Alex stepped back to admire her handy work. "You are so beautiful." She hurried Sara to gather her something new, the pearl earrings supplied by Angelica and something old and blue, all rolled into one, her sapphire barrette, the bride's favorite daily hair accessory.

"Mommy, do I look pretty?" Lizzy tugged on Alex's dress, almost tipping the basket of petals onto the floor. "Oops," She helped her daughter to rescue the basket and replied. "My little angel, you are divine."

SARAH KAGE

"Me too, Mommy, do I look pretty?" Chad waddled across the room with a pillow so big he almost disappeared behind it, the medallion pinned to the cushion waiting for its debut.

"You are so handsome, my little man." Sara scooped the small boy up and twirled him around, her veil flowing, and her cheeks rosy.

"It is time." Angelica burst into the room and hurried to recover the dress. Sara pulled the bodice up and over her hips to rest against her breast; Alex zipped the zipper and painstakingly buttoned the back.

There was a hush in the chamber. Sara turned toward the full-length mirror that rested against the wall, all lips quiet to admire the dress.

The front bodice adorned with embroidery and twisted threads like tree limbs, to end up extended across her cleavage, like tiny branches reaching out into the air. The form-fitting skirt hugged every curve, flaring just below her knees with fabric circling her legs, dripping with embroidery and crystals. "My good grief, Sara, this must be better than any image you conjured as a girl."

Everyone backed away to give her more room to admire her dress. Sara flapped her hands in front of her face to stop the waterfall building in her eyes. Then the back of the dress revealed itself as she turned her body and looked over her shoulder.

"Oh, Angelica, it is too beautiful." The cut was extraordinary, folds of satin material sculpted against the roundness of her buttocks to gather in a point and branch out into a train of material, reminiscent of a white peacock's royal plume.

The back of the bodice see-through and shimmery, revealing the sculpted lace corset rounded from her shoulder blades, ending in a point in the middle of her back. The embroidery threads coaxed together, forming branches, rising across her back in shapes of trees adorned with crystals and pearls.

A bun style veil, short and dainty to surround her curls like icing on a cake, only one layer of chiffon encouraged her vibrant crimson hair to peek out and cascade down her back in massive curls. The dress had stolen the show.

Her trance broken, Sara heard Alex instruct the children. "Okay, kids, remember how we practiced." Alex started the procession and guided the youngsters toward the aisle, Lizzy first and Chad with his pillow next. The bridesmaids took their positions, leaving room for Alex to position Sara in all her splendor.

"Oh, I have a surprise for you, Sara." Angelica motioned for everyone to be quiet and to listen. Above the murmurs of the guest, a faint and beautiful combination of harpsichord and violins drifted through the air. The music *Pachelbel-Canon in D minor* filled the chapel and coaxed the bridal party out into the aisle.

Sara's joy was uncontainable; she waved the tears away. "Angelica, you are amazing. It's a wonderful surprise."

"What would a wedding be without music?" Caleb asked as he wound the handle of the old Victorian gramophone with its golden tonearm and musical cylinder. His job to keep the music flowing.

Petals covered the aisle; Sara peeked through the curtain and noticed they were from the types of flowers in her bouquet. Her hands tightened around the replica of her proposal spray surrounded by Roses, Stargazer Lilies, and Camellias; every color reminded her of the night he proposed.

"Alright, Sara," Angelica instructed, "wait for my signal."

SARAH KAGE

Sara panicked; she straightened the trail of her dress, fluffed out the veil, took a deep breath and mumbled, "Where the hell is he?"

The hand pulled the curtain aside, and he fumbled head first into the small enclosure. Sara jerked around and scolded the shapeshifter. "Well, it's about time, really Dax, last minute." There was no time for an explanation; she took his arm along with a deep breath just as Angelica moved the curtain aside to start her entrance.

Classical music flowed through the chapel and soothed Jarrid's nerves. Nikko stood beside his son and waited for her reveal. Vincent positioned his cloak and waited under the arbor for the bride to make her way down the aisle.

Beautiful symphonic notes prompted Jarrid and Nikko to take their places on the left side of Vincent, who was busy gathering his notes for the ceremony. Father and Son exchanged glances, Nikko's heart bursting in his chest, so honored to stand by his strong son.

Soft footsteps crushed the petals strewn down the aisle as the bridesmaids made their way to the flowered trellis, with Arianna leading the group, the light lilac colored gowns mingled with their bouquets to release floral scents into the air.

Behind the procession, Lizzy scattered her petals in heaping handfuls, looking back to guide her brother balancing the pillow and looking like a fine little prince. "Lizzy," Alex whispered, following behind her children. "Just a few at a time, please."

She searched the crowd for his ashen skin, and their eyes met. No amount of hunger could keep him from this joyous occasion, and Alex's vision of perfection in the lilac-colored flowing gown. She guided the children

BLOOD MOON

to their places and gave a glance in Jarrid's direction, her approval indicated by the wink of her eye.

Tones of the music changed with the addition of a new cylinder, a simple traditional wedding march, to send the message for the bride to start her walk.

"Are you ready?" Dax asked, taking Sara's arm and counting his steps to match the beat of the music.

Soft musical notes alerted everyone that Sara was approaching, and they all stood to observe her entrance. Jarrid stared almost blindly, waiting for her vision to reveal itself.

Gasps fell upon every ear, the comments in unison, flowing like a wave rising and cresting above the pews. Jarrid fixated on her eyes, and then the beauty of the perfect dress, his knees buckled from the sight.

"Whoa, Son, steady." Nikko offered his arm, his emotions also taken by Sara's raw and dramatic beauty.

"Are you okay?" Dax tightened his grip on Sara's arm. "You're trembling." Bells started to ring softly, a background to the wedding march. Dax whispered, trying to distract her. "Do you know why the bells ring at weddings?" He pulled her closer, steadying her walk down the aisle.

Without taking her eyes off of Jarrid, she whispered back. "You're not helping!"

Aggravated that Dax had distracted her, she stared down the long aisle taking in the site of the man that waited for her at the end of the longest walk she could remember. His hair tied back and covered with a top hat, his tux caressing every part of his massive body. Her excitement rose to increase the shivers rattling the bouquet and her nerves.

SARAH KAGE

Finally, the last pew was in sight, the wedding party arranged with Lizzy squirming and Chad's pillow on the ground, his little body cross-legged on the floor.

"Okay," Dax whispered. "It's time to hand you off to Tank." He stepped aside and disappeared to take his place behind the bridesmaids.

Her fairy brother approached the aisle and offered his hand. "Someone from your fairy lineage should give you away." She gave no resistance and gladly accepted the gesture. Tank took her gloved hand and guided her toward her groom. He bowed his head and offered his queen's hand to her betrothed.

"Here, Son, let me take the hat," Nikko whispered before Jarrid turned Sara to face the altar. Jarrid tipped it toward Sara and relinquished it to his father.

"Attention, please," Vincent addressed the crowd. "Angelica has a few things to say before we start the ceremony."

The angel circled Jarrid and Sara, turned them toward the audience and folded her wings around their shoulders. "Everyone, look upon this couple to understand, they are the chosen ones."

She brought the pair closer with the loving nudge of her wings. "God chose these two young people before their conception, his weapon to unleash upon the evil of the world, before the final battle."

Her statement profound, she thrust her hands into the air to give the Father his glory. "This union blessed and rectified before you, God and Satan." She took their hands and bound them together with her kiss, and spoke words only for their ears. "The Father loves and blesses you." She took her place among the wedding party and motioned for the ceremony to begin.

BLOOD MOON

"Everyone, please be seated." Vincent pulled his book from the altar and began his words. "To God is the glory," he raised his staff in the air, "power and love, our hearts to rejoice, Amen."

"Well, I've heard you two want to get married. Is that true?" Laughter filled the room with Vincent's comment.

The redness rose in Sara's face to match the hue of her hair. "Okay, my queen, just a little joke, but I see you are not amused." He cleared his throat and continued. "We are gathered here today to unite this man and woman in holy matrimony." He looked out at the crowd and emphasized. "These circumstances are unusual; to say the least, but this couple rises to the call of righteousness, and as a team will deem to be victorious."

"Now folks, I have to ask this question to make this union legal. Is there anyone among you who can bring witness to object to this marriage?" He waited, peering out into the crowd.

"Get on with it, man." Jarrid squeezed Sara's hand and demanded.

"Yes, indeed." He motioned to the groom, his question of the vows. Jarrid nodded. "Well, it seems the couple has written their vows, so, I will relinquish this part of the ceremony over to them." He tipped his head to Jarrid and stepped back.

Jarrid cleared the emotions from his throat and proclaimed. "My love," the groom turned to Sara and took her hands. "The fire in your heart burns brighter than your crimson hair. It fuels my promise to always protect your love and honor your soul, my words so commanded."

The pause afforded him a moment to place their hands together one atop the other, his words heavy and choked. "My soul captured by the pools of green emeralds, your loving eyes to stare in them is to unite our souls for eternity."

His hand removed to take her arm and pull her closer. "Your warrior spirit and child-like wit, a contradiction that invokes my curiosity, demanding respect for all that you are."

"Hmm…" the pause momentary he brought his hand to his heart, tapped his chest, and continued. " Your everlasting capacity for unconditional love, a gift given so easily, one I gladly receive."

"Umm…wow." He used the pause to take her hands once again, fought through the emotions, and continued. "The smoldering fire just below your skin ignites passion and my vow to protect you with the essence of what I am. You have my name and the sacrifice of my body and soul if so needed."

Quietness filled the chapel, the group fully involved in the vows. Jarrid's courage mustered, strength returned, he stared into her eyes and with commitment declared. "I am yours, you are mine, and we are united as one for eternity." The embrace colored with the passion of the ages. There could be no space between them, his words to draw them together stronger than any magnet, the pull undeniable.

"Alright, Sara," Vincent spoke to direct the ceremony. "Please, offer Jarrid your vows." He touched her arm and nodded his head.

Her gloved hand, with its bare fingertips, offered her relief from the tears streaming down her face; she gathered her emotions and took Jarrid's hand. "My warrior, your quiet strength and love for family shown to me the first day we met, the confidence and valor, complimented by your moral compass, qualities all men should possess."

BLOOD MOON

A smile flashed across her face. She touched Jarrid's cheek to bring the intimate moment closer. "Always the strong leader, bold and victorious, but you take me under your arm, to love and cherish, instead of beneath your thumb to rule and dictate."

"Your ice-blue eyes," she reached and pulled his vest to bring him closer to look straight into his soul, "sparkle with the promise of adventure, our lives riddled with bursts of sarcasm… and love elevated to the highest peaks of our souls."

The body language, a dance, his yearning to embrace his bride, and start their life together, pushed him forward into her arms. She took his hands and stepped back, using the space to give substance to her words. "And with what might be your finest quality, compassion given to the small of God's creatures, all equal in your eyes, this attribute allowing me to surrender to you, body, heart and soul."

Words too strong, passion too deep, the couple embraced giving no mind to Vincent, or any person, place or thing in their universe. "Hey," Vincent chimed. "We haven't gotten to that part yet." He rustled the couple to stand apart to finish the ceremony.

"Chad," Alex whispered. "It's your turn, get the pillow and do it how we practiced." The youngster jumped to his feet and toggled the medallion over to Jarrid.

The relic clanked, the familiar glow, dark. Jarrid thanked Chad and sent him back to Alex. He turned to Sara and proclaimed. "This medallion is my promise of love, handed down from my family, my allegiance to you and God."

As soon as the disk touched Sara's skin, a burst of blue emanated from the stone in the middle and filled the room, destiny fulfilled.

SARAH KAGE

"The medallion is now the third tool you possess in the battle of good and evil." Angelica approached the couple and proclaimed, "The first tool is your love, and the second, *The Spirited Sword of Purity*, offered up this night, a loving, holy union between husband and wife."

"Chad and I have a surprise." She motioned for the ring bearer to join her. "The Father and I felt that you should have rings, the more traditional sign of your love." Chad raised the pillow to reveal two bands of rose gold, tree roots intertwined in an unbroken circle. Angelica touched them and continued. "These are blessed and sanctioned by God." She touched Chad's shoulder, escorting him back to his mother.

Cheers from the group resounded in the chapel; Vincent blessed the bands of gold and returned to the ceremony. He cleared his throat and continued. "Do you, Jarrid Knox, take Sara Ogletree to be your lawfully wedded wife? To have and to hold from this day forward in sickness and in health, till death do you part."

"Not even in death will we be parted!" Jarrid took Sara's hand and spoke the words. "I do."

"Do you Sara Ogletree; take Jarrid Knox, to be your lawfully wedded husband. To have and to hold from this day forward in sickness and in health, till death..." She turned to glare at the magician. "Yes, okay until eternity."

"I do." Her eyes burst with tears, no way to control the flood of emotion.

"And now the rings," Vincent handed the gold rings to the king and queen.

"With this ring, I thee wed." Jarrid slipped the band on her finger, "The symbol of my love eternal."

Tears flooded Sara's vision, and she fumbled with the band of gold, "Hmm, Jarrid, with this ring I thee wed."

BLOOD MOON

The warmth of his hand gave a memory, her snapshot in time. She pushed the band onto its rightful place.

Because Vincent took pleasure in being a little impish, he slowed the pace and offered his tidbit. "So, Sara, do you know why the ring is placed on the fourth finger of the left hand?"

Frustration flowed behind her green eyes, and she humored him, "No, Vincent, please enlighten us."

"Umm…" His face a little red he quickly spoke his answer. "In olden times," he stuttered. "That finger was thought to hold a vein that led straight to the heart." Her eyes could not have rolled any further back in her head, and the laughter filled the chapel.

Then, the wait was over, Vincent proclaimed. "By the power vested in me by God himself, I pronounce you husband and wife." He paused for a moment just because he could and offered. "Jarrid, you may kiss your bride."

Emotions ran through the crowd with uncontrollable gestures of affection, their king and queen united, the kiss long and sweet to usher in the dawn of their union.

"Music maestro," Dax shouted across the room to Caleb. He placed the chosen cylinder in its place and upped the volume to raise the roof. The bridesmaids threw their bouquets in the air and joined the celebration, following the king and queen down the aisle toward the feast, well deserved by two people at the start of their married life.

SARAH KAGE
Chapter 29 The Feast of Souls

The toll of the bells resounded in every corner of the Fortress. Faint music pierced the Altar Room and drove Luna to madness. Cheers of merriment, voices piled one on top of the other, telling the truth of the demon witch's darkest nightmare. It could only mean a wedding had taken place.

"It is done." Luna paced in front of Sargon, her hands in the air. "Sara and Jarrid are man and wife." Sargon was sprawled on the floor, kicking at the feet of the undead as they lazily stepped in front of him, causing them to stumble, evil laughter rising from his chest when they fell.

"You have the brain capacity of a child." Her frustration raging, she declared. "Sara gets a head councilman, and I get a partially brain dead demonic toddler." She raced to the corridor, her first impulse to rage at her demonic Father, but instead, she turned back to her grotesque spouse. "Can't you find anything better to do?"

Sargon questioned his dark mate. "Don't you have the power of vision?"

"You bumbling idiot." A frown crossed her features. She kicked his legs and pulled him up to accompany her on her fevered mission. "I can't see into the chapel. Angelica has shielded it from my eyes." She pulled on his clawed hand and guided him toward her wishes. "The best place to listen is the back stairs that lead to the closed wall in the chapel. Maybe the bricks will offer up the clues to confirm my fears."

His tail swished and took down a row of the undead; his amusement followed him to the back stairs. "Woman, so what if they're married." Sargon sat on the top landing and stared at the wall, the stairs to nowhere. "That doesn't concern us." He flicked his tail and picked his teeth.

"Animal," She nearly knocked him off the stair with her backhand. "If they are indeed married, then *The Spirited Sword of Purity* will be accomplished this very night." Sargon stood over her, grabbed her black raven hair, and started to speak, his words stolen by Luna's tongue, quick and sharp. "Shut up! You know nothing." She shook him off and pressed her ear to the bricks.

"Yes, it's true." The black-winged one snuck up the stairs and confronted the devilish pair. "I'm afraid you have lost the battle, disappointed me once more."

"You know," Luna pushed Satan against the wall, her frustration fueled her bravery, and she confronted the Devil himself. "You promised me Jarrid, but I got Sargon." She shoved him down the stairs, stopped, and articulated. "Why is it that the Prince of Darkness can't do his dirty work and get rid of the righteous pair?" Sargon rose from the stoop and stood behind his bride.

"That's an excellent question." Satan rose to the top step, brushed off Luna's confrontation, and spoke. "Her powers come from the fallen angels themselves." He started down the stairway, stopping in the middle of the staircase with his back to the pair. "The ancient ones protect her; our gifts are mutual; I am forbidden to use my powers against her." He turned to state his humiliation. "That's why you'll have to do it for me."

***

Tables laden with fruit, meat, and cheese sprawled out across the back of the chapel. A fattened pig, provided by the Father, lay in the middle of the bridle table next to the spice and rum wedding cake, two tiers. Merriment abounded in the festive atmosphere, the thoughts of the undead far away in the guest's minds.

Wine and spirits abundant, filling goblets primed for the many toasts offered to the bride and groom. Cake sufficiently smashed in Jarrid's face to linger in his long locks. The gramophone's cylinders spun the lively music to coax the guest to dance. Their celebration of the heavenly union was festive; the alcohol removing all inhibitions.

Musical notes called to the king and queen to have the last dance before retiring to the honeymoon. Their bodies intertwined, Jarrid moved his bride across the floor, stealing kisses and sharing their excitement.

"Well," Caleb and Sebastian interrupted the dance. "We feel it's time for you to consummate this union." They tugged on Jarrid's arm to prompt his intention.

"Hey, what gives you the right to decide?" Sara tugged on Jarrid's arm and asked.

"It is the tradition." Jarrid acknowledged his brothers and took Sara's hand.

Excitement flowed through the chapel, with each guest realizing it was time for Jarrid and Sara to retire to the wedding chamber. "Ouch…" Sara pulled away from the source of the pain.

"Oh…" Alex giggled, recoiling from her pinch that was landed squarely on Sara's behind. "Did I hurt you?" Before Sara could react, Lizzy and Chad joined in and landed small pinches on her arm.

"Hey, what gives?" Sara complained, turning and backing toward the stairs.

"That is also a tradition." Jarrid smiled at Alex, leaving no doubt in Sara's mind that they were in cahoots. "It is to send you off to your chamber with good luck." Jarrid gave Alex a devilish wink.

BLOOD MOON

"I think I'd take the offering, Sara." Sebastian smiled. "You might need it, being your first time and all." Laughter filled the chapel its intensity to match Sara's flushed face.

"Come, my love." Jarrid escorted his bride to the bottom of the stairs, rose to the first step, and made his speech. "Sara and I thank everyone for this beautiful wedding made possible by our friends." He put his hands on the top of his bride's shoulders and continued. "Please feel free to enjoy the party. We will be otherwise engaged."

"Oh, I think he underestimates the wedding night, you shall be on another planet, my friend." Caleb and Sebastian laughed and directed the wedding party to escort the bride and groom to their room, as tradition dictated.

"Um…" Sara stopped on the top stairs and turned back to the group, "You're not invited to the honeymoon, Sebastian." He bowed and started his retreat with the taunts rising over his head.

"If you need any instructions Jarrid, feel free to ask." Dax skipped down the stairs, proud of his one-liner. The group descended the staircase and headed for more alcohol.

"Well, Mrs. Knox, are you ready to start the rest of your life." Jarrid prompted.

She suddenly felt nervous; the mere thought of crossing the threshold and giving herself to her husband gave life to hoards of butterflies churning in her stomach. She swallowed hard, bucked up, and answered. "Yes, Mr. Knox, I believe I am."

The door shut softly of its own accord. Jarrid fought the bulk of satin and crystals, corralled Sara's dress and dropped her down ever so gently, still embraced by his arms. "Sara, you are trembling." He pulled her to his chest, an attempt to force the waves of nervousness out, to roll against his loving shore.

"Come by the fire. We are in no hurry." He escorted her to the massive fireplace, the flames roaring like the embers of his love. He fought his urge to take her in a long hard kiss, their union, once forbidden, his thoughts arguing against his need to protect and cherish her, his loving bride. He moved toward the window, a distraction to his desires.

Soft tones of blues and purples flooded the walls of the wedding chamber. The fire calmed Sara's nerves, still in her wedding dress, staring at the dancing flames, reminding her of the need she felt every time Jarrid touched her.

Victorian furniture filled the sitting area in front of the large mantel. The darkness in the room caressed Sara's anxiety and allowed her passion to rise beyond her fear. The couch rose up to meet her, embedding the crystals and pearls into her back, moving her to abandon the beautiful satin dress.

"I need just a moment. Do you mind?" Sara rose and headed toward the bathroom door.

"Of course not, my love." He moved from the large window, out of the moonlight, and opened the door for his bride.

Flowers filled the space, each of the ones that had become so important since the proposal. A small vase graced the tall round table, bottles of wine to accompany the meat and cheese carefully arranged on a platter.

It seemed like hours before the door opened and Sara appeared minus the yards of satin, crystals, and pearls. The corset and pantaloons caressed her body, now the object of Jarrid's attention.

BLOOD MOON

"Umm…" Jarrid rushed toward Sara. "You forgot the veil." He reached up to release the chiffon pulling at the barrettes and pins to allow her curls to fall on her shoulders, his nervousness coloring his cheeks.

No words, Sara felt the rush overtake her body. He lifted her face, feeling the heat rise into his hands. The scent of Lilacs overpowered his senses, the kiss tasted of strawberries, the stays of her corset dug into his chest, the room spun.

Their heads fell together, spent from the glow of the sacred kiss. "Hmm, guess I need to get this finery off as well." Jarrid moved to the closet and carefully hung up his coat and vest. He started to remove his shirt but turned to his bride and second-guessed the move.

"Would you care for some wine?" He leaped for the table before she could answer. He dropped the glass and placed his hands on the chair for stability. Sara couldn't help but smirk, and it put her at ease.

"To our happiness," He raised his glass, the ting sounded, and he spoke again. "May love, friendship, and passion follow us always?"

He moved to intertwine their glasses. Sara's eyes flashed with fire, her attempts to smolder the flames, a moot point. "So many times, my husband, we were denied carnal knowledge because of my promise." She put her glass on the table and stepped toward the window. "And now we are husband and wife, *The Spirited Sword of Purity* ours to command."

It was all the invitation he needed. He crossed the room and claimed what was his. He embraced his bride with one arm, and swept the hair from her face, buried his lips into her soul, the barrier removed, his will be done.

SARAH KAGE

"Jarrid, my love…" She whispered in his ear, his hands pressed hard against the corset, the lacy barrier between their bodies. She pushed away and started to unlace, slowly pulling at the end of the ribbon, demanding the bow fall to her will.

His eyes bore into the depth of her emerald eyes; he motioned to take the ribbon from her hand, to pull its resistance away, each tug revealing more of her ample bosoms. A sigh left her lips, the restrictive lingerie giving up its hold on her body. He dropped it to the floor, her freedom evident, allowing her to drape her arms around his neck.

"Sara, let me look at you." He gently released her arms and stood back, leaving a few feet between them. Her breasts heaved and shuttered, the nipples rising to meet his gaze. Tides of testosterone riddled his body, hands lifted, with his fingers running through his hair, his restraint lifted.

"Jarrid, it's okay." She took his hand and placed it on the rise of her breast, letting her skin conform to his touch. His finger raked across the hardened mound, her sigh followed by her head falling backward in ecstasy.

Time for restraint vanished by their vows, Sara popped the buttons on his shirt, slow at first, and then with an urgency, the apparel tossed to the ground. His naked chest, rising and falling with labored breaths fueled by passion.

He reached for the ribbon of the pantaloons, pulled and watched them pile on the floor by her feet. Her eyes followed the garment. Her head hung in shyness. "Never be shy before me, woman." He lifted her head and poured his words into her eyes. "I am your husband; there are no boundaries between us."

BLOOD MOON

The fire in her eyes burned. Jarrid's words fueled the permission to have her husband's body and soul; now. Her desire overtook her hesitance; she unbuckled his belt, pulled it through the loops, and drove her hand down against his hardness, her innocence forgotten.

Their lips came together, the kiss driven by the passion raised between them, his seed just below the surface, a reason to slow down. "Hmm…" Sara removed her hand and stepped back. "Wow, I'm not sure where that came from, husband." She picked up the wine, tipped the glass, and toasted him. "Must be the wine banishing all my inhibitions."

"Mine as well." She sat the glass down just as he took her and fell against the wall. His head buried in her neck, his hands deep between her legs. He was relentless; the intensity of the kiss only fueled the strokes. His fingers followed the shape of her mound to run its length, moist and welcoming, each stroke of his fingers bringing her closer to her release.

She grabbed his hand, her attempt to stop the sensation, and asked. And where, pray tell, did you learn to do that, my husband?" He continued, his hand starting again to pull at her need and stated. "Said I was a virgin, guess it depends on your definition of virginity?" No eye raised, just her complete surrender.

"I want to look at you, Jarrid." Her voice exasperated, he removed his hand and pulled her out into the center of the room. The wine erased all signs of her shyness.

Moments passed, not a word spoken. Sara reached for his half undone pants, finished lowering the zipper, and hinted for him to reveal his body to her.

He pulled the last resistant pant leg away and stood up straight and tall, no reluctance to the admiration of his bride. "Jarrid, you are magnificent." She circled his nakedness, letting her hand lightly touch each rippled muscle, lingering on his round cheeks, his buttocks well defined, to end up in front of his massive chest to meet his embrace, his movement swift.

Her legs wrapped around his waist, instinctively, her soul knew that the climax was imminent. Their bodies entwined the lust now prominent. The bed complained as he brought her up toward the headboard, her legs still wrapped around his waist. The moment brief, he stared into her eyes.

His kiss now fevered, he returned to her need, stirred the embers, his mouth hard on her nipples to release her acceptance. Her moistness prompted him to continue. He wet his hand with her desire, to aid against her pain, stroked his lust, and positioned his pulsing need just outside her virginity.

"I love you, Sara." He sealed his words with the kiss of no return, his lips on fire almost too much for his restraint. Her moans invited him to continue, and he positioned himself just at the breach of her virginity and whispered. "I don't want to hurt you."

His kiss relentless, her desire uncontrolled, she reached around to his buttocks, buried his lust into the full length of her desire – virginity gone with a mighty gasp.

He lay still, propped slightly on his elbow, easing the weight of his body, embarrassment nagging at his senses. "He buried his face in her neck; I'm so sorry."

"What, you think this is the only time we'll do it." She took his face in her hands, and he rolled to the side. "God, I hope not." She stated. "Look, what do you expect? You've denied your sexual urges all your life." She rose up and kissed his cheek. "Besides, we have all night." A grin covered his face, his eyes followed her round buttocks, watching it jiggle to and fro, his need raising once again, his confidence renewed.

"Let's have some more wine," Sara suggested as she pulled her cotton top around her shoulders.

"You know, I might want to hold off, I would rather enjoy the rest of the night sober." He reached and fashioned the bed sheet like a kilt, used his belt to fasten the frock, and sat down to indulge in the meat and cheese. "This is a better choice, good for stamina." He winked and placed his elbows on the table.

"I have to tell you, without sounding selfish, it was incredible." He tipped his cheese toward her and continued. "If the first time was that good, I can't imagine the next." Sara agreed, hoping to herself he was right.

"It was quite the wedding." He said nervously. Jarrid stood by the window draped in the kilt-like sheet with moonlight cascading over his massive body. Sara's passions stoked with the denial of her climactic moment. Something she planned on correcting this very second.

"Yes, it was more than I ever hoped for." She stood and let her top fall to the floor. Approached Jarrid, and swiftly released his belt, encouraging the sheet to fall around his feet.

"He needed no instructions." She pulled his hand down and guided him to search for her need, its surge lying just below the surface. He obliged while he walked her slowly toward the bed, his desire mildly satiated from their virgin voyage.

"Yes, Jarrid now," Her invitation accepted he laid her on the bed and joined her, slipping next to her porcelain skin. He took his time, memorizing each curve and nook that made up her beautiful body. The need building once again, his mind fighting to slow the impulse, lips traveling down to the edge of her island, round and tempting.

"Jarrid, please…" She tugged on his body, begging for her release, not waiting for him, she opened her legs to invite his entry. The cue accepted Jarrid braced his weight and slid in deep, her gasp of pleasure took him by surprise, his hips guiding his thrust.

"Hmm… ah…" her voice coaxed him to ride the wave of sensation just below the surface. She buried her hips into the bed, grabbed his buttocks, and guided him up, his head closer to the headboard, her purpose to fill the channel of pleasure with his full length, to ride from the tip of her delight straight on through to the walls of ecstasy.

Her direction heightened his sensation, pulling at his release, worried about pleasing his bride. Her hips rose in the air, spasms tightened, stroking him from deep inside her body. Consciousness threatened, the climax circling their bodies in unison, exploding into fits of pleasure the likes of which neither one had ever known.

"I understand the meaning of *afterglow*." Sara proclaimed, her body spent, their passion and restraint emptied into the room, its presence still vibrating in the air.

"I believe," Jarrid lay as dead, all his strength pulled from his body, used up to power his performance. "It can't get much better than that." His breathing slowed, sleep demanding its due.

"Oh, my love, but it will." Sara laid back, closed her eyes, and thanked God for her blessings.

BLOOD MOON
Chapter 30 After The Blood Moon

Quietness lingered in the wedding chamber; the embers in the fireplace glowed, popping with their attempt to live on through the darkness. The sound stirred Sara to throw her arm over Jarrid and cuddle up to his back. She was content in the shadow of their love.

The knock soft, Angelica's voice muffled by the door; she whispered, "Sara, I need to talk to you." The plea followed by a louder knock. "It is important."

Jarrid moaned and rolled to his other side, Sara slipped away, closed the terry robe around her waist and whispered, "Hold on, Angelica." Her hand pulled the massive wooden door open; she peeked out to see the angel poised on the steps.

"Sara, please excuse the intrusion, but we must speak." The angel pushed the door wider and continued. "I realize this is almost criminal, but please get dressed and meet me in front of the podium. Don't wake Jarrid and make sure you have the medallion." Angelica didn't wait for her response. Sara's mouth fell open to protest, her gesture moot; she followed the angel's instructions.

Her red hair bounced, the medallion rode her bosoms, lying cold against her skin. The frustration drove her to fly down the stairs to confront Angelica on what could be so damn important that she pulled her out of Jarrid's arms, literally.

"Angelica, what..." The concern so evident on the angel's face, Sara stopped in mid-sentence and asked. "What's wrong, are we being attacked?"

"Sara, it has begun." Her wings shuddered, and she touched Sara's arm. "*The Spirited Sword of Purity* has been accomplished; it now resides in your armory." Angelica tugged on her arm to guide her toward the back of the chapel.

"Your blessed union has stripped Luna of her greatest weapon." She pulled Sara into the shadows and continued. "The witch relied on her ability to wield Jarrid's lust to sully your love." A smile crossed the angel's lips, her statement a glorious revelation. "This power is gone. She is weaker and lacks the true ability to face you and win your souls for her master."

"I think I know where this is going." Sara's hands wrenched, the medallion started to glow a brilliant blue and hummed against her skin. She spoke her suspicions. "It's time for the final battle." Sara fell against the wall. Her head hung, her doubts written across her face.

"My child, you were born for this battle." Angelica embraced her doubts and offered. "God has chosen you to face the Devil, as God's warrior; you will be victorious."

"Okay, I'm ready; I'll just wake Jarrid and the others. It'll take an army to defeat the witch, for the Devil himself supports her." The atmosphere changed, a look of apprehension on Angelica's face, causing Sara to stop and ask the question. "What?"

"Righteous One," Angelica took Sara's hands and spoke the words of the prophecy, "You're meant to face Luna alone."

The air sucked into Sara's lungs, the fuel needed to compel the words born deep in her soul. "I can't face her without Jarrid; he is my rock." She started to pace, running small circles back and forth across the floor. "No, Angelica… that can't be!"

"It is God's will." She stood in front of Sara to get her attention. "He will not forsake you. He has given you three tools, love, faith, and *The Spirited Sword of Purity*, which you earned with your abstinence." Angelica's demeanor changed, and she demanded. "You are the Chosen One, handpicked by God, to win his final battle and close the veil of destruction."

And there it was, the familiar flood of emotion, the call to action, her Warrior-Princess screaming from deep inside to be released upon the world. "Yes, my spirit hears the call, and I will obey."

"Wow, hold on." Angelica petitioned Sara. "You must be careful; Luna and Sargon are a deadly force, even though their powers are weak. Use your head, your strength, and every tool given to you from birth."

Angelica touched the blue glow coming from the medallion. "This tool will assist you, its purpose shown to you at the proper time." The angel made one last attempt to guide Sara, her words profound. "Luna must not possess the medallion. It would be catastrophic."

"I understand." Sara reached for Angelica, the angel's smile offered as a blessing her final gift of love.

***

The medallion hummed against Sara's chest, serving as a distraction to the fear welled up in her soul. The sliver of hallway laid just ahead, the corridor the only thing between her and the battle for good and evil.

Sara positioned herself behind the boulder closest to the corridor. Her eyes focused on the red skin of Sargon lying on the altar, his tail flicking in the air while he mocked Luna, and pretended to be Jarrid. "Oh, no, I can't be with you. I love only Sara." The witch's outburst caused the undead to scatter to the dark corners of the room, her frustration visible, not amused with Sargon's theatrics.

She stopped in mid outburst. "Sara, please join us. We wish to congratulate you on your marriage." The witch slinked toward the boulder and added. "I'm sure Sargon would like to kiss the bride, his toast to Jarrid for a job well done." Her laughter filled the chamber, and her words got Sargon's attention.

"You seem so confident, Luna." Sara's legs acted like hydraulic jacks, pushing her to tower above the boulder, her courage welling up in her stomach she taunted. "Your master lies to you, makes you do his will; he is a false god." She moved past the rock and headed straight for the witch.

"You will be silent." Sargon declared as he crossed the room to close the distance between the women. He wrapped his tail around Sara's waist, grabbed her neck, and pinned her against the wall, his appendage tightened to restrain her.

Luna's laughter filled the air; she approached the couple and whispered in Sargon's ear. "Careful, my love, she is the Chosen One."

"I think it's time to enlighten you, Sara. After all, you're a captive audience." Luna slapped Sargon on the rear and moved closer to the Righteous One's ear. "My master requires the King and Queen of Light's souls," her laugh from deep in her throat, almost a growl.

"What has he promised you?" Sara's words fought against Sargon's grip, his hands running across her breast, his fingers toying with the medallion.

"Hmm, to be his equal, beautiful forever to reign over the dominions of the world, his daughter to inherit his kingdom, it will be quite the gift." Luna gloated.

Gasps fell from Sara's mouth, her breath crushed by Sargon's weight. His tail slipped over her shoulder and down her buttocks to spread her legs, his thrust against her mound, leaving no doubt of his intentions.

BLOOD MOON

"Let's get on with it." Luna's frustration obvious fueled by Sargon's advances. "We shall just wait for Jarrid to join us." Luna moved toward the altar, placed her hands on the cold stone, and spoke her revelation. "Do you know how you will die?" The question bounced off Sara's ears; she had no breath to answer.

"Sargon, back off, I need her alive until Jarrid arrives." He only released his grip around her neck but continued to grind against her body.

The air returned to Sara's lungs, her first reaction a sly laugh. "Jarrid does not know I'm here, he slumbers, exhausted from the long and successful honeymoon."

"Be quiet, you wretched woman!" Luna's frustration oozed from her pores, the words raking across her soul. Sargon's devilish intent was of no concern to the Evil Queen.

"Oh, rest assured he will come." She stood beside Sara with her back to the wall, staring at Sargon, she chided, "Continue on my red devil, do as you please. It makes no difference to me, but before you consummate this little union, I need to enlighten the queen as to how she and Jarrid will die."

"Hmm…" he slid his tail forward, pushed her legs further apart, buried his pelvis against her body, and shouted. " Make it snappy, woman. My need is upon me." Sara gasped for air, her fears mounting, and his advances frightening.

"Jarrid will rush without thought to save his wife; emotions always make people stupid. His friends will join him, but it is just a ploy to bring him to me."

Luna returned to Sara's ear. "Once he arrives, you will be bound together, one on top of the other, tied to the altar faces together, and your bodies as one."

SARAH KAGE

"Angelica sent me." Sara's words spilled through Sargon's massive scaled hand. "I am to defeat you, with *The Spirited Sword of Purity*."

"Oh, you believed that, huh?" Luna laughed and continued. "You are the first wave, my dear." She pulled Sargon away, aggravated with his lust. "A good commander always has reserves."

"Now, where was I?" The witch started to encourage Sargon, leading him to believe that his climactic moment was close at hand. "Oh yes, all of my demons will attend the sacrifice. After all, the defeat of the King and Queen of Light will be the event of the century." Sara tried to voice her contempt, but Sargon covered her mouth once again.

"The dagger will pierce your heart first, Sara. Your blood, running down upon your husband, he will have only moments to realize that you are dead before the steely blade, pushes through your chest, finding its mark, snuffing out his life."

"Enough of this, you deny me, I will take her now." Sargon's hands ripped Sara's blouse to expose her milky breast, his red hand a contrast, his touch monstrous, he pawed at his prize.

"No…" Luna chastised the demon. "I must finish, the master demands it." She pulled his massive body away and scolded. "Calm down. It will be worth it."

"Since my mate seems to be in a great hurry, I will make it short." Luna moved to the altar and continued. "Your deaths will open the veil between Heaven and Hell. We will be victorious in the battle, and my master will force God's hand. His army defeated, the Devil to reign on the earth with dominion over everything, including paradise."

BLOOD MOON

Her stride carried her across the room, resting against Sargon's shoulders. "Well, that about sums it up, and since my mate is so hell-bent on having his way…" she moved away from the scene, turned back, and continued. " Just remember Sargon, she must be alive."

Luna's laughter filled the room and echoed down the corridor, her mission to gather her army of demons to prepare for the final battle, Sargon's grunts of lust the last thing she heard before she reached the portal.

The demon's roar traveled the narrow corridor and rained down on every corner of the Fortress. "Now, woman, let's see what makes you so special."

Come on, Sara, use your cunning. Her words, floating across her mind trying to break free from the demon's grip. Sargon tightened his hold and moved to steady himself for the assault.

"Thadeous…" Sara pleaded with the soul of her friend. "Please, remember who you are?" The demon shuddered, taken back by her words. "It's Sara; please remember! I know you're still there." Her tears flowed and touched Sargon's hand. Her Fae reached down to the depths, where the essence of Thadeous's soul resided, one with the demon.

"Sara…" His voice familiar, the warrior's soul still present within the red entity, the effort to escape the demon's curse, stomped out by Sargon's evil laugh.

"Nice try, bitch, but it is no use. I will taste your nectar." He released his grip from her neck, removed his tail from between her legs, and stood back to admire his prey.

The knee was swift and accurate, to land squarely between Sargon's legs her response to his lewd remarks. His reaction immediate, he bent over to absorb the mighty blow, writhing in pain curling up in the fetal position. She bent down to taunt the demon. "Guess that's what makes me so special." She kicked him for good measure and started after Luna.

"Oh, my," Luna declared, walking with the undead, marching into the room just in time to see Sargon writhing in pain. "Well, guess that wasn't what he hoped for." A smirk of contentment framed her face. "Score one for the queen."

"Take her and bind her to the wall," Luna demanded. Sara lunged toward the altar, with the medallion glowing royal blue, the tingling rising in her stomach. "Do it now." The undead jumped into killer-mode and subdued Sara before she reached her adversary. The tiny webs of electricity pulsed in and out, running down the length of Sara's arms, but didn't affect the zombies.

The undead worked fast, tying her hands together with a knot, laced and positioned on the meat hook mounted on the wall. Her struggle futile, Luna's confidence tingled with the sight.

"You will regret this, you evil witch." Sara spat in Luna's direction, the anger fueling the electricity from deep in her core. No matter how hard she struggled, the ropes would not relent.

"Release her!" Jarrid's voice demanded his body flew through the slim corridor, birthed into the room with his sword pointed in Luna's direction. He ran across the room. His presence demanding his words be obeyed.

"Sargon, take him." Jarrid's entrance so abrupt he didn't notice the red devil coming up from behind. He towered over the warrior and quickly subdued him, sword and all.

One by one, the Army of Light exploded into the room, each warrior taking a stance against the evil witch. "Release him..." Caleb demanded, his Wolfen eyes flashing amber, just this side of a full transformation, his teeth revealed to confront Sargon.

The back of the demon's hand a sufficient blow to knock the Wolfen off his feet, winding up in a heap against the wall. Sebastian's fluid moves quicker than the assault, lessening the blow, cradling Caleb's head against the impact, and even quicker to walk between Sargon and Jarrid to assist in his escape.

"Everyone, please, can't we just get along." Luna passed by Sara, smacked her, and addressed the guest. "Let's all calm down and try to come to an understanding."

"I will tell you what I understand, witch." Jarrid rushed the altar and met Luna just before she stepped in front of Sara. "You have already lost." He stopped short, moved up into her space, and whispered in her ear. "You should have been there, the moment of our union, sweet and explosive, my thrust that took her virginity and made you the loser of this battle."

His words fell upon the witch with such force; each syllable chimed with musicality, the spell broken and cast down to the depths of Hell from which it came. Luna's agony pushed from her lungs, the audible response deafening. The spell reversed her transformation complete.

Soft whimpers escaped through the witches' mouth, and her hands clamped across her face to hide the results of the demonic reveal. Her skin stretched across skeleton arms, the bones white, her fingers clawing at her eyes.

"See what you truly are, you demonic bitch!" Jarrid forced the withering old woman to the mirror hung by the altar.

"No, I can't…" She fought to hide her hideous face; Jarrid's strong hands forced the reveal.

SARAH KAGE

"Look to see your master's handiwork." Gray matted hair clung to bits of rotting skin, her face sunken and unrecognizable, the vision of her beauty gone. The consumption of her soul, the obedience to the Dark Prince, its price paid forevermore.

She wept, inconsolable, the will to fight gone, her rewards stripped, and now only demonic anger remained to fill the space where her lust and hate had fueled her attack. "Sargon, take them." Her eyes distracted from the mirror to see Caleb cut the ropes and free Sara. Sebastian and Nikko tackled Sargon with Vincent speaking spells of containment over the red devil.

"Sara," Jarrid spoke into her ear, lowering her to the ground, feeling the burst of electricity stinging his arms. The flash of light filled the room, Sargon broke Vincent's spell and marched across the floor to take Sara, but came up against Jarrid's sword. Caleb jumped onto the demons back, riding the beast to the other side of the room.

A scream broke the air; Luna lunged for Sara's throat, pushing her into the wall, choking the life from the queen. The medallion's blue light directed into a beam to blind the hideous witch and force her to release Sara.

"You will not win." Sara declared, turning the witch and pinning her to the wall. The medallion shone bright, its blue light flooded into Sara's being, shining through her skin. Electricity flowed from her fingertips and poured into Luna's eyes, gouging and burning, she screamed in pain.

Ancient words of incantations spilled from Luna's lips in between her screams. Sara's powers wiped away; Luna struck with evil intent. The witches' curse heavy upon the medallion, all of its powers gone.

"Hmm, take that, my queen." Luna moved her decrepit body toward the altar and commanded her army.

BLOOD MOON

Bring them. The time is near. Thunder rolled through the Fortress, windswept down through the hole in the roof. Every eye directed to the window. "Quick," Luna screamed, "it has started." She moved to the altar and proclaimed, "The Blood Moon of prophecy is beginning."

In the window, framed by the panes of glass, the full moon shone with brilliance and magic. The faintest hint of red covered the celestial body, the beginnings of an eclipse foretold by divination, the beginning of the end of days.

Once again, Sara took advantage of her power and shot a lightning bolt in Luna's direction. It lifted her off the floor. Sara spoke as she pinned the witch to the wall. "I decide prophecy, and I say you will reside in the bowels of Hell."

Then the bolt was gone, sputtered like lights in a storm. Luna's strike deadly, her aim perfect to bring the Righteous One to her knees. The warrior's protection demanded they ran to their queen.

A mighty roar cleared the air, the shadow of a large cat jumped over the approaching saviors, the shine from his black coat blinding their sight. Sara turned just in time to move out from under the cat's attack. She rolled across the floor, her eyes fixated on the neck of the beast with hints of purples and blues rippling across his neck. She recognized the colors and called out, "Dax, no."

The fierce beast jumped up and pinned the witch to the wall, the sound of crushing bones mingled with the thunder. His face only inches from the witch, his teeth snarling, and his claws anchored into the stone wall.

"Dax, I have to be the one to send her back to Hell." She pulled on the muscular shoulder of the larger than life Black Panther and pleaded. "Just hold her there until

I figure out what to do." Bouts of purring rattled the cat's chest, content to do the queen's bidding.

"The spell is working." Vincent proclaimed, waving his wand in the air over Sargon. "It should hold, go, and help Sara." The thunder roared again, their attention once more directed to the window to see the eclipse more than half accomplished. "Whatever you're going to do, Sara, you need to hurry." Vincent encouraged. "The eclipse is almost over; you must send her back to Hell before it becomes a true Blood Moon."

The clicks and calls flooded up from the portal, the undead immobilized by Vincent's magic. The shadows in the corridor obscured the vision, each warrior glaring to recognize what evil demons conjured from the pits of Hell.

They came forward in groups, hanging on to one another. Hoards of gray, wrinkled trolls, inquisitive by nature they sniffed the air and moved into the room. Sara stood and recognized one immediately, "Jarrid that is the gray troll from the night of the attack in the clearing." He motioned his understanding and moved to stand by Dax, the cat's paws still sequestering the hag.

"This one," Sara moved toward the leader of the gray entities and spoke. "I think it was this one. His eyes seem familiar."

"Sara, watch out," Vincent's voice raised to alert her of the attack.

Sargon broke through the wizard's magic and headed straight for the Righteous Queen, but before the red devil made his mark, Thadeous's voice reached out to her. "Sara, please help me." Sargon's face fluttered, changing between the demon and the strong face of Thadeous.

"Quick, hold him down," Vincent screamed from across the room, speaking the words to bind the demon.

BLOOD MOON

Caleb and Sebastian forced Sargon to the ground. At the same moment, Dax's spell broke, and the form of the cat gave way to loosen his grip on Luna. She jumped forward just as the gray troll leaped and grabbed her arm.

The group watched as the gray demon drug her kicking and screaming toward the portal, her Father demanding her retreat. In a flash, the demons cleared the room, except for Sargon.

"Sara," Jarrid flew across the room and gathered her into his arms. "Are you okay?" She smiled and fell into his strong arms, her gift controlled. For just a second, he recoiled from her touch, remembering the lightning bolt, he asked, "How are you controlling it?"

She smiled, proud of her answer, "It is mine to wield," a hand to his face gave him the confidence to kiss... "What's happening?" The thunder rolled across the room, the floor shook, and the altar tipped over.

"It's the eclipse." Vincent pointed to the window and continued. "We must go. Luna's fall into the portal should have stopped the Blood Moon." He motioned for everyone to follow. "Something is wrong."

The windowpane framed the moon, red like blood, the eclipse wiping out all but a small crescent of its milky hues. The floors shook and caused the small corridor to close. The walls slid together like the earth's tectonic plates rubbing against themselves, cutting off their escape.

"We have no choice but to use the back steps." Jarrid motioned for the men to help Sargon to his feet, hoping against hope that Angelica could reverse the demonic spell.

Vincent offered Dax his cloak, "This is becoming a thing you know." He dismissed the shapeshifter and led the way to the stairs.

440

SARAH KAGE

Screams and haunts belched up from the portal, demons being pulled back into the depths of Hell. "How will we know when Luna is past the portal?" Sara asked, climbing the stairs behind Jarrid.

"I am not sure, but we need to get back to the safety of the chapel, in case something has gone wrong." Sara just stared at him, unable to even entertain the idea of facing Luna again.

The red hue of the moon shone through the window at the top of the stairs. Thunder still quaked, and the eclipse marched across the moon to seal their fates. Sara couldn't take her eyes off the celestial event, counting the moments until the Blood Moon would be accomplished.

"We cannot carry Sargon up the stairs," Caleb exclaimed. "Vincent, can't you wake him up just a little."

"Sure, can't you be a wolf, just a little," Sarcasm rolling off his tongue.

The staircase shook, and a bright, blue light lit each step. Angelica floated down and stood in front of Sargon, slumped on the floor. She touched his scaly skin, took his head in her hands, and spoke a blessing to banish the demon back to Hell.

Slow at first, the scales disappeared; his horns and tail gave way to the muscular body of the man the group had come to love. Sara ran down the stairs and grabbed her friend. "Thadeous, its Sara, snap out of it." She slapped his face and raised him to his feet.

"Welcome back, my friend." Jarrid moved to embrace the warrior and helped to steady him against the wall.

Thadeous shook his locks, ran his hands over his face, and asked, "What happened?"

"Just a little snafu," Vincent offered his observation. "You were a demon for a day." He slapped the warrior on the back and started up the stairs.

BLOOD MOON

"Let's get out of here," Caleb complained. "We have to figure out why the eclipse is still happening." The Wolfen passed Sara and headed for the top of the stairs only to be met by a brick wall. "Hey, whose bright idea was this? Anyone have a clue how we walk through a wall."

"We've done it before," clambered Sara pushing her way to stand in front of the barrier.

The witchy scream rose up the corridor straight out of the portal, coming closer and closer bouncing off each stair to collect at the top, its rush pushing Sara against the wall.

Luna materialized in a burst of dust to stand in front of Angelica's outstretched wings. "You cannot protect her, angel." She stepped around her, the confrontation pushing the winged entity further up the stairs. "My Father demands her soul."

"Are you waiting for an invitation to break through that wall?" Caleb confronted Sara, coaxing her to use her light to break through the bricks. She looked at her fingertips, the electricity jumping between her hands. "Now Sara, do it now."

The air left the room, only to re-enter in a gush of wind. The vortex, wide and swirling conjured in the corner. Luna slumped against the wall, fearing the repercussions of her Dark Prince, the Father of evil, her judge and jury, his judgment swift.

"Do not be afraid." Angelica put herself between the vortex and her Army of Light. "He cannot harm you."

"Luna, my daughter, you have disappointed me for the last time. We have been defeated; you will join me in Hell for the next thousand years." Her wretched body pulled into the vortex, to reign with her evil Father, until the next end of days.

SARAH KAGE

The snap so loud it broke the window above the stairs, the glass tumbling outward to accent the moon in its full splendor, the eclipse no longer controlling its path across the sky.

A burst of blue electric light accompanied by a cataclysmic explosion rocked the stairs, the portal closing, the Fortress washed of evil and all demonic entities. Jarrid fought through the cloud of dust and took Sara into his arms. "You did it, my queen." Cheers rose up in the stairwell, accolades to the Righteous One.

It didn't matter, the eyes that stared upon the kiss, a seal of righteousness, their burden lifted. "Um…" Angelica tapped Sara on the shoulder. "What do you say; put that energy to good use, open this wall, and let's go home."

Energy flowed around the group, Sara backed away from Jarrid, placed her hands on the wall, called on her power, and blew a hole straight to the other side. Caleb went through first; Jarrid stood in a trance, remembering Angelica's words, "Home…" His puzzled look accompanied him through the wall.

BLOOD MOON
Chapter 31 The Homecoming

The smoke and chaos surrounded Sara on the top of the staircase, with dust circling the piles of bricks strewn on the landing and the church bells tolling in the distance. "So why do the bells toll at weddings?" Sara asked Dax "Why to ward off the evil spirits, of course," He answered, taking her arm to direct her toward her adoring fans.

"Here are your heroes," Angelica announced, walking down the steps in front of Caleb and the other councilmen. Alex gathered the others in front of the stage, the sound of the explosion brought them running just in time to see the wall at the top of the stairs to nowhere, crash in, revealing their victorious queen.

"Thank you, Dax, but I think I can take it from here." Jarrid took his queen's arm, and walked down the stairs to join Angelica on the stage, the bells tolling the news of their victory over Luna, and the Army of Darkness, all evil banished to Hell.

Roughhousing prevailed, taunts and victory cries rolled out into the crowd. Sara was lifted on their shoulders and paraded across the stage for all to see, with the chants of Sara, Sara, Sara echoing through the chapel.

"Come and join me." Angelica motioned to Jarrid and Sara. She stood by the king and queen and spoke to assure the crowd. "The Army of Darkness has been banished to Hell for a thousand years. Blood Moon set until the next end-of-days."

"So, what exactly does that mean?" One of the men in the group yelled out. Agreements flowed into the air, and uncertainty drifted through the crowd.

SARAH KAGE

"When can we go home?" Alex asked, standing in front of the stage, her arms folded, resting on the stage floor, her eyes fixed on Sebastian's face longing to touch his ashen skin.

"How do we get back across the veil?" The men in the group questioned.

"You have all been through a traumatic time." Angelica moved to the front of the stage to address the crowd. "All will be revealed to you in due time." She took Sara's hand and continued. "Please take this opportunity to relax, give thanks for the victory and de-stress from this life-altering event."

"Jarrid, take your queen, and be an example to everyone, enjoy your honeymoon, make the best of the coming days." She gave Sara's hand to Jarrid and started to walk off the stage.

"Home…" Jarrid touched Angelica's arm. "Will we be able to go home?" Sara joined his question and stood by him, waiting for her answer.

"The veil is still open," Angelica turned toward the crowd, "but it is up to the heavenly Father. I will plead your case before him, commune with the angels, and petition for him to grant your wishes. Only he can part the veil." She patted Jarrid on the arm and floated away with her familiar light fading toward the ceiling.

"Alex," She knew the vampire's voice, so in tune with his presence. His gentle touch, his face only inches away from her ear. "Will you come to my chamber after you put the kids to bed?" He wrapped his arm around her waist; she pulled it close and nodded her head. Then he was gone.

"Well, gentlemen," Caleb addressed the councilmen. "I think our victory calls for a beer." He turned to the

BLOOD MOON

kitchen and called out, "Wench, a round for your heroes."

"I will not join you." Jarrid proclaimed with Sara's eyes shining in his direction. "We will bid you goodnight." Caleb lifted his beer in a toast, "To the bride and groom and the continuation of the honeymoon." Jarrid raised his hand to acknowledge their good wishes and hurried his bride up the stairs. The men jeered and downed their well deserved cold ones.

The stories got taller as the beer got warmer, each version of the battle more fierce than the last. Cheers and laughter filled the chapel. Caleb noticed the light coming from the shadows and left his beer to investigate.

Her silhouette against the wall, Caleb recognized it was Angelica. "I'm sorry to interrupt your festivities, but I must speak with you and Sebastian in the Sun Dome, later when everyone has gone to bed."

Her eyes shone with urgency too strong for him to refuse. "Is everything alright?" he petitioned the angel.

"Do not be alarmed, I will explain later." She turned back into the shadows and left him bewildered in the darkness.

***

Candlelight poured from the crack in Sebastian's chamber door, his open invitation to welcome Alex into his room. The light shone out into the chapel, acting as a beacon to guide her to his arms. The distance between them was obvious due to the return of his hunger. She had respected his wishes to put space between them but now was happy he had summoned her.

"Sebastian," she called softly, pushing the door open and slipping into the room. He turned, his face radiant with his happiness to see her, the ashen tone draining from his cheeks.

446

SARAH KAGE

"Please, sit down." The vampire ushered her to the bed, took her hand, and kissed it gently. "I have missed you." He pulled away, a slave to his blood lust. "We must talk."

The passion would not let her sit still; she jumped up and embraced him with no hesitation. He buried his face into her hair and then pushed her away. "Please, Alex, you must listen." He walked to the wall and leaned against it. "Tonight, in the battle, I betrayed my Pendas bloodline." He walked to the bed, leaned his head against the bedpost, and continued. "My ancestor blood dictated that I stop the queen's victory against the Devil, to let the Blood Moon reign and usher in the days of the dragon, so commanded by Uther Pendas, my alien ancestor."

He crossed the room, took her by the shoulders, and turned her into his confession. "I denounced my vampire heritage; my actions disgraced my family and erased all ties to their history." The emotions flooded his demeanor, and he took her in his arms. "Alex, I want to be mortal, to live and love as a human."

An understanding was the reaction she wanted to convey, but her words just blurted out. "Sebastian, who would you be without the vampire?"

Frustration riddled his face, "hopefully, your husband." He stood frozen, he had risked it all, exposed his underbelly, spilled the truth about his desire to marry her. He waited for her reaction.

"Man and wife," she approached him, his skin warm and rosy. "How would we deal with the hunger?" Her hand caressed his face, and she noticed the warm and flushed skin, the sign of his arousal.

"I promise you I will find a way." His voice riddled with conviction.

BLOOD MOON

She relented, felt his need, and gave in to the fiery passion, the kiss bringing back the memory of their first union. "The hunger," She pulled away, curious about his restraint.

His answer strong and filled with confidence, "The satisfaction of your love is the only hunger I feel." He took her face in his hands and proclaimed, "I will find a way to be mortal." His lips raked across her mouth, his fangs lightly pricked her skin, and he whispered the words, "Alex, will you marry me?"

**

The fire dried the tiny rivers cascading down Jarrid's muscular chest, his hair wet and dripping. The fireplace embers cracked and accented the sound of running water from the bathroom; Sara's humming relaxing any anxieties that flooded his soul. He stood naked, his skin glistening in the firelight.

Sara stood in the doorway, towel-drying her hair, the terry robe pulled across her breast, admiring the physique of her beautiful husband. "Are you waiting for me?" She inquired, dropping the towel to the ground and joining him in front of the fire.

"I see," he joked, "It is only our second night of marriage, and you bring out the terry robe." He tousled her damp hair. "Is the honeymoon over already?"

No answer, just a reaction, she reached down the length of his body and took matters into her own hands. "Do you have an objection to terry robes?" Both of her hands explored his answer. She pulled away and guided him to the couch, gently shoved him down and seduced him with her words. "I will have you now, husband."

She lowered the shoulder of the robe to expose her breast, rubbed them slowly, moving to straddle his lap, being careful to keep the robe tied around her waist. She hovered over his need, teasing with the slightest touch, her moistness calling to his desire.

The robe soft and warm between his hands and her breast, the fuzzy barrier to her skin, she watched his frustration rise in the corners of his eyes. "Do you still have a problem with the robe?" Before he could answer, she slid her body down to envelop his entire length. His shudder priceless, her release almost instant, she shimmied the robe up to her thighs, bent toward his ear, and asked, "Shall I take it off?"

He was gone, impervious to her questions, a slave to his desires. His hips rose to meet her rhythm, his hands grabbing her shoulders, robe and all to bury his seed deep, her cries of release only building the intensity, they fell together; spent.

Moonlight spread across the bed, their bodies intertwined in the afterglow of the terry robe thrown to the floor. The knock was soft; Sara stirred, pulling the sheet over her naked body. "Sara, its Angelica." The voice quietly calling from behind the door, followed by a louder bang.

"This is getting to be a habit," Sara mumbled, grabbing her discarded clothes from the closet. "Hold on, Angelica. I'm coming."

Her face bright, the angel tried to ignore Sara's frustration, she moved to flow down the stairs, but turned back on the step and proclaimed. "Sorry, but this is important." She continued down the staircase and stopped at the bottom.

Aggravation oozed from Sara's mouth. "Do you have something against me spending a quiet moment with my husband?" Sara flopped down the steps and turned into the angel's path.

BLOOD MOON

"I wouldn't bother you if it weren't of the utmost importance." Angelica stepped in between the pews and walked to the back of the chapel. "There is some unfinished business we must address."

"Something else you require of me?" Sara spoke with sarcasm in her voice. Her head bowed to escape the angel's glare.

"Do not make light of my request," Angelica demanded. "I need your help with a matter concerning Caleb."

"The Wolfen, what has he done now?" Sara asked with pettiness in her voice. She crossed her arms and waited for the angel to enlighten her.

"Sara, sarcasm will not help your plea to go home." The one thing she could have said to grab the queen's attention, her desire to leave the Fortress foremost on her mind.

Shudders of pearlescent wings drove home the fact that Angelica was agitated with Sara's mannerisms. The angel's voice exasperated, the tone short, she demanded. "Meet me in the Sun Dome. Caleb and I will be waiting for you."

In a flash, the white light appeared and was gone to leave Sara standing in the chapel with her ego bruised, and her will commanded.

She walked past the bedchambers and turned down the hall toward the Sun Dome. Sebastian opened his door and spilled out into the corridor right in front of Sara. "What are you doing roaming the halls, don't you have better things to do?"

"Not according to Angelica." Sara snorted, brushing past the vampire. "I've been summoned to the Sun Dome."

SARAH KAGE

"What a coincidence, that's my destination as well." He moved to the side of the hall, bowed, and offered his arm. "I would be honored to escort you, my queen."

"Oh, why not," Sara quipped. "Let's get on with it. I want to spend the rest of this night with my husband, in the wedding chamber celebrating my honeymoon." She took his arm and huffed loudly, her frustration palpable, and her green eyes flashing.

The Sun Dome was formidable, a circular room rising three stories high. The copper dome constructed to open like the lens of a camera, to focus the mid-day sun in a beam, the destructive end to any vampire.

Creaking of the large hinges anchored to the heavy wooden doors announced the arrival of the vampire and the queen into the ancient chamber of death. Caleb knelt by the large cross erected in the center of the room, rising from the middle of a large pentagram painted on the floor.

"Was it your idea, Wolfen, to pull me away from my husband's arms?" She stood over the alien, her foot tapping, the patience draining from her face with each tap of her foot.

"Caleb and Sebastian are here at my request, a matter of grave importance that involves the triangle of your souls." Angelica touched the scorched wood of the sacrificial cross and continued. "Before I can petition the Father to open the veil, I must have atonement for the alien's sins."

"Yes, your sins Wolfen, her demise, your responsibility," Sebastian spoke as he turned to face Caleb. "It was your war against our people, the excuse to execute the vampire race for dominance of this world, to reign superior over the humans and taint their bloodline." The ashen skin of his hand, monochromatic against the

451

BLOOD MOON

burned wood of the cross, his accusations now silent, he bowed his head and spoke the words, "My wife, Victoria, your conquest for the cause."

"Sebastian's ancestor Uther Pendas made a deal with the Devil," Angelica moved between the two aliens and continued her story. "A prophecy that Sebastian would fulfill, by stopping the Righteous One from saving the world, allowing the Blood Moon to usher in the age of the vampire, but Sebastian refused this legacy."

"I'm sorry," Sara touched Sebastian's sleeve. "I didn't know." She moved to thank the alien vampire.

"It would be wrong for me to say I did it entirely for my queen," He walked past Sara and stared into Caleb's eyes. "The truth be known, it was a selfish act." He patted the Wolfen on the back and acknowledged the brotherhood formed in protecting their queen. "We must let the past die with the Blood Moon." He turned toward Angelica and added. "I want to be mortal and reasoned that fighting next to you, Sara, and denying my duty would atone for my alien sins."

"Your loyalty didn't go unnoticed, my friend. The Father will consider your sacrifice when he decides your fate." Angelica beamed with the possibility of Sebastian's mortality.

The stare was intense; Caleb's eyes honed in on Sara, even with Sebastian's confession of betrayal still hanging in the air.

"Yes, Caleb," Angelica broke the stare. "You are drawn to her, your instinct of imprinting driving you to madness." Angelica moved across the room to confront Caleb. "Your honor, tearing at your soul, for she belongs to another, your spirit cries for understanding."

The room spun with Angelica's words falling on Sara's ears. Her mouth opened to form her protest. "It's not me he seeks, but the communication of his dead wife, Raven."

"Ah, and that is the very reason I brought the two of you together." The angel touched Sara's hand and guided her toward Caleb. "We must accomplish this connection, but Raven's spirit is not strong enough to get her message across the veil."

She moved in front of Sebastian, and brought him into the circle, joined his hand with Sara and instructed. "It's imperative that Raven brings her knowledge to Caleb, the only way he will be able to move forward."

The Sun Dome draped in its history of death and torture, acting as a conduit to the other side. "Caleb, take Sebastian's hand and form a circle around the cross. Make sure your feet are not touching the pentagram." Angelica commanded, her voice compelling Sara, she continued. "Give us a small amount of your lightning bolt, Sara, just enough to boost the connection to Raven." The angel came behind Sebastian and instructed. "Bring them into your mind; meld them together so Raven can reveal her directions for Caleb."

Small currents flowed through Sara's fingertips, her mind tingling with the intrusion of Sebastian's brain waves intermingling with her thoughts, connecting her telepathically with Caleb, their minds connected like a three-way call.

Electricity sparked the voltage low enough for the vision of Raven to cross the barrier and flow into Caleb's mind, executed as a holograph projected between Sara, Caleb, and Sebastian.

Raven's projection turned to Sara and spoke. "Caleb can't help himself. His alien bloodline dictates that he mates with only someone he imprints on." Raven's words spilled into the space between the three companions. "He's drawn to you, but he does not understand."

"What Raven?" Caleb called out to the ghostly image floating above their heads. "I love you..." his voice cracked with the frustration of his feelings for Sara and the love for his dead wife.

The current circled the cross and connected the energy between the vision and her intended audience. "Listen to me, husband!" The ghostly form stopped in front of the Wolfen. "You are drawn to Sara's future, not her present. Honor is how you present your love." The vision started to fade; the connection broken with a clap of thunder. Sara and Sebastian fell to the ground and watched Caleb fall to his knees, his hands outstretched to the air in front of his trembling body.

"Yes, my love..." Caleb's words offered to the air. "I understand, thank you for releasing me."

The Wolfen collapsed forward, his head hung toward his lap. "Caleb, snap out of it." Sebastian pulled him to his feet and leaned him against the cross.

"Sara..." Caleb moved to embrace his queen. "I understand now, Raven eased my mind and gave me the answers to soothe my soul." He held her for a moment, his future now secured in his mind, the revelation bound by love, honor, and the promise of things to come.

"Now..." Angelica touched Sara's arm and spoke. "You must return to Jarrid and wait for my instructions, the future set in motion, the Father's grace bestowed upon all in his Army of Light." Sara wiped the tears from her face, addressed her friends, and left to return to Jarrid.

The Angel followed Sara to the door, watched her leave, and then turned back toward the cross. "Sebastian and Caleb, you will be the first to know about the gift that has been given to see everyone safely home." She moved in front of the cross and continued. "God has forgiven your sins; your prayers answered. But there are stipulations to this reward."

His response instant Sebastian dared to ask, "Home to the mortal world, as what, vampire or man?" Angelica's eyes softened, she knew his only prayer was to be human, to walk the earth as a man. She moved closer to the sanguinarian and proclaimed, "As flesh and blood, to walk beside Alex with all the frailties of the human condition, as a mortal man."

She reached out, bringing the vampire closer and touching his face, giving her words power. "You can have children and grow old, along with all the conditions of mortality." Her eyes connected with his stare and proclaimed. "The real sacrifice comes in the form of time lost. When you cross the veil, it will be twenty years in the future. Your memories will be intact, as if you lived each one of those years, in the blink of an eye. Do you accept these terms?"

His arms gathered around the angel, to lift her toward the dome, laughing, he proclaimed, "Yes, I accept. It's a small price for mortality." He lowered Angelica in front of the cross and fell to his knees, giving thanks. "I give glory and honor to God. Thank you for this blessing."

"Everyone will receive the same opportunity to go across the veil, each one with their sacrifice and condition. Do you understand?" She walked Sebastian to the door his nod of understanding the last thing he offered before he left the Sun Dome.

"Are we really going home?" Caleb petitioned the entity. The Wolfen's eyes flashed with excitement. "Raven showed me the future, and it takes place in the village with Sara. Is this my destination?"

BLOOD MOON

"Raven gave you a glimpse into one possibility." The angel walked Caleb toward the door. "You must choose your previous life or a new existence in the village with your friends, twenty years into the future."

She turned to him and offered the Father's gift. "If you choose the village, your alien bloodline will be lost; you will walk as a man, all traces of the alien wolf gone. You won't have memories of the lost years, your connection to the present minus the history of the days past." She stopped and took his hand. "You need to understand that you will be human in all respects." She lowered her head and waited for his response.

"Let me understand your words." He corralled his excitement and spoke slowly. "When the others become conscious of their choices, they will have twenty years of memories; a seamless transition of their lives lived, no knowledge of the time warp, the memories of the Fortress in tack." The Wolfen paused, and then continued, "But, my sacrifice is to lose all memories and connections to my past."

His face beamed with anticipation, the weight of the revelation fueling his joy. He waited for her answer, the words explaining the transition. "Yes, seamless is a good word. Your sacrifice demands the absence of memories. Your first conscious thought will be to remember the day you came back across the veil, an orphan residing in the village." The angel answered with compassion. "Your memories gathered and erased, lifting the burden upon your heart."

"There's one more condition for you, my Wolfen friend." She put her arm around his shoulder and escorted him toward the door. "You'll cross the veil as a six-year-old boy." The door groaned, she pushed it open and continued. "This is necessary so you can grow in stature as a human. The Father commands it."

"But how will I survive without family?" Caleb petitioned the angel. "Who will be responsible for this young boy?" Fear poured from his amber eyes, the sacrifice frightening.

"That is for the Father to know, he will protect you always. You must have faith in his grace."

She positioned her body against the door and pleaded with Caleb. "Think about Raven's prediction. How could it be if you went across the veil as a grown man?" Angelica knew the truth of Raven's prophecy and spoke with great conviction. "She will be worth the sacrifice, wouldn't you say? Remember, you will have no memory, only the muted vision of yourself as an orphaned boy."

"I understand," A smile came across Caleb's face. "Whatever the Father deems necessary, it will be a sacrifice I am willing to make." He bent on one knee and proclaimed. "I accept the terms."

***

The moon shone through the stained glass windows in the chapel and caused hues of blues and greens to dance against the bedchamber doors. Slumber was the spell that fell across the rooms, each member of the Army of Light dreaming of going home. The quietness haunted Sara's thoughts.

"Sara, is that you?" The door opened, and Alex stepped out into the chapel. "What're you doing?" She caught up with the queen and touched her shoulder.

"Its okay, Alex, go back to bed." She patted her arm and turned to go.

"Wait, I need to tell you something." Alex stumbled over her words, her body interpreting a version of the 'pee-pee dance.' "I've been busting to tell you, but I didn't want to interrupt your sleep," her smirk telling in the moonlight.

"I wish Angelica had shared your restraint." Sara crossed her arms and tried to listen patiently. "Well, spill it girl, I have a husband waiting for me."

"Okay, you might want to sit down for this one." Alex tugged on Sara's arm and fell backward onto one of the pews. "Wait, Angelica. What did she want?" Alex wiggled around on the seat and blurted out. "No, wait, I have to tell you first."

"I'm not getting any younger here," Sara exclaimed, grabbing Alex's shoulders to anchor her to the pew.

"Sebastian and I are getting married." The words spilled out into the quietness of the chapel, only making them more profound. Alex stared at Sara, waiting for her reaction.

"Marrying a vampire, are you nuts?" Sara bolted from her seat and stood in front of her friend in the moonlit shadows.

"No, wait, you don't understand." Alex jumped up to come face to face with Sara. "Angelica told him that the Father had granted his desire to become mortal. He will cross the veil as human, all of his alien traits gone; no more blood curse."

"Wait…" Sara's hope welled up in her stomach. "We're going home?"

"Yes, Angelica is going to talk to each of us individually about the conditions of breaching the veil." Frustration welled up on Alex's face. "Aren't you happy for me?"

"Yes, and I will be there for you on your day, Alex, but we're going home I have to tell Jarrid." Sara pledged her heart and blew kisses in her friend's direction, turned, and ran toward the stairs taking them two at a time.

SARAH KAGE

The warmth of his body cured Sara's chills. She slid in beside his warm thighs, reached around his waist and whispered in his ear. "Wake up, my love." She touched his cheek and kissed his lips, covering his face with butterfly kisses; she spoke the words, "Jarrid wake-up. We are going home!"

BLOOD MOON
Chapter 32 Thanks For The Memories

The lanterns in the hall flickered, their shadows casting ghostly forms on the walls. Lizzy coaxed Chad down the corridor, pulling on his hand and talking non-stop. "We are going home, Chad." She skipped along, tugging on her brother until he dropped her hand and ran to his mother.

"Alright, Lizzy," Alex scolded her daughter. "Try and control your enthusiasm." Sebastian took Alex's hand and walked beside his family.

"Come on, you guys." Alex taunted Jarrid and Sara. "You'd think you would be chomping at the bit to get back to the village." She corralled Lizzy and followed Angelica.

"I am so excited," Sara exclaimed. She pulled on Jarrid's hand, compelling him to walk a little slower. "Are you sure about the sacrifice?" She snuggled under his arm. "We made the best choice, right?"

"We talked about this, Sara, and agreed it is the only choice." He took her hand and twirled the band of gold on her finger. "We will be home, no sacrifice too great for that miracle."

The wall loomed, the same stack of bricks that started the nightmare and had controlled their lives since walking through the wall. They stood in silence; even Lizzy was at a loss for words.

"Mommy, I am scared." Chad pulled on his mother's arms, climbing up to rest in her embrace.

"I'll be with you, Chad." Angelica reached out to take the little prince and put her hand out to Lizzy. "I'll take you to the other side, wrapped in my wings, you will be safe." She lowered Chad to stand with Lizzy, knelt to comfort their fears, and glanced at the adults.

"Okay, let's just get on with it." Alex protested. "I want to go home."

"I'll take the children," Angelica instructed. "Alex and Sebastian will join me to walk through first." The angel rose and addressed Sara, "You and Jarrid will wait for my return, and we will travel through the vortex together."

"Alex, wait," Sara pulled on her arm. "I'm sorry about my reaction to your news. I want to be there when you walk down the aisle, so wait for me on the other side; agreed."

The hug riddled with tears and heartfelt sobs, Jarrid and Sebastian rolled their eyes, and Jarrid complained. "Geez, you would think we weren't going to see each other for twenty years."

"That is not funny, Jarrid." Sara quipped as she glared at the jokester.

"See you on the other side." Alex nodded toward Sara and joined Sebastian waiting for Angelica to gather the children.

"Okay, Caleb is waiting for you two on the other side. His sacrifice made, the memory of the Fortress wiped away. All of his alien Wolfen tendencies gone." Angelica moved to take Alex's hand. "He is just a small, scared boy with no memory of his past, lost without a home, his mortal form void of all Wolfen characteristics. He will need your unconditional love."

Sebastian stepped forward to speak, "We will raise him as our own. I will be his father in every sense of the word."

Alex took his hand and committed to her vows, "And I, his mother, he will be loved."

BLOOD MOON

Angelica folded the children under her wings and motioned for Alex and Sebastian to join her. Their commitment to Caleb sealed before God, they followed the angel and stepped into the wall as if there was nothing there. No fanfare or disturbance. One moment they were there and the next they were not.

The lanterns hissed and broke the silence in the hall. Jarrid leaned back against the wall and pulled Sara into his embrace. "I love you, wife." He lowered his face into her curls and let a sigh rush past his lips.

His touch ignited the memory, "I will never forget the second I saw you waiting for me at the altar, husband." She buried her face into his chest, breathing in his very essence.

The bright flash accompanied Angelica: her radiant body slipped through the wall with little effort, the glow lasting on the bricks, hiding the image of three people painted on the wall.

"Jarrid, the wall, who…" Sara rubbed her eyes, trying to focus on the vision of the faces that graced the bricks. "Angelica, what… Who are they?"

"It's you, Jarrid." Sara ran her fingers over the image of his face. Only he was older. The sheen too strong, the other faces obscured.

"Here, let me help." Angelica waved her hand over the wall. "Now Sara, look upon your future."

Her gasp was so strong it almost stole the oxygen from the lanterns. She stood close to the wall and touched the image of her eyes; they were older, years in the future.

"Who is the little girl?" Sara searched Angelica's face for an answer. The queen turned to Jarrid and started to smile.

SARAH KAGE

"This is a glimpse into your hope." Angelica moved behind the couple and guided them closer to the wall. She placed her hand on Sara's stomach, looked into Jarrid's eyes, and proclaimed. "Sara, Jarrid, the young girl is your daughter. Her name is Chloe." She brought Sara's hand up to her stomach and delivered the joyous news. "Sara, you are pregnant."

The face of the girl on the wall glowed, standing in between her parents, curls of strawberry hair with the impish smile of a ten-year-old, her ice-blue eyes piercing; the spitting image of her father.

"There will be time for rejoicing once we breach the veil. Are you ready to go home?" Angelica waved her hand over the wall, and the bricks seemed to vanish, the village begging from the other side.

Jarrid gathered Sara into his arms with tears streaming down his face and answered. "We are ready."

***

TWENTY YEARS LATER

In a blink of an eye, the time was accomplished. The village bustled with tourist, Jarrid and the councilmen had worked hard over the years to bring the village current with the addition of electricity and running water for the entire community.

Mr. Choate's storefront updated and brought into the twentieth century, Sebastian's talent for business evident, alongside his flamboyant wife whose flair for adventure gave the shop an air of the exotic, "Hurry, my love." Sebastian stood at the door with the bell ringing overhead, the one item left to remind them of the village's past. "We must not be late for the celebration."

Caleb locked up the newspaper's storefront and took Chloe's outstretched hand. "Hey, Alex, are you guys going to Mom and Dad's for the celebration?" They hurried across the street, intertwined, arm in arm.

"Yes, indeed." Sebastian chimed. "We wouldn't miss it; the meaning of this celebration affects us all." Alex took her husband's arm, and he continued. "Will we see you there?"

"Yep," Chloe answered, hugging Caleb as they walked, "Wouldn't miss the joyous event."

"Wait up, guys," Lizzy called from down the block. "Chad is giving some last-minute instructions to the front desk for the night. What time are you going to the cabin?"

"I guess we might as well go now," Chloe answered. "Mom won't care if we're a little early." Her strawberry curls bounced in the wind, her eyes fixed on Caleb, her answer direct.

"Okay, guys, go on ahead, we will be right along." Sebastian directed Alex onto the street to start their stroll to the cabin.

"Chad, did you take care of the front desk?" Lizzy tugged on his sleeve and complained. "You know, as proprietors of The Thornfell Village Hotel, we are expected to hold our employees to a high standard, and sometimes you lack strong managerial leadership."

"I do not. My abilities are legendary," Chad quipped. His aggravation was evident, with the roll of his eyes.

"Come on. We don't want to keep Queenie waiting." Lizzy said, ignoring his protests and heading toward the cabin.

"You know, Sara does not like that nickname," Chad laughed with a snort, passing his sister, on his way toward the path.

SARAH KAGE

Lizzy rolled her eyes and huffed, "You are impossible, little brother." She grabbed him by the arm and trudged up the hill to the cabin, scolding him the entire way.

"Twenty years later and nothing's changed with those two." Alex declared, "Yet, I'm terribly proud of them." Sebastian agreed, his arm draped across his wife's shoulders.

Even though Mary's cabin now had electricity, Sara opted for the ambiance of the flickering candle. Each room of the quaint dwelling bathed in the glow of the romantic light.

Shadows danced down the hall to illuminate the wall of love, Mary's title for the rows of family pictures hung the entire length of the corridor. Sara peeked over her shoulder, watching Jarrid standing in the light of the hall. "Where are your thoughts tonight, my husband?"

He moved across the kitchen and let his actions answer her question. Jarrid's embrace was swift to push Sara's hips against the sink, his hands following a path well known, and frequently traveled, exciting his bride of twenty years. "Jarrid, hmm… stop, our guests are arriving at any moment."

"And whose idea was it to invite them, woman?" His head buried in her neck, nibbling on the areas of lust he knew so well.

"Honey," She turned to face his ice-blue eyes and pleaded. "They'll be gone soon, and we can celebrate our anniversary our way, hmm." She patted him on the arm and slipped away to spin the bottles of wine resting in their ice bath.

The cabin door burst open with the laughter of young people spilling into the small parlor. Chloe's strawberry curls glistened in the candlelight, her familiar voice calling toward the kitchen. "Mom, Dad," She stopped just in the light of the kitchen. "Geez, you two, aren't you over each other yet?"

Sara placed Jarrid's hands next to his side with an exclamation. "Chloe, sweetie, you are early." She moved to hug her daughter and invited their friends, now pouring in for the celebration, to come in and join them in the kitchen.

"Can you believe that it's been twenty years?" Sebastian asked, moving past the women, heading for the snacks laid out on the table.

"No, friend, it still haunts my dreams, the details so crisp and clear." Jarrid poured some wine and handed it to the councilman. "I just try to focus on the miracle, my wife, and children and the opportunity to raise Caleb from a small boy, one of the good things to come from the nightmare."

Sebastian's manner inquisitive, he asked, "Speaking of miracles…" He raised his eyebrow and continued, "I have always wondered, did Sara's gift survive when she crossed the veil?"

A chuckle rose in Jarrid's voice, and he declared, "Yeah, sure, only, now we call it PMS." It was a joke between all men and a perfect answer to Sebastian's question.

"Well," his friend offered the comeback, "I guess we can call it another of the miracles we received that night."

"Yes, and true blessings, they were." Jarrid raised his glass to Sebastian and moved toward the parlor.

From the corner of the room, behind the couch, their shadows mingled, her strawberry curls complimenting his yellow eyes. There were no signs of the alien attributes shrouding his sight. Sara motioned to Jarrid and whispered. "Those two are inseparable; I do think it is love."

SARAH KAGE

"Please, woman, you are talking about our little girl." He dismissed her observation and traveled across the room, his intention to distract Caleb from his daughter.

The cabin door burst open, Ted, Sara's old boss, strolled into the center of the room. Jarrid's eyes caught the look on Sara's face, it was her disbelief of him busting through her door. "Ted, what..." She met him with curiosity in her eyes. "I haven't seen you in years, why..."

Every eye was on the older man, his demeanor shy and apologetic. "I have thought of you often, Sara. The stories of your disappearance, the manhunt initiated when you vanished." He offered his bottle of wine. "This is for your anniversary. May you have twenty more years of wedded bliss?" He dropped his eyes, her stare relentless.

"Everyone..." She cleared her throat, gathered her wits, and continued. "This is Ted Williams, my boss from *The Daily News,* where I worked before I married Jarrid." The man nodded his head to address the greetings from the room.

"Thank you, Ted." Jarrid moved to shake his hand. "How have you been?"

"Hmm..." Sara glared at her husband and quickly escorted Ted to the kitchen. "Help yourself; I'm glad you could make it." She hurried off to place distance between them. She hadn't seen him since resigning from the paper but heard that the disappearance of the video ruined his career.

Friends and family toasted the couple, wine poured freely, and time passed. Jarrid pulled Sebastian to the side and pleaded. "Take your wife and go home."

"Well, I never..." Sebastian smirked, realizing Jarrid's intent he surrendered. He gathered Alex's arm, his coat, and announced it to the room. "It is getting late. Thank you, Jarrid, and Sara for including us in your celebration. I think we should all take our leave and allow this loving couple to usher in their next twenty years." He motioned for the group to follow suit.

"Ted, thank you for coming, I hope you hold no ill will toward Alex and me." Sara ushered him to the door.

"Too many years have passed, Sara. We all did what we had to do." He stood in the door and offered his words of celebration, "Blessings to you and yours." The broken man bowed and took his leave.

The goodbyes filtered through the air, and the door shut, leaving the candles to flicker and set the mood.

"Leave those for later." Jarrid coaxed, taking the glasses from Sara's hand. "Here, sit with me." He guided her to the parlor, where he had set up the wine and two glasses. She fell onto the couch, exhausted from the day's preparations, glad that the cabin was quiet and the family had retreated.

"A toast to my beautiful wife, whose fire still lights my flame." He intertwined their arms and sipped the wine, his smoldering eyes evident of the fire that burned deep in his soul.

The lusty blaze that fueled his need now burned a steady flame, allowing for the rise and fall of the intimacy that came from the love and sacrifice of a mature union, his words falling soft just beyond her ear. "Your love is overwhelming; my soul immersed in your eyes."

"My love..." She wanted this time to last forever; her desires rising to the surface she proclaimed. "We have all night, let's celebrate our love, the memories that make up the stories that are our lives."

"I have an idea." She embraced his face between her hands, kissed his lips, and jumped from the couch to retrieve Mary's scrapbook from the cabinet. "I know, this is not a real gift, but humor me." She flopped down next to him with the platter of snacks and another bottle of wine.

Laughter colored the room to mingle with flickering candlelight. Their memories preserved so carefully by Mary's caring hands, a snapshot of the years lived since their escape from Luna and the Blood Moon.

"Oh, this is my favorite picture." Sara pointed to the photo of the bridal party. Mary had been so excited when the couple had announced their wedding plans, none the wiser of the ceremony that took place inside the Fortress before God and the Devil.

"I loved my wedding dress. It was such a gift from Angelica to bring it through the veil, one of the most important pieces of the ceremony performed on this side of the fortress wall." Her eyes filled with tears, remembering the day.

"There were so many twists and turns in our fate." Jarrid took her hand and continued, "Have you ever wondered who was responsible for the notes that directed us to meet that night?"

Sara's eyes bulged, and she answered, "No… I'd forgotten about that night." She put her hand over her mouth, remembering the truck stop.

"You were so beautiful, parting the sea of truckers." A smirk preceded his reveal, "I know who wrote the notes."

"Okay, my husband, you've been keeping a secret." She rose up, placed the scrapbook on the table, and waited for his answer.

"Not a secret," He leaned back against the couch, "just did not feel the need to tell you." His eyes met hers, and he proclaimed, "It was Nikko."

"What!" She sat on the edge of the cushions and directed her surprise into his face. "I didn't even know

BLOOD MOON

him then." A few seconds passed, and she asked the obvious question, "How?"

"Angelica told me after I found out he was my father." Jarrid sat forward and continued, "Nikko had seen your face on a wall, in his dream, and recognized you from the news."

The flame from a candle cracked and broke the silence. "Nikko told me later that it was his destiny to make sure we continued our relationship. His way of manipulating us, making sure we came together to face the impending battle."

"Wow!" Sara played the events in her mind, filling in the mystery of the yellow note. She sighed and brought the scrapbook back into her lap. "I would have never guessed it was Nikko."

Jarrid took a sip of his wine, the photo directed his attention, and the mood took on a lighter tone. "Look at Caleb." Jarrid pointed to the snapshot of a young sixteen-year-old boy, sitting next to Chloe. "That young man was relentless. Wherever Chloe was, you were sure to find Caleb."

"Nothing has changed in that story," Sara said, pointing to the next photo. "This wedding was pretty special too." She removed the picture to get a better look. "Alex was such a beautiful bride. Sebastian looks so happy and mortal."

"What is that look on Alex's face?" He pointed to Sebastian standing by his bride. "Looks like he goosed her, I wonder where Sebastian's other hand is?" Sara almost lost it, spilling her wine over her hand.

"We have so many memories of the people who came across the veil with us." Sara lay back against the cushions; a saddened look crossed her face. "I wish Mary and Nikko were still alive to celebrate with us."

SARAH KAGE

The mention of his mother and father edged Jarrid from his seat. He walked over to the table, where Mary kept her beloved photos. "This is my favorite picture." He picked the frame from the group on the small table. A close up of pink roses covered in the morning dew. "I wonder when she took this, must have been in her garden."

"That was Lizzy's picture." Sara joined Jarrid, took the picture from his hand, and held it to her heart. "Mary had distracted Lizzy from wanting to go with Alex that night to the Fortress. She promised her that if she stayed, they would go to the garden the next morning and take a picture of the roses with the early dew."

The memory of that day became a sad reminder to cause a frown upon Sara's face. She put the picture back in its place and moved toward the couch. "I guess Mary took that photo without Lizzy."

"Don't be sad, love." Jarrid sat back down and gathered her into his arms. "Mom and Dad had a wonderful life filled with grandchildren. They lived to see their two sons marry and have families of their own. This cabin full of the laughter of children, and Mom's lifelong dream of being united with Nikko, they were blessed."

"And so are we." Sara pulled herself together and returned to the scrapbook. "Speaking of family, I missed your brother tonight." She lovingly touched the photo of Joshua and Tara, his wife.

The photo was taken in front of Joshua's house in the city. His wife, Tara, and the two boys, William and Nicholas, were standing proudly beside their father. "Did you talk to him?"

"Yes, he was sorry that he would miss the celebration, but his work schedule demanded his time," Jarrid interjected.

BLOOD MOON

"He works far too hard." Sara interrupted. "Do you think he's happy with his decision to leave the village?"

"Like father like son, or so they say." Jarrid sat back and continued. "Only Joshua could answer your question."

There was silence in the parlor, Sara's question lingered in the firelight until she spoke to break the spell. "You know, I have often wondered about our friends from the Fortress and the choices they made. I envision Thadeous battling some ogre in his native land, his sacrifice to return to his past, without knowledge of the Fortress and the evil that touched his life."

"Me as well, I remember Arianna, I never heard what her destiny held, did you?" Jarrid refilled his glass and sat back to reflect.

"No, I hadn't thought of her in years. I hope she is happy."

"Tank and Dax were probably the least affected by the whole situation." She cuddled under Jarrid's arm. "They are still free to cross the veil, Tank's ancestors have had that privilege for centuries, and I'm convinced that I have heard the call of the peacock on quiet days in the forest and have found feathers caught in the branches of trees." She curled up further into his embrace and continued. "I must admit my imagination runs away with me, and I see his face in the squirrel that runs across my path or a familiar tone to the owl's hoot."

"Yes, my wife, I miss our friends and family, as well." He slipped to the edge of the couch and poured the remaining wine into their glasses.

"We cannot celebrate our wedding without thinking of Vincent and our ceremony. He was so colorful, not many people can claim to have been married by a wizard." His laugh resounded in the glass, a snicker across its rim.

"His choice may have been the most difficult to understand. To stay with the Fortress and guard its walls, ushering in any soul that is unlucky enough to find themselves' lost in the Fortress." Sara finished her wine, set the glass on the table, and exclaimed, "The Knight of the next Blood Moon, sacrificing his future; his contribution to the cause as the watchdog of the portal." She moved to the edge of the couch and proclaimed. "He is truly missed."

A strange look overtook Sara's face. The look prompted Jarrid's question. "What troubles you, my love?"

She shuddered and asked, "Do you think about... I mean, those evil things really happened. We don't talk about them, but they are our past." She searched his face for his reaction, but continued, "So many questions still haunt my dreams. Why did Anuk bring the children into the Fortress?"

Her eyes compelled Jarrid to answer. "I asked that question of Angelica. Her answer was very troubling."

"Something you're not telling me, my love?" She braced herself for his answer.

"Another Blood Moon is imminent, and Chloe, Lizzy, Chad, and Caleb are somehow tied to the event." He stopped to evaluate her reaction.

"When, how?" Her words spilled into the air.

"Sara, I do not know. Angelica only said Anuk had no choice in her decision to bring the children that night. She was compelled to bring them into the Fortress."

His wife's face told the story. The fear of the nightmare once more was enveloping the village.

BLOOD MOON

The choice of denial filled Sara's thoughts. She waved away the knowledge that her daughter was somehow involved in the second Blood Moon and declared, "Okay," She moved to distance the thought from their celebration, "enough of dread and doom. Our lives are in God's hands, and he will protect us." She picked up the scrapbook, wiped her eyes, and looked for a distraction in the form of a memory.

"We must not forget the one true sacrifice," Sara put her hand over her heart in reverence, and an attempt to forget Jarrid's words. "The selfless gift that Anastasia gave all of us, her life for our protection during the Days of Peace, the only reason we were able to defeat Luna. Without her, there wouldn't have been a wedding."

"It was a true gift of love," Jarrid said, pausing for a moment of reflection.

"Look how handsome Caleb was in this picture." Sara balanced the scrapbook on her lap and pointed to the photo of Sebastian and Caleb. "He must have been about sixteen." Sara touched the photo and sighed.

"I am glad that Angelica wiped the children's memories clean, the trauma of that experience would have changed who they are." His face solemn, he continued, "I wonder if they have any spark of memory, leftover from the days inside the Fortress."

"That's why I told them the stories when they were little, hoping that it would fill the void with fantasy." She brought Caleb's photo closer, a distraction to Jarrid's questions, "You know husband, Caleb could very well be our son-in-law, it's a distinct possibility."

Jarrid cringed at Sara's words, took the scrapbook from her lap, and said. "At least we know he had a good childhood, Alex and Sebastian raised two fine young men."

SARAH KAGE

The glasses empty, Jarrid put the food away, blew out the candles, and met Sara in the hallway. She stared at the groupings of pictures hanging on the wall, a representation of the family she had come to love. Her robust laughter filled the hall. She pointed to the photo of Zeus and her mother. He was sprawled in her lap, being rocked back and forth like a baby. "I'm so glad I left him with Mom. They kept each other company for many years. He was a happy kitty."

"Yeah," Jarrid added. "He came around eventually, and we became best buddies." He straightened the picture on the wall and declared, "They will both be missed."

A feisty mood struck Jarrid, and he snuck in behind Sara, his strong hands enveloped her, and he asked. "Can you conjure up images of our wedding night, see the fireplace roaring, the lace corset dropped to the floor, the moment you relieved my body of its makeshift kilt." He pressed his need against her round, firm buttocks, and turned her around to lean against the wall.

"Yes, my husband, with deep clarity." There were no more words between them, only the memory of a night spent so many years ago with deep passion and love for one another. This night was a celebration of their union.

***

The night sounds of the forest echoed through the trees and bounced off the fortress wall. Four childhood friends walked in the cool air, calling to one another through the trees and taunting the spirits with their chatter. "Chad, you did not catch me." Lizzy scolded her brother. "I totally beat you up the hill."

"Oh, Lizzy, leave him alone. Sometimes you are too much." Caleb exclaimed. He came from behind and

BLOOD MOON

scooped Chloe up, pinning her against the wall. "Shall I kiss you?" He pressed his weight gently against her body.

She gave a shove and proclaimed. "Not if you want to live beyond this night." She slipped under his arm and headed toward the path. Her motion stopped, the dust rising from her stride. "Do you hear that?" She motioned for them to be quiet. "There beyond the trees, someone is coming."

Meanwhile, Ted wandered through the forest on the way to his car. "Fortress indeed, it's just an old building with a wall, nothing evil about it," Ted spoke out loud, trying to comfort the uneasy feeling picking at his mind. The newsman pushed his way through the bushes, missing a step to end up off the path. "What was that?" He spoke out loud, moving behind a tree for protection. The snarling coming from the bushes in front of the wall, its gray body glistening in the moonlight, the troll stood staring at Ted, its red eyes glowing.

Oh my God, it's the troll. The newspaperman recognized the entity from Alex's description and fumbled for his phone. "If you want something done right, you must do it yourself." He repeated the age-old saying, his fingers flipping the phone into the air. His hands felt through the dry leaves, struggling to keep his eyes focused on the troll just feet away and snarling.

"Ted, is that you?" Chloe called into the darkness. "Do you need help?" Her eyes focused on the shadow of the small creature. "Guys, look, it's one of the trolls from Mom's stories." She rushed the creature just as Ted turned to flee. "Wait, don't go," Chloe called after him. His arms flailed, his feet marking the path to his car, and he was gone.

SARAH KAGE

The four young adults stood on the path staring at the troll, his teeth bared to enhance the red glow from his eyes. "Everyone, back up slowly," Caleb demanded.

"No, I want to see if he is friendly." Chloe knelt and coaxed the bizarre creature. "We won't hurt you." She motioned toward the group to stay behind her.

Her mouth opened to address the others when the troll made his move and leapt over the fortress wall disappearing behind the stones. Chloe ran to the wall and tried to peer over. "Dang, I guess we're going to have to go in and investigate. Who's with me?"

"Do you remember all the stories Mom used to tell us at bedtime, Chad?" Lizzy turned to face her brother.

"Sure, about the Blood Moon and how they defeated the Devil and saved the world, I seem to remember a troll in those stories." He looked at Lizzy's face for confirmation.

"Yes," Chloe interrupted. "I got the same stories about angels, demons, and the fight of good and evil." Chloe looked at Caleb and asked. "They were fairy tales, right?" Caleb shrugged his shoulders, growing weary of the girl's games.

"Mom always played the hero. I thought she was just showing me that women could be strong. The story was over the top, something about her face being on the wall in the Fortress." Chloe stopped and shook her head. "Mom really knew how to tell a story about how they walked through a wall and saved the world."

"Yeah," Lizzy answered. "I got the same story from my Mom." The girls' locked eyes and Lizzy proclaimed. "Do you think they were true stories?"

"Chloe that gleam in your eye is starting to worry me." Caleb protested, "What do you have up your sleeve?" She ignored him, took Lizzy's hand, and headed toward the old gate to the Fortress.

The hinges groaned as the group made it into the corridor that led to the inner walls. "Chloe, what are you planning?" Lizzy pulled on her sleeve and demanded to be answered.

"Mom's story always included Dad finding the magic brick that gave them entrance to the wall that framed Mom's face." She patted the bricks, up and down, heading down the hall to the end of the walkway.

"Chloe, we should not be in here." Caleb stood in her way before she grabbed for the next brick.

"Listen, Caleb, if you are afraid, you can go back." She pushed him aside just as her hand felt the protruding brick.

The group was not the only visitors to the Fortress. Alex and Sebastian had wandered toward the old castle on their way home lost in each other's company. "Do you ever regret becoming a mortal?" Alex asked her husband. "I mean, are there things about the vampire that you miss?"

"What a strange question, my love. Do I sense regret in your words?" Most of his attributes had fallen away with the blessing of mortality. "The question is, am I enough, I mean as a man."

"No, oh please, I'm happy that we are human together." She took his face in her hands and declared. "Although I must confess, I would love to know what you are thinking, to know your mind just one more time when we join." She stared in his eyes and proclaimed. "You are all I need, husband."

The kiss soft and sweet, her words assuring, Sebastian reached up to touch her lips with the familiar buzz of the vibration, her favorite attribute.

SARAH KAGE

The sound of scraping concrete broke the spell. "Sebastian, did you hear that?" She rushed to the old gate. "It was coming from in there." They slipped down the hall to investigate the source of the disturbance.

It only took a few moments for the wall to swing open on its hinges. The brick pushed against the wall to beckon the young people to enter the inner sanctum of the Fortress.

"Chloe, no," Caleb called after her, making a split-second decision to follow her into the dimly lit chamber.

"Well, come on, Chad. We can't just stand here in the hall and let them have all the fun." She grabbed his arm and pulled him into her mayhem.

"Caleb, what is wrong." Lizzy ran right into his back. "Snap out of it." She stopped to see Chloe standing in front of the wall, motionless and fixated on some unknown object.

"Oh, my God..." Lizzy gasped, coming up from behind to see the wall, the image of Chloe's face painted on the bricks, to fill it from side to side. Her strawberry red curls framing her face with the light pouring from her ice-blue eyes. "Chloe, what is your face doing on the wall."

Before the words fell from Lizzy's mouth, Alex and Sebastian pushed through the opening in the wall and stood in front of the new prophecy.

The light flooded the chamber. An image of a beautiful fairy materialized in the corner. Alex screamed from across the room, "Chloe, what in the name of God is happening?"

The fairy's voice called out, "Chloe, I am Lucinda, your Fairy Grandmother. We need to talk!"

BLOOD MOON

Before the fairy's words were acknowledged, Caleb blurted out, "I remember everything." He looked at Alex searching for an answer. "What does this mean?"

Alex moved to take Caleb's hand, glanced at Lizzy and Chad, taking Chloe's arm, she exclaimed. "I am afraid it is the beginning of the end!"

***

Ted threw open his office door, stumbled to his desk, and tried to bring up the picture on his phone. "I know I got it this time. The photo of the creature will vindicate me and bring my career back from the dead." He declared out loud, his demeanor was that of a mad man, fumbling through the pictures of his mother's birthday and his dog's attempt to roll over.

The frustration riddled his soul, every wrong picture that slid by raised his blood pressure until the blood vessels in his forehead bulged.

There was a ruckus just outside his office. The news teams were loud and boisterous, the voice of the rival station's anchorman bellowed through the newsroom:

This just in, a body has been found outside the walls of the Fortress located just outside of town. The Sheriff's department and local authorities are on the scene. It seems the victim has suffered multiple, gruesome injuries, speculated to have been caused by some sort of animal. This scene is eerily familiar to the unsolved murder that took place in the same location over twenty years ago. Stay tuned to this station for any further developments.

The commercial poured from the multiple screens across the newsroom. Ted stood in the doorway of his office, numb and defeated, the picture of the troll wiped from his phone, the evidence once more eluding the middle-aged anchorman.

SARAH KAGE

***

The inner walls of the Fortress trembled and creaked. Vincent steadied himself against the wall just as Tank and Dax rounded the corner. Feeling urgency, the wizard asked, "Do you still have the backpack and memory card, Tank?" Vincent shot a wizardly glare at the fairy.

"Yes, you know I retrieved them from the inner chamber before the walls closed in." Tank answered, his wings flitting in annoyance. "I have protected the memory card ever since the night I retrieved it from Alex's room." The fairy's wings smoothed into place, and he declared. "It is one of my jobs to make sure the mortal world doesn't have proof of the existence of the entities that exist behind these walls and…"

Vincent interrupted the fairy's words, "and the video will be instrumental in convincing Chloe that her mother and father were telling the truth about the Blood Moon."

The fortress walls began to rumble, "What the hell was that old man?" Tank asked, breaking Dax's stumble against the wall.

"Nothing to concern yourselves with, I'm sure it's just the old bones of the castle settling in for the winter." Vincent flicked his cape and headed down the corridor, past the duo, mumbling to himself, "Or the new prophecy of another Blood Moon."

THE BEGINNING OF THE END…